MW00476589

Guardians of Dawn: Ami

ALSO BY
S. JAE-JONES

Wintersong

Shadowsong

Guardians of Dawn: Zhara

Guardians of Dawn:
Ami

S. Jae-Jones

WEDNESDAY BOOKS
NEW YORK

First published in the United States by Wednesday Books, an imprint of St. Martin's Publishing Group

GUARDIANS OF DAWN: AMI. Copyright © 2024 by S. Jae-Jones. All rights reserved. Printed in the United States of America. For information, address St. Martin's Publishing Group, 120 Broadway, New York, NY 10271.

www.wednesdaybooks.com

Designed by Devan Norman
Endpaper map illustration by Rhys Davies
Sunburst illustrations © Diana Kovach / Shutterstock

The Library of Congress Cataloging-in-Publication Data
is available upon request.

ISBN 978-1-250-19145-8 (hardcover)
ISBN 978-1-250-19147-2 (ebook)

Our books may be purchased in bulk for promotional, educational, or business use. Please contact your local bookseller or the Macmillan Corporate and Premium Sales Department at 1-800-221-7945, extension 5442, or by email at MacmillanSpecialMarkets@macmillan.com.

First Edition: 2024

10 9 8 7 6 5 4 3 2 1

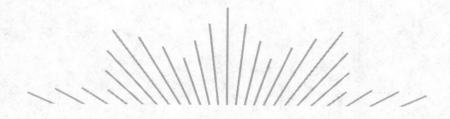

For Lemon,
WHO HAS READ MORE WORDS OF MINE THAN
LITERALLY ANY OTHER PERSON IN THE WORLD

May your good deeds return to you thousandfold.

**—WAY OF SAYING THANKS
AMONG THE FREE PEOPLES OF THE WEST**

Part I

The Pillar

ON THE EIGHTH DAY OF THE OSMANTHUS month, Ami's fairy tree unexpectedly produced a miniature flower.

It was the fragrance that caught her attention first—a rich, subtly musky perfume that brightened the heavy animal smells of livestock and overripe humans in Kalantze's village square. Ami set down her begging bowl and picked up the tiny brass vase containing the fairy tree. She touched a gentle fingertip to the delicate white petals, letting her magic mingle with the plant's ki. "Little Mother," she murmured. The tree shivered and shimmered as another minuscule bud emerged, quivered, and blossomed in the blink of an eye.

"Doom!" Beside her on their shared woven blanket, Ami's father preached his usual dire prophecies to anyone who would listen. "Doom upon all the world!"

Although the villagers of Kalantze had long since learned to ignore Li Er-Shuan's dire rantings and ravings, a few pilgrims who had come to pray before the Pillar eyed him askance. Nearby, a handful of castle guards on their rounds paused, ever watchful for signs of unrest.

"Shush, baba," Ami murmured, eyeing the guards. "Not now." She picked up her begging bowl once more and adjusted the wooden sign propped up against her legs. SCRIVENER, it read, in three different languages—the syllabary of the common tongue, the alphabet of the Azure Isles, and the Language of Flowers. Beside her, Little Mother produced another bloom.

"Rinqi?" Li Er-Shuan sniffed the air in surprise. "You haven't worn that perfume in years, darling."

Ami flinched as her father's gaze met hers and flitted away again without recognition. "Ami, Ami, I'm Ami," she reminded him through clenched teeth. "Mama's been dead for twelve years."

A misty expression crossed Li Er-Shuan's face as he struggled to reorder his mind and find the correct moment in time. Ever since the two of them fled Zanhei, he had become increasingly unmoored from the present, forever wandering the halls of memory or the branching pathways of the future. "Oh," he said vaguely. "I forgot."

Ami pushed her glasses up her nose and sighed. "Alms, alms for the needy," she called, tapping the side of her begging bowl with her knuckles. She nodded her head at the passing pilgrims, trying her best to ignore their pity.

There wasn't much use for a scribe's services in the remotest parts of the Zanqi Plateau—the Free Peoples had their own systems of writing, if they were literate at all—but it was all she had left to sell. Most refugees from other parts of the Morning Realms had not stayed long in Kalantze, either young and able-bodied enough to travel with the nomadic clans as apprentice or itinerant magicians or else skilled in some way aside from magic that allowed them to adapt or assist with the way of life in the outermost west. Woodworkers. Weavers. Herbalists. Healers. Hunters. Only the very old, the very young, the disabled, the infirm, and the useless were left behind to survive on charity—begging for grace in the village square. Like Li Er-Shuan. Like the orphans of the Just War.

Like her.

"Doom!" Li Er-Shuan bellowed. "The Guardians awake and demons walk among us!"

"Baba," Ami pleaded, looking toward the castle guard once more. Their increased presence in the village set her teeth on edge, the memory of black wings etched onto leather sleeves ground into the overtight muscles of her jaw. But these guards were no Kestrels; they were merely dispatched from the nearby fortress-monastery of Castle Dzong to protect villagers from the growing crowd of restless pilgrims come from far and wide to pray before the Pillar.

"When the Pillar blooms," Li Er-Shuan called, "the end of the world is not far behind."

One of the pilgrims, a tall yak-herder with a gold devotional shawl about their neck, gave the astrologer a sharp glance. At their feet, a small child peered at Ami with a curiously flat gaze that lifted all the hairs on the back of her neck. Her magic tingled, itching like a rash. "The Pillar has bloomed?" the yak-herder asked fearfully. "But the sacred tree has not blossomed in over two thousand years!"

A ripple of anxiety fluttered through the crowd. "The Pillar, the Pillar," the pilgrims murmured. "Why won't the Qirin Tulku let us pray before the Pillar?"

For the past several weeks, the gates of Castle Dzong had been shut to any and all supplicants seeking solace before the most sacred relic in the realm. The Pillar was the only living sapling of the mythical Root of the World, also known as the tree of life. Stories and rumors had run rampant throughout the streets of Kalantze as to the reasons why, and the mood of those encamped in the village was tense and volatile, like tinder just waiting for a spark.

"Proof!" Li Er-Shuan moaned. "We need proof." He clutched a leather folio filled with papers and notes to his chest. "For though it is written in the stars and in the book, we must see the Pillar for ourselves!"

The crowd murmured in restless agreement.

"Ho, beauty," said the nearest guard. Raldri, one of the youngest members of the castle guard, and the only one she knew by name. He was a familiar face around the refugee shantytown after sundown. "Keep that old man of yours quiet lest we arrest him for disturbing the peace."

Ami bowed her head and kept her gaze lowered. "Of course, Excellency."

Raldri said nothing, and she could feel his eyes on the back of her neck like the burning rays of a too-hot sun. "No need to be so formal with me, beauty," he said in an entirely different tone of voice.

She didn't respond. She never knew how to respond in the proper way and had learned long ago that silence was better than erring.

The guard stepped closer and knelt down before her. "Business is slow, I take it?" he asked. "Tell you what, I'll give you a coin in exchange for a kiss."

Ami furrowed her brows. "No."

"You're no fun." Raldri pushed out his lower lip in a pout, but his eyes were hard. The mismatch made everything he said and did feel like a lie. It made Ami squirm with discomfort, her magic writhing in her chest in warning. He crouched down beside her with a grin, teeth flashing white. "Don't you find me handsome?"

He was so close she could smell the sharp stink of old sweat and stale beer beneath the champaca and cinnamon perfume oils he wore. "I acknowledge that Raldri's features are symmetrical and balanced," she said, leaning back and trying to create space between them without having to get to her feet, "which other people find attractive." It wasn't a lie, and Ami didn't think Raldri would find offense in the statement.

"You're an odd one." His smile grew wider, even as his eyes grew meaner. "Beautiful, but odd." He reached for the spectacles on her face. "And you'd be prettier without those on, owl eyes."

She ducked her head, partially to avoid his touch, partially to hide the green-gold glow blooming about her cheeks. "But I can't see without them." Ami picked up Little Mother's bowl from the blanket, turning it round and round and round, letting her overworked magic unspool into the fairy tree's ki pathways. Three more miniature flowers blossomed in Little Mother's tiny branches, bursting like tiny fireworks against a dark green canopy.

"Raldri." A gloved hand came down hard on the guard's shoulder and pulled him aside. "Enough." A short, slim youth in the nondescript brown tunic and trousers of the castle barracks stood behind him, a stern expression on their scarred face. "Your attention is unwanted."

Raldri scoffed as he got to his feet. "My attentions are always wanted. It's not my fault you have a face like a cowpat."

The left side of the stranger's face was mottled and twisted with uneven flesh, a crescent moon of burned tissue curving down from above the brow to end at their lips, pulling one side up into a perpetual smirk. Theirs was not a beautiful face by any objective standard, but neither were they displeasing to the eye. The stranger caught Ami's gaze and smiled. It matched the kindness in their gaze.

"And it's not my fault you have the personality of yak cud," they said, pushing Raldri down the path ahead of them. Although the scarred youth stood nearly a head shorter than the other guard, they radiated such a sense of calm authority and charisma that Raldri complied without protest. "Go. We've got rounds to make." They gave Ami a wink as they left.

She set down Little Mother and picked up her begging bowl again. "Alms, alms for the needy."

"Here." The tall yak-herder dropped a few coins into her begging bowl. "May the Wheel turn and fortune smile upon you again soon." Their eyes slid to Li Er-Shuan, who had ceased preaching and was now frantically scribbling notes on the pages in his folio.

Ami lifted the bowl and pressed it to her forehead as she bowed. "A thousand, thousand thanks, kind stranger."

The yak-herder shook their head with a soft laugh. "We don't hold with that fancy hierarchy nonsense the rest of you lowlanders like to sprinkle into your speech," they said. "Be easy, friend, and take care of yourself."

Back home in Zanhei, she had been too blunt. Here in the farthermost reaches of the empire, she was too formal. "Thank you," Ami said again. "May your good deeds return to you thousandfold." It was the customary response among the followers of the Great Wheel, and one she was still getting used to.

The yak-herder smiled. "Come along, Chen," they said to the child clinging to their legs. "Let's see if the Right Hand will grant us passage today, lah?" They glanced up at the fortress built into the outcropping of rock above their heads, the golden flat-topped roofs glinting in the late-morning sun. "Perhaps today will be our lucky day."

"Not today," Li Er-Shuan muttered. "The stars say my luck is crossed today." He squinted into the clear, cloudless sky, as though he could read the heavens hidden by daylight. In a world long since gone, her father had been an imperial astrologer, interpreting the heavens in order to make sense of the events on earth. But the night he fled the imperial city all those years ago, the night he broke his vow of loyalty to the Mugung Emperor and stole a fragment of *Songs of Order and Chaos,* had shattered his sanity like a flawed vase in a kiln, leaving him a ranting, raving, rambling wreck ever since. "Proof," he said to himself, frantically scanning the papers spread out before him. "I need proof."

"Careful, baba." Ami grabbed several loose sheets before they fluttered away in the breeze.

"Shush," Li Er-Shuan said impatiently. "I am deciphering the commandments of the gods."

Ami closed her eyes against the sting of loneliness and resentment burning her lower lashes. She might have lost her mother when she was only four years old, but her father had been lost her entire life. To the stars, to the labyrinth of his fractured mind, and to the past. She carefully tucked the pages back into their folio, a faded leather wrap inscribed with a bisected symbol of concentric circles, half embossed, half engraved.

"Hold!" A deep, booming bass voice rumbled over the crowded square. "I said, *hold*!"

At the foot of the 888 Steps of Meditation that led up to Castle Dzong, the crowd of pilgrims pressed against an enormous black-skinned man—Captain Okonwe, head of the castle guards—demanding entrance to the fortress.

"The Pillar!" they cried. "Why won't you let us in to pray before the Pillar?"

"The Qirin Tulku will hear everyone's petition in due time, never fear." Beside Captain Okonwe was a slim, stooped figure draped in the sage-green colors of a cleric and a heavy badge of office on an enormous wooden beaded chain. The Right Hand of the Unicorn King, the highest-ranking official in Castle Dzong. "He only asks for everyone's patience."

"Patience?" said the tall yak-herder. "My daughter is dying and you ask for patience?"

"Ami-yah," Li Er-Shuan said. "Hide your light."

Panic ran ice through her veins as she yanked her magic back beneath her skin, holding it close to her bones. Moments passed, but no Kestrels came to drag them away. All magicians were free in the lands protected by the Unicorn King, but the instincts of a lifetime of terror were hard to overcome.

"Let us in!" the pilgrims demanded. "Why are we left out in the cold while a blight ravages our lands?"

"Blight?" Li Er-Shuan stirred, nervously picking at the skin around his nails. "No, no," he murmured to himself, "not a blight. A curse. But it's not in these pages. It's not in these pages." Without warning, he scattered the pages of his leather folio in a rage, sending the leaves fluttering in the mountain breeze. "Useless!" he cried. "It's all useless!"

"Baba!" Ami scrambled to her feet and scrabbled for the loose sheets before they blew away. The notes on *Songs of Order and Chaos* were Li Er-Shuan's life's work, and the only thing holding the last of her father's sanity together. "Please!" she called to the nearest guard as the papers fluttered down the street. "Raldri!"

Raldri took one look over his shoulder, paused, then continued on as though he had not heard nor seen her. The deliberate, spiteful way he met her gaze, then turned away struck Ami like a slap across the face.

"Here."

Startled, she turned to find the scarred guard behind her, the scattered pages in hand. Their cheeks were bunched in a smile, evening the mismatched sides of their face into temporary symmetry. They were handsome when they smiled.

Ami gathered the offered pages together with a bow. "May the kind stranger's good deeds return to them thousandfold."

The scarred stranger laughed.

She looked up. "Did I get it wrong?"

Their eyes twinkled. "No. It's just that we're not so formal here in the outermost west."

"I know," Ami said. "I keep forgetting."

The stranger tilted their head, eyes flitting to the painted sign advertising her services propped up on her blanket. "You would think someone who speaks so many tongues would have a better grasp on different customs."

She cringed. More times than not, Ami found herself on the outside of social customs, struggling to understand a tongue everyone spoke but her. "Pardon, pardon, a thousand pardons."

They frowned in confusion. "Why are you apologizing?"

"In case I've offended the kind stranger." It was easier to apologize than keep pretending she understood everyone else's language. She caught herself. "I mean . . . in case I've offended you, friend."

The scarred youth smiled. "Friend," they mulled. "I like that."

"Is that not the right word either?" Ami asked in dismay.

Their smile widened. She liked their smile; it felt honest. "There is no right or wrong," they said. "Friend." They bowed. "My name is Gaden."

Ami returned their courtesy. "Ami," she said shyly. "Li Ami." She smiled back.

The tips of Gaden's ears turned pink and they quickly looked away. Ami remembered to avert her own eyes. People often found her gaze too intense. Just another thing about her that made others uncomfortable, and another reason she preferred to keep her glasses on her face.

"Is this yours as well?" Gaden held a piece of leather in their hands—the folio in which Li Er-Shuan kept his notes.

"Yes, thank you." Ami tucked her father's pages into the leather, rolling everything up and wrapping it with a frayed suede cord to keep it closed. She caught sight of Gaden studying the symbol on the folio's cover.

"That sigil," Gaden said quietly. "I've seen it before. What is it?"

Ami was surprised. "You have? Where?"

They said nothing at first, their gaze searching her face for some answer to a question she did not know. She tried not to show any discomfort; too often people read her discomfort as smugness or hostility, especially if she didn't understand what was wanted of her.

"In the castle library," Gaden said at last. "There is a text with this symbol stamped into its cover, just like this."

All the hairs stood straight on the back of Ami's neck, tingling in anticipation. "And the pages? What do the pages say?"

Gaden frowned. "I don't know," they said. "I can't read it." Their eyes flicked to the painted wooden sign boasting SCRIVENER in three different languages. "I know a little bit of the Language of Flowers, but the writing on the pages seems older. More stylized, perhaps."

The tingles spread down Ami's spine and limbs. "It *is* the Language of Flowers!" she said excitedly. "Oh, I would love to see what it says!" The scarred guard took a step back, before Ami remembered to rein in her zeal. She could be overwhelming at times. "Sorry."

"It's all right." They smiled at her. "I find your enthusiasm charming."

It didn't sound like a lie. Warmth kindled in Ami's chest. "May your good deeds return to you thousandfold," she said, and this time she was certain she had gotten it right.

Gaden bowed, then met her gaze as they straightened. They were both of the same height, she realized, and their eyes were level with each other. Gaden was the first to look away again, and with a sheepish shuffle, they hurried to join the other castle guards patrolling the market square. Ami tucked the folio beneath her arm and headed back to return it to her father, excited to tell him that another fragment of *Songs of Order and Chaos* had possibly been discovered in the library. His life's work, and by extension, hers.

Only the blanket was empty.

"Baba?" Ami looked around, unease creeping up her neck, muffling her ears with ringing dread. She rarely left her father unattended, as he had a tendency to frighten those who were unaccustomed to his manic behaviors, but neither was Li Er-Shuan inclined to wander far. "Baba?"

Her father was often easily overwhelmed by a mass of people— their smells, their sounds, their textures, their closeness—unable to handle the tide of sensations that frequently threatened to drown him. The last thing Ami needed was the castle guard arresting him for disorderly conduct again. She had had to borrow butter from one of the barley aunties to pay the bribe last time, and she didn't want to be any more of a burden on them than she already was.

"Baba!" she called. "Li Er-Shuan!"

But no one responded. No one even gave her a second glance. Ami swallowed, trying to find her voice. She had spent so long hiding that she had not realized how hard it would be to be seen again. Her magic writhed in her chest, but she resisted the temptation to use her power to rifle through the ki of those around her for her father's.

Hide your light was his oft-repeated refrain. As much as Ami loathed hearing those words, they were the only times he was present with her. *Hide your light, lest the others discover what you really are.*

She had been called many things her entire life—odd, eccentric, unusual, strange, different—but those words only ever got at the barest hint of what she truly was. The thing that kept her distant and apart from everyone around her, even other magicians. Ami picked up Little Mother from the ground, turning the vase round and round and round in her hands. More and more blossoms bloomed as her power entwined with that of the little tree.

Unnatural.

2

IT WAS IMPOSSIBLE TO ESCAPE THE GOOD-LOOKING Giggles while traveling with the Bangtan Brothers.

"What's so funny?" Mihoon, the troupe's composer, percussionist, and second-oldest member, had been tasked with teaching Zhara how to cast spells, as he was the most patient and practical of the Brothers. He sat beside her in the back of the Bangtan Brothers' cramped and crowded covered wagon as they worked on her magic lessons, and their physical proximity made Zhara both giddy and giggly.

"N-nothing," she replied.

Mihoon lifted a sardonic brow, which only made the Giggles worse.

The problem, Zhara decided, was that there were seven of them—Junseo, Bohyun, Mihoon, Sungho, Taeri, Alyosha, and Yoochun. She could handle one good-looking person at a time, perhaps even two, but seven at once was both overwhelming and exhilarating.

"Yah!" came a shout from outside the wagon. "That was my shirt, you fiend of a feline!"

Well, eight people. Zhara sneaked a peek out the back as a half-naked prince tore down the road after a small, gleeful ginger cat. Wonhu Han, the Royal Heir to the throne of Zanhei, had many admirable attributes. His back muscles in particular were quite well-defined.

"Admiring the view?" Mihoon asked drily.

Zhara coughed. "Right, binding spells." She returned to the torn halves of the mulberry paper before her, her brush poised above the jagged edge. Zhara studied the character for *mending* in *The Thousand-Character Classic,* trying to remember the order in which the strokes were drawn. Mihoon held the paper together on the seat between them. Zhara felt her way along the void that existed between all things, and drew.

Nothing happened.

"I must be a dunce," she groaned. "Why can't I get this right?"

"You are not a dunce." Zhara's cheeks warmed. Mihoon wasn't especially demonstrative, so any bit of praise—however slight—was incredibly validating. "Some people are good at some things, but not good at others. You could be like Junseo, who easily grasps the most complicated and complex magic but struggles with the simplest spells."

"If only I had Junseo's brain," Zhara muttered. The leader of the Bangtan Brothers, being the quickest and cleverest of the members, had initially been assigned as Zhara's magic tutor, but they soon discovered that impressive intelligence did not readily translate into equally impressive teaching.

"Some people learn by reading, some people by doing, and still others by watching." Mihoon gently took the brush from Zhara's hand and drew the glyph across the torn edges of the paper, his sharp, confident strokes leaving a trail of black light edged with white. The tear sealed itself, and the paper was whole once more. "Here." Mihoon handed Zhara *The Thousand-Character Classic* and the sheets of mulberry paper they had been working on. "Keep practicing."

Zhara sighed and took back her brush, flinching when her fingers brushed the page Mihoon had bespelled.

"Is something the matter?"

Frowning, she lifted the page to the sun. She swore she could see the faintest glimmer of black edged with glittering white where the tear used to be. The color of Mihoon's magic. "Can you see it?"

"See what?" His arm brushed hers as he leaned in close and Zhara flinched again. "Beg pardon," Mihoon said, giving her space, but she stopped him with a touch.

"Wait." Beneath her fingertips, she could sense his ki, the essence that was Mihoon, and realized with a start that she had felt that same essence when she picked up the mended piece of paper. "Here," she said, placing the page in his hand. "Do you feel it?"

The composer blinked. "What am I supposed to be feeling?"

"The magic."

He tilted his head at her, much the way Sajah did when he was confused. "I don't understand."

"Maybe it doesn't work if you did the spell," Zhara said. She leaned out the back of the wagon and hailed the nearest Brother. "Junseo," she called. "Can I ask you a favor?"

The troupe's tall, lanky leader jogged up to join them. "What is it?"

Zhara tore a fresh sheet of paper and handed him her brush case. "Can you make this whole again?" she said, holding up both halves.

"Better ask one of the others," Mihoon advised. "Junseo has a tendency to make things explode. Born with Yuo's brush in his hand, but his big brain tends to overcomplicate things. Sungho!"

The troupe's slim stage director popped up beside their leader with a cheery smile. "At your service! How many I help?"

Zhara repeated her instructions and Sungho obliged, his brushstrokes leaving trails of bright red before dissipating as the paper seamlessly mended itself. "Here," she said, handing the page to Mihoon. "Can you feel it now?"

"Feel what?" Junseo asked.

"Magic, apparently." Mihoon passed the paper to the leader with a shake of his head. "I don't feel anything. It just feels like paper to me."

Junseo studied the sheet and turned it over a few times before handing it back to Zhara. "I don't feel anything either."

Again, that startling sensation of resonance—of recognition—flooded her bones. This time the paper *felt* like Sungho—his bright and sunny disposition, his ambition, and his surprisingly dark inclination toward perfectionism. "It feels . . ." Zhara began, trying to find the right words. "It feels as though Sungho left traces of his ki in the spell."

Junseo frowned, his chin jutting forward with concentration. "Perhaps sensing ki is a sort of Guardian power," he mused. Zhara could almost see the quickness of his thoughts flickering behind his eyes. "If a magician's ability is to manipulate the void," he murmured, more to himself than to the others, "is a Guardian's ability to manipulate ki?"

Zhara looked down at the brush in her hand. It had been a gift from Jiyi, one of the members of the Guardians of Dawn back home in Zanhei and a good friend. Huang Jiyi came from a long line of spell-mongers, or people who traced and maintained the etymology of each glyph and occasionally created new ones as necessary. *You're a magician,* Jiyi had said. *And you should have the tools of one.*

But what good was a tool if she couldn't even use it properly? Zhara tucked her brush back into its case and slid it into her waist-pouch, glancing up at the winged white shape circling overhead. Temur, the Eagle of the North and their ever-present watchful tail. Temur was the celestial companion of Princess Yulana, the other Guardian of Dawn—the elemental warrior, that is. Yuli was the only other person who might help her make sense of elemental powers, but unfortunately, the northern princess was currently en route to Urghud.

Not that it stopped them from communicating. Yuli's Guardian gift was spirit-walking. She could send her spirit far and wide, or at least wherever Temur happened to be. Once they were settled in Mingnan, Zhara hoped the princess would have time to catch up.

"That blasted cat!" Han returned from chasing Sajah down, still shirtless. "This was my last clean shirt," he moaned, holding up a stained and crumpled piece of fabric. "And Sajah peed all over it."

"Well, they say animals pee on things when they're feeling territorial," Mihoon remarked.

"Are you saying Sajah thinks of me as his property?" Han asked with dismay.

The barest hint of a smile twitched at the corner of Mihoon's lips before they smoothed back into an expressionless line.

Han sighed. "Can I borrow a spare shirt, gogo?" He had quickly fallen into the habit of calling the members *brother,* adopting an easy intimacy with them that Zhara sometimes envied. With her, the Bang-tan Brothers were nothing but polite and ever-so-slightly distant, as though *she* were the noble and Han the commoner.

"Your biceps will burst the sleeves to shreds," Sungho said to the prince, even as Mihoon began rummaging through his things.

"You could also just go shirtless until we get to Mingnan," Zhara remarked, opening up the canvas flaps at the back of the wagon. Mingnan was the largest of the border towns along the foothills of the Zanqi Plateau that dominated the western part of the empire, the last stop on the road before entering the lands ruled by the Unicorn King. "Some of us wouldn't mind the view."

Han startled to see Zhara twinkling at him. "Oh," he said, flushing a deep plum red, hands scrabbling to cover his bare chest. "I, er—haha," he said, voice cracking. "Um, so—"

"Oh, just take it, Master Plum Blossom." Mihoon tossed his shirt at Han, where it landed on his head. "Spare me your maidenly blushes."

Zhara politely averted her gaze as Han got dressed, swallowing down the temptation to tease him. There was very little privacy on the road, which made Han's inherent modesty both adorable and just a little bit frustrating. She had hoped that once the other refugees from Zanhei left their party, he would open up, but if anything, their increased proximity had turned him even more shy. Zhara touched the rose quartz bangle around her wrist.

Rrrrrip!

"Mother of Demons!" Han looked sheepish as he fingered the shredded sleeves about his arms. "Sorry, gogo," he said to Mihoon. "I'll buy you a new shirt."

"Mah!" came a voice from the front of the wagon. Taeri, the third Choi brother and the group's main tumbler, sat on the driver's bench, directing their elderly nag, Cloud, along the road. "There's Mingnan!"

As the group crested the hill, a river valley plain came into view, a glittering ribbon of silver running down the foothills of the Gunung Mountains straight ahead to the west. Nestled in an emerald-green pine forest was a collection of brightly painted roofs, scattered among the canopy like gems in a mine. Unlike the walled cities of the south, Mingnan had no stone borders but the sheer cliffs on either side of the river tributary on which it had been built. There were no walls, no watchtowers, nothing that marked the boundaries of the border town, so different from the carefully constructed cities of the south and east. Strung in the treetops were lines of prayer flags, carrying wishes from the people to the ears of the heavenly Immortals. Prayer flags were not common in Zanhei, but Zhara had seen more and more of them on the road to Mingnan, as they drew nearer to the land of the Qirin Tulku and the Free Peoples of the outermost west.

The Bangtan Brothers gave a cheer at the sight of the jewel-colored roofs and Sungho began clapping. "*We're here, we're here, the good time boys are here!*" he chanted. "*We're here, we're here, the good time boys are here!*"

The others immediately took up the song. "*Good! (Good!) Time! (Time!) Good! (Good!) Time! (Time!) Come now join in our shine!*"

Everyone's spirits were high as they drew ever closer to Mingnan. The road had been long, dusty, dirty, and occasionally dangerous, with bandits and Kestrels to avoid. Thankfully, they had not encountered any abominations along the way, although they had come across rumors of other . . . unnatural and uncanny encounters. Stories of hungry ghosts devouring the souls of the living, tales of empty cairns and tombs, of the dead rising once again. But thus far, the rumors were just that—rumors. Information to bring to the Guardians of Dawn once they reached the safe house.

"I'm starving," Yoochun said, rubbing his stomach plaintively. Youngest though he might have been, Yoochun was also the biggest member of the Bangtan Brothers, a rapidly growing boy of fourteen who—despite his well-developed muscles and surprising height—had the lean, hungry look of a child who never got enough to eat. Zhara had been sneaking him part of her road rations at almost every meal, only to discover that everyone else was secretly doing the same. "The first thing I'm going to do when we get to the safe house is eat twenty bowls of Mingnan's famous red sauce noodles," he declared.

"I heard all the food in Mingnan is red," Taeri said. The region was famous for its ice-fire peppers, which were said to tingle the taste buds with a numbing sensation. "Anyone want to place wagers on who can win the title Sovereign of Spice? Loser has to dig the latrines wherever we camp next."

"I'm out," said Sungho. "I can't handle spicy food."

"Same, same," said Alyosha. Mihoon and Bohyun, the eldest, also demurred.

"I thought all Azureans had a high tolerance for spice." Zhara grinned. "I'm in."

"Not me," Han said. "I value my guts too highly for that."

The prospect of a hot meal after weeks of road rations—rice and fermented soybeans supplemented with whatever game they could catch and greens they could forage—raised everyone's mood. "I hear the Le sisters keep a good table," Junseo said. "We should be in for a treat."

"The Le sisters?" Zhara asked.

"They run the Guardians' safe house in Mingnan," the leader said. "A message outpost on the outskirts of town."

"Message outpost?" Zhara was disappointed. She had hoped it was a bathhouse. They could all use a good scrub. Even Sajah was starting to smell rather ripe, and he was an immortal celestial animal companion. This close to the source of the Red River, the waters were a fast-flowing, creamy turquoise, rich with the mineral smell of hot springs and steam. The border towns along the foothills of the Gunung Mountains were famous for the natural baths, and as they approached the freestanding vermillion gates to Mingnan, Zhara didn't know what she was looking forward to the most—a hot meal, a bed, or a bath.

The group fell into comfortable silence as they traveled down the river valley and along the riverbanks toward the town itself. The western bank rose sharply into sheer black cliffs as the foothills gave way to the Gunung Mountains themselves, the border between the Zanqi Plateau and the rest of the Morning Realms. Zhara craned her neck, trying to envision what the lands of the outermost west looked like on the other side. On the maps of the empire she had seen, the Zanqi Plateau was a vast plain of highland pastures and snowcapped glacier peaks, nearly as large in mass as all the other provinces put together. The prospect of trying to find Li Er-Shuan within miles upon miles upon miles upon miles of land was overwhelming, so she tried not to think about it.

"One step at a time," she said quietly. "One step at a time."

The Bangtan Brothers' covered wagon stuttered to a sudden stop.

"Mah!" Mihoon pulled the curtain aside to peer outside. "What's going on?"

"Shh, shh, shh." Alyosha stood by Cloud, stroking her nose and murmuring in her ear. "What's wrong, girl?"

The troupe's faithful old nag was trying to back out of her harness, the whites about her eyes visible with fear. Not even the second-youngest Brother's soothing words could calm her, and he was the group's most effective hostler. In Zhara's lap, all the hairs on Sajah's back stood on end, his tail puffed out with alarm. Lightning flickered in the depths of his golden eyes, and a ripple of flame stirred the edges of his fur. Within a blink, the cat transformed into a red bird and fluttered out the back of the wagon, disappearing into the forest outside.

"Yah!" Alyosha cried, and the cart shuddered. "What—"

Zhara crawled out of the wagon with Mihoon to see Cloud galloping away as well, dragging the hitch behind her. The ordinarily placid nag had somehow managed to kick herself free of the cart, and was running away faster than Zhara had ever seen her move.

"Cloud!" Alyosha started after her, but Bohyun stopped him with a warning hand, giving a subtle shake of his head.

"Hold." Junseo held up a fist, reaching into his sash for his brush with his other hand. The Brothers all pulled out their brushes, and Han slid a bo staff out from the back of the cart, gripping it easily in both hands. Slowly, hesitantly, Zhara pulled her own brush out from its case, but it felt awkward and stiff between her fingers.

The leader pressed a finger to his lips and cocked his head, listening to sounds in the woods. Zhara strained her ears, but couldn't hear anything.

Then she realized that what she was hearing was nothing. No bird-song, no late-summer cicadas, no distant sounds of life at all coming from either the town up ahead or the forest behind. The silence was heavy, dense, and unnatural.

Junseo nodded, and they all followed quietly behind him on foot, passing beneath the freestanding vermillion gates that marked the entrance to Mingnan. The town was empty—no people, no livestock, nothing but cobwebs and gathering dust.

"What happened here?" Zhara breathed. The buildings and storefronts were mostly undamaged, and it didn't appear as though the border town had fallen prey to attack. Looters and bandits had made off with valuables a while past, judging by the broken windows and doors, but apparently Mingnan had been abandoned long before opportunists came to scour the place clean.

"Sickness?" Sungho asked fearfully. He had his nose buried in the crook of his free arm, brush hand shaking. "Some sort of plague?"

"Maybe." Junseo frowned, pulling his shirt over his nose and mouth. "Does anyone else smell that?"

Zhara sniffed, then coughed. A strange, almost sickly-sweet scent hovered in the air, coating the back of her throat like chalk. It was the smell of spoiled meat, of something rotten, of decay and death.

Yoochun wrinkled his nose. "It smells like an abattoir," he said.

Han gripped his bo staff even tighter, slowly moving his feet into a defensive stance. "Something's not right here," he said in a low voice. "It all feels very . . . ghoulish."

And that was when the undead attacked.

THE SUN WAS STARTING TO SLIP BENEATH the horizon, but Li Er-Shuan was still nowhere to be found.

Kalantze wasn't a large settlement, and there weren't many places a small, frail southerner could go without standing out like a weed among wildflowers. Ami had gone to each public establishment several times over, asking for her father, but each time, no one could remember having seen him, and Li Er-Shuan was anything but forgettable. He was a thin, bald-headed, birdlike figure with thick black spectacles that made his eyes seem enormous and owlish, frequently flapping around Kalantze's market square in oversize robes . . . if he remembered to clothe himself at all. On ordinary days, Li Er-Shuan's wandering off would be concerning enough, but Ami couldn't help but think of Raldri's veiled threat earlier. Her father's fragile wits could scarcely manage the sights and sounds of Kalantze; imprisonment would break him entirely.

Perhaps he had gone home. Ami packed her things and made the hike down to the refugee settlement at the foot of Grombo Hill, trying to remain hopeful. Perhaps one of the barley aunties had found him and brought him to their little shanty on the outskirts.

But he wasn't there either.

"Maybe your father is out in the fields?" one of the barley aunties suggested unhelpfully. She sat with the others on a woven mat atop a wooden platform, sorting and bundling together stalks of barley for threshing. "Helping with the harvest?"

Li Er-Shuan had never once performed a day's work, not manual labor, at any rate. She wasn't sure she would trust him with a sickle in his hand either, even if he knew what to do with it. Her father had never handled a tool less refined than a scholar's brush even before his mind was broken. Most refugees coming into Kalantze worked in the barley fields to start—tilling, planting, cultivating, harvesting, milling—before moving on to other situations in the lands of the outermost west. Ami had done her share of work in the Poha Plain with the others when she first arrived, but her father's unique caretaking needs had taken precedence. The barley aunties had all been so kind and so gracious and so supportive that guilt still burned her throat like bile whenever they spoke to her.

"We've got enough hands working the yield," said Auntie Tsong. She was the oldest of the barley aunties, and the kindest, the one who always made sure they had enough to eat, even though neither Ami nor her father had been able to meaningfully contribute to the village resources. "A full third of the harvest is gone."

Ami was taken aback. "A whole third?" She glanced at the rippling beige waves surrounding them, plains of grain on which the village depended to survive through the long, harsh winters on the Zanqi Plateau. Bits of gray and black curled in from the edges of farmland— crumbling and rotten barley stalks, the unmistakable signs of a blight. "Will there be enough for everyone come winter?"

There was no answer. The specter of starvation hovered over every exchange, every conversation in recent days. It was the reason pilgrims had been pouring in from all over the outermost west and even from the border towns in the Gunung Mountains, each hoping to pray before the Pillar. Ami thought of the yak-herder and his strangely listless daughter, Chen. Perhaps the child's listlessness had been due to hunger. Pity twisted Ami's stomach with sympathetic pangs.

"What are you going to do about your father?" Auntie Tsong asked. "Shall we send a search party?"

"No, no," Ami demurred. "I don't want to trouble you. My father is my responsibility."

Auntie Tsong's lips thinned. "Burdens are meant to be shared," she said gently. "We must do all we can to look out for each other."

It was one thing to share burdens with others, and another thing to *be* the burden. "Please don't waste your time on our account," Ami said. "I'll return to the village and keep looking." She picked up one of the blighted stalks from the woven mats and bid a hasty retreat, steeling herself to make the climb back up to the village. Although Ami had long since grown accustomed to the thinness of the air atop the Zanqi Plateau, the path up to the village was not an easy one to make on an empty stomach.

She wiped away the sweat that trickled down her brow as she studied the barley in her hand. At first glance, it seemed merely rotten—the golden brown of its stalks and grain turned ashen and gray. Brittle, almost like stone. Petrified, yet still living.

Curious, she probed the stalk with her magic, seeking its ki the way she did so effortlessly with Little Mother.

Ever since she was a little girl, Ami had been able to twine her power with the threads of ki that bound the world together. It was easier to do with the living: their ki was vivid and bright and easy to find with her magical senses. If the ki was weak or thin, she could fill the emptiness with her power, like water filling a vessel. Ami had used her gift to help the herbs and flowers of their garden grow back home in Zanhei; perhaps she could do it with the barley now. Concentrating, she let her magic flow from her veins to the stalk in her hand, finding the wounds her power could heal within the plant, enveloping the little branch in a green-gold glow.

With a hiss, Ami dropped the barley plant in shock.

For a moment, it was as though her magical senses had been entirely snuffed out, as though someone had flashed her eyes too quickly with a bright light and now everything was dark. Only instead of light, whatever was within the barley plant was the complete absence of light—a dark so opaque it almost hurt. It pulled at more than her power; it pulled at her very soul. Her ki.

And now her magic was numb. Ami tried to call forth her power, but there was nothing. Although she still had use of her physical eyes, ears, nose, tongue, and touch, she felt as though she had lost some vital, crucial part of herself with which she had navigated the world. "No," she murmured, tugging at the skin of her lip over and over again, to remind herself that she could still feel, that she was still alive. "No, please." She tried to bring up her magic, but there was nothing. No light, no glow, no warmth. "Please."

Clang, clang, clang, clang.

The sudden clamor of bronze sent Ami clapping her hands over her ears, her entire body ringing with alarm. Waves of terror washed over her again and again and again, and she crouched down in the middle of the path, just within view of the village gates. Unable to feel her magic, she felt strangely vulnerable to every sensation, as though experiencing the entire world anew. Everything was raw. Everything hurt. She wrapped her arms about her middle, where Little Mother was tucked into a blanket tied about her waist.

"Are you all right, friend?" It was the yak-herder with his dead-eyed child.

Ami gritted her teeth and nodded, swallowing down the tongue that seemed to have suddenly swollen in her mouth. In her hands, Little Mother stirred and produced another flower. Little by little, her power began to return and Ami felt herself inhabit her body again as the same soul, the same ki she always was.

"Friend?" The yak-herder placed a gentle hand on her shoulder. "Are you all right?"

Ami startled at their touch as her power roared back to life, coursing through her veins again. "Yes," she gasped. "Yes, yes, a thousand thanks."

"I didn't even do anything." The yak-herder looked amused. They pressed their palms together and touched their thumbs to their nose, sticking out their tongue in greeting in the manner of the Free Peoples. "My name is Sang, Chen's father, should you need a friend." It was the customary greeting of the plateau peoples.

Ami bowed in return, hands held out before her in the southern style. "And I am Li Ami, should Sang need a friend." She glanced at Chen, but the little girl did not seem inclined to introduce herself. Instead, her eyes were fixed on the fairy tree in Ami's hands with an expression almost akin to fear.

The yak-herder grinned. "We'll break you of that habit of formality yet, scrivener." He glanced up at the castle towering over Kalantze. "Do you know what all this bell-ringing is about?"

Ami shook her head. Unlike the watchtower drums of Zanhei, ordered and predictable with their own rhythms and patterns to signal *fire* or *invasion* or *plague,* the bells of Kalantze rang for any occasion: happy, sad, terrifying, and trivial. "The bells could signal danger," she said. "Or the announcement of a betrothal. The only way to find out is to gather in the square and wait for someone to step on the crier's platform."

"Well then," said Sang. "Lead the way, Li Ami."

By the time Ami, Sang, and Chen arrived at the market square, a vast crowd had already gathered, scarcely leaving any room for stragglers. Ami took the opportunity to scan the assembly for her father, hoping he too had heeded the call to gather. But his distinctive bald pate and owl spectacles were nowhere to be found, and her heart sank with both dread and disappointment.

"What's going on?" people murmured to one another when several moments passed and no one stepped onto the crier's platform. "Why have we been called here?"

"I heard they caught someone trespassing in Castle Dzong," someone else replied.

"Kkgggghh." Another made a guttural sound of disapproval. "That would be exile. Who would risk that? It's hard enough surviving out there with a whole clan around you. You wouldn't last long on your own."

"Especially with the undead prowling about," Sang muttered beside Ami.

She gave the yak-herder a sharp glance. "The undead?"

Sang's lips tightened, along with his grip around Chen's arm. "I know what it is I saw," he said. "And my own daughter bears the marks of their violence. Don't tell me the dead coming back to life is impossible; I've heard it enough already."

Ami frowned. "But I wasn't going to—"

"Look!" came a voice from the front of the crowd. "The sages!"

All heads turned to the 888 Steps of Meditation, where a procession of clerics in sage-colored robes was making its way from the castle gates to the village square. At the head of the procession was the Right Hand of the Qirin Tulku, the highest-ranking cleric in the castle and the shaman-king's emissary to the public. Following behind was Captain Okonwe, instantly recognizable by the color of his dark skin and the breadth of his shoulders. Beside him was a guard in some sort of animal or ritualistic mask, and between them, a frail, stumbling figure limped along with their hands bound. Cold, icy unease dripped down Ami's back; the prisoner was bald. She squinted as she pushed her glasses farther up her nose, trying to make out their features from afar.

"The Right Hand," Sang said gratefully. "Perhaps the Qirin Tulku has relented and will let us pilgrims enter hallowed ground to pray before the Pillar at last."

"I doubt that," said another pilgrim to Ami's right. "Do you see the masked guard beside the captain? That's the Left Hand of the Qirin Tulku."

A chill deeper than the growing cold descended over Ami's shoulders. They said the Qirin Tulku had two Hands to do his bidding: the Right Hand to write the sentence, and the Left Hand to execute it. Unlike the Right Hand, the Left Hand was not a cleric, which allowed them to dirty their hands with death. And unlike the Right Hand, whose face was known to the public, the Left Hand wore a wooden mask carved with the features of a boar chimera to hide their face.

Sang sucked in a sharp breath. "The Beast?"

Ami knew little about the Beast, although rumors ran rampant among the pilgrims and refugees. The Beast was a tame demon, a fairy servant from the otherworld, the true inheritor of the Sunburst Throne. They wore a mask because they were monstrously ugly, or to hide their fairy marks—feathers for hair or tiger eyes or a blue tongue. Ami knew little about the Beast, but she did know one thing.

Their presence never presaged anything good.

The procession had reached the crier's platform at the bottom of the 888 Steps, and with sudden, awful clarity, Ami finally understood where her father had been all day.

"Doom!" Li Er-Shuan moaned as Okonwe and the Beast pushed

him onto the crier's platform. "Doom upon all the world! Beware, for when the Pillar blooms, the end of the world is not far behind!"

The Right Hand waited until Ami's father had fallen to his knees before raising his hands for silence from the crowd. "Hear my voice and heed my words, one and all," the cleric said in a thin, reedy voice that did not carry. "This knave kneeling before me stands accused of trespassing on hallowed ground and defiling a sacred object."

A ripple of confusion stirred the crowd. Behind the Right Hand came a soft cough.

"Defilement of a sacred object can only be a crime if sacrilege is a crime." It was the Beast. Unlike their counterpart's, their quiet voice did carry over the crowd—light, husky, and oddly familiar to Ami. "Sacrilege does not exist in the teachings of the Great Wheel." The Beast tilted their head. "But surely the Right Hand would know this."

The cleric glowered at the Beast. "Desecration of castle property," they amended. The Right Hand lifted their arm high above their head, holding what appeared to be a twig capped with a cascade of pure white star-shaped blossoms. "Behold this branch taken from the Pillar by"—they brandished the twig at Li Er-Shuan—"this cowering criminal!"

There was a collective gasp of shock from the assembled. "The Pillar," they murmured. "The holy tree." The crowd stirred, becoming restless and agitated. Ami clutched Little Mother tighter to her chest, trying her best to keep her nerves contained. She had not anticipated this; why had she not anticipated this? How could she have been better prepared?

"I would hardly call picking a flower from a tree an act of desecration," the Beast remarked in a mild voice.

The Right Hand gave a strangled squawk of frustration. "I would remind you," the cleric said icily. "That I pass the sentence and you execute it, Beast."

The masked guard gave a slight nod of their head. "I apologize, Jetsan," they said. "Pray, continue."

The cleric cleared their throat. "For the crime of trespass and desecration," they went on, "I sentence you, Li Er-Shuan, to exile."

"No!" The cry burst from Ami's lips as she elbowed her way to the front of the crowd, ignoring the shouts and cries of indignation. "You can't!" She tripped as she reached the platform, falling to her hands and knees before the cleric. "Please," she said. "My father is unwell. He would not survive exile."

"What is this?" the Right Hand said with disgust, backing away from her grasping hands.

"Please," she said again, turning from the cleric to the Beast. "I am his daughter and I am telling you my father will not survive exile. If you must write the sentence, then let me carry it out in his stead."

At the Beast's feet, Li Er-Shuan moaned. His thick black-rimmed spectacles were cracked, and his threadbare tunic and trousers were tattered and torn. The Beast looked at Ami's father, then looked at Ami. Although the expression on the boar-chimera mask was fierce and forbidding, she thought she sensed hesitation behind it. She dared not read it as kindness.

"If the criminal cannot survive exile," they said at last, "then the sentence is tantamount to death." They looked from Ami to her father and back again. "The law is clear: the punishment for trespassing is exile, not death. Therefore, we will not carry out the sentence."

Ami collapsed to the platform in relief.

The Right Hand threw up their hands in exasperation. "Then what would *you* do with the criminal, O Compassionate One?"

The Beast turned to Ami. "What would you have me do?"

"Me?" Startled, she got to her feet. "Why am I the one being asked, Excellency?"

"Because," the Beast said, "you are his daughter. You would know best."

She looked to her father on the platform. Li Er-Shuan had retreated to the mists, his gaze vacant, his face slack. He rocked back and forth mindlessly, soothing himself with the repetition. There was so much he needed and so little she could ask for. Her father needed a proper place to live, not a shanty in a refugee town on the outskirts of a remote village. Her father needed to be fed, his meals prepared for him by someone else, someone who would not harm themselves in the process of cooking. But more than anything, her father needed to be afforded the dignity to be who he was without contempt or pity or judgment.

"If it please the Beast," Ami said hoarsely. "I would ask for some form of steady employment, so that I might be able to provide the care my father needs." She grabbed at the sign around her neck. "I know there is not much need for a scrivener in these parts," she said. "But I can read and write in the syllabary of the common tongue, the alphabet of the Azure Isles, and the characters of the Language of Flowers."

The Right Hand gave a derisive snort. "The clerics in the monastery can already do all that."

The Beast held up a gloved hand to silence the cleric. "Are you able to translate older forms of the Language of Flowers?"

Ami was surprised by the question. "Yes."

The Right Hand laughed. "What sort of question is that?" When the Beast did not reply, the cleric waved a dismissive hand. "Fine. Go on then, hire your little scrivener and her deranged father for your pet project. Come," they said, clapping their hands and gesturing to the other clerics. "Let us return to the castle."

As the sage-cloaked clerics turned to head up the 888 Steps, the crowd in the village square also thinned. The drama was over, and there was no more entertainment to be had.

"Ami." The Beast's voice was gentle. "We will take your father up to the monastery for the night, as I don't know if he will make it to the shantytown. Will you meet us at the castle gates tomorrow?"

Alarm raced up her spine. "The Beast won't throw him in a cell, will they?"

"Only a monk's cell." The mask shifted on their face, as though moving with cheeks bunched in a smile. She thought she caught a glimpse of strangely textured skin beneath. "With a warm meal and a clean bed." Their voice softened. "So," they said. "Do you accept my offer?"

"Why"—Ami licked her lips—"why would the Beast do this for me?" She thought of Raldri and what he would expect in return for the slightest sliver of kindness.

They shook their head. "Ami," they said, sounding hurt. "You don't recognize me?"

She blinked. "No."

Slowly, the Beast removed the mask. Behind the fearsome visage was another others would call ugly or monstrous, but to Ami, it was the most beautiful face she had ever seen. "Gaden," she breathed.

"Do you accept my offer?" they asked again. "I might have a particular folio of work I am especially keen on getting you to take a look at."

Despite everything, despite how wrung out her nerves felt, Ami felt the edges of her lips curl up into a smile. "I accept."

4

THE MOST TERRIFYING THING ABOUT THE MONSTERS was their silence.

They made no noise as they emerged from the abandoned bath-houses and buildings of Mingnan. They made no noise as they dragged their feet, mangled and torn, over the dirt-paved paths. They made no noise if they stumbled and fell, cracking a tooth or breaking a rib. No noise but the shuffling, dragging sounds of undead bodies twitching and jerking as they crawled on broken and shredded hands and limbs toward Zhara, Han, and the Bangtan Brothers.

But the most horrifying thing of all was how human they looked.

"Junseo!" she cried. "Han!"

Out of the woods came a crimson bird, its throat hoarse with warn-ing, before it fell to the forest floor and transformed into an enormous leonine beast—Sajah, in his true shape as the Lion of the South, a crea-ture with fur of crimson, scarlet, and vermillion, a peacock's tail of rippling candle flame, and a mane of fire. He roared and leaped at the nearest mass of the undead, gleaming silver claws ripping and tearing through their flesh as though they were paper.

Without words, the Bangtan Brothers had already formed a pro-tective circle around Zhara and Han, the tips of their brushes glowing with colored light as they cast spells left and right. The stench of rot-ting meat was overpowering now, and almost more disabling than the horror of the monsters themselves. Zhara stumbled back, arm over her nose. The people—bodies—undead were too dreadful to even look at. Chunks of flesh were missing from their limbs and their torsos, as though they had been picked over by wild animals. Bits of sun-bleached bone were visible through the patches of leathery, gray, and withered skin, but the worst were the eyes—empty save for bits of tendon and sinew that trailed down their desiccated cheeks like tears. To her left, Bohyun swiftly sketched the glyph for *severing,* which hovered in the air before him, glowing pink, before he pushed the spell toward the nearest oncoming monster. Deep slashes appeared all over the creature's body, as though it had been sliced open by the keenest blade of the finest swordsman, but the monster kept coming, kept advancing despite the injuries, having no more blood or life to spill.

"We have to run!" Junseo shouted from Zhara's right. "There's too many of them!"

Sajah roared again and thunder rumbled in the distance, though the skies were clear and cloudless. Zhara shrieked as a corpse crawled toward her. She fumbled with her brush, her mind wiped clean of every character, every spell she had ever learned. She backed away from its grasping hands and gaping maw, tripping over a rock and tumbling to the ground, flinching as the monster drew close. Suddenly, Han appeared before her, swinging his bo staff with a grunt and sending the creature flying.

"Go!" Sungho shouted. "Take the Guardian of Fire to the safe house. Taeri and I will cover you!"

"No!" Zhara cried. "We all run together!" She felt useless. Some Guardian of Fire she was, scarcely able to string two characters together into a coherent spell.

"We have to move. Fast," Junseo said urgently. "Before the path is overrun by these . . . these . . ." He couldn't bear to finish.

"Watch out!" Zhara shouted as a graying hand burst out of the ground beside them, followed by the top half of a snarling corpse. There was a sudden explosion of blue light as Junseo cast a defensive spell, and they were both showered in bits of dirt and mud.

"Augh!" Han frantically brushed at his robes and skin, as clumps of wriggling, writhing dirt fell to the ground. "Entrails!"

To Zhara's horror, she realized what she was covered with was not mud. It was blood, rotten blood, curdled to the texture of pudding. She shrieked and gagged as the stink of putrid flesh filled her nose. She clawed at her sleeves, clothes, and face. Was that a . . . *finger*? Zhara yelped as the finger wriggled, crawling over her foot like a worm. She immediately set the thing ablaze with a thought.

Of course.

Zhara thrust her brush back into her sash. She might not have an arsenal of spells, but she *was* the Guardian of Fire. She was an elemental warrior, even if she didn't feel like one in the moment. Drawing in a deep breath, she looked inward to that wellspring of fire, that furnace of power she called her magic. As she exhaled, she released her terror, her doubt, her restraint. She removed the shackles she kept bound about her power and let go.

The world turned inside out.

Distantly, she could hear shouts of alarm and awe from the Bangtan Brothers as she went up in flame, but she was engulfed in a different universe altogether. From within the column of her power, the town of Mingnan looked very different. The entire world was sewn together with ki, and she could see the lines that connected everyone and everything now. Through her magic, they appeared as glowing threads of various colors, threads she could twist and tie and manipulate as she chose. Zhara reached out and ran her fingers along the nearest one—the ki of a fallen branch, roughly the length of her arm and glimmering with the pure white light of life.

She imagined it turning into the dull, glinting ki of metal, of steel, of a blade.

"Zhara!"

A shimmering figure of royal blue jumped in front of her, swinging a bo staff with a yell and knocking away another one of the undead. Han. With a start, Zhara realized she was looking at *Han,* at who he was at the core without any of the handsomeness that she so often found distracting. He shimmered with royal blue, and she recognized his ki—his soul—straightaway. The kindness, the loyalty, the sweetness, and that beautiful, innocent heart she didn't think he would ever outgrow.

All around her, the world revealed itself to her in an entirely new light. The Bangtan Brothers and the colors of their magic—Junseo indigo blue, Bohyun pink, Mihoon black edged with white, Sungho red, Alyosha green, Taeri gold, and Yoochun purple.

And the undead.

Through her column of fire, they were nearly invisible to her—no ki, no soul, no light, no life. Except for one thing: where their souls had once glowed, there was a darkness so deep as to have its own presence. Anti-light. Anti-ki. It burned her eyes to look at them, leaving hazy trails of an afterimage etched behind her eyelids. The monster nearest to her snarled and lunged, but Zhara awkwardly knocked it out of the way with the fallen-branch-turned-blade in her hand, her knuckles grazing the creature. As her skin came into contact with it, her mouth immediately flooded with bile and the taste of a memory. Of being in Teacher Hu's apothecary and touching another magician for the first time. But not just any magician. A possessed child. It was the taste of corruption. The taste of the void.

Demon.

She lost her grip on her magic, and the world returned to normal.

The blade in her hand thudded to the ground, much heavier than she realized. The undead lunged for her again, but the sword was too big for her to swing, so she merely threw up her hands. The corpse instantly disintegrated into ash the moment it came into contact with her skin. Another monster appeared over her shoulder and she whirled around, shoving it away. It burst into flame a few feet away. Another at her opposite ear. She kicked out with her back foot and missed, but somehow managed to catch it with her flailing elbow. How did she have so many limbs and knees and elbows? How had she wrangled them into doing her bidding before? Zhara felt stiff, awkward, panicked, and overwhelmed as more and more revenants crowded around her.

A firework of bright blue and another spatter of blood and guts. Junseo. Pink slashes of light sliced through the shambling void and the creatures fell to the ground in pieces. Bohyun.

"Watch out!" Han picked up the blade at Zhara's feet and chopped off the hand wrapping its dry, grasping two fingers about her ankle. "Wow," he said in amazement, twirling the sword with a practiced turn of his wrist. "The balance is incredible on this thing." And then he proceeded to expertly wield the weapon against any and all oncoming undead.

"We're going to have to make a run for it!" Junseo panted. "We can't fight off this many!" On the edges of the melee, Taeri gave a shout of pain as one of the creatures managed to sink its teeth into his shoulder.

Then came a roar that split the heavens.

An enormous streak of lightning struck the middle of the field with earth-shattering force, sending a ripple of jagged fire through every monster around it for several yards. Sajah.

The Lion of the South leaped over the heads of the Bangtan Brothers and landed beside Zhara, his padded footfalls light and silent. His magnificent mane was the corona of the sun, his brilliant tail fanned out behind him, and his very presence seemed to give the creatures pause. He roared again, the tips of his small rounded silver horns crackling, and another bolt of lightning came down, making everyone's hair stand on end. The force of Sajah's power sent the revenants flying in every direction around them, clearing space around Zhara and the others.

"That way!" Sungho shouted, pointing toward the water. "Upriver! Upriver!" In the distance, the revenants were slowly pulling themselves together, both literally and metaphorically. "We need to run while the path is clear!"

"Wait!" Mihoon slung Taeri's arm around his shoulder. "He's injured!"

Sajah galloped to the tumbler's side and knelt, offering his broad, plush back to the boy. Mihoon climbed onto the cat behind Taeri, wrapping his arms about the boy's middle to grab Sajah's mane. "It . . . it doesn't burn," he said in astonishment.

Sajah huffed impatiently and shook his enormous maned head, clearly eager to move on.

"Sungho's right," Junseo said. "We should get out of here."

"And go where?" Bohyun asked quietly. "If Mingnan is overrun, then who is to say the safe house is secure?"

"We'll take it one step at a time," Sungho said. "Stay alive, that's the first one."

"And get Taeri-gogo some help," Yoochun said, large eyes shiny with tears.

"What about Cloud?" Alyosha asked. "Will she be okay?"

"She'll find us," Bohyun said gently. "She always does."

"Leave everything behind," Junseo ordered. "We look for the safe house first. As Sungho says, one step at a time."

Zhara and the others followed Sungho and Junseo's lead as they ran along the river path. The Le sisters' message waypost was a league or so outside the town of Mingnan itself, halfway between the edge of the Zanqi Plateau and the rest of the Morning Realms, near to the edge of the tree line before the forest fell away to shrubs and grass.

"Follow the sounds of the forest" had been Alyosha's suggestion. "The birds and Cloud were scared to even go near the village. Where there is life, there is safety."

Remembering the unnatural silence surrounding Mingnan, they heeded his advice.

The flight from the border town to the safe house was uneventful, but everyone had their weapon of choice at the ready—the Bangtan Brothers held their brushes, Zhara had her hands, and Han gripped the sword Zhara had forged, which glowed faintly with a rose-gold light in the deepening twilight. The sun had already slipped behind the tall peaks of the Gunungs, and the shadows blurred everything around them into darkness.

"Look," Han said, twirling his blade over and over again. "Who needs a torch when you've got a magic sword?"

"Would you stop that?" Mihoon complained. "You'll take someone's eye out."

"Yah, I'm an excellent fencer, I'll have you know," Han pouted. "I even bested Princess Yulana herself in combat once."

Zhara snorted, her mood lightening despite her fear. Out of habit, at the mention of Yuli's name, she glanced at the skies above, searching for Temur acting as the princess's eyes.

And there she was, the Eagle of the North, circling in serpentine motions overhead, her white feathers tinged a bloody red by the light of the setting sun. Zhara wondered if Yuli knew what had happened to them. She wondered if the northern princess herself had encountered any trouble on the road to Urghud. It had been over a week since the two of them last spoke.

Presently they arrived at the safe house, which was less a message station than a defensive fortification on the edge of the woods. Several stacked logs formed a barrier around the perimeter of the property, topped with sharpened rocks and bits of what looked like ancient farm tools. A moat had been dug around the fortification as well, filled with stakes. There was a haze that hung about the place, and a smoky smell, as though there had been a recent fire.

"Well," Bohyun remarked as they approached. "Let's not go overboard. Get it?" He laughed hysterically to himself, slapping Sungho beside him with mirth. "Boards?"

Everyone else groaned at the bad pun.

"Hullo?" Junseo called. "Is anyone there?"

No answer.

"Do you think . . . do you think the Le sisters were killed by those"—Yoochun swallowed—"monsters?"

It was difficult to tell. There was a makeshift drawbridge of rickety planks and rotting rope crossing the moat, and the door to the fortification was open. There were no remains of bodies in the moat itself.

"I'll check it out," Junseo said.

"Wait," Bohyun cautioned. "It could be booby-trapped." Lifting his brush, he painted the character for *unveiling* in the air before him. The pink light of his magic shimmered as it encompassed the entire fortification before dissipating entirely. He frowned. "No spells."

"Hold a moment." Alyosha bent down and picked up a rock. With careful aim, he tossed it over the moat and across the open threshold gate.

Whoosh! Thud! A large boulder dropped out of nowhere as the stone tripped a pressure plate hidden by a woven rush mat covered by sand.

"Mechanical booby traps," Alyosha said. "Not magical."

"Then how do we check it to see if it's safe?" Sungho asked with dismay. "We need a place to rest so we can take a look at Taeri's injury."

Zhara glanced up at Temur again, wishing that she could call Yuli to her somehow. The princess's spirit-walking would come in very useful at the moment. "What are our choices?" she asked.

"It's either the mechanical traps or be caught in the open after dark," said Junseo.

Han shuddered. "After our brush with the undead, I would rather the mechanical traps."

The group was in agreement. Bohyun and Alyosha agreed to take point, as the two of them had good instincts for treachery.

"Especially when we play games," Yoochun whispered conspiratorially to Zhara and Han. "They always cheat."

"I heard that," came Bohyun's voice from inside the compound. "And it's not my fault I was born lucky." Then, after a few moments, he called back, "Clear!"

Carefully, the others followed suit—Sajah with Taeri and Mihoon on his back, Zhara bringing up the rear.

Zzzzzzthunk! An arrow struck the plank in front of Zhara.

"Go no farther," came a new voice from above them. "That was a warning."

Immediately the group sprang into action, brushes and swords and hands at the ready.

"Who's there?" Junseo cast the spell for *light,* and a soft blue glow emanated from the tip of his brush like a torch. "Who are you? Show yourself."

"Who are *you*?" the voice demanded. It came from the treetop canopy, and Zhara squinted into the shadows, trying to find the source. "Identify yourself first."

"We are the Bangtan Brothers," Junseo said. "We are a traveling troupe of performers." He nodded to Yoochun, who sang a few lines from the Guardians of Dawn code song.

"*Summer, fall, winter, spring,*" the youngest sang, his voice sweet, high, and clear. "*Guardians rise and . . .*" He trailed off at Junseo's signal.

There was no reply from the trees. At their leader's nod, the rest of the Bangtan Brothers slowly closed in around Zhara and Taeri, brushes at the ready. Han brandished the enchanted blade, which glowed brightly in the deepening dark.

A sigh emanated from the treetops. *"And justice sings,"* came the reply, the speaker not even bothering with the tune. "Are you happy now?"

Junseo nodded at the others to stand down. Han lowered his weapon and Sungho and Mihoon cast their own spells for light, brightening the clearing beneath the trees. Two people dressed in nondescript green with paint over their faces were perched in the branches, one with a javelin aimed at Sajah's heart, the other with another arrow nocked in their bow.

"And these charming birds are the Le sisters, I presume?" Junseo asked.

"Yes," said the one with the bow. "I'm Trac, and that's my sister, Nhi." She tilted her head toward the girl with the javelin.

"Pleased to make their acquaintance," said Junseo with another bow. He cleared his throat. "I hope we are not trespassing on the sisters' goodwill overmuch," he said politely. "But we could use a place to shelter for the night and tend to our wounded friend."

Trac exchanged a glance with her sister, who gave a slight shake of her head. "Your injured party," she said. "How did they get hurt?"

Zhara looked to Taeri in Mihoon's arms on Sajah's back. The boy was sleeping, but restless. Sweat beaded his forehead, and his skin had a slight gray tinge to it. "We were attacked," she said. "By the undead."

A sharp intake of breath from Nhi, who made a move to throw her javelin, but Trac raised her hand to stop her sister. "Then I am afraid we cannot let you in to shelter. Not unless you leave the injured person behind."

"What?" Yoochun cried. "You can't!"

Junseo silenced the youngest with a look. "Surely the Le sisters wouldn't be so cruel as to ask us to leave our Brother out in the cold. He will die!"

"Yes," came the inexorable reply. "And once he does, we must burn the body immediately."

"What?" Han exclaimed. "Why?"

A beat. "All those bitten by the undead turn into the undead themselves," Trac said, and Zhara thought she could detect a hint of sorrow in her words. "As we have learned the hard way."

"No," Yoochun said, looking to Junseo with pleading eyes. "We can't."

The leader met Zhara's gaze. "What of the other safe houses?" she asked.

Trac shook her head. "We lost contact with them weeks ago. They've succumbed to the revenants, or they have gone and joined the cause of the Heralds of Glorious Justice. Either way, we are all on our own."

Zhara frowned. *The Heralds of Glorious Justice?* she mouthed at Junseo, but the leader mouthed back, *Not now.*

"The boy must be slain," Trac decreed. "And his body burned to ash. Otherwise," she said grimly, her eyes flinty even in the dark, "your journey ends here."

5

8**88 STEPS WAS A VERY LONG WAY** to climb.

And it was an even longer way to climb with a reluctant, recalcitrant child in tow.

Ami had set out for Castle Dzong before dawn, making the ascent between the refugee shantytown and Kalantze before readying herself to make the climb to the fortress at the top of the mountain, but was surprised by the gauntlet of eyes gathered in the square at the entrance to the Steps of Meditation. She shrank back from the pilgrims' stares, unable to read their expressions. Jealousy? Fear? Contempt? A faint green-gold glow heated her cheeks, and the eyes of the pilgrims turned suspicious.

Hide your light, her father had said.

Ami tugged at the short, shorn hairs at the back of her neck, trying to pull her wayward magic beneath her skin. Her unique powers—like so much else about her—had been one of the reasons she was singled out by others her entire life. But her magic she could understand; it was the other reasons she could not, for they never seemed to be consistent from one occasion to the next. When she was a child, the other children her age had been unable to understand the intensity of her desire to know and collect and memorize every little detail about her hobbies—languages, history, the taxonomies of plants. They found her odd and off-putting, but no matter how much Ami tried to rein in her enthusiasm, to become acceptable to her peers, they could see through whatever masks she wore.

"A moment, friend." Sang stopped her at the entrance to the 888 Steps of Meditation, pressing his palms together and touching his thumbs to his nose and forehead in greeting. His ever-present shadow of a child was beside him, even more listless and gray than ever. "I would beg a favor of you."

"Of course." Ami thought of the coins he had dropped into her bowl the first time they met. It was time to repay his good deeds thousand-fold.

The tall yak-herder pushed Chen forward. "Take my daughter with you," he begged. "Please. Bring her before the Qirin Tulku and beseech him to let us pray before the Pillar for her health. Or if he won't let us do that, then to have the castle healers examine her."

"Is she ill?" Perhaps that would explain why the child looked so haggard. By her size, Ami guessed Chen was six or seven years old, but the slackness of her face and the knowingness of her gaze made her seem much older.

The yak-herder's lips thinned. "She was attacked," he said in a grim voice. "By the undead." He pushed up the girl's sleeve, revealing what looked to be a human bite mark on her arm. Ami sucked in a sharp breath; the injury was old, but the wound wept black blood and smelled of rot.

"The undead," she murmured, studying the bite. "But that's impossible."

"So everyone says," Sang said in frustration. "Only I have seen the dead rising from their graves with my own eyes!"

"No, it's not that." Ami shook her head. "It's just that the art of necromancy was lost with *Songs of Order and Chaos*. Not even my father has been able to recover the fragment containing those rituals."

Sang blinked in surprise. "I, uh—" He frowned. "The *art* of necromancy?"

Ami glanced owlishly at him from beneath her spectacles. "Did I say the wrong thing again?"

The yak-herder pinched the bridge of his nose. "Never mind all that," he murmured. "If you believe me, then you must believe how urgent it is that my daughter get before the Qirin Tulku. The library at Castle Dzong may not compare to what was lost when the Great Library at Buotaka Palace was burned to the ground, but there are many ancient texts of magic in there. Surely someone at the monastery must know what to do!"

An entire library full of magic texts. The hairs at the back of Ami's neck tingled, and for the first time since she and her father fled Zanhei, she felt something like excitement stir her heart. Books. Lots and lots of books. No wonder Gaden needed a scrivener. A rush of warmth flooded her body, and eagerness twitched her fingers with anticipation. Ami surreptitiously ran her finger along the bowl of Little Mother's vase, safely tucked into the blanket bundled with all her belongings tied about her torso.

"I've been hired by the Beast to work in the library," Ami said. "I promise I'll do whatever I can to find a cure or treatment for whatever ails your daughter."

Some of the tension eased in Sang's face. "May your good deeds return to you thousandfold, friend," he said softly. He looked to the little girl at his side, who had yet to say a single word. "But still, I would beg of you to take my child with you."

Which was how Ami found herself climbing the 888 Steps of Meditation with a young child who refused to be carried, but was also not at all capable of scaling the nearly one thousand stairs on her own. The steps themselves had been carved directly into the rock of Grombo Hill, and the stonemasons of years past had made them neither even nor of equal size, and at parts it was almost more like climbing a ladder than stairs.

"Not long now," Ami said for what felt like the twentieth time. Her glasses were sliding down her nose from the sweat, so she took them off and tucked them into the bundle about her torso. The world without her spectacles was just a little blurred, and Ami sometimes preferred it that way; it was easier not to see how little she fit in with the rest of society with such ruthless clarity. "Not long."

She could see the gates of Castle Dzong up ahead, and smell the overwhelming perfume of magnolia and sandalwood wafting from the fortress-monastery. The primary industry of Kalantze was incense, used in prayer and purification rituals all throughout the Morning Realms. The region was famous within the Zanqi Plateau and beyond for the plethora of fragrant flowers and aromatic woods and resins, which the clerics of Castle Dzong turned into sticks, cones, powders, and ropes to be traded throughout the empire and with its neighbors.

"Do you see, mimi?" Ami asked, coming a little short of breath. She had kept up an entire conversation on the ascent—first asking questions about the undead attack, and then, when it was clear Chen would not be forthcoming, switching to asking questions about the girl herself in an effort to get her to open up. But neither tactic worked, for Chen was as silent as a stone. "The bell. They were ringing it last night."

Beside the castle gates was an enormous bronze bell, taller than a full-grown adult. A log suspended horizontally by two chains on either end hung beside it, which was used to ring the bell itself, Ami supposed. How exhausting, she thought, to have to climb nearly one thousand steps if one wanted to make an announcement to the village.

When at last she and Chen crested the mountaintop and entered the castle, she was surprised to find no one at the gates, not even a sentry. No guards and no gatekeepers patrolled the outer walls, no lookouts but a handful of dozy dogs who pricked their ears and lifted their heads as they approached. Ami had grown up with cats both on the street and in the homes in Zanhei, but the idea of a canine companion was still somewhat new to her. The Free Peoples allowed their livestock guardian dogs to freely roam in and out of homes, taverns, eateries, and sacred spaces, while clerics were frequently seen in the village carrying fluffy little pups in their arms the way a small child might carry a doll.

"Good morning, venerable one," she said with a bow to the majestic pony-sized guardian with the grizzled muzzle at the door. He sniffed, then nuzzled her fingers in a gesture of tacit approval. The other dogs immediately lowered their heads and returned to napping in the late-morning sunshine.

But the instant Chen crossed the threshold, the old dog let out a warning growl. The girl did not react, merely staring at the dog with a tilt of her head. Neither fear nor confusion crossed her face.

"It's all right, venerable one," Ami said to the dog. "It's only a child."

But the dog's growling only intensified, curling its lips and baring its teeth in an unmistakable sign of aggression. It heaved itself to its feet, and without thinking, Ami threw out her hand, her fingers glowing green-gold as her power took hold of the dog's ki, keeping it still, keeping it back. The dog whined in protest, but let both Ami and Chen cross the threshold unharmed.

"It's all right," Ami said to the girl. "The dog won't hurt you."

But Chen didn't seem at all interested in or concerned about the dog; instead, she was gazing at Ami with the first recognizable emotion she had seen on the girl's face since they met—horror. Chen's eyes were fixed on Ami's hands, where the green-gold glow was unmistakable, even in the bright morning sun.

"That light," the girl said hoarsely, the first words she had spoken all morning. "It's you."

Hide your light. Ami immediately tucked her hands behind her back. Something about Chen's tone made the hairs at the back of her neck stand on end. There was an intimacy to the girl's words that—while not uncommon among the Free Peoples, who abhorred hierarchy—seemed pointed, aggressive, and . . . old. They had been complete strangers an hour before, but Chen spoke to Ami as though they had known each other for millennia.

Behind them, the old dog continued to growl.

"Ami?"

Whirling around, she caught sight of Gaden standing behind her, maskless and smiling. When they smiled, both sides of their lopsided face pulled together, and she found them handsome in the morning light. "Gaden!" She felt her own cheeks pull upward in a grin.

"My apologies for not greeting you at the gates," they said. "I overslept." The truth of those words lay in the bluish smudges beneath their eyes and the puffiness of their eyelids. "Bad dreams." They scratched at the skin of their left hand, which Ami noticed was gloved, unlike the other.

"It's all right," she said. "I was delayed anyway." She turned to introduce Chen, but to her shock, the little girl was gone. "Where did she go?"

"Who?"

"There was a little girl with me," Ami said, frantically scanning the buildings. "Chen. Her father is one of the pilgrims seeking entrance to pray before the Pillar." She had told the child to call her *nene,* and she already failed in her first duty as an older sister figure. She glanced at the elderly dog at her feet, its hackles raised, its upper lip curled. What if it attacked the child? What would she tell Sang? What was wrong with her? Why couldn't she fall into the roles everyone else seemed to occupy with ease? "She's been injured."

"The child will come to no harm in the monastery." Gaden placed a reassuring hand on her shoulder.

Ami shook her head. "The dogs don't like her."

"She'll be safe," Gaden repeated, a bit defensively. "Our castle guardians are scarier than they look." Their smile turned wry. "Like me."

A cacophony of barking rose in the distance, not the sharp, high-pitched alert barks of a watchdog, but the deep, snarling noises of an animal under attack. Gaden's expression sobered, looking both surprised and concerned. "I've never heard them sound like that before."

All around them, clerics began emerging from doorways and thresholds as one by one, their canine companions worked themselves into a frenzy, their sounds of terror and alarm echoed and amplified by the acoustics of the fortress itself. Castle Dzong was built into a crater on top of Grombo Hill, with each level of the fortress built into the side of the mountain like the terraced rice paddies built into the slopes of Shangnan in the southeast. Broad, paved steps led straight down to the middle of the crater on all sides like an enormous open-air theater, where a single, miraculous tree grew from solid rock.

The Pillar.

"There!" Ami pointed at a small figure running down the steps toward the sacred tree. "Chen!" She hurried after Chen, who moved far more quickly than she would have thought a child with a week-old injury could manage. "Chen!" she called. "Mimi!"

As she ran past the snarling dogs and their surprised clerics, she released her hold on her magic, letting it trail behind her like faint, shimmering ribbons in the air. The dogs ceased to bark as she passed, the effect of her power on their ki settling them down, although she could feel their fear coursing through their bodies. Something dangerous, something wrong, something *unnatural* was in the castle, and they did not know or understand what it was.

"Chen!" Ami finally caught up to the little girl in the middle of the massive circular paved courtyard at the center of the fortress, standing beneath the shade of the holiest site in the realm. "There you are, mimi."

Chen stood still before the Pillar, face turned upward as if to study its branches, which towered far over her head. They towered far over Ami's head. The tree was enormous—taller than eight people standing atop each other's shoulders, and the spread of its umbrella-shaped canopy was so wide it had seemed like a forest from afar. The girth of its trunk was similarly broad, as big as six people standing with hands clasped in a circle about its base. What looked like the hardened vines of a banyan tree were wrapped about the trunk, winding their way upward like a rope to the tree's crown. She marveled that her frail, fragile father had managed to scale this tree to steal a flower from its branches, until she noticed the scattering of twigs and blossoms at her feet. Although the air still held the vestiges of night's chill, beneath the shade of the Pillar, the air was warm, filled with a bright, musky fragrance that was both light and heavy at once. The perfume of incense did not penetrate this space. It might have been summer. It might have been autumn. It might have been any season in the presence of the holy tree.

"Here." Gaden appeared on the girl's opposite side, holding a thick woven mat in their hands. "Have you come to pray?"

But Chen did not appear to hear them, her gaze transfixed by the sight of the star-shaped blossoms above her spangling the greenery like constellations in a forest-dark sky. "When the Pillar blooms," she whispered in a cracked voice, "the end of the world is not far behind."

Again, the brush of the uncanny raised goose pimples along Ami's arms. Chen's features were more animated than she had ever seen them, but the girl's eyes were still empty, vacant, dead. A slight breeze stirred the leaves of the Pillar, ringing the prayer bells strung from its branches.

"A once-in-a-lifetime event," Gaden agreed. "The librarian says that the last time the Pillar bloomed in recorded memory was over a millennium ago." They knelt beside the girl and smoothed the mat on the ground. "Here, mimi," they said kindly. "You can use this for your prayers."

Ami had noticed the stacks of woven prayer mats along the steps and beneath the bronze wheels inscribed with mantras encircling the courtyard. She was not a follower of the Great Wheel, but had seen the villagers of Kalantze circumambulate the fortress during morning and evening prayers often enough to know what their rituals entailed.

Again Chen ignored Gaden, walking forward to place her hand on the Pillar's trunk. Ami started forward to stop her when Gaden shook their head.

"It's all right," they said. "There's no proscription against handling sacred things in the faith of the Great Wheel. If she wants to pray in this manner, she is free to do so."

Chen closed her eyes and leaned her forehead against the hardened banyan vines twining about the sacred tree's base. Curious, Ami placed her own hand on the Pillar's trunk, reaching out with her magic for the tree's ki. It was sometimes easier to meet and understand living things that were not human; she didn't need to explain herself. She didn't need to figure out their social mores, their unspoken languages. She pressed her palm against the banyan vines, wondering if a holy tree—the only living sapling of the Root of the World—would feel any different from an ordinary tree.

Beneath the banyan, something moved.

Ami snatched back her hand. Above her, more flowers blossomed in the Pillar's dense, dark greenery, rapidly growing from bud to bloom in the blink of an eye. More and more and more and more flowers burst like fireworks against the foliage, a spontaneous eruption. Beside her, she heard Gaden suck in a sharp breath of surprise, catching their gaze before they quickly looked away, as though they had been caught in the middle of some furtive act.

"Amazing," Gaden murmured.

Ami wrapped her fingers around Little Mother's brass bowl, turning it round and round in her hands. She was shaking.

"Is something the matter?" Gaden caught sight of her expression and stepped closer. Because they were the same height, she found that she could look directly into their eyes without effort.

"Is"—she swallowed—"is the Pillar . . . dying?"

Their lashes fluttered in surprise. "How—how did you know?"

Ami looked down at Little Mother. There were more tiny white blossoms scattered among its branches as well. When had they grown? "There are blight-like growths on the tree beneath the banyan vines," she said quietly. "Growths like the ones on the barley plants out on the plains."

It was not a lie, yet it felt like one on her tongue. She couldn't figure out how to describe just what she had felt—sensed—beneath her fingertips. She had a difficult enough time explaining her unusual powers to other magicians, let alone ordinary people—and she had no words that could adequately encompass the *wrongness* at the heart of the Pillar. For as long as she could remember, she had been able to sense the life—or non-life—of everything in the world around her. All magicians could recognize each other by touch, but for Ami, everything in the world was vibrant or dull with the potential for existence. She could pour her magic into places where there was potential—in stone, in wood, in inanimate objects—and make them dance. Where the places were already full, she could mingle her power with their ki. Like she had with the elderly dog at the gates. Like she could with Little Mother.

In her hands, the fairy tree quivered and produced another bloom.

But the Pillar was not dull. It was not a vessel, with finite edges and definite boundaries. It was an abyss, an endless emptiness she could pour and pour and pour and pour herself into until every last drop of her magic—of her ki—was gone and it still wouldn't be enough to fill the void. The last time she had felt such depthless nothing was when her mother had died.

The Pillar was dead.

And yet it still lived.

"The Pillar is afflicted by the same cursed blight that has decimated the crops of the land, yes," Gaden said quietly. "We are searching for a cure." They met her gaze, and again, Ami was struck how their eyes were perfectly aligned in height with hers. "That's where I hope you come in, scrivener."

"Me?" She looked back up at the holy tree. "But I don't know anything about plants or blights."

"Probably not," they agreed. "But I'm betting you can translate some ancient texts that I am praying will hold a clue."

Are you able to translate older forms of the Language of Flowers?

Ami turned Little Mother's bowl round and round and round some more between her palms. "I see." She tilted her head back to study the Pillar's canopy, where the white of the star-shaped blossoms was beginning to crowd out the emerald green of the leaves. "Is that why the Qirin Tulku has not let the pilgrims pray before the Pillar?" she asked. "Because he does not want them to know the tree is dying?"

The muscles along Gaden's jaw tightened. "No," they said. "That was the Right Hand's decision. He thinks that if they find out, chaos will overtake the land."

Chaos. In all the stories her father had told her about the creation of the universe, the world existed in perfect harmony between Jun and Yan, the personifications of Order and Chaos. But when the scales tipped too far one way or the other, then a divine reckoning was due.

"When the Pillar blooms, the end of the world is not far behind," Chen repeated.

Startled, Ami and Gaden stepped back from each other. They had both forgotten the existence of the little girl, who remained with her hands pressed to the tree, eyes closed.

"We should take her to the infirmary," Ami said, somewhat reluctantly. She wanted to linger here, beneath the shade of the Pillar, and speak with Gaden some more. "She was injured in an attack by the undead. It's why her father asked me to bring her to the monastery."

Gaden raised their brows but did not remark on the matter of the dead coming back to life. "Come, mimi," they said instead, placing a hand on the little girl's shoulders. "Let's get you to the castle healer."

But the little girl did not move, pressing her entire body to the trunk of the tree instead. Ami and Gaden exchanged glances.

"Mimi," Ami said, wrapping her fingers lightly around Chen's arm. "Come."

The world turned upside down.

What was light was dark, what was dark was light, and before Ami's eyes, it was as though everything had been reversed. Colors were inverted, and she felt as though she were in a mirror realm, where rivers ran into mountains and roots grew toward the sky.

"Mimi," Gaden urged the little girl, gently pulling her away from the tree. "Let's—"

Chen screamed when her hands broke contact with the Pillar's trunk, then collapsed into a heap on the ground.

"What is it?" Gaden asked in a panic. "What is it?" They looked to Ami, the whites about their eyes showing in fear. "Help me!"

But Ami could not bring herself to touch Chen. Not again. Not ever. She clutched Little Mother's brass bowl to her chest, trembling with terror. Within the child had been the same emptiness that hollowed out the Pillar, the same endless nothing that no life could fill or escape.

Chen was dead.

And had been dead for a long time.

6

THE **B**ANGTAN **B**ROTHERS' MARE, **C**LOUD, FOUND THEM all the next morning.

Zhara, Han, and the Bangtan Brothers had slept in a nearby barn after the Le sisters denied them shelter for the night. While the days were still warm, this far into the foothills of the Gunung Mountains, the nights were chilly, and the Brothers and Han cuddled together, despite the reek of the undead and several days' travel. For both modesty's and privacy's sake, the boys let Zhara and Sajah sleep in the loft, apart from the others, but it had been so cold in the middle of the night that she had rather wished she were in the middle of the smelly puppy pile below. Needless to say, it had been a restless night, full of anxiety, shivers, and loneliness.

She had just managed to fall asleep when a whicker and a snort sent everyone scrambling for their brushes and Han reaching for his blade.

"Cloud!" Alyosha cried, leaping to his feet. He threw his arms around the mare and buried his face against her neck, heedless of the filth that streaked her coat. "I was so worried."

The horse flicked her ears forward and nuzzled the boy, leaving slobber all over his mop of dark curls before pulling back as though spooked, her eyes wide, her nostrils flaring.

"I know, I know," Alyosha said. "I taste of foul. We'll get a clean soon, I promise."

The second-youngest Bangtan Brother sometimes had an unusual way of speaking that made Zhara wonder if he was from beyond the Morning Realms. He said he had been raised with Taeri and Yoochun in the same orphanage, which was why the Bangtan boys referred to the youngest three as the Choi brothers, but Alyosha's name and looks were strikingly different from the others. His eyes were hazel and his hair was curly, features that weren't commonly seen in the rest of the empire.

"Yah, didi," Bohyun grumbled. "Get back here and snuggle. It's too cold to be getting up just yet."

"Taeri?" came Junseo's hoarse voice. "How are you feeling?"

"Junseo," Sungho said quietly, murmuring something to the leader that Zhara could not quite hear. She rolled over and tried to bury herself deeper into Sajah's plush fur, to the Lion's rumbling protests.

"You are the companion of the Guardian of Fire," she griped. "But I swear I would be warmer in the pile of hay."

Sajah slapped her with his fiery peacock's tail.

"Aiyo!" she hissed, feeling the heat of his flames sting her cheek. He slapped her again, this time without malice.

"Is he all right?" Yoochun cried from below. "Is Taeri-gogo all right?"

With a start, Zhara sat bolt upright and immediately descended the ladder to join the Bangtan Brothers and Han on the ground. "What is it?" she demanded. "Has anything happened?"

The four oldest members were gathered around the eldest Choi brother. Taeri lay in Sungho's arms, having lost all color during the night, his lips gray, his features slack, his heavy-lidded eyes staring sightlessly into a middle distance. If it weren't for the shallow rise and fall of his chest, Zhara would have worried they had lost him entirely.

"He'll be all right, yes?" Yoochun repeated in a stricken voice. "Taeri-gogo will be all right?"

Han gently placed his arm around the boy's shoulders and cradled Yoochun's head against his chest, the way Zhara had seen him do with his own little brother back in Zanhei. Anyang, the Second Heir.

Junseo knelt and placed a hand on the injured boy's forehead. "No fever," he said in a low voice. "No infection?"

"I don't know." Sungho bit his lip. "I applied a healing spell to the wound this morning, only . . ." He trailed off.

Junseo gently pushed Taeri's shirt collar aside to reveal the bite mark on his shoulder. The monster's teeth had broken skin, and now the wound was inflamed—red, angry, and weeping a black viscous fluid. He sucked in a sharp breath through his teeth. "And it didn't work?"

Sungho shook his head. "Mihoon-gogo said he also applied a healing spell in the middle of the night."

"So did I." Junseo's voice was calm, but his eyes were worried. "What do we do?"

"We should keep the wound clean, at least," Bohyun said.

"With what?" Sungho asked. "We left the wagon behind with all our supplies."

"I'll walk to the river," Bohyun said. "We'll use our clothes as bandages if need be."

"What about a bathhouse?" Han suggested. "Surely there must be one close by. Closer than the river at least."

Alyosha, who had wandered off outside during the conversation, presently returned with a damp cloth. "There's frost on the ground already," he said at everyone's incredulous looks.

Sungho dabbed at Taeri's wound with the cloth. "Didi," he said, gently shaking him. "Wake up."

But Taeri wasn't asleep. There was something in the way he stared at each of them that made the hairs on the back of Zhara's neck stand with recognition. The sense that another intelligence—one older and inhuman—looked back through Taeri's eyes.

She drew in a long, slow breath, trying to sooth her nerves. "May I take a look?" she asked, coming to kneel beside Junseo. If the leader was surprised, he said nothing, only moved aside so Zhara could place her hands on Taeri's wound.

When she touched him, she was immediately thrust into that world of magical sight she had discovered on the battlefield, when she had fully surrendered herself to her Guardian power. Now that she understood what was happening, she studied the boy in Sungho's arms with new eyes. Taeri's magic—a beautiful gold she would now recognize anywhere—was riddled with what looked like spots of disease or blight. She had seen this before, in Teacher Hu's apothecary, what now felt like a lifetime ago.

"What is it?" Sungho asked. His keen eyes missed nothing, and he noted the trembling of her hands. "What's wrong?"

Zhara pulled back and steeled herself to focus directly on Taeri's wound with her power. As she had suspected, it was like staring into the abyss, an endless yet depthless dark that pulled on her power. Tendrils of black rot snaked through the ki pathways of the boy's body from where he had been bitten, the source of the demonic infection. Bile coated the back of her throat as she watched the darkness slowly snuff out Taeri's light.

"Possession," she whispered.

A cry of alarm and grief rose from the Bangtan Brothers. "No!" Yoochun cried. "Not Taeri-gogo!" Bohyun wrapped his arms around the youngest, but the lad was strong and nearly overpowered him. "Please," he said, voice cracking, eyes misty with tears. "Not him."

"How?" The anguish in Junseo's voice was so raw it hurt to hear. "How?"

Zhara thought again of the revenants they had fought when they first arrived in Mingnan, of the darkness so opaque that it nearly burned her eyes with cold. The dead were riddled with demonic energy, she realized. The dead were *possessed*.

She started trembling.

"Zhara is the Guardian of Fire," Han said quietly. "If anyone can save Taeri, it's her."

She hesitated. The Le sisters had said that a person bitten by the undead became one themselves after they died. Zhara could turn monsters back into magicians, but she wasn't sure if she could transform the dead back into the living.

"Nene," Yoochun said tearfully. "Please. You must."

Startled, she looked at him, then quickly away from his doe-eyed gaze. Six other pairs of eyes stared beseechingly at her, and the full weight of the enormity of her responsibility as the Guardian of Fire settled over her shoulders. Zhara wasn't sure what terrified her more—how little she knew, or how little she felt capable of living up to everyone's expectations. At the back of her mind, she could hear the Second Wife's voice, whispering poison in her ear. *Worthless, worthless, worthless.*

Someone laid a gentle hand on her left shoulder. Han. She knew his touch immediately, that muted magical resonance between them, that feeling of utter safety. Han was an anti-magician, and the first person she had met whom she had not burned with her power. He had always sympathized with her magic, even if he had not understood. She turned to him and saw the royal blue light that illuminated his ki pathways, soft as though seen through crystal instead of glass.

"You can do it," Han said quietly. "I believe in you."

It was not his words but the intensity of his faith shining from his large, dark eyes that gave her strength. Taking another deep, slow breath, Zhara closed her eyes and exhaled, pushing her power through Taeri and sweeping his ki pathways clear of demonic presence. With her magical vision, she could see the wound on his shoulder diminishing and she imagined the bite like a doorway to another realm that she was slowly drawing shut. She magically cauterized the portal closed with her Guardian fire and made another sweep of Taeri's magic, making sure everything was clear.

Taeri gasped and started in Sungho's arms, color suddenly flooding back into his face. Junseo quickly applied a healing glyph to the boy's shoulder and the puncture marks disappeared, his flesh knitting together and smoothing back into unblemished skin.

"Taeri!" Yoochun ran forward and grabbed his hands. "You're all right!"

The boy in Sungho's arms shot the youngest a stern look. "Mah, who said you could address me so informally?"

Junseo smiled. "He's definitely fine now."

Taeri sat up. "Where are we?"

"Somewhere along the Red River between Mingnan and the outermost west," Mihoon said. "Closer to Mingnan than to the outermost west."

"I know *that*, gogo." Taeri glared. He looked around at Cloud and Alyosha and the others still filthy from the aftermath of battle. "Well, did we win?"

"We ran," Han said.

"We survived," Zhara corrected.

Taeri blinked with surprise when he turned to her, and with some embarrassment, Zhara realized she was still glowing. She pulled her magic back beneath her skin, but the awed, almost shy way he had looked at her made her feel a bit exposed and vulnerable. Before, she had just been a girl to him and the other Bangtan Brothers. An extraordinary girl, perhaps, but a girl nonetheless. But now . . . she was afraid of the distance her power had put between her and the other magicians of the world.

While Sungho and the others filled Taeri in on what had happened since he had been attacked, Bohyun and Mihoon went in search of food and water. Junseo pulled Han and Zhara aside.

"We need to make a decision," the leader said quietly. "About our next course of action."

"Getting to Kalantze and the seat of the Unicorn King," Han said.

Junseo nodded. "Yes. We can go back to the Le sisters with proof that Taeri will not become one of . . . one of them." He swallowed, and looked sick. Even now, hours after their ordeal, Zhara tried not to think of the horror of what they had all witnessed. None of them were strangers to death, not even Han, but there were no words to describe the utter, full-body revulsion of the walking dead. It was not the rot nor the decay nor their decomposing bodies that turned the stomach, but the knowledge that there was no rest, no end, nothing but inexorable hunger from which nothing—not even death—could escape.

"But?" Han prompted.

"But I don't know if we can trust them," Junseo said in a low voice.

Zhara thought of the sisters disguised in the canopy of the trees, of the terrible cold ruthlessness with which they had intended to cut Taeri down before they would even consider extending a helping hand. "Agreed," she said. "Even if they do aid us now, I don't like how willing they are to kill someone just because they might present potential danger."

"Good, I was hoping you would say that. I propose we strike out for Kalantze on our own," Junseo said. But even as he suggested it, he looked pained.

"But?" Han prompted again.

The leader tugged at his hair sheepishly. Like most other Azurean men, he wore the backs and sides of his hair shorn close, tying the rest of it back into a neat bun. "Unfortunately, I'm not entirely sure of the way. But I'm certain we can figure it out. There is only one road out of Mingnan and onto the Zanqi Plateau, after all."

"What of the others?" Zhara asked, glancing at the rest of the Bangtan Brothers. "What would they say?"

"They will follow your lead, Guardian of Fire," Junseo said. "That is what we have sworn to do, after all."

Again, the terrible weight of that responsibility and the dreadful distance of awe between them. "We'll strike out on our own then," she said, hoping she wasn't making a mistake.

"What of these—what was it?" Han scratched his head. "The Herders of Magnificent Glory or something like that? The Le sister said something about the other safe houses being slain or joining their cause."

Zhara looked to the leader, who sighed. "The Heralds of Glorious Justice," Junseo said. "They're a fringe group within the Guardians of Dawn, but I don't think we have anything to fear from them. I'm more worried about the undead."

"What of supplies?" Han asked. "We left the wagon back in Mingnan with all our provisions and camping equipment. And," he said after a moment, "all the volumes of *The Maiden Who Was Loved by Death*."

Junseo smiled. "I'll take Bohyun and Yoochun with me back to Mingnan to bring back the wagon," he said, "if"—he nodded to Sajah still resting in the hayloft—"the Lion of the South agrees to accompany us and help us bring the cart back."

Sajah rumbled his assent.

"Good news, kids!" Bohyun came striding back into the barn with Mihoon on his heels, both of them looking scrubbed pink, cheerful, and *clean*.

"You found us something to eat?" Yoochun asked hopefully.

"No, even better." The eldest's eyes were shining. "We found a *bathhouse*."

The prospect of a bath—a real bath—palpably lifted everyone's mood. Out of courtesy, the boys let Zhara bathe first, and she followed Mihoon out of the barn down the road while Junseo, Bohyun, and Yoochun took Sajah to Mingnan to retrieve their wagon.

"Mihoon," she said quietly, once they were out of earshot of Taeri and the others. "Do you . . . do you know anything about necromancy?" While Junseo might have been the most intellectual of the group, it was Mihoon who had the most worldly knowledge, having survived on the streets of Kasong, the capital city of the Azure Isles, since he was a child. Of them all, he was the only one who had ever mingled with the dark underbelly of black-market magic, a secret trade conducted by Azurean nobles that not even the majority of the members of the Guardians of Dawn on the mainland had known existed.

"My dear friend," he said, "perhaps you should learn how to properly mend a sheet of torn paper with magic before you attempt something so complicated as raising the dead." But when Zhara did not laugh, he sobered. "No, I don't know anything about necromancy," he admitted. "The black market mostly trafficked in ancient artifacts, bits and pieces of enchanted jewelry, armor, and weaponry, that sort of thing."

The word *enchanted* sent a ripple of recognition through her body. She thought of the blade she had forged from a fallen branch, and how it glowed with her magic in the dark. "What does an enchanted object do?" she asked. "And how do you know something is enchanted?"

In response, Mihoon carefully, respectfully wrapped his long fingers around Zhara's wrist. The resonance that rang between all magicians flowed through her body.

"Ah," she said. "I see. The chaos within our blood resonates with the enchantment."

He nodded. "We can all feel the magic within the artifacts. According to legend, these objects were enchanted by the Guardian of Fire over a millennia ago. We don't know what they do, but certain discerning collectors among the nobility—even members of the Warlord's court—will pay a premium price simply for the prestige of possessing such an item." Mihoon released her wrist with a laugh. "I doubt the enchanted artifacts are real, though. It's much more likely that they're cursed. Before *Songs of Order and Chaos* was destroyed, there were tales of magicians summoning spirits to bind to vessels." He tilted his head at her. "There is one thing I do know about necromancy, though," he said.

"What is that?"

"That raising the dead—like any other form of dark magic—requires summoning a demon."

Zhara thought of the abominations that had plagued Zanhei, of the demon wearing the skin of her friend Xu's father. The Chancellor had sought to summon *her*—the Guardian of Fire—all those years ago, only to become possessed by a Lord of Tiyok. For so long, the Morning Realms had believed that only magicians were susceptible to possession, because of the void between matter they were able to manipulate. The chaos void.

But perhaps they had all been wrong.

"Do you think a demon can possess someone who isn't a magician?" she asked.

Mihoon looked thoughtful. "I'm not sure. Isn't that why we're looking for Li Er-Shuan and *Songs of Order and Chaos*? Because that's where we'll find the answers?"

"Yes," she said. "But I mean . . ." She trailed off as they rounded the path to find a small collection of turquoise-blue pools and milky-white springs, around which several wooden pathways and a pavilion had been built. It was not quite a bathhouse, as Bohyun had said, but it was close enough.

"We're here." Mihoon smiled. "The bathhouse. You can bathe in the pools here, but we also found a cave a little farther upstream with a wellspring of warm mineral water that flows into a waterfall. No soap, though, I'm afraid."

"I don't care," Zhara said fervently, nearly swooning at the thought of a long soak in hot, bubbling waters, washing away weeks' worth of grime and travel. "This is paradise enough."

"I'll leave you to it then," Mihoon said. He pointed to a copse of trees not far away. "I'll wait there until you're finished. Take your time."

"One more thing before you go." Zhara bit her lip. "Do you . . . do you think a demon can possess a dead body?"

At that, the composer fell silent. The specter of the undead hung in the air between them, and the blight they carried in their bite.

"If they can," Mihoon said softly, "then we are all in more danger than we thought."

7

AS FAR AS **K**UNGA, THE HEALER, COULD tell, there was nothing wrong with the girl.

Dead, the odd but beautiful scrivener had said. *Chen is dead.*

But as far as Kunga could see, Chen was alive and well.

Well, perhaps *well* wasn't quite the right word. But the girl was certainly alive. She was ambulatory, and she had no sign of a fever or an infection that could have caused her to swoon before the Pillar that day. In fact, if anything, her temperature seemed cooler than it ought to be, and her pupils did not respond to the light of a candle. Kunga hadn't been able to find her pulse either, which had been mildly alarming, but as everything else seemed to be in working order, he figured it was simply due to his inexperience and lack of practice that he had not been able to find it.

"We'll keep the child in the infirmary for now," he had told the Beast and their beautiful but odd scrivener. "And monitor her through the week to see if she improves."

"What course of treatment will the healer be giving her?" the scrivener asked. Their dark eyes were intense behind their spectacles. "The injury on Chen's arm has become septic."

It had taken all of Kunga's strength not to vomit as he unwrapped the little girl's bandage to examine her wound. He had always been the squeamish sort, and the smell alone was enough to turn anyone's stomach.

Kunga had never wanted to be a healer. When he first joined the monastery at Castle Dzong as a novitiate, he had intended to work with fragrances. Kalantzean incense was famous throughout the Morning

Realms, and he had thought to possibly expand the castle trade into cosmetic perfume oils for rich nobles and pampered peers. Unfortunately, the Qirin Tulku had not been interested in such an endeavor, and had thought Kunga's gift with herbs and flowers might be translated to a skill with tinctures and tonics. The Qirin Tulku was not often wrong, but in this instance, the shaman-king had erred in his judgment.

For five years, Kunga had been apprenticed to the previous castle herbalist, an old woman with a gift for healing in her fingers. She could place her hands on various different meridian points of the body and diagnose what ailed a patient simply by touch, pulse, and the color of a person's tongue. Old Sritee claimed what she did was not magic, but as far as Kunga was concerned, it might as well have been. Although all magicians had the potential to manipulate the void equally, Kunga found healing spells difficult to wrap his mind around, but then again his paltry skills with magic had not been considered significant enough to apprentice with his clan shaman. It was just that there was so much to *learn* and *remember,* and while he could extensively catalog every single strand and strain of flower and herb, he could care less about which tendon attached where on the hand, foot, elbow, whatever. He had no feel for the human body and its various idiosyncrasies; he was far more comfortable with plants. Plants he understood; people he did not.

But at least he knew what to do with an infection. "I'll brew her an anti-inflammatory tincture of Solomon's seal and burdock root," he said. "And encourage her to rest and eat."

"She's dead," the scrivener said again. "She won't do either." They turned to the Beast. "We should fetch her father, Sang. Ask him where their ancestral lands are so that her heart seeds may be buried with the rest of her people."

"But the Right Hand won't allow any pilgrims into the castle," Kunga had protested nervously. Sometimes he didn't know which Hand of the Qirin Tulku he feared more, the scarred Beast before him or the officious official who ruled over the castle in the Unicorn King's time of illness. The Right Hand was a rigid, unforgiving sort; at least the Beast could be prevailed upon to be reasonable, even if they evinced no remorse in carrying out the Qirin Tulku's dirty work.

"I'll ask Teacher for an exception," the Beast said quietly.

"In the meantime," the scrivener said, "we should see if we can't find some sort of explanation or even a cure for Chen's condition in the library."

The scrivener was rather blunt, bordering on bossy, but to Kunga's surprise, the Beast did not seem to mind. In fact, they seemed to rather like it, if the slightly besotted expression on their scarred face was anything to go by.

"All right," the Beast said equably. "In fact, I do have a title that I've been wanting to show you."

And the two of them disappeared off to the library without so much as an acknowledgment or a farewell, leaving Kunga and the girl alone.

That had been a week ago and Kunga had not seen either of them since. Probably having too much fun flirting with each other in the library, he thought. And ordinarily he wouldn't have minded being left alone—it gave him more time to experiment with different fragrance profiles at his still, but after a week alone with Chen, he had to admit that there was something . . . not quite right about the child.

She didn't eat, for one.

He didn't notice at first. He dutifully brought her bowls of tsampa porridge and butter for her tea at every meal before leaving the child to her own devices while he attended to his own. The one advantage of being a healer in a castle monastery was that he rarely saw injuries worse than the occasional paper cut from the library or an accidental bruise or burn from the kitchens and incense workshops.

Then he began to notice the bowls returned just as full as they had been dropped off, dried barley meal crusted around the edges as though the child had simply sloshed the tsampa around. At first he had thought it simply the work of a child being a child. Refusing to eat anything that did not suit their fancy.

But as the days went on, Kunga grew worried when he too saw just how little she was eating. How little she was eliminating. If it weren't for the fact that he could occasionally hear Chen shuffling back and forth in the infirmary by herself, he would have thought he was entirely alone.

He began conducting daily examinations of the girl, even though he did not know what he was he looking for, nor how to treat it if he did find something unusual. He wished Old Sritee were still alive. He wondered if the Beast and their scrivener had found anything to help her.

"How are you feeling today, Chen?" he would ask.

But the little girl would never reply.

That was the other thing that unsettled him most.

Her silence.

Kunga, like many other children of the outermost west, had grown up in large tribes and clans, with dozens upon dozens of other children. Cousins. Siblings. Half-siblings. His own mother had five husbands, and Kunga's fathers had each fathered several children of their own. If Kunga was unfamiliar with the body in its illness, he was incredibly familiar with birthing, babies, and children.

And children did not act like Chen.

Children were not silent.

Then there were the moments she did speak. Sometimes, in the middle of the night, Kunga would hear muttering and murmuring coming from the infirmary, an unfamiliar, eldritch language. There were no words in her speech that he understood, but neither were they the nonsensical babbling of a baby. They sounded almost like incantations or prayers, but to who—or what—he did not know.

He thought that perhaps it was time to swallow his fear and ask the Right Hand and the Beast to let the girl's father into the castle.

"Chen," he said to the girl one day. "Are you missing your baba?"

As per usual, she did not reply. But today, things were different.

Today, when Kunga walked into the infirmary with a tray of tsampa, butter, tea, and a bit of honey he had managed to beg from the kitchen cleric to tempt the girl's palate, Chen's eyes were bright, and for the first time since he had met her over a week ago, he thought he could see a distinctly inhuman intelligence shining out of them, staring intently at him.

"Chen?"

And then she sank her teeth into his arm.

8

GADEN STARED AT THE MANUSCRIPT PAGES BEFORE them, the script blurring together into an illegible scrawl, trying their very best not to look at the pretty girl sitting scant inches from them at the adjacent desk. They both sat on threadbare silk cushions on the library floor, their knees just barely touching as they made notes, searching for a reference or a mention of necromancy or the undead in their respective texts.

Or at least, that's what Ami had been doing. Gaden admired her single-minded focus; once she set her mind to a task, the scrivener was determined to see it through.

But they, on the other hand, had a difficult time concentrating because they were sitting in the library, next to the most beautiful girl they had ever seen.

Gaden had seen beautiful people before, of course. For all its remoteness, Kalantze had been a hub of commerce and trade of the Zanqi Plateau since before the fall of the old capital of Ngasa. They had seen beautiful people of all shapes, sizes, and skin colors come and go, some from places as far away as the kingdom of the Sindh, the desert empires beyond the Dzungri basin, and the tropical isles from beyond the Nameless Sea. Ugly people were keenly aware of beauty, because they saw how the rest of the world turned its eyes away from ugliness. Gaden had spent much of their childhood struggling to find beauty in their own scarred and damaged face, to find some semblance of light to draw the eye. When they failed, they turned to seeking it out and admiring beauty in others.

Ami looked up from her work with a puzzled expression. "What?" she asked. "Have I got something on my face?"

"Oh, um, ah, no. Just, er, thinking." Blushing furiously, Gaden wrenched their attention back to the text in their hand. They hadn't even made it past the title page.

She peered over her spectacles at their translation. "Oh, the title is *Visions of a Bloody Chamber,* not *Dream of a Red Room,*" she said, pointing to one of the characters with the tip of her charcoal pencil. Gaden quickly withdrew their gloved left hand, clenching and unclenching their fingers beneath the low desk. "In this context, *red* means *blood.*"

Gaden dutifully made the correction with their right hand, feeling slightly sheepish. Because Gaden was not a magician, none of the clerics had taken it upon themselves to teach them the intricacies and nuances of the Language of Flowers, leaving them to learn as best they could from *The Thousand-Character Classic* themself. "Have you made any progress in your translations?" they asked, clearing their throat.

A few weeks before their encounter in the village square, Gaden had found a stained leather folio containing several disintegrating pages in a rubbish heap outside the castle walls. They wouldn't have given it a second thought if it weren't for the strange symbol stamped into the water-stained cover—a series of concentric circles of alternating dark and light, bisected vertically so that each half was a mirror inverse of the other. It had reminded Gaden of the all-seeing eye of Mara, or the sigil of the Seventh Immortal of magic. Not many people in the outermost west worshipped at the mansions of Reason, and the unusualness of its iconography made Gaden think it had been thrown away by accident.

That had been before they noticed the long, jagged slices and slashes that marred the symbol, as though someone had taken a blade to it in order to obliterate or obfuscate the symbol.

The book had definitely not been thrown away by accident.

"Some," Ami said, bringing Gaden's attention back to the text before them. "But I can't quite figure out the meaning of this phrase. This"—she pointed to the first character—"means *ki.* But this radical here"—she circled part of the glyph with her fingertip—"means *against.*" Picking up her charcoal pencil, she started sketching down her thoughts on a piece of paper. "Against ki," she murmured. "What does that mean?"

Gaden wouldn't be of much use to her. When they had opened the folio for the first time, they had been confronted with pages upon pages of incomprehensible nonsense. The characters resembled the Language of Flowers, but they had not been able to read any of it. An ancient form of the magician's script, Ami had said later, from before the standardization of the writing system during the reign of the sixth Mugung Emperor.

"My father would know better than me how to translate this," Ami said with a sigh, closing the folio and removing her spectacles. Without the barrier of glass between her eyes and the rest of the world, Gaden was struck anew by how beautiful they were—large, lambent, and intense. "But . . . I suppose he's not quite in his right mind at the moment." She scratched at the back of her neck, looking embarrassed.

The specter of Gaden's last encounter with Li Er-Shuan lingered between them. Once Ami had arrived at the castle, her father had taken one look at his daughter, then at Gaden, then screamed at them to stay away from her. They had been masked at the time, and thought removing their guise as the Beast would help matters.

It had not.

Instead Li Er-Shuan's wild eyes had gone even wilder with fear at the sight of Gaden's scars. "No," he said in a strangled voice. "Not you. Not you!" With a shriek, he had fallen to the ground, pounding the dirt with his fists. "I have broken my will on the wishes of tyrants my entire life," he moaned. "I cannot bear Their Majesty's radiance."

Gaden had looked to Ami in bewilderment, but she had been equally flummoxed. In the end, Okonwe and the castle healer, Kunga, had taken Li Er-Shuan to a spare bed in the dormitories with a sedative in his butter tea.

"You're still here?" Zerdan, the librarian, emerged from the catacombs beneath the library, carrying armfuls of scrolls. The texts the clerics had managed to save from the fall of Ngasa were stored in the vast, labyrinthine stone passageways beneath the library, and while the Qirin Tulku might have been incredibly motivated to save as much knowledge as he could, he had been less motivated to organize it. The task had fallen to the castle librarian, who might have possessed the wisdom of the ancients but unfortunately had the bones of one as well. "It's late. Shouldn't you children be in bed by now?"

With a start, Gaden realized they had been staring at Ami the entire time they were lost in thought, although thankfully she had not noticed. They wrenched their gaze away and back to the present. "Sorry, Zerdan," they said. "We won't be here too much longer. I know how much the elderly prize their sleep."

"Psh," the librarian scoffed. "I'm afraid you have it the wrong way round, child. It is children who must be put to bed early and soon."

Ami looked up from her notes and frowned. "I am not a child," she said seriously. "I'm sixteen."

Zerdan chuckled. "When you get to my age, everyone else is a child, no matter how old they actually are."

"Just how old is the librarian?"

Gaden raised their brows at the directness of Ami's question, but Zerdan did not seem to mind.

"I'm older than Lo's mountain but younger than the birth of the universe." The librarian smiled. "Which is to say, I don't remember."

No one knew Zerdan's true age. He had been at the monastery of Castle Dzong since before the Qirin Tulku had made Kalantze the Unicorn King's seat-in-exile, and he had been ancient even then. The librarian was small, wizened, with spindly grasshopper limbs and bright, nearly bulbous eyes. He might have been fifty. He might have been five hundred.

"So," Zerdan continued, peering over Gaden's shoulder at the pages of notes scattered across the stone floor and wooden desktops of the library. "Riveting read?"

"Yes." Ami ran her hands over the symbol stamped into the cover of the folio. It was twin to the symbol on the folio that she had brought to the castle, the very folio that had made Gaden think that they could trust her the first time they met. "Extremely."

Zerdan froze at the sight of the symbol. "Where did you find this?" he whispered. "Do you know what this is?"

Gaden frowned, studying the little librarian. "Do you?" They resisted the urge to cover the defaced leather cover with a spare sheet of paper. Someone had not wanted the book to be found, and as fond as Gaden was of Zerdan, that was enough to give them pause.

The librarian hesitated. "This," he said, pointing to the symbol on the cover with a quivering finger, "is a *taikhut*."

Gaden blinked. "*Taikhut?*" They had never heard the word before. There were many dialects and languages spoken throughout the Morning Realms, and they thought it might be a word from one of the clans on the Zanqi Plateau.

"The word has roots in an older tongue lost to time," Zerdan said. "But it means *Great Absolute*."

"Oh!" Ami scrabbled for a loose sheet of paper and jotted down something in the Language of Flowers. "*Daeghuk*," she said, writing a variation on the glyph for *large* or *great,* followed by one unfamiliar to Gaden. "It's a version of the symbol for the followers of the Way." She drew a bisected circle, coloring half of it dark, leaving a bit of the dark blank and adding a drop of black to the blank space. It looked like a half moon with opposite stars on the black and white sides. "The priestesses of Do say it means the Supreme Ultimate, and represents order in chaos, chaos in order. It must be the same root characters."

Zerdan nodded. "Just so," he said. He gave Gaden a sidelong glance. "They're clever, this one." He twinkled, and Gaden tried not to blush. "I like them."

"But hold a moment, something doesn't make sense," Ami murmured, studying the *taikhut* and her drawing. "Why would *Songs of Order and Chaos* have this symbol on its cover? It has nothing to do with the philosophy of the Way."

"Does it not?" Gaden asked. "I'm no priestess of Do myself, but I believe the Way has a god of Order and a god of Chaos. Jun and Yan."

"That's not entirely accurate," Ami said. "Jun and Yan are just names for the principles of Order and Chaos."

Zerdan had been studying them with an unreadable expression on his ancient face, lips thin and eyes sharp. "*Songs of Order and Chaos,*" the librarian said slowly. "What is that?"

Ami's eyes widened in surprise. "Surely the librarian knows of *Songs of Order and Chaos?*"

He shook his head. "I'm afraid not, my child."

"It's a book of demonology, cosmology, and the rituals, spells, summoning, and binding of spirits."

"Ah," Zerdan said. "Is that what the people call it these days?" The librarian laughed. "I had always heard it called *The Book of Beginnings and Endings.*" He grew serious. "I thought every extant copy had been destroyed."

Ami glanced at Gaden. "So did I," she murmured. "But I'm glad to know there are others like my father in the world who are more interested in the preservation of knowledge than its destruction."

"What do you know of this book, Zerdan?" Gaden asked. Not many clerics had access to the catacombs beneath the library where all the rescued texts from Buotaka Palace were stored aside from the librarian, and if Zerdan had been the one to toss it out, Gaden wanted to know why.

The librarian shrugged. "Not much, I'm afraid." He gave them a sheepish grin. "A librarian I might be, but I'm not much of a scholar. The traditions of magic I come from don't have much use for texts, you see."

Gaden frowned. "I thought you studied the Language of Flowers at the imperial university before the Just War."

Zerdan nodded. "And so I did. But I was already a man grown when I began learning to read; such things don't come so easily to the elderly. I know enough to catalog and organize what we have, but not so much as to comprehend it all." He smiled ruefully. "So much for my librarianship."

Gaden smiled back. "You're still the most learned among us, after the Qirin Tulku."

The librarian snorted. "That's a function of time, not intellectual capacity, my young friend." Leaning over, Zerdan peered at the pages laid before Ami's desk. "So," he asked in a tremulous voice, "have you discovered anything interesting in this forbidden book of yours?"

"Not much," Ami admitted. "We only have fragments of what seems to be a much longer text. See?" She removed a page from Gaden's folio and a page from her father's and set them beside each other. "Without the other, most of what is written here is nonsense. But when put in context, we can find a much bigger picture. Instead of phrases, we have entire sentences. Instead of oblique references, we have actual explanations." She tilted her head as she scanned the work. "This says something about calling upon the spirits of"—she squinted and brought the paper closer to her nose—"elemental warriors? These look like ancient forms of the characters for fire, wood, wind, water, and . . . oh. I think I'm reading these incorrectly. These are ancient ways of writing the Celestial Symbols, I think."

"Celestial Symbols?" Gaden asked.

Ami nodded. "There are four stars that rise and fall according to the seasons in each of the cardinal directions," she said, clearly an astrologer's daughter. "Sajah, the red star, which lives in the asterism of the Lion of the South. Temur, the white star, which resides in the asterism of the Eagle of the North. Yongma, the azure star, which resides in the asterism of the Dragon of the East, and . . ." Her brows furrowed. "I can't remember the name of the yellow star, but it is said to live in the asterism of the Unicorn of the West."

"The Unicorn of the West?" Gaden sat up straighter on the floor. "It's a constellation, not a creature?"

"Well . . ." Ami bit her lip. "The stories say that they *were* creatures, whose bodies were placed in the night sky by the Immortals to protect each of the cardinal directions over which they watch."

"I thought the Unicorn of the West was said to reside by the Root of the World," Zerdan said. "They were the sacred tree's holy protector in all our legends."

"And the healer of all illnesses," Gaden said, resisting the urge to scratch at the scars beneath their left glove.

"Yes." Ami frowned. "I can't be sure, but it seems like the yellow star is called . . . *nameless*? That can't be right." She looked to the librarian. "Can you read it?"

Zerdan shook his head regretfully. "Remember, child, I had the education of a yak-herder's son until I came to Castle Dzong."

Ami drew her brows together. "Do you think someone else in the monastery might be able to decipher this then?"

Gaden gave her a sidelong glance. "If there were, I wouldn't have needed to hire your services, Li Ami."

The librarian gave her a kindly smile. "Kalantze is not the capital city of Ngasa, and never was. The clerics here might have magic, but it's only ever been in the service of growing sweet flowers and aromatic woods. Incense is the lifeblood of this monastery, not institutional knowledge."

"Oh." She sounded disappointed. "I suppose I wrongly assumed a place with such priceless texts would have scholars to match."

Gaden laughed. "We have rare texts of magic aplenty around here, but a new romance serial or a light detective novel would be worth more than its weight in perfume around these parts. I heard Jae Hyun is publishing a new love story."

"Yes, *The Maiden Who Was Loved by Death*," Ami said dismissively.

"You've read it?"

She shrugged. "My last job was copying out romance novels in a bookshop."

"You don't sound all that impressed."

Ami made a face. "Once you've read one romance novel, you've read them all, to be honest."

Zerdan chuckled. "Are all love stories the same to you, child?"

She frowned. "I suppose not," she said. "It's just . . . the endings are all the same. They all end with a kiss."

Gaden swallowed hard, imagining what kissing someone would be like. They wondered if Ami knew, but didn't dare imagine kissing her. No one had ever touched them comfortably, let alone romantically, their entire life. They scratched absentmindedly at the skin beneath their glove, trying not to touch the scars on their face. "Do you like to be surprised?" they asked instead.

Ami tilted her head. "No, but I like when things are . . . different,

I suppose. Out of the realm of the ordinary." She bit her lip, looking at them, then looking quickly away. Gaden felt a flutter of something like hope brush their heart. She cleared her throat. "Like this." She tapped the fragment of *Songs of Order and Chaos* with the non-charcoal end of her pencil. "Every version of history is different when told through the eyes of a different person."

"What do you mean?"

"Well, in the south we are taught that the Sunburst Warrior saved the Morning Realms from the Mother of Ten Thousand Demons with the help of the Guardians of Dawn, the elemental warriors of legend. But here"—she pointed with her pencil—"there is no mention of either, only the Star of Radiance."

"I've always heard the Bangtan Brothers put on an amazing rendition of the Sunburst Cycle," Gaden said wistfully. "But they've never made it to the outermost west."

Ami was mystified. "Who are the Bangtan Brothers?"

"You've never heard of the Bangtan Brothers?" Zerdan was astonished. "Even I know who they are, and I've got one foot in my grave."

Just then, the doors to the library blew open.

"My liege!" It was the healer from the infirmary, Kunga. "You must come quickly. It's the girl, Chen."

"What is it?" Gaden asked, immediately getting to their feet.

"She's . . . she's dead."

9

IT TOOK **Z**HARA **AND THE OTHERS A** little more than a week to cross the Gunung Mountains and enter the Zanqi Plateau.

Although Zhara had been warned about cloud sickness by her old mentor, Teacher Hu, nothing could prepare her for the actual reality of traversing across the highlands of the Gunung Mountains, so short of breath and lightheaded she feared she would pass out at any moment. Of their party, Yoochun and Han fared the best, their robust athleticism serving them in good stead. Sungho and Mihoon suffered the worst, experiencing crippling bouts of nausea and piercing headaches, to the point where they had to take two days off for them to recover.

But now, at last, they were in the lands of the Unicorn King, the outermost west of the Morning Realms.

The landscape of the outermost west was nothing like the city-born-and-bred Zhara had imagined it: vast and stark, filled with scrubby shrubs and hardy grasses instead of the lush grazing fields she had envisioned. The Gunung Mountains ran all the way to the Dzungri basin in the north and the Kimanayas, also known as the Ever-Whites, in the south. The tops of the peaks were glazed with glaciers, a pure, blinding white that was so crisp and clean it hurt to look at, flowing into the rivers that watered the rest of the empire. Zhara had thought weeks on the road had inured her to the emptiness of the rural parts of the empire, but even in the remotest parts of the lowland provinces, there was always a lonely trading post, a lonely roadside guesthouse, a lonely traveler. But atop the Zanqi Plateau, she could see no path, no road, no markers to lead the way to

Kalantze. Nothing but gentle rolling hills and vast grassland as far as the eye could see.

So *much* nothing. She felt both vulnerable and isolated at once beneath the too-wide sky.

"Well," Junseo said. "This might be harder than I expected."

"Surely we have a map," Han said.

"Of course we have a map," Mihoon said. "Unfortunately, they all stop at the borders of the Zanqi Plateau."

"You mean to tell me we don't know where we are?" Han asked in dismay.

"Well, we know where we are," Mihoon said. "We're somewhere between the desert to the north and the sea to the south."

"Could be a song," Junseo murmured, humming a little to himself. "*Between the desert and the sea, I'm still wandering, not knowing where to go.*"

"Focus," said Sungho, snapping his fingers before their leader's nose. "We're not here to perform; we're here to make sure the Guardian of Fire and her escort get to Kalantze safely."

"And after that?" asked Han. "What will the Brothers do after we get to Kalantze?"

Sungho looked around, taking in their tired horse, the thin, wan, and exhausted faces of the Choi brothers, and even Sajah's dimmed and dulled fur. "I don't know," he said. "We've always gone where we were needed. This is the longest we've been out of contact with our mentor in the Guardians of Dawn, Lee Banghyuk. We were supposed to have received a message from him in Mingnan with our next course of action." He gave a hollow laugh. "I suppose it's up to us to figure out the next step after Kalantze. If the safe houses in the border towns have been compromised by the undead or the Heralds of Glorious Justice, I don't know where we can go."

"One step at a time," said Bohyun. "First things first. I propose we find a good place to camp, get a full meal into our bellies, and have a nice long rest. We've earned that much, at least."

"Did someone mention food?" Yoochun called hopefully from the back. "We never did get to eat a single bowl of Mingnan's infamous red sauce noodles."

"The battle for the title of Spice Sovereign will have to be tabled for another day, I'm afraid," Zhara said with a smile.

The troupe went about the business of finding and setting up camp, a routine that they had all honed to perfection by then. Junseo, Han, and the Choi brothers played a game of *frog, fly, net* to determine who would have to dig the latrine trenches while the others set up tents. Sungho went to settle Cloud and Sajah down for the evening. Zhara assisted Bohyun and Mihoon with supper, throwing together a quick noodle soup with fermented chili paste and water for broth and reheating preserved deep-fried noodles.

"Nooooo!" came an anguished groan from the setup cohort. It appeared as though Yoochun had lost.

"You know what they say, didi." Alyosha grinned. "The loser always starts it."

"It's they who have the most to lose will lose." Junseo laughed.

"Don't worry, didi," Han said, clapping a hand on Yoochun's shoulder. "Taeri and I will help you dig."

"We will?" Taeri was surprised. He had entirely recovered from his ordeal with the revenants—physically at any rate. Although he seemed to have returned to his usual, cheerful self, there was a darkness that occasionally shadowed his eyes now, and sometimes, when he looked at Zhara, she could feel the force of his mesmerizing stare like a stab to the gut.

"Of course we will," said Han. "As long as you do us a favor in return."

Yoochun sighed. "Why do I feel I will regret this?"

"I'll read *The Adventures of the Pirate Baron* if you read *The Maiden Who Was Loved by Death* with me."

"Aw, gogo." Yoochun groaned once more. "Not again."

Zhara laughed quietly as she listened to Han try to cajole the others into reading his favorite romance serial for the thousandth time. When he tried to introduce the Bangtan Brothers to *The Maiden Who Was Loved by Death* several weeks before, their reception had been less enthusiastic than he had hoped.

"Does it have pictures in it?" Alyosha had asked. The Choi brothers loved illustrated adventure serials, and their current favorite was about a boy on a quest to become a pirate baron of the Jade Flotilla.

"No, but it has . . . feelings!" Han had begged to no avail.

Alas, the Bangtan Brothers had remained unmoved.

"*Frog, fly, net!*" Han and the Choi brothers chanted, now arguing over whether they were going to read *The Maiden Who Was Loved by Death*. The playground hand game was the way the Bangtan boys settled any dispute in camp, a habit Han had also picked up. "*Frog, fly, net!*"

"Yes!" Han shouted, pumping his fist in triumph. "Frog eats fly. I win. You boys will have to read the first volume now."

The Choi brothers gave theatrical moans, then laughed as Han pouted.

"Just you wait!" he called as they began to dig the ditches. "You'll be basing your next play on this, mark my words!"

After dinner, Zhara declined Han's offer to practice fencing with her enchanted blade and curled up in the covered wagon with Sajah and a sheet of paper instead. He had insisted since Mingnan on teaching her the rudiments of swordplay and self-defense, and although she did not mind watching him strip down to his undershirt and work up a sweat, she was less enthusiastic about working out herself. Besides, she had promised to write Suzhan while they were apart, and this was the first opportunity she had had in weeks to send her sister a letter. She smoothed out the paper and readied a charcoal pencil to write.

Except she didn't know what to say.

Tell me stories, nene.

Zhara had plenty of stories to tell Suzhan, only she wasn't sure what she could put in a letter that would be read aloud by an attendant at the academy in Jingxi. What could she say about her ability to become a living being of flame? How would she describe to her blind sister what things looked like when she was in Guardian form, the colors, the lights, the threads of ki that bound the world? Or the fact that she had discovered a side effect of her transforming objects from one form to another was enchantment? She looked to the sword she had carried with her since Mingnan, propped up in the corner of the covered wagon along with all the other theatrical props used by the Bangtan Brothers. If it weren't for the faint glow of magic along the length of its naked blade, it wouldn't look any more convincing than the others.

I only know love stories, I'm afraid.

Zhara smiled. Warmth kindled in her chest, as it always did whenever she thought of Han, but lately another feeling was starting to mingle with the heat: frustration.

Tell me stories, nene . . . as long as all the love stories are yours.

Zhara stared at the blank sheet before her, twisting the rose quartz bangle about her wrist. She had so much to say, but so little to tell. In all the romance novels she had read, after the kiss came intimacy, but the closest she and Han had gotten to any sort of skinship was a few chaste handholds. And while Zhara respected his modesty, she was beginning to wonder if he didn't see her more as a friend than a lover.

The uncertainty hurt.

"The problem with love stories," Zhara said aloud, "is that no one ever writes about what happens in the ever after."

"That's because the ever after is for grown-ups, and grown-ups are boring."

Zhara whirled around to find Yuli's spirit-ghost lounging on some props and costumes in the corner of the wagon. "Yuli!" Pushing off her intentions to write for another night, Zhara threw her arms around the spirit girl.

"Well, well, well, Bubbles," twinkled the tall redhead. "I never knew you felt this way about me. Whatever will Prince Rice Cake say?"

"Shut up." But Zhara couldn't stop grinning at the sight of her friend. It had been weeks since they had seen each other last, either in person or in spirit. "It's good to see you."

The smile that Princess Yulana returned was genuine, entirely without her customary irony or smirk. "You too," she said softly. "I was worried. Temur lost track of you in Mingnan. What happened?"

Zhara sobered. "We were attacked by the undead."

Yuli's spirit-ghost flickered in surprise. "So the rumors are true."

"Rumors?" Zhara sat back on her heels. "You've heard then?"

The redhead nodded. "Stories of attacks from border towns all the way to the westernmost regions of the Middle Kingdom." She tilted her head as she studied Zhara. "Are you all right?"

Zhara bit her lip. "We are now, although one of the Brothers got bitten during the attack."

"Who?"

"Taeri."

"The sexy one?" At Zhara's expression, Yuli shrugged. "What? I may like girls but I have *eyes*."

"I just said he was bitten and that's the first thing that comes to mind?" Zhara rolled her eyes. "He's fine, by the way."

"He sure is." Yuli winked. "Aiyo!" she cried as Zhara pinched her leg. "I keep forgetting you can do that," she muttered.

"Can you *please* be serious for once?"

"Being serious makes me itchy. I think I'm allergic." When Zhara glowered at her, Yuli sighed. "All right, all right. Tell me what happened."

Zhara repeated the events of the past several days, including her suspicion that the undead were possessed by demons.

"What?" Yulana shook her head. "But that's impossible. Only magicians can be possessed by demons."

"We don't know that," Zhara said. "Without *Songs of Order and Chaos*, we don't know what the limits are to the demons' chaos magic. If there even is a limit." She fell silent, thinking of the enormity of what they were up against. The return of the Mother of Ten Thousand Demons. Finding the locations of the portals to the chaos realm. Closing them. Banishing any Lords of Tiyok they might encounter along the way. The weight of it all made Zhara want to lie down for a nap and never get up.

"I might have some leads on that front, if you don't find Li Er-Shuan out here in these hinterlands," Yuli said.

Zhara sat up straighter. "What do you mean?"

Yuli removed her distinctive pointed cap and raked her hands through her tangled, ruddy hair. It always amused Zhara to see Yuli treat her spirit-self like a physical body; there was neither hair nor hat for the northern princess to fuss with. "It was rumored," she said, "that in the days before the Just War, the Mugung Emperor ordered four of his greatest magicians to try to summon the Guardians of Dawn in order to combat the growing instability in the Morning Realms. There are spirit-summoning rituals in *Songs of Order and Chaos*; they believed the Guardians could be summoned. But that gambit obviously failed. His magicians became possessed by greater demons and the emperor himself turned into an abomination. So the prime magician ordered the book to be struck into four pieces and scattered to the four corners of the empire so that no one would be able to play with forces beyond their ken ever again."

"Hold a moment," Zhara said. "You never told me this!"

Yuli looked sheepish. "I only just recently discovered this myself, otherwise I would have told you before. It was the real reason Auncle Mongke thought sending me south was a good idea—not only to get me out of the reach of the current kang's claws, but to possibly look for one of the pieces in Zanhei's palace library."

"So that's why you agreed to the engagement with Han." Although Zhara knew now that their marriage arrangement had been a sham from the very start, she couldn't help but feel a small twinge of resentment about it. Han had lied to her for so long about his true identity as a prince, and it had taken her finding out about the betrothal for him to come clean.

Yuli nodded. "We knew that the southern piece had been found. There were rumors surfacing all over the black markets of the realm that a southern astrologer had discovered a copy of *Songs of Order and Chaos*. But because we knew it was incomplete, there wasn't much this astrologer could do with it."

"Why did your auncle want to find *Songs of Order and Chaos* anyway?" Zhara asked.

The tall girl sighed. "Each of the pieces supposedly carries a different piece of information. The southern piece supposedly has all the knowledge about demonic summoning and possession, and my auncle is very keen to find some sort of way to either cure or prevent possession among our people."

"Do you know what the other pieces contain?"

Yuli shook her head. "Only that all together, the four pieces of the book would tell the totality of Tiyok's first rise and defeat, as well as the entire truth of the Guardians of Dawn. Us," she added. "Not the mutual aid society."

"You mean to tell me that even if we find Li Er-Shuan and his fragment of *Songs of Order and Chaos,* we still might not know how to defeat Tiyok anyway?" Zhara asked in dismay. "What do we do?"

"It may behoove us to start a search for these other fragments," Yuli said. "Conducted by the people we trust." Her copper eyes glinted. "*Only* by those we trust."

Zhara was silent for a moment. "You mean to ask the Bangtan Brothers."

"Yes."

An unexpected lump rose in her throat at the prospect of saying farewell to the Bangtan Brothers. She had come to respect and adore them in their journey west together—not just as artists she idolized, but as friends. "Well," she said, trying hard to keep her voice from wobbling, "they were in search of the next course of action after Kalantze."

"Perfect." Yuli peered at Zhara. "Oh, I'm sorry, I didn't mean to make you upset."

"It's all right." Zhara wiped at her tears. "I've just grown fond of those chaos clowns, is all." She cleared her throat. "But enough about me," she said. "What about you? What's happened since we last spoke?"

Yuli rolled her eyes. "Well, it might not be as dramatic as being attacked by the undead, but we've been harried by the Heralds of Glorious Justice the entire journey north."

"The Heralds of Glorious Justice?" Zhara had heard the name a number of times now. "Just what are they?"

The princess sighed. "They are a fringe faction of the Guardians of Dawn," she said, "who believe in magician liberation by any means necessary. Including"—she made a face—"violence."

"Violence?" Zhara stirred uneasily, thinking of the Le sisters saying the other safe houses had either been overrun by the undead or recruited to the cause of the Heralds. She then thought of Junseo downplaying the danger of the Heralds as they traveled west, and felt a sinking sensation in her stomach. "In what ways?"

"Small acts of guerrilla warfare, mostly," Yuli said. "Setting magical traps, attacking prominent people in my grandfather's court, taking people hostage and press-ganging them into their organization, that sort of thing."

"You say *guerrilla warfare* like it's nothing," Zhara said.

Yuli shook her head. "I don't mean to. It's just that I think I would rather these small acts of sabotage to the bigger threat they pose to the empire."

"Which is what?"

The princess met her gaze. "Civil war."

Zhara was taken aback. "What are their aims?" she asked. "If the Heralds of Glorious Justice are looking to wage war?"

"They ride under the banner of the Four-Winged Dragon," Yuli said. "The Mugungs' old battle standard."

"Do you mean to tell me," Zhara said incredulously, "that these . . . these, uh, insurgents are looking to restore the *Mugung Dynasty*? The one your grandfather destroyed twenty years ago?"

Yuli nodded.

"But there's no one left," Zhara said. "All the Mugungs were killed. They found the infant Princess Weifeng's remains in the palace."

"They did find fragments of bone consistent with that of a small child in the imperial quarters," Yuli said. "Next to the charred corpse of her mother." She heaved her shoulders. "There are whispers," she said wearily, "that the young princess was actually smuggled out of the palace the night my grandfather razed the imperial city to the ground."

Zhara frowned. "What makes people believe that?"

"Because the Star of Radiance was never found."

"The imperial gem?"

Yuli nodded again. "Legend says that the Star of Radiance is what gives the Sunburst Throne its true claim because it was used to seal Tiyok back into her realm all those years ago."

"But that's just a story," Zhara said. "A gem doesn't confer a divine right to rule."

"No," Yuli agreed. "But it was an enchanted object, and one tied specifically to the Mugung bloodline. The fact that it's disappeared and not shown up on the black market indicates to some that perhaps the heir did indeed survive somehow."

Another enchanted object. There was so much of ordinary magic she did not know, let alone the powers of the Guardians of Dawn.

"It doesn't help," Yuli continued in a low voice, "that my grandfather is ill and that the issue of succession is far from secure."

"Ill?" Zhara was startled. The Warlord's presence had loomed over her entire existence so that it was impossible to think of the Great Bear of the North as anything but larger than life and undying.

"He's old," Yuli said. "And he hasn't yet named his heir, to either the Sunburst Throne or the bear claws of the Gommun Kang." The northern princess looked grim. "It may be that civil war is on our doorstep, with or without the help of our insurgent friends in the Heralds of Glorious Justice."

Zhara knew very little of northern politics, but she did know that a succession crisis and a civil war would throw the Morning Realms further into chaos. "*They say when the world is out of balance, the souls of the Guardians of Dawn are reborn,*" she murmured.

Yuli made a face. "If it comes to fighting the Mother of Ten Thousand Demons or the Lady of Wild Things, I would rather face Tiyok than the head of our rival kang."

Zhara shook her head. "One step at a time," she said, echoing Bohyun's oft-repeated refrain. "One step at a time."

10

BY THE TIME AMI AND GADEN ARRIVED at the infirmary, Sang
and the Qirin Tulku were already praying over Chen's dead body.

"You!" The tall yak-herder got to his feet when Ami walked through
the door. "I thought you were going to look after her!" Sang clawed at
his face in grief. "Look at her. *Look at her.*"

The little girl lay supine on a pile of blankets on the floor, hands
folded over her stomach, eyes closed. Despite the unnatural pallor of
her skin, it was the first time since Ami had met Chen that she thought
the little girl looked . . . human. In death, she was just another body
whose ki had gone, her features slack and empty.

"I—I'm sorry," Ami said, stumbling over her apology. "I meant to
look for a cure in the library but I got . . . I got distracted." By the
stricken look on Sang's face, she knew she had said the wrong thing
yet again. She had thought the yak-herder deserved the truth of her
failings, that he would account for her honesty, but the bereaved father
looked as though he would burst with rage instead.

"I thought you cared about her!" Sang clenched his hands into fists.
"You promised!" he shouted, throwing his hands down to his sides.
"You promised!"

Ami shrank back at Sang's outburst, resisting the urge to use her
power against him the way she had the dogs in Castle Dzong when she
first arrived with Chen. To her surprise, Gaden stepped in front of her,
arms outstretched to protect her from any harm. But the yak-herder
only turned his violence on himself, beating at his chest with his hands
and wailing. Sang fell to his knees, wrenching, heaving sobs racking
his body with such anguish that Ami felt the ache of it in her own ribs.

His grief was raw and terrible and overwhelming, and Ami wanted to scratch at her skin to alleviate the discomfort, at the green-gold glow that clawed at her from within.

Quietly, the Qirin Tulku came to kneel before Sang, wrapping his hands around the yak-herder's shoulders and resting his forehead against his, their faces meeting nose to nose. They stayed together in an act of communal grief, rocking back and forth in time with Sang's sobs until they subsided.

"May her soul return to the Great Wheel of the universe——" the Qirin Tulku began the benediction.

"——and keep the spokes turning," Sang, Gaden, and Ami finished softly.

This was the first time Ami had ever laid eyes on the reclusive shaman-king of the outermost west, under whose protection she was so graciously living. He was far more unassuming than she thought he would be, his sage-green robes indistinguishable from a common cleric's. She might have even mistaken him for an initiate, if it weren't for the crown he wore on his shaven head——made of lacquered wood and topped with a polished piece of crystal. He was younger than she expected, although it appeared as though rumors of his illness were true; his features were drawn and haggard, his limbs wasted.

Slowly and with intention, the Qirin Tulku took a small, bone-handled knife from within his robes and reached for the small pouch about Chen's neck. With another whispered prayer, he cut the pouch loose and handed it to Sang with two hands and a bow. The father received the pouch with two hands and a bow.

"May her heart seeds nourish the next generation," they all intoned. Ami sensed Gaden's curiosity that she knew the ritual words.

"My mother was from the outermost west," she murmured, wishing she had Little Mother with her. The little fairy tree had been grown from her mother's heart seeds and her mother's ashes. Neither Ami nor her father had known from which people or what place Rinqi had come. Otherwise she would have planted Little Mother in its home soil already.

"Chen will lie here until the next full moon," the Qirin Tulku said to Sang. "And then we shall have a funeral pyre for her remains."

The tall yak-herder nodded, tears still coursing down his sun-seamed cheeks.

Ami studied the little girl laid out on the floor with arms crossed over her chest. Although she knew that life had departed the body, she couldn't help but feel as though Chen would stir and wake up at any moment. There was something about the twist of her lips or the tension of her face that made Ami feel as though the child was asleep; in fact, Chen was more animated in death than she had been in the last few weeks of her life.

Her power prickled and Ami resisted the urge to scratch. She felt cold and clammy all of a sudden, as though someone had thrown a damp cloak over her magical senses. In the distance, a lone dog began to howl and dread gathered in the pit of her stomach.

"Farewell, daughter." Sang leaned over and pressed a gentle kiss to Chen's brow. "Until the next life."

The girl's eyes snapped open.

Howls erupted from every dog within the castle.

"Chen?" Sang asked in disbelief. "Chen?"

The child blinked, then turned her head to look at Ami, gaze falling to the green-gold glow about her hands. There was a profound emptiness within Chen's eyes, a darkness like the abyss she had sensed in the roots of the Pillar.

"Chen!" Sang cried, flinging his arms about his daughter, laughing with joy. "Chen!"

"Wait!" Ami cried. "She's—"

The girl launched herself at the yak-herder, a child throwing herself into her father's embrace. Then the force of her lunge brought them both crashing to the ground. All around the fortress, myriad snarls, growls, and barks erupted from every corner as every faithful hound tried to bang down the doors to the infirmary and attack the unnatural presence within the castle.

"Child!" The Qirin Tulku tried to pull Chen off her father, but her teeth were sunk deep in Sang's throat—ripping and tearing at his flesh, sending arterial sprays of blood everywhere. "Chen!"

Gaden rushed forward and threw their arms about the Qirin Tulku's waist just as the girl turned her eyes on them both. "Kunga!" they shouted for the healer. "Kunga, go fetch the Right Hand! Now!"

The healer, who until that moment had been cowering in the corner, clutching their injured arm to their chest, took off with alacrity.

"My brush," the Unicorn King said weakly. "In my . . ."

Ami grabbed her own brush and brandished it at Chen, her mind suddenly blank. She knew hundreds of thousands of characters in the Language of Flowers, and several more hundred variants in other dialects, yet not a single one came to mind as she faced down the approaching child. Her hand trembled as she sketched the first spell she could think of—the opening line from *The Thousand-Character Classic.*

The heavens were black, the earth gold.

Green-gold light hovered in the air, the glyphs shimmering until they faded into nothing. At once the skies grew dark, although the day remained cloudless and clear. Beneath her feet, the ground buckled and roiled and danced as the dirt turned to gold, molten and liquid and pliable in her magical grasp. With a gesture of her hand, Ami pushed a wave of transformed earth at the child, engulfing Chen's feet in a cast of gold that solidified immediately, rooting her in place.

But that did not stop the child from advancing.

Slowly, inexorably, Chen kept moving forward. The sounds of breaking bone and tearing muscle were dreadful, the crackle of snapping tendons and the slop of blood and flesh turning Ami's stomach as the girl left her feet cast in gold on the floor. She didn't know what was worse—the sound of bodily torture or the utter silence from Chen herself.

"Fire!" Gaden shouted beside her. "Set her on fire!"

Their voice galvanized Ami, and she wrenched her mind away from the unspeakable horror before her and dredged up the character for *fire.* She traced it in the air with wide sweeps of her brush, and as the green-gold light hovering before her faded into flames, she shoved the fiery net at Chen with all her magical might.

But even fire did not stop her. Even as parts of her body began to char and drop off, she continued to advance toward them, stumbling a bit as first her fingers, then her toes, then her hands and feet disintegrated into ash. When she could no longer stand, Chen continued coming on wrists and knees, grinding the bone to nubs as she left a trail of sparks.

"We have to get out of here!" Gaden shouted. "She'll set the entire place aflame!"

The blankets from her bed were already burning, and fire was licking up one of the wooden support columns toward the thatched roof of the infirmary. This time Ami quickly drew the character for *water,* directing the flow of liquid toward the roof, the blankets, the floor, soaking the wood, straw, and stone so they wouldn't catch.

"Her father," the Qirin Tulku began weakly, coughing as smoke began filling the room. "We can't leave him."

Sang lay on the dirt floor, a fountain of blood bubbling from the wound in his throat. Without thinking, Ami reached out with her power, feeling for the yak-herder's ki, then filled the pathways of his body with herself. With a gesture of her fingers, Sang heaved himself to his feet. "Hurry!" she called. "Follow us!"

Gaden had the Qirin Tulku slung on their back and ran out of the infirmary, with Ami puppeting Sang on their heels.

"The fire brigade!" Gaden yelled. "The fire brigade! Someone ring the bell!"

The castle dogs had not ceased barking as Gaden, Ami, and their respective burdens made their way to the central courtyard of the Pillar. The crazed, frantic frenzy echoed off the stone walls of the amphitheater, louder than the sound of any bell. Clerics began gathering, pointing fingers and crying out in alarm at the sight of the infirmary on fire. Some of the clerics who were magicians began working together to put out the flames—casting and chanting, casting and chanting, a rhythm and a wave of motion and music and magic. Water ringed the building, sending up billows of steam as it came into contact with the heat, but slowly, oh-so-slowly, the fires began to die down, as the last of Chen's remains dissipated into smoke.

Beneath the shade of the Pillar, Gaden, Ami, the Qirin Tulku, and Sang all collapsed to the ground. Ami released her hold on the yak-herder's ki, and Sang fell limp, no longer able to move or speak, although through her eyes, Ami could still see the clear brightness of life shining through his veins, growing fainter and dimmer by the moment.

"I'm sorry," she said hoarsely. "I'm so sorry."

More blood bubbled from his throat as he tried to say something.

"My brush," the Qirin Tulku said. "It's broken." He turned to Ami. "May I borrow yours?"

She relinquished it immediately, startling as her fingers came into contact with the Unicorn King's. "Holiness," she began, but the Qirin Tulku gave a subtle shake of his head.

Taking Ami's brush, the shaman-king quickly drew the characters for *flesh, seal, mend,* and *whole* over Sang's wound. The spell glowed jade green before sinking into the yak-herder's skin, and Ami watched as the torn muscle and tendon knit together.

"Shh, shh," the Qirin Tulku soothed. "It won't be long now. But before you return to the turning of the Great Wheel, my child, give me the heart seeds of you and your daughter, so that we may bury them in your ancestral lands to nourish future generations to come."

Sang nodded his consent and once again, the Qirin Tulku took his small knife and cut the leather cord that kept a pouch full of seeds close to the yak-herder's chest. Sang also handed Chen's pouch to the Unicorn King. He whispered something, and the Qirin Tulku leaned in close.

"The Pochezin lands," Sang rasped. "My homeland."

The Qirin Tulku put his hand over the yak-herder's. "I will make sure your seeds will be planted there, my child. You may rest now."

With another nod, Sang relaxed, his face and body going slack as one last breath rattled out of his ravaged body. The Qirin Tulku gently closed his eyes. "May his soul return to the Great Wheel of the universe," he said softly.

"And keep the spokes of fortune turning," Ami and Gaden replied.

They sat in silence for a moment. The flames had been put out in the infirmary, and the dogs had finally fallen silent. In the distance, they could see curious clerics coming down the amphitheater stairs to join them at the Pillar, Li Er-Shuan and Zerdan among them, with the Right Hand in his emerald-green robes at the head of the procession.

"Burn the body," the Qirin Tulku said in a low voice to Gaden. "Tonight."

Gaden looked shocked. "But what about the rites? His soul won't have any time to leave his body."

The Unicorn King shook his head. "We cannot wait for the full moon and risk the body coming back to life and attacking more of us."

Gaden narrowed their eyes. *More of us?* they repeated.

Ami met the Qirin Tulku's gaze. She had known the moment their fingers touched that the shaman-king had been bitten. Gingerly, he pushed the sleeve of his robe up over his bicep. Gaden sucked in a sharp breath at the sight of a bite mark on his arm, already turning black and septic.

"Child," the Qirin Tulku said to Gaden. "You have always been my little star."

"No." They shook their head. "No. I won't hear this, Teacher." Their voice broke. "We'll find some cure. I will search the plateau far and wide, even if it means finding the Unicorn of the West for you."

"There is no cure for the undead, or if there is, I don't have enough time before I turn into a revenant like this unfortunate father and his daughter." He tilted his head toward Sang. "My little star," the Qirin Tulku said again. "You know what to do."

The shaman-king reached for his own heart seeds and pressed them, along with Sang's and Chen's, into Gaden's hands. "Fulfill my last promise to the yak-herder," he said. "And take my heart seeds and bury them at the place where the sky was held back."

"Teacher?"

"At the foot of Mount Llangposa."

"Mount Llangposa?" Gaden was confused. "I've never heard of it before."

The Qirin Tulku smiled. "Ah, well, burying my heart seeds at the foot of Mount Llangposa fulfills a promise I made to someone else a long time ago." He patted Gaden's glove hand. "You will honor that for me, yes? My last request?"

"Stop." Tears clotted Gaden's voice. "I can't lose you."

"Hush," the Qirin Tulku soothed. "You won't lose me." He wiped a tear from the scarred side of Gaden's face. "You'll meet me again," he said. "Bonded souls find each other throughout many lifetimes. You'll find my next incarnation."

"But it won't be the same," Gaden said, and their voice was thick with tears.

"Of course not," the Qirin Tulku said. "That's the beauty of this cycle of life, death, and rebirth. My soul will return to the cauldron of the universe to be remade in a different form, to carry the lessons of this life into the next. Perhaps in the next incarnation, you will be my teacher, as I have been yours, my child."

Gaden was sobbing openly now. "I'll find you," they said. "I promise."

"Good," the Qirin Tulku said. "Good." He closed his eyes. "Now, promise me one last thing, my star."

"Anything, Teacher."

"Promise me you'll kill me."

"No." Ami recognized the stricken look in Gaden's eyes. "Teacher, please—"

"Do not let this vessel go corrupted," the Unicorn King said. "Please. Let me die with dignity, and let me die a final death."

But Gaden was beyond reason, their grief too overwhelming to think clearly. "No, no, no," they repeated. "There has to be some way. Some cure."

There was no time. The Qirin Tulku knew that, Ami knew that, and deep down, so did Gaden.

The shaman-king reached into their robes, pulling out the ceremonial bone-handled knife from their robes that they had used to cut the bags of seeds from Sang's and Chen's necks. Ami had never seen a knife like it before—the ivory was nearly translucent, a milky-white jade instead of bone, and the blade was made from sharpened stone. The shape and materials were crude, like the tools used by the ancients.

"Drive this into my heart," the Qirin Tulku said, pressing the knife into Gaden's gloved hand. "Be swift, and be strong."

But Gaden continued to shake their head, trying to refuse the weapon.

A knife blade to the heart would not be a swift death, Ami thought. Although she was no healer like Kunga, she knew how stubborn the threads of life could be, how hard they resisted being cut off by death. A wound to the heart would be drawn out and painful, even if life lingered on for only a few more breaths.

Then she looked to Gaden. The agony on their scarred face was palpable, and the horror of what their teacher and mentor was asking of them was writ large across their features. To kill someone you loved with a knife . . . the intimacy of that action sent a shiver of revulsion down Ami's spine. You would be close enough to feel the life drain from their body, to see the light leave their eyes.

She knew firsthand what that was like. She had held her mother's hand as Rinqi died from a wasting sickness, had felt the terror and world-ending trauma of grief, and the desire to chase a loved one down into oblivion. Ami would spare Gaden that. She would spare anyone that if she could.

Kneeling beside them, Ami wrapped her hand over theirs, gently pushing the knife away and placing her hand on the Qirin Tulku's brow.

"Ami?" Gaden asked in confusion. "What are you doing?"

She ignored them and closed her eyes. She couldn't save her mother, but perhaps she could save the Unicorn King. Letting her magic unfurl, Ami imagined that green-gold glow filling her blood, her bones, her ki pathways with light. She imagined herself blossoming like the flowers on Little Mother's branches, blooming power in her wake.

When she opened her eyes, she could see the world anew.

Beneath her hands, she could see the jade green that was the Qirin Tulku's magical gift inextricably wound with the bright life of life. But there was also a shadow on that light, something that was dimming it, draining it.

It was the wound.

Through her magical sight, she could see the bite mark absorbing light the way a locust devoured crops. As it swallowed life, it grew, larger and larger, beginning to encompass the whole of the Qirin Tulku's forearm. Ami moved her hand over the bite, flinching as her magic came in contact with it. The wound was more than a wound; it was a tear in the fabric of reality, beyond which she could sense something deep, something ancient, something so vast as to rip at the seams of her sanity. It tugged at her power, a bottomless, insatiable hunger that wanted more and more and more. But if she pushed, if she poured herself into it, she could sew—

"No," the shaman-king rasped. "Do not let the darkness take you too."

Ami met the Qirin Tulku's gaze.

"You," he said. "I know you for what you are. I see your light."

Hide your light.

"Teacher?" Gaden asked.

"Listen," the shaman-king said, grabbing Ami's hand. She flinched as his nails dug into her flesh. "You alone can defeat this. Whatever is in me, it's dead. Bring it back to life, so that I may die. Do you understand?"

But she didn't. With a cry, the Qirin Tulku slapped her palm over the wound and Ami cried out as her magic went numb. "I will help you," he said. "Now heal me."

Through the blankness, she could sense the light of his ki hovering on the edges of her magical senses. She drew on it, folding the strands of life over the abyss, weaving and stitching the hole closed. She could feel the Qirin Tulku's own gift guiding hers, and beneath her fingertips, she began to understand. The darkness fed on death and the more she drew death away from the wound, the weaker it grew. Her power returned to her, drawing strength from the Unicorn King's own magic.

The wound was sealed, leaving clean and unblemished skin in its wake.

The Qirin Tulku went limp in Gaden's arms.

"Teacher!" they cried. "Teacher!"

The life was fading fast from the Qirin Tulku's body, his energy spent. "My little star," he said again, lifting his hand to cup Gaden's cheek. "Remember my words. And may we meet again in my next life."

Before she could stop it, the light within the Unicorn King went dim, and he was gone.

She slumped over, exhausted.

"Ami!"

Presently, she became aware of whispers rising around her, a susurrus of suspicion. As she returned to herself, she noticed a crowd of clerics gathered about her, murmuring among themselves. Expressions of shock, terror, and even a bit of awe were writ on their features.

"Her eyes—"

"Did you see? They glowed."

"What is she?"

Ami closed her eyes and turned away. She knew what the next words out of their mouths would be.

"Uncanny," they murmured. "Unnatural."

"What is this?" the Right Hand cried upon seeing the Qirin Tulku's body. "What have you done, scrivener?

"What have you done?"

PART 2

The Root of the World

11

KALANTZE SMELLED LIKE FLOWERS.

Zhara was amazed at the beauty of the fragrances that permeated the air around the little village, a heady mixture of perfumes
both familiar and foreign to her. The only flowers she and the Bangtan
Brothers had passed on their way to the Qirin Tulku's seat-in-exile
were cosmos flowers growing wild along the edges of the pastures and
plains, a pretty proliferation of pink, white, and purple, but they were
scentless.

But here, in this tiny, isolated village halfway up a lonely mountain surrounded by nothing but fields of barley, Zhara's nose was overwhelmed with the smells of home. Ylang-ylang, jasmine, lemongrass,
sandalwood, osmanthus, and even Buri basil, a sweet, minty scent that
suddenly made her very hungry for the bowls of noodle soup that the
canal vendors of the Pits sold every morning, noon, and evening.

"Kalantzean incense is quite famous throughout the Morning
Realms," Mihoon remarked as they wound their way up the hilly path
from the plains to the village gates. "The clerics at Castle Dzong have
been making it for thousands of years."

"Do the clerics make perfumes too?" Han asked curiously. "I would
like to send Xu a little gift if I can."

Mihoon shook his head. "I don't think so, but maybe the vendors in
the market do."

"*Shopping,*" Sungho breathed, closing his eyes in excitement. "I haven't
been shopping in so long."

The word *shopping* sent a thrill of pleasure up Zhara's spine. She had never had much coin for selfish pleasure; the vast majority of the wages she had earned had disappeared straight down her stepmother's gullet. What little she could scrimp and save for herself had gone toward her little stack of romance novels she kept under her pallet by the hearth, but she had always loved to *look*. She had grown up in a port city, and one of the few free pleasures she had had in life was browsing the goods and wares from all over the world on display in the covered market at the Pits. After weeks upon weeks upon weeks of the same food and the same scenery, she was yearning for something different. Something new.

"What sort of food is Kalantze famous for?" Yoochun asked, rubbing his belly. "I'm starving."

"You're always starving." Bohyun sighed. The eldest wrapped an arm about the youngest's shoulders, ruffling his hair affectionately. "I'll buy you some flatbread when we get to the village. I hear they make it out of barley here."

Although Zhara had grown accustomed to the thinness of the air on the Zanqi Plateau during their travels, the path to the village was still quite steep, and soon it was too hard to keep talking. The trail was surprisingly empty, considering that Kalantze was also considered a place of holy pilgrimage for many in the Morning Realms, but perhaps the lands of the outermost realms were just so vast that it was impossible to run into a crowd of people. In the ten days it had taken them to get to Kalantze from Mingnan, they had not run into a single other soul. Zhara glanced at the skies above, where the ever-present serpentine flight of Temur could be seen. The Eagle of the North had been their guide in the past week, pointing the way to the seat of the Qirin Tulku from her perch overhead.

It had nearly been a pleasure jaunt for Zhara and Han—ten days of travel with the Bangtan Brothers, during which they had not encountered any trouble—but a mournful air had started to permeate the group. They were fast approaching the moment of parting, and although the Bangtan Brothers had been eager and willing to journey north to Urghud to help Yuli look for the northern fragment of *Songs of Order and Chaos,* no one wanted to say goodbye.

To Zhara's surprise, this funereal air also seemed to permeate the town of Kalantze.

"Who died?" Bohyun muttered, eyeing the somber-faced residents of the village, who eyed them back with haggard and weary expressions as they passed through the main gate toward the market square. There were no guards posted at the entrance, and Zhara was uncomfortably reminded of the last time they had entered an unfamiliar town with no defenses. Thankfully, the people of Kalantze were alive, although they weren't exactly *lively*. If it weren't for the gloom, Kalantze would have been one of the prettiest towns Zhara had ever come across—the entrance marked by a freestanding lintel and posts made from stone, painted dark red, bright blue, and yellow-gold, which stood in stark contrast to the beige-brown of the landscape. The village itself was filled with square, flat-topped buildings with whitewashed walls and brightly painted trims. Some homes even boasted murals by talented artists, most of which appeared to depict scenes from the life of the Sunburst Warrior, the Sunburst Cycle.

"Not a bad likeness," remarked Han as they passed one mural depicting the Sunburst Warrior with all four Guardians of Dawn. "Although you are far more majestic in person, Mistress Brandy." He pointed to the warrior wielding a fiery sword, hair streaming out in flames behind them, eyes aglow, riding astride an enormous leonine creature. "But you, on the other hand," he said to Sajah, dozing in ginger cat form in the cart, "are rather less impressive in person."

Sajah opened one baleful golden eye, gave a perfunctory hiss, then resumed napping.

Zhara studied the mural. Parts of it were vibrant and vivid, while others were faded and forgotten. It appeared as though the villagers freshened the paint from time to time, and the main figures of the Sunburst Cycle had been the beneficiaries of the most care. Yet as she looked closer, she could make out other scenes and figures—a volcano in the distance, a banyan tree ringed by clouds atop a glacier peak, and a crater lake surrounded by plum blossoms. Streaks of colored light flowed from behind a black thundercloud with glowing red eyes, and beneath it, a frog, a locust, and a moth.

"I never realized how much the sigil of the Sunburst Warrior looks like the Great Wheel of Virtue," Junseo remarked, coming to stand beside Zhara. On the central figure's golden breastplate was the familiar sunburst symbol of the Mugung Dynasty and the Guardians of Dawn society, but in the middle of the device were eight spokes like a wheel. Zhara was unfamiliar with the faith of the Great Wheel, although she had seen that eight-spoked wheel on prayer flags all over the western part of the empire.

"They say it was the Sunburst Warrior who brought the teachings of the Great Wheel from the kingdom of the Sindh into the Morning Realms," Mihoon said.

"Is that why the Free Peoples acknowledge no sovereign but the person on the Sunburst Throne?" Yoochun asked.

"But I thought the Qirin Tulku was their sovereign," Han said.

"Why are you asking me?" Mihoon looked bemused. "I don't know anything about the politics of the outermost west."

"Because you know the most random things, gogo," Han and Yoochun replied together. They looked at each other and grinned.

"Speaking of the Qirin Tulku," Zhara said quietly, "we should move on to the castle and ask for an audience."

Silence fell over the others as they all craned their heads to gaze at the fortress-monastery towering on an outcropping of rock over Kalantze. From their vantage point, all they could see were gleaming white walls and glimmering golden rooftops.

"How do you get up there?" Taeri asked.

One of the pilgrims in the village square overheard his question. "The entrance to Castle Dzong is here," they said, pointing to a stone post and lintel carved with characters from the Language of Flowers that Zhara could not read. "The 888 Steps of Meditation. But you'll not find entrance to the Pillar today. Or any day," the pilgrim said angrily. "The Right Hand has been denying everyone the right to pray, even those of us who have just lost loved ones. Two of our own have died, and they won't even return their bodies." They shook their head. "It's not right. It's not right!"

Zhara glanced at the 888 Steps, which seemed to be carved of stone directly into the hill. At the front of the entrance were two large biers of aromatic woods and pressed flowers. White banners had been draped over them both, and with a start she realized she was looking at two funeral pyres, although there were no shapes of bodies beneath the cloth. "My condolences for the pilgrims' losses," she said. "May the souls of the departed find peace." She had given the benediction of those who worshipped at the mansions of Reason, and wondered a breath too late if she had committed an egregious offense.

But the pilgrim seemed mollified. "May your good deeds return to you thousandfold," they said. "I appreciate your heart, friend." They glanced at the castle overhead. "That's more than I can say for the clerics cloistered behind the walls of their fortress."

At last, it was time to say farewell. From this point on, the Brothers would be going their way, and Zhara and Han to see the Qirin Tulku.

"I'll miss you all," she said softly, taking each of their hands in hers as she said goodbye. She memorized the feel of their ki, the exact shade and tint of their magic, and engraved them all onto her heart. Indigo blue, cherry-blossom pink, glittering black, fiery scarlet, shimmering gold, forest green, and iris purple. Junseo, Bohyun, Mihoon, Sungho, Taeri, Alyosha, and Yoochun. "Take care of each other."

"You too." Junseo gave her a side hug before Han came up behind and threw his arms around them both. Zhara gave a watery laugh as the top of her head accidentally knocked into the taller boy's chin.

"Stay safe," Han said, his voice muffled as he buried his face in Junseo's jacket.

"One last cheer before we bid each other farewell?" Junseo asked.

As one, the nine of them gathered in a circle, their hands meeting in the middle.

"Bangtan, Bangtan, Bang-Bangtan!"

"I know it's an honor meeting the Unicorn King and all," Han panted as he steadily climbed the 888 Steps. "But"——he wiped at the sweat pouring from his brow—"right now I would rather have someone else have the glory instead and be eating some of those yak dumplings they were selling in the village square."

Zhara said nothing on the ascent, conserving her breath. She too had quickly worked up a sweat beneath the fierce sun as she walked the steps, although every once in a while, a bitter breeze would blow through her damp jacket, sending chills and shivers all through her body. Although she had adjusted to the thin air of the high plains, it was the chill she wasn't sure she would ever get used to. It was late in the osmanthus month, and already the air had a bite, even as the sun's rays seemed harsher on the Zanqi Plateau. The back of her neck still stung with the burn of wind and travel, even as her brown skin had protected her from the worst of it.

At last the two of them summited the steps and arrived at the entrance to the castle. The enormous wooden gates were closed, with no sentry posted on either the wall above or on either side of the doors, although a handful of dozing dogs were scattered about the place. They pricked their ears and sniffed the air curiously as they approached, then returned to their naps. A white banner with the device of a single-horned gazelle-type figure was draped over the doors—the unicorn sigil of the Qirin Tulku, Zhara supposed.

"I guess they don't need to worry about invasions up here," Han said. "You could see anyone coming from miles away." The view from the castle gates was nothing short of awe-inspiring: vast plains of golden barley as far as the eye could see. He frowned. "What's that?"

He pointed to what seemed at first like a shadow encroaching on the edges of the barley plains.

"Scorch marks?" Zhara ventured. She squinted and shaded her eyes against the sun. "No, it almost looks like . . . bruises."

Bruises. The word conjured the image of the spots of blight Zhara had seen on Taeri's magic. On a hunch, she closed her eyes and took a deep breath and let herself be consumed by her own power once more.

The world was again awash in glimmering threads of ki. As Zhara gazed out over the plains, she could see the clear white light of life that wound through each barley stalk, as well as the flat, dull gray of harvested grain. When life was gone, it was simply as though the light had been extinguished from the vessel, although she thought she could still see an afterimage, a faint glow that emanated from all organic matter that contrasted with the matte sheen of rock and dirt and stone.

The dark spots on the barley were not the absence of life.

They were the void.

With a start, she pulled her power back beneath her skin, screwing her face against the pain of anti-ki burning her eyes. Han was staring at her with an expression of fascinated awe, a silly, proud little smile on his face. It made her pulse flutter faster and she fingered the rose quartz bangle at her wrist. "What is it?" she asked.

"Your eyes . . ." He took her hand in his. ". . . were glowing." His words were soft and full of amazement. "What did you see?"

Warmth flooded her at his touch, driving away the constant chill of the mountain breeze. "I . . . I know this sounds impossible, but . . . those dark spots . . . the plants are . . . possessed."

Han raised his brows. "Possessed? Like . . . people? Like"—he lowered his tone—"the undead?"

Zhara nodded. "It's hard to describe, but it's like anti-ki. The utter opposite of life and order and reason. In the undead, in abominations, and now in the barley . . . it's like there is a dark so deep as to be a void. A demonic energy."

He looked troubled. "That's definitely something we should bring up to the Qirin Tulku."

Zhara eyed the closed gates to the castle. "*If* they let us in to see the Qirin Tulku."

"They'll let us in." Han grinned. "We have a *real* Guardian of Dawn of legend."

She knew Han said it to make her feel better, yet she couldn't help but feel even more alienated and afraid than before. It was so much responsibility, and she was only a girl. An elemental warrior, perhaps, but just a girl nonetheless, just turned seventeen.

"I'm just a girl," Zhara said in a soft voice. "An ordinary girl."

Han wordlessly placed his hand over hers and the fires of her magic immediately dimmed. She glanced down to see that she had inadvertently transformed her bangle—his gift to her—into gold before it flickered and turned back into pink translucent stone. He dimpled and turned his palm over, linking her fingers through his. Zhara tightened her grip, relishing the simple act of touch. For most of her life, she had believed her touch would burn those she loved, the unusual power in her veins a wildfire that scorched everything and anyone that dared get close. The sensation of skin against skin was a marvel each and every time. Heat of an entirely different sort warmed her body.

"An ordinary girl," Han repeated. "And so much more."

Her heart fluttered at the tenderness in his tone. Han's kindness was the reason Zhara had fallen for him, the reason she had wanted to kiss him—well, one of many reasons she wanted to kiss him—but sometimes she felt incredibly vulnerable beneath his gaze, as though his empathy were somehow more revealing than standing naked before him.

Not that she would mind that. Much.

"Extra and ordinary all at once," Han said. "How can that be anything but extraordinary?"

Zhara gave a watery laugh. "Your poetry has improved."

He was confused. "It has?"

She shook her head. "Let's ring this giant doorbell, shall we?"

Han and Zhara stood on either side of the suspended log, pushing it away before releasing it to swing back and strike the bronze bell.

Presently, the doors opened, and two figures emerged—a cleric in emerald-green robes and an enormous wooden chain of office, and another figure in a nondescript brown tunic and trousers, wearing a boar-chimera mask.

"Go away," said the cleric. "Can't you see we are in mourning?" He pointed to the white banner draped over the gates.

"Mourning?" Zhara asked in surprise. She thought of the biers in the square down below and realized she had assumed the deaths were among the villagers of Kalantze or the pilgrims. "Whose passing?"

The masked figure turned to her, and although she could not see their expression behind their face covering, she could hear the grief and unshed tears in their husky voice.

"The Qirin Tulku is dead."

12

AMI SAT BENEATH THE PILLAR, LITTLE MOTHER in hand, studying assorted pages from *Songs of Order and Chaos*. All around her, the clerics milled about, preparing the Qirin Tulku's and Sang's bodies for the pyre. Gaden and the Right Hand had fought well into the night about the proper funerary procedures for the Unicorn King, as well as what was to be done about Ami herself. The Right Hand had all but outright accused Ami of murdering the Qirin Tulku, but Gaden had managed to convince him and the other clerics that the shaman-king died of his wound. Gaden had radiated righteous fury, and even Ami could feel the force of their anger compelling her to silence.

In the end, she had been cleared of any wrongdoing.

Since then, she had buried herself in *Songs of Order and Chaos,* seeking any knowledge she could about the undead. From her father's folio, she knew quite a bit about abominations, about how demonic energy infected the ki of magicians and transformed them into monsters. But she had never heard of demonic energy infecting the ki of non-magicians before, and she was troubled by the lack of information in the book.

Ami knew the text she possessed was incomplete. During the week she had spent in the library poring over the text with Gaden, it had become abundantly clear that the original book was quite literally in pieces. The two of them had spent more time trying to match the pages into some semblance of order than on translating, which was why she had not made much progress in finding a cure for the blight ravaging both the Pillar and the land.

She tilted her head back to gaze at the flower-laden branches of the sacred tree. The rot had progressed up the roots of the tree, visible as ugly growths that dotted its trunk like bruises. Although the canopy was still lush and green, the twigs and leaves that had fallen to the courtyard were desiccated, dry, and almost stonelike in texture. By now she had gotten used to the way touching the blighted parts muffled and dulled her magical senses, as long as she could run her hands over something living again shortly afterward. Little Mother bore the brunt of her experimentation, and as though in protest, several minuscule white flowers popped into bloom, saturating the air around with a bright, musky perfume.

Ami rubbed a fallen leaf from the Pillar between her fingers, trying to categorize the sensation. An emptiness like death, only deeper. Darker. An absence that was almost a presence. She had felt it across several different sources now—the barley stalks, the roots of the Pillar, Chen, and in the Qirin Tulku. She thought of the wound she had sewn up in the Unicorn King, the way her power had pushed away the darkness. Then she looked to Sang's body, remembering his torn throat. A feeling of foreboding overcame her.

You alone can defeat this.

The leaf in her hand fell to her feet, soft and green once more.

"When the Pillar blooms, the end of the world is not far behind." Ami looked up in surprise to find her father standing before her. "I wonder what the stars say about little fairy trees."

Li Er-Shuan's eyes were large and owlish beneath his spectacles, clear and lucid for the first time in a long time. His stay in the monastery seemed to have done him a measure of good, the days of consistent rest and food giving him some semblance of safety, bringing some color back to his cheeks and a soft smile to his lips. Ami couldn't remember the last time her father had seemed so healthy. She couldn't remember the last time he had smiled. Not since before they escaped the palace of Zanhei.

Not since the night Ami betrayed the Royal Consort to the Chancellor.

"The stars don't speak, baba," Ami said. She immediately regretted her words, berating herself for her bluntness. Rolling up *Songs of Order and Chaos,* she tucked it into her sash, avoiding her father's gaze.

The smile quivered on Li Er-Shuan's lips. "No, but I've learned to read their language nonetheless."

Ami picked up Little Mother from the ground and got to her feet. "You're looking well, baba," she said, wishing she had something more substantive to say. Although she loved her father, it had been years since they had been able to speak clearly with each other, and she felt herself at a loss.

Li Er-Shuan studied the fairy tree in his daughter's hands. "Your mother would have loved it here," he said softly. "Kalantze smells beautiful."

Ami thought of the little garden in their canal-house back in Zanhei. Although her mother had not been a magician, she had had a gift for growing things. Ami could force flowers to bloom with her power, but Rinqi could coax even the most stubborn plant to open up with tenderness and care. The way she could coax a smile from even the most hardened stranger in the marketplace, the way she could coax her father out of his mental terrors with infinitely gentle patience. Ami had none of her mother's gifts, only a strange and uncanny power she scarcely understood.

"Mama would have thrived anywhere there was a bit of earth," she said softly, running her fingers along Little Mother's brass vase. "Anywhere she could grow flowers."

"I wish she had told me where she was from," Li Er-Shuan said, his eyes filling with tears. "I wish I knew where to lay her heart seeds to rest. I've failed her."

Ami closed her eyes. Of all the ways her father had failed her mother, she thought her mother would have pointed out the neglect of his children as the greatest sin. Resentment bloomed beneath her skin.

"Ami-yah," her father said in a warning tone. "Hide your light."

She glanced down at her hands, the green-gold glow scarcely visible in the searing sunshine. "Why?" she asked, trying to tamp down her growing irritation. "No one will notice. Or care." Magicians were free in the outermost west; she didn't understand why he kept insisting she hide her power.

Li Er-Shuan glanced at the grand platform overlooking the court-

yard, where Gaden was overseeing the funeral preparations. "I'm trying to protect you," he said softly. "You don't know who you can trust."

Ami closed her eyes. "Not now, baba," she whispered. "You cannot
be present now and absent at any other moment of my life. I can't bear
it. Not now."

When her mother was still alive, her father's distance and benign
neglect had been, if not bearable, then simply a matter of everyday
life. Ami's older half-sisters were already married and gone by then,
but her childhood had not been empty or lonely. The moments Li Er-
Shuan was present had been a gift, an unexpected treat, like a bit of
dragon's beard candy from a kindly shopkeep.

And then Rinqi died.

And Ami had been searching for home ever since.

Li Er-Shuan blinked his owlish eyes. Unlike his daughter, he was
farsighted, able to see at great distance but unable to make out much
of the world just beyond the tip of his nose. Perhaps that was why he
never seemed to much care about the world in front of him, for it was
only the stars that mattered. But to her surprise, Ami could see him
try to bring his vision into focus, to look at *her,* and be present with *her.*
"Ami-yah," he said again. "I never told you . . ." He trailed off, fighting
the urge to go vague again. "I never told you about the night I fled the
imperial city."

The night he broke faith with the Mugung Emperor. The night his
mind broke. All the hairs stood straight on the back of her neck. "No,
baba," she said quietly, not daring to breathe lest she lose him to the
mists once more. "You didn't."

"That night . . . when you were born, the stars . . ." Li Er-Shuan
struggled to pull himself together, to remain coherent. Ami could see
the effort her father was making, and tried not to hope. "You were
reborn. You and three others. I tried to hide you, but the Mugung
Emperor compelled me to give you to him. With the Star of Radiance.
It burned out my mind."

As per usual, he wasn't making sense, but for once Ami did not try
to rationalize his words, to force a logic onto his wandering thoughts.
She let him speak the way he needed to speak. She absorbed his words,

committed them to memory, and told herself she would examine them later.

"The Star of Radiance," he continued, pressing his hand to his chest. "I still feel its pull." His eyes darted back to the platform, then flickered to Ami. She saw with dismay his hold on the present slipping, as the trauma he had endured resurfaced. "It must mean that one still survives."

Ami frowned. "What does that mean, baba?"

But Li Er-Shuan was growing agitated. "You must not become ensnared." His lashes flickered. "Maintain your sovereignty, maintain your separate sense of self." He shook his head. "Hide your light! Do not allow yourself to become enslaved to their will!"

"Whose will?" she asked carefully, trying not to upset him further. "Who were you protecting me from?"

A sudden *gong!* rang across castle grounds. Li Er-Shuan gave a cry and clapped his hands over his ears, crumpling to the floor as the giant bell outside the castle gates sounded, rattling branches of the Pillar, shaking loose several white petals, which drifted down like rain. Across the courtyard came an echoing cry, but the sound was ripped from a human throat.

"Kunga!"

Ami jerked her head up sharply to see several clerics surrounding the healer, who seemed to have gone into a sudden fit of convulsions.

"Kunga!" someone cried. "What's wrong? What is happening?"

Another scream, but this time, the sound was no longer quite so human. It sounded more like the whistle of a teakettle, or perhaps the shrill shrieking of a wooden flute blown at the highest pitch. Shouts of alarm rose from the clerics surrounding the healer, as several fell back in fear.

Kunga was hunched over as though in pain, the muscles of his back and shoulders rippling and bulging beneath the sage green of his monastery robes. A cacophony of growls, barks, and howls arose all around them as the dogs were once more whipped into a frenzy at the sight and scent of something uncanny in their midst. Kunga's robes burst at the seams, his dark brown skin darkening even further, forming what looked like . . . knots or eyes all over his spine. There was an awful cracking, stretching, tearing sound as the healer screamed again, only this time, it sounded like the hollow whistle of a large wooden pipe.

The healer straightened, then turned.

And Ami tripped and stumbled back in horror.

Where the healer had once been now stood a monster.

The abomination was enormous. Its body was shaped like that of a tree—its legs like forked roots, its arms like hardened vines, its head a crown of branches. Something writhed in its branches that made Ami feel sick and unsettled, as though spiders were crawling up and down her spine.

"Guards! To me!" boomed the deep bass of Captain Okonwe's voice. "Rally to me!"

The big dark-skinned man came barreling up from the barracks, swinging a large poleax. The abomination swung its arms left and right, catching Okonwe across the abdomen like a giant rope flail. He went flying across the courtyard, landing hard against the steps, his poleax snapped in half like a twig. Clerics tripped and screamed as they ran up the stairs, trying in vain to get out of reach of the abomination's thrashing vines, crying out in pain as they were caught and scattered across the castle grounds like seeds over a field.

"When the Pillar blooms, the end of the world is not far behind!" Li Er-Shuan shrieked, rigid with horror at the sight of the abomination. "Proof! Proof! Here is proof! Monsters run amok among us!"

At the sound of his voice, the monster turned its . . . branches? head? in their direction. It lurched and lumbered forward, using its long vine-like limbs to drag itself across the cobblestone courtyard.

"Run, baba, run!" Ami grabbed her father's hand and tried to drag him away. But Li Er-Shuan stood tall and resolute, fingers scrabbling for the brush at his waist. With swift, sure strokes, he sketched a character that Ami did not recognize. As the goldenrod glyph faded, she realized with a sinking heart that the spell was gibberish—half Language of

Flowers, half some coded shorthand only her father's mind could decipher.

The abomination swung its branches and Ami shoved her father out of the way. The vine came crashing down a hairsbreadth from where they had stood, sending a ripple of broken cobblestones everywhere. Little Mother fell several yards away, its brass vase ringing like a bell as it tumbled toward the Pillar.

"Rinqi!" A piece of rubble caught Li Er-Shuan across the temple, and blood gushed from the wound. "The heart seeds—"

"Go!" Ami scrambled to her feet and lunged for the fairy tree, rolling out of the way as another vine came whipping down. She swept Little Mother up in her arms and sprinted for her father, grabbing his shirt and dragging him behind her. But Li Er-Shuan's terror had now turned to confusion, and he fell to his knees. With a slight scream of frustration, Ami shoved the fairy tree into her father's hands. Gripping him beneath his armpits, she dug in her heels and hauled him upright. No time to think; she let her magic flood her father's bones, his blood, his limbs, filling them with her power, forcing him to move.

But the instant her gift touched his ki, Li Er-Shuan went stiff. "No," he said in a strangled voice. "Don't. Don't make me."

"Come on!" Ami ground out.

But he fought her at every turn, struggling against the invasion of his daughter's power over his flesh. Slowly, surely, she managed to get one foot, then the other, moving step by step away from danger. "One, two, one, two," she chanted, pushing her father along with her arms as well as her magic. She was so preoccupied with getting her father out of the courtyard that she didn't notice one of the abomination's vine-like arms snaking out around her own feet.

"Ami!" A shadow passed overhead, a slim silhouette soaring over the steps, wielding a threshing scythe. Gaden, she realized, masked and armed. The rusted and pitted blade sliced through the abomination's branches, sending black sap and fluid flying everywhere as branches—fingers—fell wriggling to the ground around her. Ami tried not to gag. Up close, she could see that the monster was not made of wood, but of a fleshy gray hide that seemed to pulse, flutter, and breathe. It didn't have a face, but what she had initially taken to be knotholes were eyes, each of which blinked and fluttered as lashes winked at her.

But it was the crown of branches that was the most revolting. The monster had human limbs for twigs and fingers for leaves, and the parts wiggled and waved independently of one another. The whole thing was too much for her to comprehend, and all she wanted to do was close her eyes and pretend it didn't exist.

"Child!" It was Zerdan. The librarian rushed to her side, surprisingly nimble for his advanced age, and helped Ami and Li Er-Shuan to their feet. "I've got your father," he said kindly, wincing as he picked Little Mother up from the ground. Li Er-Shuan clutched the little fairy tree to his chest like a child clinging to a beloved toy. "Come," Zerdan said to the astrologer, "follow me to the library."

"Yah!" Gaden's voice rang out. "Let go of me!" Whirling around, Ami saw the youth hacking at the vine arms with their blade to no avail. Slithering vines began wrapping themselves about Gaden's limbs, squeezing tight like the coils of a snake. They struggled in its grip as the abomination lifted them into the air.

"Gaden!" Ami cried. She pulled her brush from her sash, but her mind was blank, wiped clean of all the spells she knew. "Think, Ami, think!" she ordered herself, but the only things she could think of were nonsense, words cobbled together that had no meaning without context.

"*Cut . . . detach. . . . vine . . .*" Ami traced the characters in the air before her, leaving a trail of pale green-gold light.

But the phrase dissipated into nothing, with no intent, no magic behind them, the words were useless. What could she possibly do against an abomination? She had no weapons and no training in battle magic. The creature already had its vines wrapped around Okonwe and Raldri, with another coiling around the feet of a hapless cleric. The abomination fed the unfortunate victim to its crown of hands, where its wriggling, writhing fingers prized into the cleric's flesh and began tearing them apart, their cries and shrieks rending the air.

Scattered on the ground, the bodies of the guards lay still or groaning, their weapons cast aside or broken. She picked up the nearest staff, and realized when she lifted it that it was a glaive. A reaper's blade gleamed in the sunlight, and the balance of it was surprisingly comfortable in Ami's hands as she swung it around.

All the best spells are poetry. A spell-monger's daughter from the Pits had told her that once. Ami had never been particularly good at poetry, nor at improvisation, but let the first words and phrases come to her fingertips without agonizing over the meaning or shape or sound.

"Keen as winter night, the edges paper-thin," she murmured, writing down the characters as the spell came to her. "Whistle in the wind, straight and true."

The pale green-gold light of her magic glimmered along the blade as it became razor-sharp. With a cry, she swung the weapon over her head, letting the momentum of the glaive spin her around as she let it fly. The edge whistled as it flew through the air, a high-pitched keening—

Shnick!

The glaive sliced through the tentacle-vines holding Okonwe, and the old solider fell to the ground, gasping for air. The blade turned and sliced through Raldri's bindings before crashing into the ground, the power spent. The abomination roared with pain, spewing black blood as it thrashed and struggled, but did not lose its grip on Gaden, who lay limp in its grasp. Another vine wrapped itself around her foot and she screamed as she fell, scrambling for another weapon.

A roar split the heavens.

And then, a bolt of lightning, striking from a clear, cloudless autumn sky. It struck the abomination, which screamed its hollow wooden whistle of a scream, the tops of its branches smoking and scorched.

"Halt!"

It was a small, delicate figure. A small, delicate figure astride an enormous feline of crimson, vermillion, and scarlet. A small, delicate figure on fire.

No, made *of* fire.

Their hair streamed flames behind them, and their eyes were like two blazing stars as they and the gigantic cat paced the top of the castle walls. In their hand was a glowing blade, a sword that shimmered like sunlight ripples across the surface of a pond. In that instant, Ami was immediately reminded of the various murals of the Sunburst Cycle painted all over Kalantze and knew, down to her very ki, who this figure was.

The Guardian of Fire.

And the leonine creature they rode was the Lion of the South.

With a cry, the Guardian of Fire pointed their blade at the abomination, clapping their heels into the Lion's flanks as they charged down the steps to the courtyard. Their brilliance was almost too bright to look at, so bright the image of their body was burned onto the back of Ami's eyelids as she blinked. The Lion roared again as it circled the abomination, and the Guardian of Fire brandished their flaming sword, the edges of the blade slicing into the monster's hide. The abomination shrieked as fire began to consume it, as its crown of finger branches collapsed in on itself, its tentacle-vines withering and shrinking away.

But instead of burning away into nothing, within the flames, Ami thought she could see the shape of a human body emerging, the trunk of the abomination molding itself into a waist, the roots forking into legs as it shifted, changed, and transformed back into a person. When the flames died down at last, a naked human tumbled to the ground, unconscious, surrounded by the fallen bodies of the soldiers and clerics it had attacked.

The light died down, and although it was still bright, it was as though a cloud had passed over the sun. Where an elemental warrior made of fire once stood was an ordinary youth, small and slight, with a mass of dark hair surrounding a heart-shaped face.

"Who are you?" Ami breathed. "What are you?"

The figure looked at her, and although the flames were gone from their skin, their eyes still held all the light of their power.

"Who am I?" they said. "I am Jin Zhara, and I am the Guardian of Fire."

13

THE PILGRIMS HAD BEEN POUNDING AT THE gates of Castle Dzong for the past hour, as the sun slipped down behind the Gunung Mountains, casting long shadows over the Poha Plain.

"Let us in! There are the wounded and dying among us! You cannot be so cruel as to deny us the chance to pray before the Pillar!"

On a platform overlooking the castle courtyard, Zhara shifted uncomfortably in her seat between the Right and Left Hands of the Unicorn King. After she transformed the abomination back into the healer, Kunga, and revealed herself as the Guardian of Fire, the behavior of the clerics—the Right Hand in particular—toward her changed significantly. Where at first they had been hostile, now they were all hospitality.

"The Guardian of Fire caught us in the middle of a moment of grief," the head cleric had said. "I apologize for any offense I might have caused in my rudeness."

The death of the Qirin Tulku.

She and Han had arrived too late to beseech him for aid.

Once Kunga and the others injured during the abomination fight had been tended to, the castle resumed its funerary proceedings for the late Unicorn King. Zhara marveled at the ability of the clerics to shake off the horrors of what they had just witnessed, but the Left Hand—or the Beast, as everyone seemed to call them—had said that in times of great stress, people found comfort in the routine and ritual. She thought that the Beast was speaking as much about themself as the inhabitants of the monastery. Although it was customary to wait at least eight days after a death before burning the earthly vessel on a pyre, the Qirin Tulku's last wishes had been to cremate his remains as soon as possible.

The Right Hand had offered Zhara a seat of honor at the funerary proceedings. Castle Dzong was shaped like a giant circular open-air theater, and in the middle of the "stage" was the holiest site in all the Morning Realms—the Pillar, an enormous umbrella-shaped tree with white star-shaped flowers bursting from its branches. Zhara's seat of honor was on one of the platforms overlooking the sacred tree, along with the Right and Left Hands, their respective guards, and Sajah, back in cat form on her lap. Han was among the other mourners in the massive circular courtyard itself, easily distinguishable in his dark blue attire against the pale green robes of the castle clerics. Beneath the flowering Pillar, two biers had been hastily laid, each draped with a funereal cloth—one pure white, the other stitched with the device of a white creature with a horse's mane, a fox's tail, and a single horn against a background of sage green.

"The banner of the Unicorn King," the Beast said for her benefit, their husky voice slightly muffled by the wooden mask they wore. "For as long as I can remember, that banner has hung from the second-floor window of Teacher—of the Qirin Tulku's quarters."

Zhara stole a sidelong glance at the Beast, trying to make sense of the person behind the mask. They seemed young, perhaps near to her in age, but she had no basis for comparison. One of the guards, Raldri, had told her in a malicious whisper that the Beast was hideously ugly, and that the mask was to spare the virgin eyes of beautiful maidens everywhere so that their terrible visage would not drive them mad with fear.

Zhara didn't like Raldri very much.

"Once the banner of the current Holiness is burned," the Beast continued, "another will be stitched by the hands of the clan into which the Qirin Tulku's next incarnation will be born."

"Do you know which clan that will be?" Zhara asked.

The Beast shook their head. "In the old days, the Hands of the Unicorn King—the Qirin Tulku's personal attendants," they clarified, "would travel the length and breadth of the Zanqi Plateau for five years, searching for the soul of the person they had called Teacher. One of the Hands would then be appointed the Rygal Tulku, teaching the next incarnation all the wisdom they were taught by the Qirin Tulku in their previous life."

"How would someone recognize the next incarnation?"

"The next incarnation identifies themself for us," said the Right Hand, speaking up for the first time. "We bring them the heart seeds of their previous incarnation and ask where they should be buried. If the child gives the correct answer, then we would know."

The Beast fiddled with something beneath the neck of their shirt. Zhara noted that they had not removed their glove since she had first met them at the gates of the castle. She also noted that they were dressed in the plain brown tunic and trousers of the castle guard instead of a cleric's robes, and carried what appeared to be an ancient bone-handled knife at their waist. She wondered what the duties the office of the Left Hand came with, and tried not to wonder at the reasons the Beast had received their particular sobriquet.

Gong! Gong! Gong!

The pilgrims outside had escalated from shouting to ringing the giant bell outside castle gates. "What have you to hide?" Their voices echoed off the stones of the courtyard. "Let us in!"

Behind Zhara, Raldri stirred uneasily, hand straying to the hatchet they wore thrust through their belt.

"If you will not let us in," the pilgrims called, "return the remains of our kin! Chen! Sang! Bring us their heart seeds so we may return them to their ancestral lands!"

"What are heart seeds?" she asked. The funeral practices of the outermost west were startlingly different from the ones observed by the southern provinces where she and Han had grown up. Back home in Zanhei, a priestess of Do would arrive to say the last rites, sending the soul to the cauldron of the universe to be remade and reborn into the next life. Then the body would be burned, the cremains kept in urns. According to Jiyi, her courtesan friend in the Guardians of Dawn, before magic had been banned, many of the wealthy hired magicians to turn the ashes of their loved ones into diamonds.

Many of those diamonds sat in the Gommun Emperor's treasury now.

"We carry seeds in pouches around our necks and near our hearts our entire lives," the Beast answered quietly. "And when we die, we bury them with our remains so that our bodies can nourish future generations."

It was a beautiful sentiment, Zhara thought. To serve in death as much as one had in life. The ashes of her parents had been scattered to the winds; all she had left of them was her father's death plaque, carved with his name, safe in Teacher Hu's keeping back in the apothecary's shop in the Pits.

Gong! Gong! Gong!

"Let us in!" the pilgrims intoned. "Let us in!"

"Surely there's no harm if we let them in to pray," said Raldri. They continued to fidget with their hatchet, making Zhara nervous. She didn't know if they were expecting trouble . . . or inviting it. "The pilgrims are kin to the yak-herder, after all."

"The yak-herder?"

"The other person we are honoring tonight," the Right Hand said.

"Sang?" Zhara asked. "Or Chen?"

The Beast shifted beside her. "Sang," they said. "Chen was his daughter."

"What happened to the little girl?"

The Beast did not answer. Instead, they looked to the Pillar, at someone talking to Han. This figure was not a cleric, judging by the southern-style tunic and trousers they wore, pitifully inadequate against the chill of the mountain climes. Despite the short hair curling in ragged waves about their ears and the owlish spectacles on their face, Zhara thought they were strikingly attractive.

"She . . . there is nothing left to say farewell to" was all the Beast said.

Zhara sensed there was more that the Beast was not telling her, but for what reason she could not tell. They were hiding something in this castle, and she suspected it had to do with the mysterious nature of the Qirin Tulku's death.

"Please!" came the voices from outside castle walls. "We have the wounded and dying with us! Let us see the Qirin Tulku! Let us pray before the Pillar! Let us ask for healing!"

"Surely we could do that much," she said. "It would be cruel to deny them that."

"No." The Right Hand gripped the arms of their chair, the knuckles of their hands turning white. "To let the pilgrims in would incite a riot."

"Their Excellency doesn't know that——" Zhara began.

"Emotions run high during times of mourning," the cleric said shortly. "Grief manifests itself in unpredictable ways, and we cannot risk another"——they inclined their head at a shivering Kunga, wrapped in a woolen blanket and sitting beneath the Pillar——"abomination wreaking havoc on the populace."

"Grief does not turn people into monsters," she said softly. "Demons do."

The Right Hand flinched at the word *demon* as though they had been slapped. "But that cannot be possible," they murmured, more to themself than to her. "There have been no rituals, no spells or circles for summoning."

"Kunga did not summon a demon," the Beast said. "He was infected. By a bite."

The words *infected by a bite* sent a frisson of alarm down Zhara's spine. She thought of the undead attack in Mingnan, and the wound on Taeri's shoulder. If Kunga had turned into an abomination from a bite, then . . . then . . .

"What bit the healer?" she asked, almost afraid of the answer.

The Beast looked to the figure beneath the Pillar again. The short-haired figure was now joined by another——an ancient cleric. "A little girl," they replied at last. "Chen."

Zhara felt the blood drain from her cheeks. "The undead," she whispered.

The Beast gave her a sharp look from beneath their mask. Understanding passed between them in an instant, and Zhara knew in that moment just what strange events had passed in Castle Dzong before she and Han had arrived.

"The undead," the Right Hand scoffed. "That's impossible. The dark arts of necromancy were lost with *The Book of Beginnings and Endings,* and unless there is a hidden copy somewhere here on castle grounds, I don't think we're in any danger."

Out of the corner of her eye, the Beast's gloved fingers twitched nervously.

Zhara frowned. "*The Book of Beginnings and Endings?*"

The cleric blinked as though caught off guard. "Oh," they said. "I believe it is also called *Songs of Order and Chaos* among the lowlanders."

Zhara sat up straighter in her seat. "*Songs of Order and Chaos?* We came to the outermost west in search of that book."

The Beast clenched and unclenched their fists. "Why does the Guardian of Fire believe that a copy would be found here?"

Zhara hesitated. "Because," she said, "we believe a copy was in the possession of Li Er-Shuan, who disappeared from Zanhei some months back, along with the text."

The Beast started but quickly went still. They definitely knew more than they were letting on, and Zhara tried to figure out a way to speak to them in confidence. Perhaps after the funeral.

The Right Hand furrowed their brows. "Li Er-Shuan," the cleric said slowly. "Why does that name sound familiar?"

"Their Excellency has heard of him?" Zhara asked in surprise. "Is he here?"

The Right Hand frowned thoughtfully.

"Why is the Guardian of Fire searching for *Songs of Order and Chaos?*" the Beast asked in a quiet voice.

"Because," she said, "we believe it contains information on how to defeat the Mother of Ten Thousand Demons."

Silence fell over the viewing platform, both awkward and fearful. At the back, Raldri had their hatchet in their hands and was twirling it anxiously, before the captain of the guard reached out to stop them.

"No," the Right Hand repeated. "There have been no rituals, no summonings."

Zhara gestured to the healer down in the courtyard below. "Is not the fact that abominations and the undead walk the earth evidence enough that Tiyok has returned?" She gave a hollow laugh. "Is not the fact that *I* am on this earth enough?"

"They say when the world is out of balance, the Guardians of Dawn are reborn," the Beast said slowly. "So it's true. Demons walk among us."

Zhara nodded. "And the undead are corpses possessed by chaos. This little girl, Chen, was spreading a demonic infection with her bite. That is why your healer transformed into an abomination."

But the Right Hand was still reluctant to believe her. "The child was rabid," they said dismissively. "Happens more often out on the plateau than one might imagine. Wild animals contract the disease from each other and occasionally spread it to humans." The cleric shook their head. "A horrible way to die, but unfortunately there is nothing to be done for it." An expression of disgust crossed their face. "Another reason we should think twice before letting the pilgrims in to pray before the Pillar. Who knows what poison and pestilence they might bring into the castle?"

Zhara shuddered, thinking of the Chancellor. The Frog Demon of Poison and Pestilence, a greater demon and a Lord of Tiyok she had defeated just a few months ago.

"The girl was dead before she attacked her father," the Beast said. "Before she attacked the Qirin Tulku."

Zhara startled. "Was the Qirin Tulku also bitten?"

It was a long while before they responded. "Yes."

"And is the bite what killed him?"

The Beast looked away. "Yes. No. I don't know."

"We know what killed the Teacher," the Right Hand said in a tight voice. They pointed an accusing finger at the short-haired person beside Han. "Her. The scrivener."

"Ami did not kill the Teacher," the Beast said, and for the first time, Zhara detected a note of defensive anger in their voice. "I was there, Jetsan. The Qirin Tulku died of his injuries."

"A mere bite?" the Right Hand sneered. "The Teacher might have been ill, but he was not so frail as to succumb to death from a mere flesh wound. No," the cleric murmured, narrowing their eyes as they stared at the short-haired scrivener. "There is something uncanny about that girl. Something . . . unnatural."

Unnatural. A demon? Zhara looked at the figure next to Han down in the courtyard. She seemed so unassuming, although she supposed the Chancellor had seemed so at first as well. If this scrivener were a greater demon, there was only one way for Zhara to tell.

"Can I meet this scrivener?" she asked. "I would like to ask her some questions about the Qirin Tulku's death."

"What for?" The Right Hand looked both surprised and suspicious. "Why are you—I mean, why is the Guardian of Fire so curious?"

Zhara studied the beautiful short-haired scrivener. She was so young, too young to have been one of the four magicians who tried to summon the elemental Guardians of Dawn, only to end up possessed by the Lords of Tiyok instead. Nor did she want to accuse an innocent person of being a demon in disguise without any proof. But she couldn't be sure. Not unless she met her face-to-face.

But if she wasn't a demon, then could she possibly be . . .

"What is the scrivener's name?" she asked. "Anyone with unusual or uncanny powers is certainly of interest to me."

The Beast met her gaze through their mask. Their eyes were kind, and Zhara wanted to trust them very badly. She thought she could see an internal struggle reflected behind their mask, and she wondered whom they were protecting: the scrivener or themself.

"Her name," the Beast said at last, "is Ami. Li Ami."

14

THE CLERICS WOULD NOT LET **A**MI SEE to Sang's body.

She was no priestess of Do, but she was not unfamiliar with the rites of the dead, even those practiced in the remotest parts of the Morning Realms. Her own mother had been a member of the Free Peoples, after all. There was no proscription against a stranger observing the body before cremation; in fact, the faith of the Great Wheel believed that the body was nothing after life had fled. It was the soul that mattered, the soul for whom the prayer flags were raised.

But the clerics of Castle Dzong were infuriatingly obstinate that Ami stay out of their way as they cleansed the corpses of the Qirin Tulku and Sang with water perfumed with osmanthus and chrysanthemum flowers. *Out of respect for the dead,* they repeated. *It is what the Qirin Tulku would have wanted.*

It was *not* what the Qirin Tulku would have wanted. Ami had been there as the great sage breathed his last, as he had begged his protégé to take his life before he could be turned into an abomination or a revenant.

But it was not the Unicorn King Ami was worried about.

When Ami had helped sever the threads of life in the Qirin Tulku's body, she had seen with her magical vision the darkness that had infected his ki. An . . . infection that radiated from the bite he endured from Chen. Sang had been bitten as well, and she feared the longer he went untreated, the higher the likelihood he would return as the undead. Even from a distance she could sense the abyss within him, the hole at his throat that was also a hole in the essence of the universe itself. Something horrific was spilling out, an invisible wound that threatened to infect every ki it touched.

She had to fix it. She had to close the hole.

You alone can defeat this.

Although she did not understand how or why, she knew the Qirin Tulku was right. What were her uncanny powers for if not for this?

If only the clerics would let her get close.

"Did the scrivener know the yak-herder?" asked the broad-shouldered youth at her side. She hadn't caught their name, but they looked familiar to her. Something about their eyes, and the way dimples appeared in their cheeks when they were both angry and smiling.

"Ami, Ami, just call me Ami." She preferred the western way of eschewing honorifics altogether. "We can lower our speech," she said, using the Azurean phrase.

The youth grinned. "Oh good. I'm not that great with honorifics myself. I've never had to use it much, so I never know if or when I'm being rude or polite."

A flutter of kinship warmed Ami's heart. "Me neither."

"Yeah? Were you a prince of Zanhei too?"

She startled. "Were you?"

The youth rubbed the back of his head. "Yeah," he admitted. "My name is Wonhu Han, by the way. May I have your family name?"

Ami stiffened, seeing the Royal Consort's eyes in his face. "No. Not you."

Han looked hurt. "Yah, no need to be rude. I was just asking for a name."

No wonder he had seemed familiar. His was the face of the little boy whose mother she had inadvertently killed by revealing her magic to the Chancellor of Zanhei. His nose seemed bigger back then, but the dimples were still the same. She staggered back, feeling the weight of guilt press down on her ribs, making it hard to breathe.

"Are you all right?" Han stepped closer, a furrow of concern etched between his brows. "Do you need to sit down?"

Did he know? Ami wondered. Did Han know that she was the reason he no longer had a mother? Would he hate her if he did? "I—I—" She cast about for some excuse to get away from her cousin, and from the kindness in his eyes. "I need to see to Sang."

Han frowned. "Why are you so keen to examine the body?"

Ami wished she had Little Mother with her, but her father had taken the fairy tree with him to the library. She felt itchy when her hands had nothing to do, when anxiety was crawling over her skin like a million myriad ants. It was harder to be present when her nerves were overwhelmed. "Because," she said, "I need to sew up the emptiness inside him."

Han blinked. "I don't follow."

She resisted the urge to huff. She didn't have the patience or desire to explain, nor was she even sure she *could* explain, even if she wanted to. "There is . . . a darkness inside a corpse that has been killed by the undead," she said. "I can't explain it any better than that, only it's that darkness that takes control once life is gone, bringing the corpse back to unlife."

Her cousin said nothing, but his large round eyes were thoughtful and intense. "That sounds," he said slowly, "like possession."

"Does it?" She picked at her lower lip, glancing from the healer, Kunga, sitting beneath the Pillar, to the biers laid out in the courtyard. "How do you know? I thought a magician had to summon a demon in order to become possessed."

"So did I," Han murmured. "But there's a lot about demons and demonology we don't know. It's why we came out here, me and Zhara. I mean, the Guardian of Fire. We came in search of a book."

"A book?" Ami stiffened, feeling the leather of the fragments of *Songs of Order and Chaos* press against her back in her sash. Her hands itched terribly, and she wanted nothing more than to pluck out strands of her hair to alleviate her nervousness.

"*Songs of Order and Chaos,*" he said. "It was last seen in the possession of my uncle, Li Er-Shuan. Do you happen to know him?"

"Yes," she managed. "He is my father."

Han went very still. "Cousin Ami?" he asked, half hopeful, half disbelieving. "Is that you?"

"Yes," she whispered, and then braced herself for his hatred.

But it did not come. Instead he swept her up in an embrace, his big, strong arms hugging her so hard it almost hurt. "I can't believe it," he murmured. "Tendi's twisted luck!" His dimples were on display full force, his smile so bright that it was like looking into the sun. "I can't believe we found you!"

His enthusiasm, as welcome as it was, was starting to make her feel rather uncomfortable. Either he did not know the role she had played in the death of his mother, or those matters of trust and betrayal did not matter to other people. She wasn't sure which was which sometimes, and with people as friendly as her cousin was being, it was even harder to tell which was truth and which was a lie.

"What about Uncle Li? How is he?"

She swallowed, glancing back at the library where Zerdan had taken her father, as the infirmary had been burned down during the encounter with Chen. "Alive," she said. "He was caught up in the abomination attack."

"Oh." Han grew quiet. "I'm sorry."

Again, his kindness grated at her, because she felt worse about not responding properly to compassion than she did to cruelty or indifference. "I know. Unfortunately, it was the castle healer who had turned into an abomination, but thankfully the Guardian of Fire turned him back. I think he's recovering." But by the haunted look in Kunga's eyes, Ami knew it would be a long time—if ever—before Kunga recovered from that experience.

At the mention of the Guardian of Fire, Han glanced toward the viewing platform overlooking the courtyard. "She's something, isn't she?" he murmured, and it was a moment before Ami realized he was talking about the petite brown-skinned girl sitting on the platform between Gaden and the Right Hand of the Unicorn King. When not in her Guardian form, Jin Zhara was rather unassuming, although Ami supposed anyone would be considered unassuming when they were not a literal being of fire.

"She is . . . that, I suppose," Ami replied, although she wasn't entirely sure what her cousin was talking about. Everyone was *something*.

"So," Han said, wrenching his gaze away from the girl on the platform and looking rather pink. "What do you need to sew up this . . . emptiness?"

Ami was startled. "What?

He gestured to the corpse beneath the white banner on the pyre. "You said you need to . . . I mean . . . do you need to . . . touch the corpse? Or would you be able to do what you need to from here?"

That was not the question she had expected him to ask. Most other magicians would have pressed her on the reasons why, but Han was either indifferent or accustomed to strange magic. "I, uh," she began, trying to organize her thoughts. "I don't know," she said at last. "I think I need to be in contact, or at least close enough to"—she scrunched her nose and wriggled her fingers—"be in contact with something touching the body."

"Hmm." Han scanned the pyres. "The clerics are gone. If you need to get close, now is the time to do it."

Ami looked to see a procession of sage-robed figures making their way up the stairs to join the Right Hand, Gaden, and the Guardian of Fire on the level overlooking the courtyard. "Do you think I could?"

"Of course you *could*." Han grinned. "But whether or not you *should* is another question altogether." He lowered his voice. "Better to ask forgiveness than permission. It's a rule I used to live by when I was a child trying to escape the Chancellor's clutches."

Ami did not like breaking rules. Breaking rules brought too much attention to her and her light, but Han was right. She needed to take care of the darkness leaking from the wound in Sang's body.

"I . . . need a distraction," she said. "From the Right Hand up there."

"Hmm," he said again, looking up at the viewing platform. "I suppose I could try to declaim some of my poetry for them," he said, perking up. "I've been working on something new for Mistress Brandy. I mean, for Zhara. I mean, the Guardian of Fire."

"Poetry?" Ami looked her cousin up and down. She didn't remember often seeing him in their lessons back in the palace; he was usually off playing in the meditation gardens or pestering the guards down in the training ring. "You don't seem like the literate type."

"Don't you mean *literary*?"

Ami said nothing. Han huffed.

"Shoo," he said. "Now be off while I figure out some way to distract them." Han strode out to the middle of the courtyard and turned dramatically to face the viewing platform. "My esteemed hosts," he began, his voice squeaking a little. "In honor of this occasion, I would like to be able to recite a few poems for the deceased."

"Who is this?" the Right Hand asked. "And what are they doing?"

Beside the cleric, the Guardian of Fire palmed her face.

"*Let us walk along the path of light,*" Han said. "*But such words cannot be true. I wish I could tell you the future is bright, but I won't be the one to lie to you.*"

Ami hurried to Sang's side, pulling aside the white funeral cloth covering his face to reveal the yak-herder's body, cleaned and purified.

"Huh." The Right Hand's voice carried well in the acoustics of the castle courtyard. "Their poetry isn't half bad."

"It's because it's a lyric from one of the Bangtan Brothers' ballads," the Guardian of Fire murmured.

This close to Sang's body, Ami could see just how much the dark infection had taken hold. Closing her eyes, she called forth her power, imagining the green-gold glow as hands wrapping themselves around the threads of emptiness entwined in the yak-herder's limbs.

But the darkness was now inseparable from the body of Sang itself.

Unlike the Qirin Tulku, whose light of life had kept the worst of this . . . void infection at bay, the dullness of death had left Sang's body completely vulnerable to the emptiness. To this . . . rot. Beneath her hands and through her magical senses, this sticky darkness felt like rot—the squishy, moist, slimy bits of organic matter that had decayed. An indescribable stink filled her nostrils—no, not her nose, another sense akin to smell that existed only in this extrasensory magical realm.

The rot clung to her and her ki. Like mold slime, it slithered up her fingers and arms and tried to burrow into her body through her skin. To get at the essence that made her who she was. To . . . possess her.

She now had a name for the darkness.

A demon.

With a cry, she stumbled back. Han had stopped in the middle of reciting, leaving her completely vulnerable to curious, judgmental eyes. A storm of howling arose around her, as the dogs caught wind of the uncanny wrapped around her, slithering about her neck, tightening, choking, strangling.

"You, girl!" the Right Hand shouted from his perch atop the viewing platform. "What are you doing?"

Ami clawed at the vines of darkness that held her in their disgusting embrace. The wrongness of it made her feel sick, and she wanted nothing more than to scream and shriek and cry and throw up. She was tied up with the body of Sang and every time she moved her arm, his arm jerked. Every time she moved back, his legs twitched. A gasp of shock and fear went up from the clerics around her as slowly, surely, Sang rose from his pyre and began shuffling toward the crowd.

"Necromancer," the Right Hand hissed. "Necromancer!"

"No," she choked. "No!"

She was not a necromancer. Uncanny as her magic might have been, Ami was not a necromancer.

She wasn't.

She couldn't be.

She couldn't.

Guardian of Wood, came a high-pitched whine from thin air. Ami thrashed as she wrestled with invisible tentacles. *Guardian of Wood, I have been expecting you.*

A distant roar broke through the whine that was not a whine in her ear. Lightning crackled overhead as a small ginger shape leaped from the viewing platform, tripling, quadrupling, quintupling in size as it became an enormous leonine creature with a mane of fire. The Lion of the South. And on his back was the Guardian of Fire.

"Han!" she cried, tossing something bright, sharp, and gleaming in his direction. It landed with a thud at his feet, a glittering, glimmering blade.

Ami's cousin swiftly picked up the weapon and turned to her. "Come with me!" he shouted, holding out his hand.

But Ami could not move. The darkness had her in a hold, and she could feel the void leaking into her eyes, her ears, her mind, her soul.

"I got you!" Han struck at the threads of emptiness with his blade.

Like sunlight cutting through shadow, the sword sliced through the tentacles, freeing Ami. "Go!"

Freed from their mutual entanglement, the corpse that was once Sang sprang to life.

Or unlife.

"Ami!" Gaden shouted. "The yak-herder!"

But it wasn't Sang, not anymore. The corpse was only a vessel for the demon that wore his body like a second skin, and it crawled and shuffled and lurched toward the nearest person. A luckless cleric, who screamed as the undead Sang sank its teeth into their shoulder, spitting out bits of flesh. Another cleric blasted the corpse with a spell but missed, showering them all with an explosion of stone. The revenant then turned its sightless eyes on Ami and hobbled in her direction.

"Zanheeeeeeeiiiiiiiiiiiiii!" Han gave a great battle cry as he leaped and swung his blade, severing Sang's head from its neck. The head thudded to the ground beside her, teeth still gnashing at her ankles.

A roar, and a flash of lighting. The head exploded and Ami gagged as bits of skull spattered everywhere.

"Ami!" She looked to find Gaden and the Guardian of Fire sitting astride the Lion of the South. "Climb on!" They reached down to grab her wrist, and she clambered on behind them.

"Wait for me!" Han shouted, sprinting in their direction.

The Lion bared its teeth at him.

"Oh, stop it, you overgrown fuzzy couch," Han growled. "There's plenty of room for me too. You're the Lion of the South, you can bear the weight of one extra boy."

The Lion lashed its flaming peacock tail but allowed him to get on its back.

"Are you all right?" the Guardian of Fire murmured.

It took Ami a moment before she realized the other girl was talking to her. "Yes," she said. "I mean, no. I don't know."

"You're alive," Jin Zhara replied. "That's enough for me. Hold on tight, all of you!"

Ami barely had enough time to wrap her arms about Gaden's waist before the Lion took off. Behind them, clerics were falling to the undead blight before twitching and jerking and coming back to life. Like a swift-moving plague, the demonic infection was beginning to sweep through the castle. Han struck out at various corpses with his blade, and where the blazing sword touched the bodies, they immediately went up in flames, charred to ash within an instant.

"Wait!" Gaden cried. "What of the Teacher's body?"

Ami glanced to the bier of the Unicorn King, where the silhouette of the Qirin Tulku's body could be made out from beneath the banner.

"It's not possessed!" Zhara shouted. "The tears to the void realm are sealed."

Tears to the void realm. It was the first time Ami had ever heard someone else describe exactly what she had sensed with her magic, and she felt something stir in her chest. It was as strong as her power, but softer, warmer. It was a moment before Ami recognized it for what it was: hope.

"Let's go, Sajah," Zhara urged her mount. "Let's clear out."

More shouts, more roars, this time from the castle gates. Craning her head, Ami could see a guard—Raldri—opening the doors, letting in a flood of pilgrims.

"No!" the Right Hand cried. "Keep them back! It's not safe!"

One by one, the clerics within the castle turned on each other, as demonic infection spread from one to another and another and another. Han struck out left and right with her sword, wielding the weapon indiscriminately. Their mount—the Lion of the South—batted with its paws, sending people flying as it tried to clear a path for them to escape.

"Help us!" the pilgrims cried as Zhara and company bounded past, hands grasping at fur, at feet, at clothes, trying desperately to clamber onto the Lion's back as well. The Lion reared back and Gaden slipped off its back.

"Gaden!" Ami screamed as a tide of people swarmed over them.

Just then, an enormous man bounded through the crowd, swinging the staff end of an enormous poleax. "My liege!" Captain Okonwe called. "My liege!" He made his way to Gaden's side, twirling his weapon blade to prevent anyone else from getting close. "We must flee. The castle is no longer safe."

Zhara pulled her mount back around. "What of the village?"

"If this infection spreads," the captain said in a grim voice, "then Kalantze is no longer safe. No time to gather your things; I propose we leave now."

"What of my father?" Ami asked. "And Zerdan? They're in the library!"

"The catacombs," said Okonwe. "There is a secret passage in the catacombs beneath the library that leads from the castle out onto the Poha Plain. Zerdan would know of it."

"And what about us?" Ami asked. "Where are we going? Will we meet up with my father and Zerdan?"

"There's no time," Okonwe said. "Our first priority is getting out of here safely. After that, we can figure out where we want to go and who we want to trust."

Something about the way he said it made Ami think that he already had a place and people in mind.

"Everyone get on the giant cat," Zhara ordered. "One step at a time. Oh, stop it, you baby," she admonished the Lion of the South, who gave a roar of protest. "Turn yourself into an elephant or something then."

Ami shrieked in surprise as the fur beneath her legs rippled, then disappeared, the plush velvet of the Lion's back turning hard and bony, covered with a dry, leathery hide. She suddenly found herself several feet higher than before, and with a start, she realized that the cat had done exactly as Zhara had asked.

They were sitting on an elephant. A ruby-red elephant with golden eyes and golden tusks.

"Hyah!" Zhara cried. She turned to Okonwe. "Where to, Captain?"

"To the Poha Plain," he said. "To the Heralds of Glorious Justice."

15

They were two days from Kalantze when they encountered their first sign of the Heralds of Glorious Justice: a banner flapping in the wind planted next to a burning pile of billowing black smoke. Zhara tensed at the sight of the device, a sinuous red snakelike creature with four wings instead of legs against a golden field.

"The Four-Winged Dragon," Han murmured beside her. "The Mugungs' old battle standard."

Zhara glanced sidelong at the old soldier leading them deeper into the Poha Plain. What little she knew of the Heralds of Justice from both Junseo and Yuli had not endeared them to her, and she wondered at Captain Okonwe's motives. They had had no time during their flight from Kalantze to discuss their next course of action—any shelter in a storm—but if they had, she might have raised some objections.

Although she didn't have any other solutions to offer.

"What about the nearest Guardians of Dawn safe house?" Han had suggested.

"That would be Mingnan," Okonwe said. "Two weeks from here."

"And they've been overrun by the undead," Han muttered. "The Heralds of Glorious Justice it is, I suppose."

"Just *who* are the Heralds of Glorious Justice?" Ami had asked.

"A bunch of wild conspiracy theorists," the Beast muttered, just as Zhara replied, "Insurgents." They exchanged startled glances. Somewhere between Kalantze and the Poha Plain, the Beast had lost their boar-chimera mask, and Zhara found them both more and less intimidating without it. Without the mask, they were just another ordinary youth—near to her in age, slim, and slight. But she couldn't deny that the fearsome scars that marred the left side of their face and down their neck made her flinch with both surprise and sympathy every time she looked at them. Burn scars, although long since healed. She looked down at her hands, thinking of the fire she could summon at will.

"I didn't realize the Guardian of Fire was acquainted with the Heralds of Glorious Justice," the Beast said in their husky voice. For some reason, the ungendered timbre of their tone made Zhara want to giggle.

She touched the bangle on her wrist and cleared her throat. "I'm only repeating what I've heard from others."

"Insurgents and wild conspiracy theorists?" Ami had asked. She looked from Okonwe to Gaden to Zhara. "Then why are we seeking them out?"

"Because," Okonwe said, "they have resources we do not. Shelter. Protection. Food. Once we are safe, we can set about helping others."

None of them could gainsay the old soldier's advice, and after the days of travel without shelter or food, Zhara would have accepted aid from anyone, even the Falconer and his Kestrels. The land of the Zanqi Plateau might have been beautiful, but it was also unforgiving. Water had been easy enough to find with the many glacial rivers and streams that ran along the Gunung Mountains, but there was little in the way of edible plants to forage, and game was similarly scarce. But what Zhara had found the most unbearable was the cold.

Dusk had begun falling when they came upon the Four-Winged Dragon in the middle of a field.

Okonwe held up a fist for silence. "Hold." The big soldier surveyed the ground beneath them with a critical eye. "Something strange passed through here."

The grassy field was torn beneath their feet as though from the churning of many hooves, or perhaps an earthquake. Tremors were not uncommon in many parts of the Zanqi Plateau, but the pattern of disturbance was not the same as the others. A thick fog covered the ground, and the air smelled bizarrely of roasting meat somehow. Sajah, in his sorrel horse form, shied away from the haze, the whites showing around his golden eyes. "Look." Okonwe bent down to pull a broken shaft from the earth, the tip of which revealed itself to be an arrow. "There are broken spears and arrows littered everywhere."

"A battle?" Han asked with a frown. "If there's been a battle, then where are all the bodies?"

"And what's that smell?" the Beast asked.

Zhara glanced at the column of black smoke in the distance. The fog in the air left a thick, oily residue at the back of the throat that tasted vaguely sweet by way of bile. Okonwe sucked in a sharp breath, then coughed, bringing his hand up to cover his nose.

"Burning bodies," said Han in a hollow voice. "It's the smell of burning bodies. My mother was burned alive by the Falconer and his Kestrels for her magic. I . . . I can still smell the pyre in my nightmares."

Zhara reached out to twine her fingers in his, but he flinched and turned away. She curled and uncurled her hands, trying not to feel hurt when she saw the glitter of unshed tears in his eyes.

Okonwe cleared his throat. "Would the Guardian of Fire come look at this?" He pointed to strange black stains on the arrow's tip. "What does she make of it?"

With a frown, Zhara brought the tip close to her face. The skies were rapidly fading from blue to lavender. Twilight came early to the plateau, and the shadows blurred the edges of the world into a vague, hazy gray. "Can someone bring me a light?" she asked.

Green-gold streaks shimmered in the air as Ami traced the character for *brightness* with a brush, casting a circle of soft light around them.

Zhara pursed her lips as she examined the arrow tip. "It's blood," she said quietly.

"That's blood?" Han surveyed the scene around them in horror. Sticky black stains were everywhere, spattered over the dirt, the stalks of grass, and the shattered weapons, stringy and dripping like slime. "I thought it was tar."

"Oh." The Beast choked as they brought their hand to their nose, trying not to vomit.

What had once been a barley field was now nothing but a morass of decay. What should have been vast fields of golden grain were now nothing more than gray-brown stalks of living stone, the dirt beneath their roots a sticky, slimy swamp of rotted leaves, twigs, flesh, blood, and bones.

"Mother of Demons," Han said in a muffled voice. He had pulled the collar of his jacket over his mouth and nose, and looked as though he were trying not to breathe. "This land is more than dead; it's ruined."

Okonwe knelt and was about to clear a patch of grass of the blood when Zhara called out sharply, "Don't touch it! It's demonic."

The old soldier paused and held up his hands, rose to his feet, and backed away.

"Demonic?" Ami looked around her, eyes wide not with fear but with fascination. "How can you tell?"

"It feels . . . empty," Zhara said. "Like a hole in the fabric of the universe."

"Will we be possessed if we touch it?" Ami asked.

She furrowed her brows. "I don't know. But we'd best not risk getting in contact with it with our bare hands at any rate."

"Demonic blood." Han shuddered. "First abominations, then the undead, and now this. What's next, a hungry ghost?"

The Beast bent over to pluck a tall blade of grass from the ground. "My hand is gloved," they said at Zhara's warning glare. "Besides, I'm not a magician." They brought the blade before their nose, studying it carefully. The plant seemed almost calcified, although it remained pliant like other living greenery. "Is it just me, or is the grass . . . blighted?"

"That's what I was trying to look at," Okonwe said. "It's as though the field has been turned entirely to stone. Like coral."

"What's coral?" Han asked.

"Living stone." The old soldier reached beneath the neck of his shirt and showed what seemed to be a bright orange piece of polished rock shaped a bit like a flower and handed it to him. "We used to trade pieces like this that washed ashore back home in Masikara. The pearl divers would tell us of the vast forests of coral beneath the crystal waters, living but stone."

"How is this possible?" Zhara murmured. "What could possibly be turning the plants into living stone?"

It was a long while before anyone answered. "The blood," the Beast said at last. "It must carry the blight somehow." They shuddered as they dropped the stalk back onto the ground. "The field was soaked with it."

"Demons," Zhara said in a glum voice. "The answer these days always seems to be *demons*."

Silence fell over the group. There was nothing they could say to gainsay her.

"The question then is," the Beast said softly, "what are we going to do to stop them?"

They came upon the Heralds of Glorious Justice not long after. Night had fallen entirely before they reached the encampment, but the lights of their torches and cook fires could be seen from miles away. Sajah, as the sole incorruptible member of their party, returned to his ruby elephant form, carrying them all on his back toward the settlement.

"How did you know they would be here?" the Beast asked Okonwe in a low voice. "I thought you abjured them when we left all those years ago. When you renounced their beliefs."

Zhara's ears pricked, but she tried not to betray her interest. It was rude to eavesdrop, but she couldn't help but be curious about the connection between the Heralds and the old soldier herself.

It was a long while before Okonwe answered. "I have renounced their ways as I have promised my liege," the captain said. "But my beliefs are my own."

The Heralds' encampment was halfway up a hillside overlooking a shallow valley plain. Zhara could make out the silhouettes of two enormous, broad-shouldered figures standing guard at the entrance to the camp, each holding a wicked-looking poleax, similar to the one Okonwe carried with him. To her surprise, she thought she could make out at least one hundred tents or so, much bigger than she had anticipated considering the guerrilla nature of their tactics.

She hadn't known there could be so many people persuaded to insurgency.

It made her uncomfortable.

Zhara looked over her shoulder at the battlefield, wondering with whom the Heralds had fought, and why. The undead? Or just an innocent group of pilgrims on their way to Kalantze to pray in order to press-gang them into joining their cause? She felt the weight of the enchanted sword that Han had insisted she carry strapped to her back press against her shoulder blades.

"I don't like being so close to the battlefield," she murmured as they crested the hill leading up to the encampment.

"The Heralds have lookouts posted on all sides," Okonwe said. "They'll be able to see any danger coming long before it gets here."

"Yes," she said quietly. "But what about the danger in their midst?"

To that, none of them had anything to say. The memory of Kalantze, the attacks of the undead, the sudden eruption of abomination as the demonic infection swept through Castle Dzong, was still fresh in all their minds.

"Well," Okonwe said. "It's a good thing we have the Guardian of Fire with us, lah?"

"Halt!" called one of the sentries. "Who goes there?"

"It's me, Pang Lok," the old soldier said.

The guard relaxed. "Okonwe?" they asked incredulously, lowering their polearm. "You came back." Frowning, Pang Lok searched the faces of the rest of their party before their gaze rested on the Beast's scarred face. The guard's eyes widened.

"We did not," Okonwe said gravely, "come here entirely of our own volition."

The other guard—who was shorter than either Pang Lok or Okonwe, but bigger around the middle—stirred uneasily. "What does that mean?" they asked in an Azurean accent. With a pang, Zhara was reminded of the Bangtan Brothers, on their way north to Urghud. She hoped they were all right.

"Kalantze has fallen to the undead," Okonwe said.

The Azurean sucked in a sharp breath. "You too?"

The Beast frowned. "What do you mean *you too,* Uncle Samsoon?"

Samsoon turned his head. "Who's that?" He squinted into the

darkness, studying the scars on the youth's face. "Beast?" he said in amazement. "Is that you? By Do, but you look different now."

"It's been five years," Pang Lok said airily. "People can change a lot in five years. The Beast changed their appearance, and I got bigger and stronger."

"But not any smarter, I see," the Beast said acerbically.

Pang Lok grinned. "And your personality is just as beastly as ever."

"Hold a moment," Zhara interrupted. "As loath as I am to interrupt this reunion, can someone please let me know what happened with the undead?"

The two guards exchanged glances. "The party must have passed through the battlefield on the way here," Samsoon said in a low voice. "A scouting party of ours was attacked on their way back from patrolling the border towns. They had several new recruits with them."

"If by *patrolling,* you mean *harassing,*" Zhara muttered beneath her breath.

"What happened to the party?" Li Ami asked. "Were any of them injured?"

"A few were bitten by the revenants," Samsoon said, scratching at his shoulder.

"What happened to the injured?" the Beast asked.

"What do you mean what happened to them?" Samsoon asked, seemingly insulted. "They were tended to and cared for, of course. Most of the injuries weren't terrible, just a few bites here and there." He winced as he placed his hand on his shoulder.

Zhara stiffened, thinking of the bite on Taeri's collarbone and of the transformation of the healer back in Kalantze. "The injured need to be isolated," she said in alarm. "Immediately. Are any of them magicians?"

"A few," Samsoon said. "Why?"

She shook her head. "No time to explain," she said. "Take me to them. Now."

The two guards looked at each other. "Rather bossy for such a pretty little thing," Pang Lok remarked.

"Oh, shut up, Lok," the Beast said. "Do as she asks."

Pang Lok raised a brow. "Are you compelling me, Beast?"

Something passed between the two of them, something dark and like resentment.

"No," the Beast said. "I'm ordering you."

The burly guard crossed their arms. "No," Pang Lok said, but their refusal was tentative, as though they were probing or testing at the boundaries of something. "You forsook whatever authority you had when you left us."

Zhara was taken aback. "Beast was a member of the Heralds of Glorious Justice?"

"I was a child," they said shortly. "And I left over five years ago."

"A child?" Zhara looked to the encampment, over one hundred tents strong. "Are there children among the Heralds?"

"Not exactly," the Beast said. "I was . . . an exception."

Pang Lok gave an incredulous laugh. "You didn't tell them?"

Li Ami frowned. "Tell us what, Gaden?"

"Oh ho ho," the big guard said. "So they don't know. The truth of who you are, the—" They choked, the words suddenly cut off as their face grew purple. Zhara rushed forward in concern, but Pang Lok waved her off. "Well," they said. "I guess it still holds." The dark air between them and the Beast thickened.

The Beast coughed. "Go fetch Lee-Lee. Tell her the Guardian of Fire must see to the injured in the infirmary immediately."

"The Guardian of Fire?" Both Pang Lok's and Samsoon's heads snapped in Zhara's direction. Her power rushed to her cheeks in response, but instead of tamping down on her fire, she let the flames blossom over her fingertips. The guards' eyes widened with shock and astonishment, and Zhara stood a tiny bit taller. Perhaps being the Guardian of Fire wasn't always such a burden.

"Yes," said the Beast, giving her a slight smile. "Go on then. Fetch Lee-Lee. We need to see to the injured."

Samsoon shifted uncomfortably on his feet. "The General is not to be disturbed."

"Then send Lok. He's her nephew; she'll have time for him."

"Who is Lee-Lee?" Han asked.

"General Lee-Lee," Pang Lok said. "She is the leader of the Heralds of Glorious Justice." He gave the Beast a surprisingly pitying look. "Haven't you heard? I thought that was the reason you came back."

"Heard what?"

The two sentries exchanged looks. "Auntie Lee-Lee is dying," Pang Lok said in a soft voice. "I thought Okonwe had brought you to say goodbye. We sent word to the castle over a week ago."

The Beast looked stricken. "Oh," they said, their voice small and tight. "I see."

Li Ami placed her hand on their shoulder. "Gaden?" she asked gently. "Is everything all right?"

"Yes," they said. Then, "No. I don't know."

"I'll take the others to the infirmary to see to the injured," Samsoon said quickly. "Please," he said to Zhara and her companions. "Follow me."

Zhara paused, looking back over her shoulder at the Beast. "Will you be all right?" she asked.

They closed their eyes. "I'll be fine," they said. "Go."

And so Zhara went.

16

GADEN SAT ON A STOOL OUTSIDE AUNTIE—GENERAL—LEE-LEE'S
tent with Okonwe and Pang Lok, wishing they had the boar-
chimera mask of the Left Hand with them. They wanted nothing more
than to hide behind a frozen expression, to hide their anger and resentment from the world but especially from Okonwe. The old soldier had sworn he had severed all ties with the Heralds when they
first entered Kalantze five years before. Gaden didn't know which
hurt more—that Okonwe was still in contact with them, or that he
had lied about it.

"Why didn't you tell me about Lee-Lee?" Gaden asked the old soldier. "Why didn't you tell me she was dying?"

Okonwe met their eyes with a solemn gaze. "Would it have mattered? Would you have left the Qirin Tulku's side to come pay your
respects?"

Would they have? The filial impulse in Gaden warred with the self-
respect they had fought to gain in the years away. The larger, more
magnanimous part of them wanted to say that of course they would
have come. But the smaller, more petty part of Gaden pushed back
against that sentiment, saying that it was just another ploy by the leader
of the Heralds to guilt them into doing her bidding. Since learning
about the faith of the Great Wheel at the Qirin Tulku's feet, Gaden had
come to understand that there was an ideological chasm between them
and Lee-Lee, one that was not so easily bridged.

The Heralds of Glorious Justice were the first family Gaden had
ever known, and General Lee—Auntie Lee-Lee—had been the only
mother they had ever had. They remembered very little of their earli-

est years, not even the pain of the incident that had scarred the entire left side of their body. All they could recall was the roughness of the bandages against their raw and tender skin, the feel of Okonwe's broad back beneath their hands as he carried them from town to town to town, the iron tang of blood and blades whenever he returned from his odd jobs as a hired sword. It was how their guardian had fallen in with Lee-Lee's people; he had been hired to train them in martial arts—both with weapons and hand-to-hand combat.

Those earliest years of Gaden's life were as close to happiness as they could remember, mostly because they were as close to freedom as they could recall. The years before they knew the truth of who they were, before the need for masks dictated every aspect of their life. Before the scars on their face had any meaning or elicited any emotion aside from vague pity or disgust. Sometimes Gaden thought they preferred that to the awe or expectations that came with recognition now. The night Lee-Lee told them the truth of their destiny, the night she tried to force them into wearing the skin of someone they were not any longer, was the night they ran away from the Heralds of Glorious Justice forever.

"I don't know," they answered at last. "But I think I deserved to know."

The three of them had sat in silence for a long while, waiting for the healers tending to Lee-Lee to emerge and give them the all clear to enter. Gaden was ordinarily comfortable with silence, but this time the spaces between them were weighted with too many words unsaid. Like a tarp gathering rainwater, drops of tension had been collecting and pooling for years, and soon the foundations of their relationship would collapse under the weight, unless Gaden dumped out the tarp.

But they were afraid of the mess.

They glanced at Pang Lok, who was meditatively chewing on a piece of barley, resolutely looking anywhere but at Gaden. "What happened to Lee-Lee?" they asked the big guard. "She wasn't attacked by the undead, was she?"

It was a long while before Pang Lok spoke. "No," he said heavily. "She's been ill for ages. I think she must have been ill even before you left us, Beast, but it's only in recent years that it's gotten . . . bad."

Gaden flinched. "How bad?"

This time Pang Lok did meet their eyes, and the expression of grief on his face made them want to look away. "Bad."

Gaden frowned. "If it's so dire, then why are you lot out here in the hinterlands of the outermost west instead of back in one of the border towns? Or Kalantze or Ampo or some other village where you could find help?"

Okonwe heaved an enormous sigh. "They're out here chasing a dream," he said.

"What dream?" Gaden asked.

"The Unicorn of the West," Pang Lok said. "You know the stories."

And Gaden did. The Unicorn of the West was rumored to be able to cure any and all illnesses with a touch of her horn. The skin beneath their left glove itched as they shook their head. "A dream indeed."

"We were running out of options!" Pang Lok wrenched the barley stalk out of his mouth and threw it to the ground, trampling it underfoot.

"Do you even know where to begin looking for the Unicorn?" Gaden asked scornfully.

Pang Lok scuffed his toes in the grass. "Somewhere out west, near the place where the sky was held back. But we weren't here only for that."

Gaden raised their brows.

"As I said," Okonwe said softly. "They were out here chasing a dream."

"A dream is better than no hope," Pang Lok said sourly.

"And what hope is that?" Gaden looked from Pang Lok to Okonwe, Okonwe to Pang Lok.

The enormous youth heaved a sigh. "To see you one last time, Beast." He made a face. "Auntie Lee-Lee wants to give you her blessing before she goes."

Gaden crossed their arms. "I don't need it. Or want it, for that matter."

Pang Lok shifted on his feet. "It doesn't matter what you want," he muttered. "Or what anyone else wants, for that matter. You were ever Auntie's favorite. It doesn't matter that others have been by her side, faithful and loyal this entire time."

They were interrupted by the emergence of Lee-Lee's attendants from her tent. "The general is ready to see you," said Uncle Tama. "You and Okonwe both."

Gaden was astonished at the change the past five years had wrought in the man. Tama was Lee-Lee's older brother, and the years had not been kind. His face was haggard now, and the hair on his head completely snow-white. With a nod, Okonwe and Gaden made their way into Lee-Lee's tent.

"Beast." Uncle Tama rested a withered arm on their shoulder. "Be kind. She is dying."

A surge of resentment overtook Gaden, and the skin of their left hand felt as though it had suddenly gone up in flames. "I will be civil," they said. "I owe her no more than that."

Sorrow colored the expression on Uncle Tama's face. "She loves you, Beast."

"I know," Gaden said. "But love is not enough. Not when she would rather love the dead than the living."

Lee-Lee's tent smelled of death.

Gaden was acquainted with the charnel smell of the battlefield, the bitterness and fear of the abattoir, and the sour desiccated scent of the very old. The smell of Lee-Lee's death was like none of these; it was the smell of an internal wound slowly turning septic, rotten. It permeated the air, and made Gaden want to cover their nose, but they couldn't bear to deny Lee-Lee this one last dignity. No matter what their relationship had been in the past five years, no matter how much they had wanted to abjure and abandon their bond, Gaden could not deny how much the woman mattered to them.

How much they loved her.

They sat on the low stool next to her body while Okonwe settled his bulk on the floor near the exit.

Lee-Lee lay supine on a cot in the middle of the tent, eyes closed, arms laid by her side. Her entire body seemed ravaged and wasted, the flesh entirely gone, nothing left but sagging skin over brittle bones. Pang Lok had said she had slowly been dying for years and that no one had known until it was too late, but Gaden couldn't imagine missing the signs until she had gotten to this point. There was already a slight gray tinge to the corners of her mouth, and if it weren't for the shallow rise and fall of her chest beneath the blanket, they might have thought her spirit had flown to Do already. With a start, Gaden realized that they didn't know which faith Lee-Lee followed, if any. Was she a student of the Great Wheel? A devotee of the Way, the followers of Do? Was she a worshipper of the Immortals? Or did she perform a form of ancestor worship as the remotest parts of the empire still adhered to?

Gaden was certain of only one thing Lee-Lee believed in: the restoration of the lost Mugung heir to the Sunburst Throne.

"I can tell by your breathing you're nervous."

Gaden started as Lee-Lee's voice—while thin and labored, it was no less acerbic for her proximity to death—emerged from beneath the blanket.

"I do not know what to say."

Lee-Lee opened her eyes and turned to face Gaden. "Then why are you here?"

Why were they here? To say their farewells? To pay respect to the woman who had raised them? To have a last word with the person who would place upon their shoulders a role and a destiny they did not want nor think they could ably fulfill? "To say goodbye," Gaden said at last. It was not a lie.

Lee-Lee scoffed, then coughed. "It is said that not all goodbyes are sad or fond. Which is it for you, Your Majesty?"

Gaden tried not to cringe at the form of address, but even near death, Lee-Lee's eyes were sharp.

"Lee-Lee," Okonwe admonished.

She turned her needling gaze on the former captain of the guard. "And what are *you* doing here?"

"For the same reasons my liege is here," Okonwe said. "To pay my respects."

"To pay your respects, pfaugh!" She coughed, and flecks of bloodied spittle flew from her lips. Okonwe started for a basin, but Lee-Lee merely wiped at her mouth with a corner of her blanket. "You respected me well enough when I still full-figured. But you always did like someone with a little meat on their bones, didn't you, Koko?" She cackled until it turned into a hacking, coughing fit.

Okonwe's skin flushed darker. There was a time, back when they were still happy, when he and Lee-Lee had been together. Back before it all fell apart.

Gaden waited until Lee-Lee caught her breath again. The air in her lungs sounded wet, wheezing, rattling, as though she were drowning. "Why did you want to see me, Auntie?"

They hadn't called her *Auntie* since before they left the Heralds, and they could see the effect those words had on her. Her lashes fluttered in surprise.

"I wanted to ask you a favor," Lee-Lee said. "One last before I go."

Gaden braced themself. "Yes, Auntie?"

"I want you to take over the leadership of the Heralds."

They were taken aback. "What?"

She made a face. "Don't pretend you didn't hear me."

Gaden shook their head. "What about Lok? He is your nephew by blood."

Lee-Lee sighed, then coughed again. "Blood doesn't matter. It is a matter of who is fit to carry the mantle. I have always taught you that."

"And yet you contradicted it in the same breath," they said angrily, "by telling me I was born with a destiny to fulfill by virtue of my ancestors."

"Oh, Gaden," Lee-Lee said. "Everyone has a destiny they were born to fulfill. That yours is related to your bloodline is only a matter of bad luck."

Gaden blinked. It was the first time they had ever heard Lee-Lee address them by their chosen name instead of their dead one. The first time she had ever acknowledged the truth of who they were. Despite everything, warmth kindled in Gaden's breast. They loved hearing their name on her lips, because she had not chosen to call them that out of pity, out of political expediency, out of anything but the simple acceptance of who they were. They had wanted nothing more than this the entire time they had been with the Heralds.

But they also knew it immediately for what it was: a manipulation tactic. "I don't want a destiny," they whispered. "I want to be free. I don't want to be shackled to a future I never asked for."

"Responsibility and duty mean that sometimes we must do for others that which may run counter to our own desires," Okonwe said quietly.

Gaden rolled their eyes at the old soldier. "And what have you ever given up for someone else, Okonwe?"

Okonwe met their eyes, and for the first time, Gaden noticed the woolly gray hair peppering their mentor's temples where the braids had grown out. The captain of the guard had always seemed ageless to them, his dark skin seemingly unseamed by sun, wind, or time, but they saw now just how heavy the past fifteen years of carrying their secret had burdened him. "I gave up my place in the Heralds."

The words struck them like arrows to the chest. "I didn't think—" Gaden croaked. "I didn't think you truly believed in their cause."

It was a long while before Okonwe replied. "I don't believe in the Heralds," he said softly. "But I believe in *you*."

Tears stung their eyes, hot and blinding. "Believe in me to do what?" Gaden furiously dashed the tears away with the back of their glove.

"To save the Morning Realms."

Gaden gave a hollow laugh. "How many times must I say I don't want to rule?"

Lee-Lee shook her head. "Gaden," she said again. "Your destiny is not in the ruling of the Morning Realms, but in the protection of it."

They frowned. "What do you mean?"

"You may not see it," Okonwe said, "but you have a light inside you. A light that compels us all to follow where you will lead. I have done my absolute best to safeguard that light, ever since I rescued you as a child. I saw it even then, that endless potential within you, and have wanted nothing more than for you to embrace your destiny."

"That light," Lee-Lee croaked. "That light is your destiny. As long as the Wielder of the Star of Radiance holds the Sunburst Throne," Lee-Lee pressed hoarsely, "the realm will be protected from chaos."

Gaden pressed a hand to their chest, where something like grief or resentment or both burned like wildfire. It hurt, but they didn't know what hurt more—the grief or the betrayal. "I'm not that person," they said, "not anymore."

"No one is asking you to be that person, Gaden." Okonwe's voice was even, but they weren't sure if they could trust the use of their real name from their adoptive father's lips. "I'm no restorationist. I'm not even a revolutionary, not anymore. I'm simply a father who wishes to see their child grow up to be fully themselves. And that includes embracing who they were meant to be."

Their voice caught in their throat. "But I cannot be fully myself and who I used to be."

Lee-Lee gave them a stern look. "He said who you were *meant* to be," she said. "Who that is is entirely up to you, child."

"Princess Weifeng is dead."

"And yet," Okonwe said softly, "the heir still lives."

17

THE HERALDS OF GLORIOUS JUSTICE WERE NOT what Ami expected.

When she first heard that they were a faction within the Guardians of Dawn, Ami had assumed that the Heralds—like the members she knew back home in Zanhei—would be a collection of scholars and civilians contributing their skills to better the lives of magicians in whatever way they could.

But the Heralds of Glorious Justice were not a mutual aid society; they were a militia organization.

As Samsoon led Ami, her cousin, Jin Zhara, and Sajah—hidden up Zhara's sleeve in ruby mouse form—through the encampment, she estimated it was at least two hundred tents strong. The Heralds seemed to be comprised of a mix of all genders and ages and peoples, although she noted most of them seemed to be older than her by several decades, magicians or magician allies who could clearly recall a time Before the Just War.

In the flickering light of the campfires, Ami could also see they were a ragtag group composed of not only members of various clans of Free Peoples but also several ethnic groups from other parts of the empire. She recognized clothing styles from the Azure Isles, the southern provinces, and even some old imperial styles from the Middle Kingdom as well, now no longer in fashion at the Gommun Emperor's court. No northerners, which shouldn't have surprised her, even as it did. She would have assumed there would at least be a few who resisted the Warlord's oppressive rule. The sheer number of people of this so-called resistance faction was mind-boggling, and she couldn't help but think of what Jin Zhara had called them.

Insurgents.

"Here we are," said Samsoon, gesturing to a large circular tent supported by several bamboo poles. "The infirmary tent."

Even before entering, Ami could sense the darkness—the emptiness—within. She could feel the abyss pressing upon her magical senses, and once again, she wished she had Little Mother with her. The touch of something living always seemed to return some measure of her power back to her, and Ami glanced down at the Guardian of Fire's glowing fingertips. She wondered if it was rude to ask to hold the other girl's hand, then decided against it.

Taking a breath, Ami opened the tent flap.

And was immediately assailed by the stench of death. Not in her nostrils, but in her magical senses, but she couldn't resist bringing her hand up to cover her nose anyway. Beside her, Jin Zhara also flinched as she entered, burying her nose in the crook of her arm and giving Ami a curious sidelong glance.

"That's the injured," said Samsoon, gesturing to the people laid out on the mats on the floor. "But good luck trying to get any of them to speak."

"What's wrong with them?" Han asked. Neither Ami's cousin nor the Azurean guard seemed to be troubled by the smell.

Samsoon shuddered. "I don't know," he said in a low voice. "Trauma? We saw this after the Just War; soldiers and warriors lost in the labyrinths of their own minds from the horrors they had witnessed."

Ami looked at the approximately twenty beds—mats—laid out on the floor, each occupied by a bruised and bloodied person. Although none of the injuries seemed particularly fatal, the stillness of the bodies seemed unnatural, as though they had already succumbed to death. "Who is in charge of the infirmary?" she asked the Azurean guard.

"We don't have a healer, unfortunately," Samsoon admitted. "Most of us know field medicine from our previous experiences, but healers and herbalists are far less willing to join our cause."

"I wonder why," Jin Zhara muttered.

Samsoon frowned. "Do you have a problem with the Heralds of Glorious Justice, child?"

The Guardian of Fire shrugged. "I don't have a problem with magician liberation," she said. "Only I'm not entirely certain our end goals are the same."

The large Azurean tilted his head. "What do you mean?"

Jin Zhara straightened. "Do you honestly believe that Mugung restoration will lead to anything other than civil war?"

"Mugung restoration?" Ami was surprised. "But the line is dead." She thought of her father's enslavement to the will of the Mugung Emperor, and how it had broken his mind. "And good riddance," she said under her breath.

"Who says we're Mugung restorationists?" Samsoon asked, not quite meeting the scrivener's eyes. He scratched at his shoulder again.

"I don't know, maybe all the banners flying the standard of the Four-Winged Dragon flying about?" Han asked. "What *are* the Heralds of Glorious Justice doing? Mustering an army?"

The large Azurean laughed. "Is that what all those soft-skinned scholars back in the cities are telling you? That we are mustering an army in preparation for a revolt against the Gommun Emperor?"

Jin Zhara met Ami's gaze. "Samsoon is the one who said it," she said, "not the so-called *soft-skinned scholars* back home in the cities."

A guilty expression crossed the big guard's face. "Anyway," he said, clearing his throat, "you must all be starved. I'll head over to the mess and bring back some food."

At his words, Ami's stomach gave an audible rumble, her exhaustion temporarily pushed aside at the prospect of a hot meal. They had not had time to outfit themselves with food or other supplies when they fled Kalantze, and she suddenly found she was starving. In the distance, Ami thought she could smell something full of garlic and heavily spiced, and painfully swallowed down the want that watered her mouth. Samsoon gave them a nod and swiftly exited the tent.

The Guardian of Fire then knelt by the nearest patient, a youth not much older than her, their head wrapped in several bloodied bandages. Beneath the strips of linen, Ami could see the mangled skin and flesh of their cheek, which reminded her of nothing more than raw ground meat. She couldn't help but think of Gaden's scars then, long since healed into an almost pretty silvery pink, and winced, feeling guilty for her thoughts.

"Hullo," the Guardian of Fire said to the patient. "My name is Jin Zhara."

The youth did not respond, did not even react when she placed her hand on their arm. Ami watched with interest as a rose-gold glow bloomed where Jin Zhara's hand made contact with the patient, but the youth gave a convulsive jerk and she wrenched her hand away in dismay.

"What's wrong?" Han asked.

"He's not a magician, so I'm not sure if I can . . . if I can burn the corruption from his ki," the Guardian of Fire said softly. "My touch . . . my touch burns people who aren't magicians."

Ami glanced down at her own hands, which were faintly limned with the light of her own power. She thought of how she had sewn up the darkness in the Qirin Tulku by pushing life along his meridian pathways, then thought of Sang's body laid out on its bier in the courtyard of Castle Dzong. The yak-herder had been dead before she could sew up the corruption with her power; there was no life for her to coax into overcoming the demon. She studied the youth laid out on the mat, the shallow rise and fall of their chest.

Ami knelt beside the Guardian of Fire. "May I . . . may I try something?"

Jin Zhara blinked her large eyes at her. For a moment, it felt as though the other girl could somehow see *through* her, to the green-gold heart of her. "Be my guest," she said at last.

"Hold this." Ami pulled the leather folios from her sash and handed them to her cousin. "And be careful not to damage them—they're the only remaining fragments of *Songs of Order and Chaos*."

"What?" Han yelped, holding the folios gingerly with his fingertips. "You couldn't have told me that *before* dumping the most precious resource we have into my possession?"

Ignoring him, Ami placed her hands on the injured youth. Closing her eyes, she imagined the world and her physical self falling away in a world of pure ki. Through her magical senses, she could see the white light of life running through the patient, but it was muddied, dim, the corruption of demonic influence like sediment clouding the waters of their ki. As she had with the Qirin Tulku, she pushed her green-gold power along their bones, their blood, their body until the light of life ran clear.

Behind her, Jin Zhara gasped and Ami was startled into the present moment.

"Is something the matter?" Ami peered at the other girl over the rims of her spectacles.

"Oh? N-nothing." But Jin Zhara's face was unreadable, as she was gazing at Ami both as though she recognized her from another context and as though she had never seen Ami before. "Li Ami," Jin Zhara said softly. "Do you know what the powers of the Guardians of Dawn are supposed to be?"

Ami frowned. "Well, according to my fragment of *Songs of Order and Chaos,* the Guardian of Fire was supposed to be able to cure abominations," she said. "And lo, that is Jin Zhara's gift. It's related to her gift of transformation, or the ability to fundamentally change the nature of ki from one essence to another."

"What of the other Guardians?"

She paused. "I need my notes," she said uncertainly. "But from what I recall, the Guardian of Wind could spirit-walk, the Guardian of Wood could grant life where there was none, and the Guardian of Water could change the very nature of reality itself."

"Where does it say that?" Han asked, carefully leafing through *Songs of Order and Chaos* with interest.

Ami shook her head. "In bits and pieces, scattered throughout the pages," she said. "The problem is that none of the information is *organized*—some of it is on one page, part of it another. There must be a code, but thus far, none of us have been able to break it. It drove my father even further into madness to try."

"What about this?" Han pointed to a mark in the bottom right corner of one of the pages. It looked like someone had drawn a series of arcs, coloring in some of the blank spaces in between.

Ami pushed her glasses farther up her nose and squinted as she brought the page closer to her face. "Looks like some sort of doodle? Speaking as a scrivener, it can get boring copying out the same text over and over and you can end up doodling in the margins."

"Look, here's another one." Han plucked another page from the other folio and lined the two leaves together. "It looks like it's part of a larger design."

"The text goes this way," Ami said, turning the page around.

"But the mark would be on the opposite side then."

"Hold a moment." She lined up the two pieces of paper to make one complete half circle. She scanned the lines on both pages and realized in that moment that the text from two different folios made sense when put together this way. "Oh!"

"What? What is it?"

She scrambled for some scrap paper and a charcoal pencil, eager to make note of what she had found. "This is half of a *taikhut*! *This* is a code! Cousin, you're a genius!"

"That would be the first time anyone has ever called me that," Han said with amusement.

"What's a *taikhut*?" Jin Zhara asked.

"It's a symbol," Ami said, shutting one of the folios and pointing to the sigil inscribed onto the leather cover. "See? It looks as though it's been divided into quarters on each of the pages." She went back to riffling through the pages. "*The Guardians of Dawn rest beneath the mansions of their celestial companions*," she read aloud, swiftly jotting down the translation. "*The Mountain of Fire in the south, the Singing Skies in the north, the Lake of Illusion in the east, and*"—she squinted—"*the Root of the World in the west*. Oh, oh, oh," Ami said excitedly. "This is all beginning to make sense now!"

"Good," the Guardian of Fire said in a mild voice. "Because maybe then you can explain it to us."

"For years my father had been trying to decipher the *Songs of Order and Chaos*, and for years I thought his strange, rambling notes were simply a product of his broken mind," Ami said. "But no! The pages are divided at random across the two folios. See?" She thrust some more papers with the symbols lined up beneath the other girl's nose. "These two pages are from two different fragments—my father's and Gaden's. Alone, they're gibberish, but together"—she turned her head at an angle—"it says *and the people donated a single drop of will to the Sunburst Warrior, who gathered it with the consent of the governed to fight back the hordes of chaos.*" She knit her brows in confusion. "That sounds like it could be referring to the Star of Radiance," she said. "But the bit that would confirm it looks as though it continues on another page."

"*Songs of Order and Chaos* was divided into four so that no one would ever decipher its contents," Jin Zhara murmured. "So this must be the code the imperial magicians devised in the event they needed to!"

"What?" Ami was shocked. "There are more folios? Do you know where they are?"

"No." Jin Zhara shook her head. "But a friend told me the original text had been struck into four pieces and scattered to the four corners of the empire—north, south, east, and west. The Bangtan Brothers—"

But before Jin Zhara could explain who the Bangtan Brothers were or what they had to do with the missing fragments, a groan from the injured youth brought their attention back to the matter at hand. "Where am I?" they croaked. "Who are you?"

"Shush," Jin Zhara soothed, gently pushing the youth back down after they tried to sit up. "You're in the infirmary tent of the Heralds of Glorious Justice. You've been through quite a lot, so you need to get some rest." She glanced around the tent for medicines, but the infirmary tent was depressingly bare.

"I'll check for healing supplies," Han offered, walking to the cabinets and opening doors and drawers. "You two stay there."

"My name is Jin Zhara," the Guardian of Fire said to the patient, taking care to keep her tone as friendly and kind as possible. "And you are . . . ?"

"Tan Binh," they said. "What happened?" They brought their hand up to their forehead with a wince. "I remember getting attacked by monsters and . . ." They trailed off, their eyes going distant and haunted as they relived the memory of the undead battle. Their fingers brushed over the torn bandages on their face.

"Here, let me change that dressing for you." Ami was about to join Han when the youth grabbed her wrist.

"Wait." They began unwinding the bandage from their face and Ami braced herself for the sight of their injury. But to her surprise, the flesh beneath the linen strips was smooth, the mangled muscle and tendons of their cheek healed clean. "How . . . but I got bit . . ."

"That's . . . that's impossible," Jin Zhara breathed. "Magic can accelerate the body's natural healing processes, but . . . but it's almost as though the flesh has been given new life."

Ami could feel the other girl's curious gaze on her face, but kept her eyes averted. *Hide your light.* She pulled the green-gold glow back beneath her skin. "Let's tend to the others," she suggested, moving away from Tan Binh and the impossible healing her power had wrought. "Some of them may be magicians."

"I can't find any healing supplies," Han called from the other end of the infirmary tent.

"Leave it," Jin Zhara called back. "Why don't you bring us something to eat instead? I'm famished."

At the mention of food, Sajah poked his little ruby nose from her sleeve with interest. Scurrying down her arm, he transformed into his preferred ginger cat form and chased after Han's heels as he went out to find them all something to eat.

"Jin Zhara," Ami said quietly at the next bed. "This person is a magician."

This victim was an older magician in their middle-late years, their hair graying about their temples. They had received a rather nasty wound in the torso, deep gouging marks as though someone had tried to disembowel them with their bare hands. Bile rose to Ami's throat when she realized that was probably exactly what had happened. She drew several glyphs in the air above the wounds, and watched the flesh knit itself back together as her green-gold light dissipated into the skin. But unlike on the youth's face a few cots down, this time, the scars remained.

Ami placed her hands over the fresh scars and closed her eyes. Immediately, the sense of wrongness that accompanied all demonic influence was present, and she slowly worked to clear the void from the victim's ki.

The magician sat up with a startled gasp once she had finished. "Ti-yok!" they cried. "The undead! What—"

"It's all right, it's all right," Jin Zhara said. "The magician is safe."

"Safe?" Their eyes were wild as they stared at her—through her—to the battlefields beyond the encampment. "Demons walk among us and you think we're *safe*?"

Ami opened her mouth to reassure them, to let them know that Jin Zhara was the Guardian of Fire, that she could transform abominations back into people, but she was overwhelmed by everything they had just experienced. "We are safe for now," she said instead.

"No one is safe, not even for now." The magician gripped her hands, and Ami resisted the urge to jerk away from any and all unwanted touch. "There are demons walking among us in the encampment."

Jin Zhara went still. "What does the magician mean?"

"Not all of the injured party stayed in the infirmary after they were treated."

Alarm raced through her. "There are the bitten who are wandering within camp?"

"We have to get them," Jin Zhara said urgently. "Before—"

An ear-shattering scream rent the night apart.

18

A MONSTER WAS WREAKING HAVOC THROUGH THE CAMP.
Zhara and Li Ami ran to the tent flaps of the infirmary and peered into the night. Behind them, the injured magician was crying, "Tiyok! Tiyok! Demons walk among us!" while the others groaned and shifted and moaned in their cots.

"What should we do?" Li Ami asked.

"I have to find Han," Zhara said in panic, reaching for the blade she wore strapped at her back. Despite the lessons she had had with Han, it still felt awkward and heavy in her hands. Still, she drew the sword and held it before her like a torch as it went up in flames. "Han!" she called as she ran through the encampment. "Han!"

A roar, a flash of lightning, followed by a familiar cry, "Zaaaaaaaaaan-heeeeeeeeeeeeiiiiiiiiiiiiiiiiiiii!"

Ahead in a clearing that had once been a makeshift military mess hall was Han, brandishing what appeared to be a ladle in his hands on Sajah's back, who was in Lion form. All around him, cauldrons of rice and stew had been overturned, as well as the low wooden platforms that had served as seating for the Heralds. Before him was a giant figure made of what Zhara initially took to be mud, if it weren't for the overpowering, overwhelming smell of cinnamon, cardamom, and cumin wafting from the creature.

Curry.

The abomination was curry.

She would have laughed if she hadn't been disturbed by how hungry it was making her.

"Han!" she cried as he swung out with his ladle, taking an enormous scoop out of the monster. Bits of rice and stew went flying, spattering Zhara with the taste of game and rot.

It wasn't rice.

It was maggots.

Well, at least she wasn't hungry anymore.

"Augh!" she gagged, brushing herself off with a shudder. All around her, the maggots went up in little puffs of flame, shriveling and shrieking at an unbearable pitch as they curled and writhed into ash. "What happened?"

"I don't know," Han shouted back from the other side as Sajah paced back and forth, unwilling to cross the tide of rotten curry. "Samsoon and I were getting food for everyone and he just . . . up and transformed."

Zhara swore beneath her breath. Samsoon must have been bitten during the encounter with the undead, but it must have been minor. Too bad even minor injuries could be devastating when it came to demonic energies.

By now, the other Heralds were beginning to gather around the scene.

"What's going on—Mother of Demons." Pang Lok emerged from deep within the encampment. He lunged for the nearest weapon—a halberd—and swung it over his head, slamming the ax-head into the abomination's body.

It went straight through the monster like a knife through soup. The abomination fell and flopped and squelched into two pieces on the ground.

"Yes!" Pang Lok pumped his fist in triumph.

"Wait," Han warned as several other Heralds moved forward, brushes at the ready.

"It's dead," the other boy said, but even as he spoke, both halves of the abomination began sliding together, combining and congealing back into a single creature, thousands of rice-like maggots wriggling and writhing and climbing over one another to form the rough shape of a large human.

"I think I'm going to be sick," Pang Lok remarked in a serene voice, looking rather green. He calmly leaned over and retched into the grass.

Zhara readied herself with her blade, which blazed in the darkness with rose-gold fire. The last time she had wielded the blade against an abomination, one touch of the edge had turned the monster back into a magician. She just needed to get close enough to swipe at the creature. Not a problem. Unlike the other abominations she had fought before, this one did not appear to have fangs or claws or other dangerous bits to avoid.

She just had to fight her nausea to get close.

Gripping the hilt of her sword in both hands, Zhara raised her weapon above her head. Screwing her eyes shut, she ran forward with a yell and brought the blade down with all her might.

And missed.

"Keep your eyes on your opponent!" Han called from her left. "You can't strike if you can't see them!"

Zhara grunted and lifted her blade again.

"Are you left- or right-handed?" Han called again. "Dominant hand on top! Dominant hand on top! Aiyo!" He rubbed at his head where Sajah's flaming peacock tail slapped him reproachfully.

"You use it then!" Zhara yelled back. She swung again, keeping her eyes open this time, but the monster parted its maggots to allow the sword to pass through its body without touching a single part of its blade.

"Heralds!" Pang Lok shouted, sounding as though he were swallowing back bile. "Immobility trap!"

Immediately the magicians within the Heralds of Glorious Justice began a flurry of casting spells, brightly colored lights flashing in the air as they ringed the monster with floating glyphs in the Language of Flowers. They advanced on the abomination with left hand outstretched, palm forward, with the brushes held in their right hand at the ready by their ear. The characters floated by each magician's hand as they pressed forward, closing in on the creature with a circle of spells.

There was a wet, squelching, sucking sound and something resembling a mouth emerged in the monster's midsection. The abomination roared, its throat gargling with wriggling worms. One of the magicians near Zhara squirmed as a panicked look of disgust crossed their face.

"Heralds!" Pang Lok thumped the end of his halberd into the ground. "Hold!"

The monster hissed, or gave its best approximation of a hiss, as its writhing mass came in contact with the ring of spells.

"Now, Guardian of Fire!" Pang Lok gave Zhara the signal to move forward with her blade.

But before she could make her move, the abomination collapsed.

A shout of surprise, and the spells blinked out one by one as the magicians struggled to figure out what was happening.

The ground . . . shivered.

Sajah roared in surprise and immediately transformed into a giant bird, unceremoniously dumping Han onto the grass. "Yah!" he shouted. "Come back here, you overstuffed mattress!"

"What—" said the magician closest to Zhara's left before their words died in their throat with a choke. Their skin seemed to ripple before a stream of maggots poured from their throat, their nose, their eyes, before the abomination crawling up through the ground into the magician exploded outward in a shower of rotten spices and grubs.

"Well," said Han in a light voice. "I'm never going to eat curry ever again."

"Stand back!" Zhara brought her sword around again, wishing she had paid better attention to Han's lessons. Her weapon was heavy and unwieldy in her hand, and she was terrified of accidentally striking an innocent bystander as much as the monster.

But the encampment was chaos now. Screams poured from every corner as people fled the grain-sized worms, clawing at their ears, their noses, their eyes, to escape the maggots burrowing into their flesh.

"By the Great Wheel, have you no respect for the—" The Beast emerged from one of the tents nearby. "Mother of Demons," they breathed.

"Wait!" Zhara cried, awkwardly running forward with her sword, trying not to trip over the unaccustomed balance. "Don't—"

The abomination, sensing this new presence, seemed to shift its bulk around toward the Beast and Okonwe. The grass underfoot rippled and shivered as larvae crawled beneath the ground toward them, as the monster pulled itself forward. Like an arm or a hand, the mass of maggots wrapped itself around the Beast's ankle.

"No!" Zhara fell into her Guardian form as she ran, and the world was awash in pathways of light and dark. To her astonishment, something clear and bright was shining from the Beast's chest, a beautiful, pure glow that seemed to draw her in.

But all around them were myriad holes into the void, tiny pinpricks of the darkness that made her skin crawl with revulsion. And all those tiny tears were gathering into one large rip into the abyss, all centering around the Beast.

"Stop!"

The light from the Beast's chest flared, momentarily blinding Zhara. She blinked and flickered in and out of her Guardian form, and before her eyes, the scarred youth seemed to flash or twinkle like a star. The authority in their voice brought the entire camp to a halt, and even Zhara felt the touch of compulsion.

But more astonishingly, the abomination stopped in its tracks.

The time was now.

With extreme effort, Zhara shook off the unspoken command radiating from the Beast, and lifted her sword. With a roar, she charged forward, finally driving the blade deep into the abomination's body. Flames burst from the point of contact, immediately consuming the monster into a conflagration. The cooking smells of fats and garlic, cinnamon and cumin filled the air, and once again Zhara was reminded of how hungry she was, and how she would never, ever go near a bowl of curry ever again.

As the abomination shriveled and curled in on itself, bits of maggots crisped and flaked away, revealing a large, naked man in the middle. Samsoon.

"Gaden!" A terrified voice behind them.

"Ami?" The Beast immediately leaped forward to grasp her outstretched hands. "What's wrong?"

The scrivener's glasses were askew on her face. "The undead," she said. "The undead have risen!"

They came from the infirmary.

They came from the sleeping tents.

They came from the battlefield surrounding the encampment.

The Heralds of Glorious Justice were completely surrounded.

"We have to run," Zhara gasped. "There's just too many."

Pang Lok easily twirled his halberd in his hand. "We can stand our ground."

Han shook his head. "There is no fighting the undead. If death didn't stop them before, then what makes you think you and your rather hefty-looking poleax will stop them now?"

Pang Lok looked uncertain.

"Go," came a cracked voice from behind them.

"Auntie Lee-Lee!" the Beast and Pang Lok cried.

A thin, frail, nearly skeletal woman with wispy hair emerged from the nearest tent. She was clearly ill—dying perhaps—but she stood straight and tall, eyes alight with resolve. In her hand she held a brush, the tip already glowing with the color of her magic—a steely gray.

"Go," she repeated. "I'll buy you time."

"No." Pang Lok shook his head. "But you'll—"

"—die?" General Lee's smile quirked to one side. "I'm already dying, nephew. Let me go out in the manner of my choosing, the manner I was always meant to go: in a blaze of glorious justice, in the service of my liege." Her eyes slid to the Beast, who was resolutely not meeting her gaze.

"But we were so close," the big youth said, his voice cracking. "We were so close to finding the Unicorn of the West. To finding the cure for what ailed you!"

"You never did have your priorities straight, boy," said General Lee. "You think I came all the way out here to find some sort of miracle cure?"

"But—"

"But nothing, Lok." She took one step forward, then stumbled. Okonwe ran to her side and grabbed her arm, supporting her. "Take the gi—take Gaden, and keep them safe. At all costs. It all depends on you now."

"Go." The former captain of the guard rumbled at them. "We'll buy you time."

"The others—" Pang Lok began to protest, but General Lee cut him off.

"The others are on their own. You have your mission, Lok. Consider it the last mission you get from me." General Lee's sharp gaze moved from the Beast to Pang Lok to Zhara and the others. The tip of her brush began to glow even brighter as the ripping, gnashing sounds of tearing flesh grew louder. "Now run!"

Zhara, Han, Li Ami, and Pang Lok did not need to be told twice, immediately turning and heading out of the encampment, but the Beast hesitated. "Okonwe . . ." they began.

But the big man said nothing, only giving the scarred youth one long, eloquent look. The Beast turned their head away and swiftly followed after the others.

"Where are we going?" Han called after Pang Lok, who moved swiftly in spite of his bulk.

"To find us some mounts," he called over his shoulder. "We're going to need more speed than our feet can give us if we are to outrun the undead horde."

But when they arrived at the stables, the mounts were already gone—having broken their traces in terror and fled.

"Well, now what?" Han asked.

"I don't know, I'm all ears if you have any better ideas!"

Zhara ran to the rocky outcropping just off the side of the trail. The plains of the Zanqi Plateau were one large expanse of blackness. The night was clear, but there was no moon, no light but the soft twinkle of stars. She couldn't tell what was below them—whether sea or grass or morass.

A shout of alarm from behind her. The undead were crawling down the hillsides from the encampment. "We gotta move!" Han cried.

But no matter where they turned, more and more revenants appeared.

"They're coming from the battlefield below!" Ami pointed at the inky-black expanse below them.

"I thought all the bodies were burned!" Han looked around him, wild-eyed. "Zhara, your blade!"

She had forgotten she was holding it. "You take it!" she said, thrusting her weapon into Han's hands. Now that the abomination was taken care of, she would rather the blade be in more capable hands than hers. Besides, when it came to the undead, her actual hands would be more than enough. Gathering her power within her, she threw her arms out, sending up a wall of fire behind them.

"That should keep them for now," she said. "Let's go!"

They followed down the same path that they had taken up to reach the Heralds' encampment, but when they reached the bottom of the shallow hill, Zhara gave a cry of horror and fell back.

"What?" Han asked. "What is it?"

"The battlefield," she gasped. "The demonic blood, it's . . ."

There was nowhere to go, nowhere to step. It was nothing but a swamp of death all around them, and the demonic blood spilled from the battlefield was bringing all the dead things—including the bodies of battles long past—back to the surface. Before them, a pile of bodies the Heralds had thrown together after their battle was starting to writhe and stir. Zhara's skin crawled with revulsion to see the unnatural way the corpses moved, their arms stiff and fluid in ways backward to human movement. With a shout, she threw her hand out before her, sending the entire pile up in flames.

But that didn't stop the bodies. They continued coming even as bits of them crumbled to char, their gnashing teeth and grasping hands crawling across the muck toward them.

"This way!" Han called. The enchanted sword shone in his hand like a torch lighting their path. In the light of the blade, they could see a path illuminated with rosy-gold fire, and the party followed Han as they hopped from island to island in the cursed land.

The ground roiled and rumbled beneath their feet.

And with an explosion and a shower of mud and flesh, several more revenants shredded themselves as they tore out of the earth.

"Ugh!" The Beast kicked at a corpse crawling out of the ground, shattering its skull with a sickening crunch. The revenant kept coming, opening its jaw impossibly wide so that Zhara could hear the snap and crack of tendons and skin as it unhinged its jaw, lunging to try to sink its teeth into the Beast's leg.

A blazing arc of light and Han was suddenly beside them, swinging his blade left and right. Although Zhara had seen him wield weapons with far more finesse than this before, he struck out indiscriminately, mowing down undead bodies like a reaper with a scythe, trying to clear them all a path to escape.

But it was no use.

They were surrounded, they were being swarmed, they were going to be torn apart. Zhara felt the press of bodies on her stomach, her throat, her ribs, and gasped as she struggled to breathe. If she wasn't going to be torn apart, then she was going to choke to death beneath the tide of the undead.

And then . . . everything stopped.

It was as though time had halted, for the revenants were paused in their attack as surely as if someone had frozen them in ice. The previously black ki pathways of the undead were now filled with a glowing green-gold light. She recognized this color. She recognized to whom this ki belonged.

Turning her head, she saw Ami as a being made entirely of light.

And she recognized her.

Deep down, on a level beyond that of the body but of that of the soul.

Slowly but surely Ami was pouring herself into the nothing and filling it with herself. Every place her green-gold glow touched was healed, first turning into the dull matte gray of inanimate matter, then filling with the clear light of animate matter.

Of life.

Ami was bringing the cursed land back to life.

The Guardian of Wood could grant life where there was none.

Zhara watched with amazement as the world burst into bloom around her, the barley stalks ripening, long-dead cosmos flowers lifting, growing, blossoming. Like fireworks they opened all around her, pink and white and purple and before long, the land was healed.

Beside her, Li Ami collapsed to the ground. With the last of her strength, Zhara ran forward to haul the unconscious scrivener out of the way of the melee. As soon as her hands touched the other girl's skin, her power surged to meet Li Ami's, like a faithful companion greeting an old friend. The girl moaned as Zhara dragged her beneath an outcropping of rock before collapsing onto the ground beside her.

"You—" she breathed, both joy and recognition battling the fatigue within her.

The scrivener struggled to open her eyes, the corner of her of spectacles cracked and askew. "Me," she said faintly, her fingertips resting on the back of Zhara's. "You."

She knew who Li Ami truly was.

"Hullo," she said softly. "It's nice to finally meet you . . . Guardian of Wood."

19

AFTER TWO OF THEIR REFUGES HAD FALLEN to abominations and the undead in nearly as many days, Gaden was beginning to wonder if they weren't the problem.

In the immediate aftermath of battle against the undead, the surviving Heralds of Glorious Justice—Okonwe, Samsoon, and Uncle Tama among them—tallied their losses and began the slow, unforgiving work of burning the dead at the Guardian of Fire's behest, the General's remains included.

"We can't risk the dead coming back," she said. "And the easiest way to ensure that is to burn the remains." Her eyes had been bright—more than bright—they burned with a rose-gold fire in their dark brown depths, practically a source of light in themselves. Gaden thought of the brilliant, blazing figure who had stormed onto the castle grounds atop a fiery Lion with a flaming sword in hand, cutting down abominations and the undead left and right. For someone so powerful, the Guardian of Fire was remarkably unassuming, and they couldn't help comparing the reality of the girl before them to the images of the murals painted all over Kalantze's village walls. In real life, Jin Zhara was short, slight, and seemingly scarcely able to hold a sword, let alone wield it. She was shy, sweet, and not a little silly, if her propensity for giggling at the oddest moments was anything to go by.

The smell of smoke and cooked flesh remained in Gaden's nose for days. It inflamed the lining of their throat and made everything itch. Gaden stripped the glove off their left hand and looked down at the scaly, bruise-colored growths covering the scar tissue on their arm. The entire left side of their body—their face, their leg, their waist, and their arm—had been badly burned when they were a baby, and they had lost all sensation in the skin as the scars healed. But in the past several months, a strange infection had started calcifying the dead flesh of their fingertips, reigniting the nerve endings in their hand.

And they wondered if the infection might be spreading.

No, they reasoned, shaking their head to dislodge the low, persistent headache that had been troubling them for days. Just some sort of allergic reaction. They shouldn't—couldn't—worry about it now. Gaden replaced the glove and rubbed at the pressure between their brows.

Besides, none of this was as troubling as what was to come.

They were at a crossroads.

"We can't stay here," Gaden said to Okonwe. "Who knows what other terrors we will encounter out in the open?"

The Heralds were agreed, but what none of them could agree on was the next course of action. After the work of cleaning up the bodies had been finished, they gathered together what little foodstuffs they had left. No one had much appetite, but neither Gaden nor the others in their party had eaten in days, and they were in desperate need of sustenance.

"I say we head for the lowlands," said Pang Lok through a mouthful of tsampa gruel. "We have allies in the border towns; surely we can we recuperate and recoup our forces there."

The Guardian of Fire made a face, although whether it was from their tasteless meal or what Lok had said was difficult to tell. "How, by press-ganging people to your cause?"

"If necessary." The big boy gave her a hard look. "We believe in magician liberation," he said. "At all costs."

"Including violence?"

"Don't you understand the meaning of *at all costs*?" Pang Lok said in frustration, shoving down another large mouthful of tsampa. "The Warlord had no compunction in destroying all magicians to further his own ends. We should merely return the same courtesy. We cannot sit idly by and let the northerners dictate the parameters of battle."

"But we are not at war," Jin Zhara protested.

"Yet," Pang Lok said in a dark voice.

"Look," Samsoon said in a placating tone. "We are all on the same side. We are all in opposition to the Gommun Emperor. We just differ as to the ultimate ends."

But the Guardian of Fire and her companion had refused. "We came to the outermost west in search of a way to defeat the Mother of Ten Thousand Demons," she said. "We cannot turn back and fight for a lost cause."

"Lost cause?" Uncle Tama said incredulously. "She speaks of demons, yet ours is the lost cause?"

Jin Zhara gestured to the smoking ruins of the field below the encampment. "You cannot deny the truth of what we've all just experienced!" she said heatedly. "Magicians turn into abominations and the dead come back to life! How could that be anything but the work of demons?"

There wasn't a single voice that could be heard to contradict her.

"All I ask," she said in a softer tone, "is that you give aid and join us in our quest to seal the portals to Tiyok."

"Does the Guardian of Fire even know where these so-called portals might be?" Samsoon asked.

"No." Jin Zhara glanced at Ami. The scrivener had said little during these conversations, having passed most of her time with her nose buried in the fragments of *Songs of Order and Chaos*. "But I think we know where to start."

"*The Guardians of Dawn rest beneath the mansions of their celestial companions*," Ami said quietly. "*The Mountain of Fire in the south, the Singing Skies in the north, the Lake of Illusion in the east, and the Root of the World in the west.* The first portal was at Mount Zanhei, the resting place of the Lion of the South. We think the tree of life is the source of the western portal, the mansion of the Unicorn of the West."

Silence fell over the survivors.

"You chase a fairy tale," Samsoon said softly.

"No more than the rest of you," Jin Zhara retorted. "You believe the Mugung heir still survives."

"But that's not a fairy tale," Pang Lok protested. "The heir—"

Gaden stiffened, silently willing him to *shut up*. The words suddenly died in the other boy's throat as his face went purple.

Wonhu Han coughed. "My friends," he said. "The Guardian of Fire *and* the Lion of the South stand before you. They are not fairy tales; you've seen their power."

The survivors shifted uncomfortably in their seats.

"What say the Beast?" Uncle Tama asked, turning his eyes on them. He had the same eyes as his younger sister, the late General Lee-Lee, and it made Gaden's heart twist in their chest. "The Heralds follow your word."

They shook their head. "Let the Heralds do what they will." They looked to Jin Zhara. "I will follow the Guardian of Fire."

"No!" Pang Lok burst out. "Auntie Lee-Lee bade me protect you, and little though I like you, Beast, I cannot let you go wandering the wilderness alone."

"Besides," added Samsoon before Gaden could make their retort, "no one even knows where the Root of the World is. We wouldn't know where to begin."

Uncle Tama held up a crooked finger. "Ah, but our stories tell us where the Unicorn of the West resides. At the place where the sky was held back."

Gaden started, their hand going to the Qirin Tulku's heart seeds they wore in a pouch about their neck. "Mount Llangposa?"

Pang Lok gave them a sharp glance. "What?" They looked to Uncle Tama, who seemed similarly astonished.

"The place where the sky was held back," Gaden said, "is Mount Llangposa. That's what Teacher—what the Qirin Tulku told me before he died."

The big boy was taken aback. "We know where that is!"

Gaden blinked. "You do?"

He nodded. "Auntie Lee-Lee, Uncle Tama, and I are from the Gyasol lands," he said, naming a province farther to the north. "And the elders always spoke of *the pastures of Mount Llangposa*. I always assumed it was a Zanqian name for the Skyhold, the tallest peak of the Gunung range.

It was only a league or so from where I grew up, and visible for miles around."

Gaden sat up straight in excitement. "Then that's where we shall start our journey."

"But hold a moment," said Pang Lok. "That's in the opposite direction of the imperial city. Where we should be headed instead of on this fool's quest."

Wonhu Han made an indignant noise, but Jin Zhara placed a hand on his wrist to quiet him. "I cannot compel anyone to follow," she said. "I am not the Sunburst Warrior, divinely gifted with one drop of will from every person in the Morning Realms to seal Tiyok back in her domain. I'm just a girl. Despite it all, I'm just an ordinary girl who needs your help."

"I'm going with Jin Zhara," Gaden repeated, setting down their bowl of barley meal. "The rest of you can do what you will. Besides," they said, palming the Qirin Tulku's heart seeds at their throat, "I have errands of my own to fulfill."

"What errands?" Pang Lok scoffed. "Your destiny is here with us, whether you like it or not, Beast."

Gaden could feel ire rising in their bones. The dead skin beneath their glove itched furiously, and resentment burned white-hot in their chest. "You know nothing of my destiny, Pang Lok," they snarled. "So take your assumptions and shove them up your——"

"My liege!" Okonwe said in a reproachful voice.

"And you!" Gaden whirled on their mentor and guardian. "Don't pretend you know what's best for me either when you've never once told me the entire truth!"

There was a sharp intake of breath from the Heralds. The survivors had known Gaden their whole life, and they had never heard Gaden raise their voice to anyone, let alone the man they considered a father figure.

The skin beneath their glove felt as though it were on fire, and the urge to tear it off and scratch and scratch and scratch was nigh unbearable.

"Beast," said Uncle Tama. He held his hand outstretched, as though trying to soothe a spooked horse. "We know you're grieving——"

"You know *nothing*." The rage bubbling up within Gaden felt both cleansing and toxic at once, and they felt almost as though it were a force beyond themself.

"Beast—"

"Shut up!" Unable to bear the itching in their hand any longer, they ripped off their glove and began raking at their skin. A cry of shock and surprise rose from the crowd at the sight, but Gaden was beyond caring. "Leave me alone, all of you," they said in a savage voice. "I don't want *anything* to do with *any* of you." A burst of rage exploded from their chest like ray of light, and everyone's mouth immediately clamped closed.

And with that, they stalked off into the darkness.

No one followed.

Gaden didn't know whether to be grateful or insulted, but for the time being, they were simply glad of the peace. The itching in their hand had subsided along with the rage, and they regretted the harsh words they had hurled at everyone just moments before. They would have to find Okonwe and apologize later, but not before they made sense of what they had just experienced.

Gaden rubbed at the spot on their chest where they had felt the ripple of energy explode from their body, and the strange subsiding of the anger that had so fiercely burned them from the inside. It was almost as though they could see light pass from their body and through each and every person around them, connecting them all with myriad invisible strings of energy. If Gaden concentrated, they could feel the tugs on the ends of them all—Pang Lok, Okonwe, Uncle Tama, and the others—like fish on the end of a hook. With a start, they realized that they had always been able to feel these minuscule tugs on their consciousness, the pulling and subconscious reining in they were constantly engaged in. They thought of the last time they had seen Lee-Lee, five years before her death.

I forbid you to tell anyone who I really am. Who my parents are. Who my grandparents are. Forget my name and tell no one about me.

Wei—

Princess Weifeng is dead!

They had felt that same ripple and burst of power explode from them then, that same feeling of rage. No, not rage. Not anger. *Will.* The overpowering sense of dominance and domination, the desire to bend the desires of everyone around them into a shape of their own making.

You have a light that compels us all to follow where you will lead, Okonwe had said.

That light is your destiny.

"No," Gaden murmured, walking as far away from the center of the Heralds' encampment as they could go. Toward the edges of the settlement, toward the darkness, and toward oblivion. They needed to be away, to come to terms with a destiny they had so desperately tried to avoid, but that seemed to have followed them nonetheless. Sitting down on the edge of the hill overlooking the battlefield, they studied their scarred hand, bruise-like growths dark in the moonlight.

Wielder of the Star of Radiance. For the longest time, they had thought it was merely a title, a role to which they had been born but could not fulfill. Not their true self.

"Gaden?"

They whirled around to see the familiar short-haired silhouette and the glint of moonlight off the edge of a pair of spectacles. "Ami?"

"Is everything all right?" They saw that the scrivener held a bowl in her hand, along with a spoon. "I brought you the rest of your supper. You should eat." Her eyes slid down to the rough skin of Gaden's exposed left hand. "Unless you want to be alone."

They did want to be alone, but they found that they did not mind Ami's company. "It's all right," they said. "You can stay."

Ami handed Gaden their bowl and sat down on the ground beside them. She said nothing, waiting for them to speak. Or not. There was no judgment in her waiting, and they appreciated that. The villagers of Kalantze had called her odd because she did not often meet people's gazes or say the most politic things, but with her, Gaden thought they could trust her honesty.

"I shouldn't have yelled at them." They pushed the barley meal around in their bowl with their spoon, their appetite gone. "I'll go back and apologize in a bit."

"Why?" To their surprise, she seemed genuinely confused. "You didn't do anything wrong."

Gaden gave a humorless laugh. "No, but I was rude."

She shrugged. "I don't think rudeness always warrants apology. Not if they weren't listening to you."

"Yes, but that's no excuse for how I behaved toward Okonwe." They took a listless bite of their now-cold tsampa, made a face, and set the bowl aside. It could have used some seasoning. "He's only ever had my best interests at heart." Gaden sighed, rubbing at the growths on their hand. "Do you know why they called me the Beast?" they said softly.

Ami shook her head.

"Because I used to have a beastly temper, you see. I said what I wanted, damn the consequences or feelings of others."

Ami tilted her head as she studied them. She was extraordinarily beautiful with her clear skin and fine features, but where Gaden might have found other pretty girls intimidating, there was something about the earnest openness of her expression that made her seem approachable. "I like you," she said bluntly, and Gaden felt a stab of shock and pleasure spear them through the stomach. "You're the only person I've met who never seems to hide what they mean behind codes or manners."

"Oh." The spear turned to icy disappointment in their gut. Of course Ami wouldn't mean what they had hoped. "Well, I like you too," they blurted out, feeling the heat rise in their cheeks. Contrary to what she had said, they meant something else with their words.

She smiled and took Gaden's hand in her own. They tried not to flinch as her flesh brushed the scaly growths erupting along the scarred tissue, shivering as the nerve endings came alive beneath her touch. "Oh," she said, snatching back her hand. "Did I hurt you?"

"N-no." There was no point in hiding it now, no point in trying to hide what was truly a hideous, ugly deformity from the prettiest girl they had ever known. They had long ceased to be self-conscious about their looks when it came to the scarring they received as a child, but this . . . this *blight* was something else. It made them feel tainted. It made them feel *dirty*.

She frowned. "Why does that sound like a lie?"

Gaden looked down at their hand. Even in the past days since they had left Kalantze it appeared as though the blight had gotten worse—the scabs darker, the texture rougher. It was even getting difficult to curl their left hand into a fist now. "It's the truth," they said. "You didn't hurt me. But I would be lying if I said it didn't occasionally cause me pain."

Ami frowned, rubbing her fingers against her palm. "What happened?"

They looked away. "I don't know," they said softly. "But I had hoped you could find out."

"Me?"

"Do you remember the bruises on the roots of the Pillar?"

She nodded.

"The day I discovered the Pillar was dying was the day I discovered the first spot on my hand. And I can't help but think they are related somehow."

Understanding dawned on her face. Her expressions, her moods, were so *clear* to Gaden. It was part of the reason she had seemed so approachable to them that day they met in Kalantze's village square. "So that's why you wanted me to translate *Songs of Order and Chaos,*" she said.

They studied her. "Are you upset?"

"Why would I be upset?"

"That I wanted to use you for my own ends."

She scoffed. "Of course I'm not upset. I'm a very gifted linguist, you know. Skilled with tongues."

Gaden grinned.

"Why are you smiling?" she asked in confusion.

They shook their head. "Nothing." They looked down, feeling shy all of a sudden.

She peered at them with suspicious eyes. "Now why does *that* feel like a lie?"

Gaden laughed. "May your good deeds return to you thousandfold," they said softly.

She frowned. "What are you thanking me for?"

They shrugged. "For . . . lifting my mood. For making me feel better. For making me laugh."

Ami smiled then, and Gaden felt a little flutter in their rib cage. They resisted the urge to cough.

"What do you want to do now?" she asked.

Gaden sighed. "I suppose I should return to the others with my apology."

She rolled her eyes. "No, I meant what do you want to do about"—she gestured vaguely to the scene around them—"all this? Will you go where you will? Or will you follow your duty to the Heralds?"

Gaden tugged thoughtfully at the pouch around their neck. "I want to follow the Guardian of Fire," they said slowly. "I want to go"—they swallowed—"where you go."

Her smile widened. "Me too," she said. "Me too."

20

FOR THE FIRST TIME IN A WEEK, Ami was able to relax on a bed, and yet for the first time in as many days, she found herself unable to sleep.

In the end, the surviving Heralds had agreed to accompany Jin Zhara on the quest to seal the portal at the Root of the World. It had taken surprisingly little persuading; Okonwe, Pang Lok, and the others meekly following Gaden's orders without protest. At Pang Lok's suggestion, they decided to travel to the Gyasol lands to begin preparations for their journey to Mount Llangposa and the Root of the World.

From that point on, sleep had been strictly a matter of survival. Pang Lok and Okonwe set up a watch rotation between them all, and everyone participated, sleeping in shifts of four hours each. Traumatic survival, as it turned out, took up an enormous portion of the body and mind, to the point where she felt neither hunger nor exhaustion whenever she had a real moment to rest.

They had come to the Gyasol lands, in the shadow of the Skyhold, the highest peak in the Gunungs.

The first thing Ami noticed when they crossed into Pang Lok's ancestral home was the smell of wildflowers and sweet grasses. Their entire flight from the site of the demon-blighted lands had filled her nose with the stink of spoilage and rot to the point where she had grown accustomed to breathing through her mouth.

The demonic blight had not touched these lands.

The Gyasol lands weren't much compared to the grandeur of the southern cities, but to Ami, it was the most beautiful place on earth. The Gyasol were cultivators of aromatic flowers and woods, not nomadic yak-herders like so many other clans of the Free Peoples on this part of the Zanqi Plateau. The settlement was somewhat more permanent than some of the others she had seen in the past—buildings made of stone and wood instead of mobile tents made of yak-hide and bamboo. Purple and pink and white cosmos flowers, geraniums, and other blossoms decorated the whitewashed walls and brightly painted eaves, a splash of color on an otherwise dreary landscape. There was no freestanding gate leading to this village like there was in Kalantze, but there was a small stone stupa with the Gyasol name written in the Language of Flowers and the indigenous writing system of their people carved into the base. With a start, Ami realized that the stupa was their version of the Lion Temples she had seen littering the roads around the south, only instead of an everlasting flame, the offerings were bursting with a plethora of flowers.

"Lok-ah! Tama-yah!" A small, slight figure standing beside the stupa had hailed them joyfully as they approached. The figure had been Pang Lok's grandmother, a youthful woman in her late-middle years, who looked scarce old enough to have as many grandchildren as she had claimed. Her name was Tenno, the clan leader, and she was an incredible host.

"Come, come," she had called. "Come sit with us, we have made you food."

"Wah, something smells really good." Han's nose quivered. "Is that . . . rice?"

A moment later, the slightly sweet and fragrant scent of rice had struck Ami's nose, causing her eyes and mouth to water with want so hard it almost hurt. They hadn't eaten rice in . . . she couldn't even count how many days. The smell of fats, garlic, onion, and even cardamom, cinnamon, and cumin from the kingdom of the Sindh were strong in the night air, so strong Ami could practically taste them at the back of her tongue before she had even taken a bite. Everything was so rich, so vivid, and she was so hungry she nearly felt sick with it.

"What is it?" Han asked, accepting a bowl from the Gyasol leader. He surreptitiously wiped at a bit of drool that had dribbled down his chin. "It smells delicious."

"It's called curry," Tenno replied, handing another bowl to Zhara and one to Ami. "We got a shipment of spices from Dzungri basin traders last week."

"Oh," he said, looking slightly ill. "Perhaps I'm not as hungry as I thought."

"Same," Samsoon said glumly. The memory of the rancid abomination he had transformed into hung in the air between them all, but hunger was a stronger sauce than revulsion, and soon they had all eaten their fill.

"Go, go to bed," Tenno had said when their eyes had drooped with exhaustion. "To bed. You can all catch me up on the morrow, when you are well rested." And with that, she had led Ami and Zhara to the barn to sleep—*clean and empty, and I figure you girls would rather have some privacy*—and led the boys away to stay at the dormitories. The Gyasol were one large family spanning several generations, and they lived, worked, and slept in common.

That had been several hours ago, and Ami had failed to fall asleep ever since. There was a point past nervous exhaustion where sleep was not forthcoming and everything hurt. Her flesh felt flensed, her skin stripped and raw, as though she were one giant open nerve. Every sense was overwhelmed; her eyes hurt from all she had witnessed, her nose hurt from all the smells that had assaulted her, her ears hurt from trying to parse all the unspoken languages thrown at her, her tongue hurt from all the new flavors she had tried, and her body ached from . . . everything. The woven rug serving as her bed linen was scratchy, the yak wool rough and itchy beneath her tender skin. The night was freezing this far up in the mountains and smelled like frost, the dry sereness of autumn dissipating into nothing. She was both too cold and too hot, the fur blankets beneath which she lay both too warm and not warm enough. Ami shivered, trying not to let the sensation of free fall beginning to open up inside her overtake everything.

Hullo, it's nice to finally meet you, Guardian of Wood.

"Is everything all right?"

Jin Zhara's silhouette turned over and sat up in the semidarkness.

The other girl's long, wavy hair was a lion's mane about her head, and images of Sajah kept assaulting Ami's mind's eye. She squeezed her actual eyes shut, but the afterimage was burned into her lids. She just wanted some peace. She just wanted to be somewhere cool and dark and alone.

"Li Ami?"

Ami gritted her teeth. "Give me a moment," she ground out. "I need—" But she couldn't finish her sentence, the words weighing down her tongue and choking her.

Without another word, Jin Zhara rose from her own bed—the warm, plush flank of the Lion of the South—and crawled to the corner of the loft where a jug of water and some cups had been laid on a stool. Presently, the other girl returned to her side with a damp rag, which she gently placed over Ami's eyes. Beneath the other girl's light touch, she immediately felt a surge of recognition so great it nearly moved her to tears.

It's nice to finally meet you.

"I—" Ami began.

"Shush," Jin Zhara soothed. "When the scrivener is ready."

Ami thought of Little Mother, the desire to run her hands along the outside of the little fairy tree's bowl causing her fingers to twitch and itch. The pang of sorrow she felt at losing the little fairy tree grown from her mother's heart seeds and her mother's ashes nearly overwhelmed her with its sharpness. She had lost so much—her mother, her sense of safety, her father . . .

She wrenched her thoughts away from Li Er-Shuan, trying not to spiral out of the moment and into anxiety. Okonwe had said Zerdan would have led her father out of Castle Dzong through the catacombs beneath the library. But her father was ill, his needs particular, and—no. She needed to be present. In her body. She took a deep breath and turned her attention to the damp rag over her eyes, the difference between the heat of her body and the coolness of moisture. Once the temperature between the rag and her skin had become one, Ami pulled it off her face and sat up.

"Better?" Jin Zhara asked. "Can't sleep?"

Ami shook her head. "I keep getting caught in . . . waves of memory. Kalantze, the Heralds, and . . ." She trailed off. "It's all . . . very overwhelming."

Jin Zhara clucked sympathetically. "I know. I can't sleep either. I thought about trying to write a letter to my little sister before bed, but I don't know what to say."

"Jin Zhara has a sister?"

"Well, stepsister. Suzhan." The other girl's eyes went soft with affection. "She's studying the zither at the academy in Jingxi."

Ami thought of her own sisters—Chenmi and Yumi—and wondered if there was something wrong with her that she had never been especially close to them. She was the youngest child of Li Er-Shuan, born twelve and fifteen years after her older sisters, daughters of her father by a wife who had died of a fever long before Ami was born.

Baba's pet—

—thinks she's so special—

—she's not even that pretty.

"My sister asked me for love stories," Jin Zhara continued, "but"— she gave a rueful laugh—"I don't have much to report on that front lately."

Ami grunted. "If the Guardian of Fire wants, I could copy out the entirety of the first three volumes of *The Maiden Who Was Loved by Death*. I've copied it out so many times I could probably re-create it word for word."

Jin Zhara sat up straight. "Li Ami has read *The Maiden Who Was Loved by Death*?"

"Yes?" Ami pushed her cracked glasses up her nose. "It was part of my job at Master Cao's bookshop."

"Do you know what happens in the next installment?" the other girl asked excitedly.

Ami shook her head. "My father and I left Zanhei long before we received the master copy of the last installment. I imagine it ends like any other romance novel," she said, waving a dismissive hand. "With the two leads together."

"Yes, but it's the *how*, not the *what*, that's important," Jin Zhara protested. "Everyone reads romance novels knowing what will happen in the end. It's the *journey* that's thrilling. Besides," she said, "if Little Flame stays with Lord Death, she will die! I need to know how the author will resolve that dilemma."

Ami fell silent, thinking about what the other girl had said about journeys instead of endings. She thought of Gaden that night on the edge of the Heralds' encampment, the feel of their rough hand beneath hers. For the first time, she considered where her friendship with them was headed, about the sense of momentum and inevitability between them she had felt then. She remembered all the descriptions of falling in love she had copied out endlessly during her tenure at Master Cao's and wondered if there wasn't something to romance novels after all.

"Li Ami?" Jin Zhara studied the other girl. "Is the scrivener all right?"

Ami blinked. "Yes," she said. And it was true. She forced herself back to the present, to the moment she was in with Jin Zhara—with the Guardian of Fire—and smiled.

The other girl looked uncomfortable. "Is the scrivener sure? She looks like she's grimacing in pain."

Ami let her face go slack. "I'm fine." She felt the impending awkwardness between the two of them hover like a storm cloud, growing thicker and heavier by the moment. It was always like this with people, especially with people her age. They found her odd or off-putting, and she could never quite figure out why. "May your good deeds return to you thousandfold, Jin Zhara."

"Just Zhara is fine." The brown-skinned girl smiled, and even in the darkness of the barn, she seemed to glow. But perhaps it was just the contrast of the whiteness of her eyes and teeth against her complexion. "What is it the Azureans say? We can lower our speech. Especially after what we've been through together." She tilted her head and Ami could feel the intensity of her gaze on her face. "Can we . . . can we talk about what happened? That night we fled the Heralds of Glorious Justice?"

And there it was. The thought and memory she had been avoiding looking at all night. The night she revealed the uncanniness of her power to the world, and the night Jin Zhara had reached out and touched her soul, naming her for who she was.

The Guardian of Wood.

Ami sat up and tucked her knees to her chest. "Yes," she whispered.

Zhara placed a gentle hand on her wrist. Again that surge of recognition, beyond that of another recognition, lit Ami's soul with joy. "You don't have to if you don't want to."

"I do," Ami said. "Want to talk about it, that is. It's just . . . it's just . . ."

"Too big," Zhara finished.

Ami nodded. "I'm . . . I'm frightened. Of the possibilities. Of what it all means."

And then, before she could blink or think, the other girl had wrapped her arms around her in an embrace. Ami stiffened, but before Zhara could pull away and apologize, she forced herself to relax and returned the hug. If Zhara had been anyone other than the Guardian of Fire, Ami might not have let them touch her. Unbidden, the image of Gaden's scarred face rose up in her mind.

"I'm frightened too," Zhara said, her voice muffled against Ami's shoulder, and for the first time since the two of them had met, Ami felt—truly felt—the terrible weight of what the Guardian of Fire must be going through. To know that she must be responsible for saving the world, for stopping the Mother of Ten Thousand Demons. And now that burden was also Ami's, and it was a burden both unwanted and unasked for.

And yet, here they were.

"When did you know?" Ami asked when they pulled apart. "That you were the Guardian of Fire?"

Zhara looked thoughtful. "In some respects, I think I must have always known. My magic was always . . . unusual, I suppose, but then again, I had no basis of comparison. My father was a magician, but he died in one of the purges after the Just War, so he didn't have much chance to teach me regular magic. So what I learned, I learned on my own. What I *didn't* know," she said ruefully, "was that it was different from the magic used by nearly everyone else in the realm. It wasn't until I came across the Guardians of Dawn—the mutual aid society—that I realized I was something other than yet another girl with powers. And then"—she laughed, but it didn't sound mirthful—"I encountered my first abomination." Zhara looked at Ami. "What about you? Have you always known that you were the Guardian of Wood?"

Again Ami's fingers reached for Little Mother, only to curl in on themselves when she remembered Little Mother was gone. "Yes and no," she said. "Like you, I was always . . . unusual. Uncanny. That was the word people used. I was always *uncanny.*" To Ami's surprise, she found Zhara's fingers entwined with hers. For a moment, she thought of drawing back, for the shock of the other girl's touch was nearly scalding in its power, but she tightened her fingers around the other girl's hand, reminding herself that it was *this,* this touching of souls and the meeting of minds, that she had always craved, and Zhara's hand was the physical manifestation of it. "I never had any friends because of it."

"I'm sorry," said Zhara. "It must have been a lonely existence. I at least had my little sister and Sajah." Behind her, the Lion rumbled. Zhara snuggled farther into the celestial creature's flank, inviting Ami to lie down beside her and drawing the furs close over them both. "Come, it'll be warmer with the three of us beneath the blanket."

Ami hesitantly accepted the invitation, feeling both hopeful and uncomfortable at once. She had always been sensitive to physical sensations—to the textures of fabric and wood and even occasionally the food in her mouth. There was muchness to the sensations of everything around her, but it wasn't overwhelming. Not yet.

"Did you have a pet?" Zhara asked, nuzzling her nose against Sajah's fur.

Ami, who had been expecting an animal musk from the Lion of the South, was pleasantly surprised that the enormous cat smelled faintly of the air before a storm—clean and almost sweet, like sun-bleached linens after drying on a laundry line. "No," she said, thinking of her father. It had been hard enough keeping him alive, let alone the few plants they had in their garden. "Although I think it would have been nice to have one."

"Don't all Guardians have celestial companions?" Zhara asked. Her words were beginning to slur together with sleep, and Ami herself felt the heaviness of the day begin to weigh down her eyelids. "I have Sajah, and Yuli has Temur."

"Yuli?" Ami felt the waves of sleep momentarily retreat. "Who's Yuli?"

Zhara yawned. "The Guardian of Wind."

"You mean there are others like us? In the world?"

The other girl blinked, her gaze glassy-eyed. "Yes," she said. "Stands to reason, doesn't it? If the Guardian of Fire and the Guardian of Wood are reborn in the world, then all four of us would be? We've discovered three of us now—Fire, Wind, and Wood. All that's left is Water."

Ami settled back against Sajah's warm flank. She thought of what Zhara had said, about each of the Guardians of Dawn having a companion animal, but she couldn't remember any stories of the Guardian of Wood with a companion at all. Perhaps that knowledge was in the pages of Gaden's folio of *Songs of Order and Chaos* she hadn't yet had a chance to translate. Perhaps they were in the pieces of the book that were yet to be found, scattered to the four winds of the Morning Realms.

"Do we know where to start looking for the fourth?" Ami asked.

The only response from Zhara was a gentle snore. Ami hadn't known the other girl had already fallen asleep; their hands were still clasped, as though Zhara were a drowning sailor who had finally found a lifeline to shore. Ami supposed she felt the same.

As she slipped into slumber, Ami dreamed of a bright flowering tree, star-shaped blossoms in a forest-green canopy. The Pillar? Or was it Little Mother, all grown? The scent of rice water and warm skin was everywhere, the perfume of her fairy tree, and beneath the tree was a creature. Try as she might, Ami could not make out the features or the shape, only the vague impression of pale fur and a horn. But more than the fact that she could not make out the form of the creature before her in a dream, she was surprised that the animal was without the clear, bright light of any other living creature, but neither was it the dull, flat gray of stone or earth or rock.

It was waiting, she realized, for someone to come and bring it to life.

21

ZHARA AWOKE TO THE SOUND OF LAUGHTER.

It took her a moment to orient herself—where she was, what had happened—but the thing that puzzled her for the longest time was the chorus of light, bubbling giggles punctuated by deeper guffaws. She lay awake, trying to figure out what sort of birds made such strange calls before she realized it was the sound of children. Children shrieking. Children playing. Children laughing.

She sat up.

Beside her, Li Ami was still asleep, curled up beneath the furs against Sajah's warm flank. By the position of the sun streaming in through the windows of the barn, she figured it must be midmorning. Her stomach rumbled as she crawled down the ladder from the loft, shivering in the crisp autumn morning air. Zhara hoped she hadn't missed breakfast.

The Gyasol lands were more of a homestead than a settlement, she realized as she walked down the main dirt thoroughfare to the village square . . . if the meeting place could be called that. By the light of day, Zhara could see that the members of the Gyasol clan numbered in the hundreds, although their buildings were not differentiated by families but by function. The buildings were clustered around a common open-air area in the middle, where children were laughing and playing a sort of game that involved a ball and two sets of goals in the grassy field in the center. Zhara recognized the enormous broad-shouldered silhouette of Pang Lok playing with the children, letting the little ones get the better of him during the game, comically falling down and feigning injury any time he was "beaten."

Zhara looked up to the heavens. For the first time in days, she saw the white serpentine shape of Temur flying overhead.

Passing the field, she approached a number of seating platforms arranged in a loose semicircle, where several elders of the clan and other adults appeared to be eating, gossiping, sewing, and laying out aromatic flowers in the sun to dry. With a pang, Zhara was suddenly reminded of the parks back home in Zanhei, where the elderly would congregate throughout the day, drinking tea in the gardens, having their ears cleaned, and making matches for their grandchildren playing at their feet. She recognized Tenno Grandmother holding court in the center, surrounded by several lit charcoal braziers, each cooking something different.

"Good morning!" the Gyasol matriarch called. "You are the first of the young ones to wake. Your elders have been up and about for a long while since. Come, come, eat, eat!"

Zhara needed no further urging. Sitting down on the nearest platform, she was handed a plate and some grilled chicken skewers, along with several loaves of flat barley bread and a cup of ginseng chutney, spiced with onions, garlic, yogurt, and a minty herb she did not recognize but devoured all the same. She declined the tsampa and yak butter tea offered, but accepted a cup of water, which was icy and tasted of mountain minerals. She had not eaten so well in weeks.

"Who's up already?" she asked.

"Tama and Captain Okonwe decided to return to the Poha Plain in search of survivors from Kalantze," Tenno replied. "The captain mentioned something about catacombs and refugees." The Gyasol matriarch took a large bite of bread and chutney. "Evidently the lot of you have been through quite a trial," she said with her mouth full.

Presently the two of them were joined by Han and the Beast, who trundled up the mountain path rubbing sleep from their eyes. Zhara made a note to leave some of her meal aside for Ami, in case the other girl woke up too late to join them for breakfast.

"Good morning," Han said sleepily. And it was a good morning, for his dimples were on full display. They had been missing for the past several days. "Is there anything to eat?"

Shortly thereafter, Pang Lok jogged up to the seating platforms, panting and sweating, to steal a grilled chicken skewer off one of the braziers. "Yah!" Tenno Grandmother admonished. "You already ate, you big overgrown lummox. These are for our guests."

Pang Lok grinned, and Zhara thought it was the youngest she had ever seen him look. In this setting, in the lands of the Gyasol, Zhara realized he couldn't be much older than Han, who would reach the age of majority just before midwinter. His scowling demeanor and enormous size had disguised much of his youth, and she was surprised someone so young would have joined the Heralds of Glorious Justice. To her surprise, she realized he was handsome. She averted her gaze and took another quick sip of her water to swallow down the giggles.

"Ah, fresh meat," he said, giving Zhara a flirtatious wink.

"Where?" Han asked, looking around hopefully for more.

"Right before my eyes," Pang Lok said. "One beauty sits before me, while the other slumbers away in her bower, waiting to be awakened with true love's kiss."

The Beast rolled their eyes. "Don't be disgusting, Lok," they said in a mild voice.

"Well, you can't blame a boy for trying," said Pang Lok, "especially when the vast majority of other options around him are his cousins—aiyo!" He flinched as Tenno Grandmother struck him playfully across the shoulder.

"You mind your manners, young man," the Gyasol matriarch said sternly. "And know that no matter your size, you will never be too old or too big for an ear-boxing, lah?" She sat down on the platform next to Zhara. "So, my friends," she said. "Now that you've eaten, tell me: what brings you all to the outermost west? Based on your accents and fancy ways of speech, I take it you're all southerners."

Han caught Zhara's eye with a questioning gaze. She knew he was asking permission to reveal who she was to Tenno Grandmother, that the real reason they were out in the outermost west was to find some way to defeat Tiyok. Although she had revealed herself to others before this, the thought of being perceived—of being *known*—to people just beyond her closest, most intimate circle was still terrifying, but she knew it was something she would have to overcome sooner rather than later, especially if she were to garner allies in her quest to defeat the Mother of Ten Thousand Demons. She gave an infinitesimal nod.

"When the world is out of balance," Han said, "the Guardians of Dawn are reborn."

The Gyasol matriarch gave him a startled look. "What was that, young man?"

"He means," came a quiet voice from over their shoulders, "that demons and demonic energies flourish among us."

Zhara turned to find Ami coming to sit down beside her, her short hair charmingly mussed and her eyes bleary with sleep. The scrivener accepted a plate from Zhara and began tucking in ravenously. She spied a corner of the leather folios containing *Songs of Order and Chaos* peeking out from the back of Ami's sash.

Tenno Grandmother studied them all with sharp eyes. "Well, now that you've rested and eaten, perhaps it's time to explain yourselves."

Immediately, Han, Ami, the Beast, and even Pang Lok turned their heads to look at Zhara. "Me?" she asked in surprise.

"Yes, you." Han took her hand. "You've led us all this far."

A flush stained her cheeks, stark and hot against the morning chill, as she felt the weight of their trust in her. She thought of Junseo then, and wondered if he ever felt inadequate to the task of being the leader of the Bangtan Brothers. Zhara had spent her entire life shrinking herself down, and this sudden space to fully express herself was both terrifying and exhilarating.

"We are," Zhara began, "members of a magical mutual aid society called the Guardians of Dawn."

It took the better part of the morning to tell her—their—story, from the moment the first abominations appeared in Zanhei to the confrontation with one of the greater demons at Mount Zanhei and the revelation that an attempt to summon the Guardians of Dawn had gone terribly wrong. Ami and the Beast chimed in with some of the parts she had not known or witnessed—the blight afflicting the barley yields, the undead attacks that had driven them from Kalantze to the Heralds of Glorious Justice, and the demonic infection that seemed to be affecting both the living and the dead.

"I see," Tenno Grandmother said once their tale was finished. "So what do you and your companions intend to do now?"

What did they intend to do indeed? Zhara glanced at the others—Han, Ami, and the Beast. "We don't intend to trespass long on Tenno Grandmother's hospitality," she said. "We need to find the location of the portal in the west and seal the entrance to Tiyok."

The Gyasol matriarch's expression was unreadable. "And where is that?"

"At the Root of the World," Ami said quietly.

"At the place where the sky was held back," the Beast murmured. They glanced over their heads toward the peaks of the Gunung Mountain range towering in the distance. "Mount Llangposa."

Silence fell over the seating platforms, and even the sounds of the children playing in the distance seemed to fall away.

"The Skyhold." Tenno Grandmother's youthful face suddenly seemed old and haggard, the flesh sagging about her eyes and cheeks. "You do not know what you seek, children."

"The resting place of the Unicorn of the West." Pang Lok shook his head. "Grandmother, you never told me that Mount Llangposa and the Skyhold were the same thing."

The Gyasol matriarch gave her grandson a stern look. "If you didn't know that, then you weren't paying attention to the stories."

"But," Pang Lok said with a frown, "why have we never seen the Unicorn of the West if we live in the shadow of her lands?"

Tenno Grandmother gestured to the land around her. "Do you not see the bounty of the Unicorn here?" she asked. "Our lands are fertile, and thus far we have been untroubled by the rumors of the undead and abominations plaguing the rest of the realm. Think you that this bounty comes without cost?"

Pang Look looked stricken. "What cost?"

Tenno Grandmother looked away. "The cost of living with a demon."

"A demon?" Zhara shifted uneasily in her seat. "What do you mean?"

The Gyasol matriarch sighed. "It's not a pretty story, children. If what you say is true, then our lands may have been protected by the bargain a member of our clan made all those years ago." She looked toward the Gunungs, at the tallest peak shrouded by clouds. "But I fear the rest of the realm may be paying the price."

"Then it is a good thing we are here," Ami said. "For we can close the portal to Tiyok and hopefully set the Morning Realms to rights."

Zhara smiled at the other girl, feeling an odd sense of both pride and relief at knowing that she was not alone in this journey. While Yuli was also a part of this fight, the northern princess had other priorities, other matters to attend to, including finding the other two parts of *Songs of Order and Chaos*. But here, in this moment, in this particular battle against the forces of chaos, Zhara had more than an ally; she had a friend.

"Close the portal?" Tenno Grandmother said in alarm. "No. You can't. Without the demon's protection, we will no longer be safe!"

"And you would rather our family thrive while the rest of the people die?" Pang Lok asked angrily. "Grandmother, how could you?"

She looked away.

Zhara slid closer to the Gyasol matriarch on the seating platform. "Tenno Grandmother," she said softly, "I know you care about your people. I would too, if I were in your shoes. But trust me that leaving the portal open would eventually endanger your clan, even with your bargain with a demon. The portals to Tiyok are open, and through them, the Mother of Ten Thousand Demons comes into the world, destroying the balance between order and chaos." With that, Zhara let her power blossom, letting her Guardian form show.

The old woman looked terrified. "What are you?"

"I am," Zhara said softly, "the Guardian of Fire, and I have been reborn." She glanced sidelong at Ami. "And I'm not the only one."

Han, the Beast, and Pang Lok turned their heads sharply to stare at the scrivener.

"And I," Ami said in an even softer voice, "am the Guardian of Wood."

"What?" Han burst out. "You are?" He eyed the Beast and Pang Lok suspiciously. "And what of you two?" he said. "Are either of you hiding any secret identities as well?"

Pang Lok laughed, but the Beast looked uneasy.

Tenno Grandmother looked to the Gunungs again. Less than a league away was a steep peak—the Skyhold, Pang Lok had called it, or Mount Llangposa. If the legends were correct, then the location of the Root of the World was somewhere within that peak, although how to get there was still a mystery. "Tenno Grandmother," Zhara said. "Has anyone actually *seen* the Root of the World?"

The old woman closed her eyes. In the harsh light of the sun, Zhara could see the fine lines of worry about her mouth that had been disguised by playfulness and laughter when they first came upon the Gyasol lands. "Let me tell you a tale," Tenno Grandmother said hoarsely. "It all began with the great famine of twenty years ago."

Tenno Grandmother's tale was neither pretty nor heartening.

"Here in the Gyasol lands, we have always worshipped at the altar of the Unicorn of the West," she began, nodding her head to the stupa overflowing with flowers at the entrance to their settlement. "She Who Gives Us Life."

Zhara glanced at Ami. *The Guardian of Wood could grant life where there was none.* Were the Guardian of Wood and the Unicorn of the West one and the same?

"The sacred home of the Unicorn of the West was always said to be at the Root of the World, which is planted in the place where the sky was held back." This time Tenno Grandmother gestured to the tall mountain peak in the distance. "Mount Llangposa, although that name had been long forgotten, along with the tongues of old. If one wanted to beseech the Unicorn for aid or healing—for she was said to cure all illness and even bring people back from the dead—then all you would have to do is summit the mountain, find the Vale of Eternity, and pass through three trials to stand before the Unicorn of the West, who would deem you worthy or not by the light of her horn."

Bring people back from the dead. Before their encounters with the revenants, Zhara would have said this was a miracle worth pursuing. She thought of her father, Jin Zhanlong, and thought of how much she had longed to speak with him, especially in the wake of discovering the truth of who she was. Had he known she was the Guardian of Fire? Is that why he had taught her all those years to *be good, and be true*?

"If you were found worthy, if you were pure of heart with pure intentions, then the Unicorn of the West would let you pass to lay your offerings at the Root of the World," Tenno Grandmother went on. "But if you were deemed unworthy, then she would turn you to stone."

"What are the three trials the pilgrim is supposed to endure?" the Beast asked.

"The Gate of Faith, the Gate of Humility, and the Gate of Reckoning," Pang Lok said quietly, surprising everyone present. "See, Grandmother?" he said with a half-smile. "I *do* listen to the stories sometimes."

The Gyasol matriarch shook her head. "All right then, child, go ahead. Prove yourself further. What do these trials entail?"

"The Gate of Faith is where you are to face your worst fears," Pang Lok replied. "The Gate of Humility is where you face your worst guilt. But no one knows what you face at the Gate of Reckoning. No one's survived that far and returned."

"Except for Dzenar," Tenno Grandmother said. "My great-uncle. He was a chieftain of our clan, and a great shaman. Unlike many of us out here on the Zanqi Plateau, he had been educated in magic at the imperial university, studying the Language of Flowers and learning about the lowland ways."

Zhara couldn't help but be fascinated about the workings of magic in other parts of the empire. She knew so little, but in her travels with the Bangtan Brothers and the Guardians of Dawn, magic as an ability was the only constant; the culture around its use varied from people to people and place to place. Yuli spoke of shaman magicians in the north who augured by reading patterns of clouds in the sky, who cast spells not with words or language but with melody and song. In the Azure Isles, the Bangtan Brothers said it was dance. The shamanistic practices of the west seemed to be rooted in the earth, in nature. The Warlord might have burned the books of magic, but he couldn't completely eradicate its practice.

"He even brought back part of a book that he claimed could tell him how to summon a Guardian of Dawn." Tenno Grandmother wrung her hands, staring into the middle distance before her.

Beside Zhara, Ami started. "Was it *Songs of Order and Chaos*? Do you still have it with you?"

The Gyasol matriarch shook her head. "Even if I could read the Language of Flowers and could tell you the title of that magic text, it would still be of little use to you, for we do not have it anymore," she said. "It was lost, along with Dzenar."

"Why did Dzenar want to summon a Guardian of Dawn?" Zhara asked. "Why didn't he just beseech the Unicorn of the West himself?"

"He thought that he would not be found worthy." The Gyasol matriarch hung her head. "And so he thought that summoning the Unicorn's legendary companion warrior instead would give us a greater chance at survival." She laughed, but this time the sound was bitter. "He was right. For as he returned, flowers blossomed in his wake, and the land woke to life again." Tenno Grandmother stared into nothing, reliving that moment her great-uncle returned from the mountain. "Everyone rejoiced. Everyone but me."

"What happened?" Zhara asked softly.

"He was my favorite uncle, you see," the old woman said. "And we had been especially close. And while he could create flowers to grow in his wake, the flowers were strange. Twisted. More like living stone than anything else."

"Coral," Han whispered.

"He came back . . . changed."

Zhara already knew the outcome of that story. She had lived the outcome on the slopes of Mount Zanhei, when she had faced the Frog Demon of Poison and Pestilence in the body of the Chancellor of the city. "He was possessed by a greater demon."

"The Locust Demon of Starvation and Scarcity," Ami said quietly.

"How do you know which one?" Zhara was curious.

Ami hugged *Songs of Order and Chaos* tight to her chest. "Each of the Guardians of Dawn had a counterpart in the Lords of Tiyok," she said at last. "The Frog Demon of Poison and Pestilence is the Guardian of Fire's. The Moth Demon of Discord and Dismay is the Guardian of Wind's. The Ancient One is the Guardian of Water's. And the

Guardian of Wood's nemesis is the Locust Demon of Starvation and Scarcity."

"If I were the Ancient One," Han remarked, "I'd be furious the other three got cool alliterative names while I got stuck with *the Ancient One*."

Zhara was impressed. "You know what *alliteration* means?"

"Yah," Han said. "I do write poetry, you know."

"And it's pretty good," the Beast added to a stunned audience.

"Have you heard his poems?" Zhara asked incredulously.

"I have. Prince Wonhu recited some for us last night."

"Including *Odes to Physical Pleasures*?"

"I admit I haven't heard that one." The Beast laughed. "Sounds racier than I'd be comfortable with. But Master Plum Blossom there showed me some romantic poetry he wrote for you, and honestly, it was really quite good."

At the words *romantic poetry,* both Zhara and Han turned matching shades of deep red.

"I don't know whether to thank you or strangle you, Beast," Han muttered.

"Grandmother," Pang Lok said reproachfully. "How have you never told me this before?"

The Gyasol matriarch shook her head. "It is a secret and the shame that must be carried by the head of the Gyasol clan," she said. "I am breaking years of tradition and promises to tell you this. But," she said, looking to Zhara, "if you truly are a Guardian of Dawn, then I am trusting you to do what is right and right the wrongs of my ancestor."

"What happened to Dzenar in the end?" Zhara asked.

"He disappeared." Tenno Grandmother's voice was scarcely audible. "I think . . . I think whatever sliver of humanity was left knew he was a danger to us. So he left, taking that cursed book of summoning spells with him. I don't know what happened." Her face was grim. "But I can guess. The blight. Although our lands remain untouched, it sounds like the flowers that grew in his footsteps."

The Beast looked hopeful. "Do you think that closing this portal will destroy the blight?"

"I hope so," Tenno Grandmother said. "I hope so."

22

ON THE DAY THEY WERE TO SET out for Mount Llangposa, Gaden noticed the bruise-like growths on their arm were beginning to spread.

Truth be told, that infection had been spreading for a long time, but Gaden had ignored it until now, hoping it would fade away of its own accord. Deep down, they had known that would not happen, but for a long time, the infection seemed to be under control.

Until the return of the undead.

They had first noticed the patch one morning, many months ago, when the first star-shaped blossom appeared on the Pillar in Kalantze. At first Gaden had thought it was an ink stain on their littlest left finger—they had just been in the library, helping Zerdan catalog the inventory—but when the stain did not go away after washing their hands, they wondered if it wasn't some sort of mole, only the discoloration was on the scarred part of their left hand. Over time, the dead flesh from their burn accident all those years ago had healed into a silvery map of webbing and constellations across their ruined skin, an effect that Gaden had ceased to feel self-conscious about and had come to admire about themself over time. Their scars glistened in the light. The spot, on the other hand, did not glisten. It was dark, squat, and ugly.

But the spot persisted.

And grew.

At first it was just discoloration. But the longer it persisted, the more the spot . . . proliferated. It began to take on heft and weight, the dead flesh growing bulky, scaly, stony. Like the blight-afflicted barley stalks growing in the field surrounding Kalantze. Like the roots of the Pillar.

Calcified. Dead but living. What had begun as a spot on their littlest finger had grown to cover their wrist, but the first time they came into contact with Chen and Sang, the infection had grown past their elbow. And it was definitely affecting only the scar tissue down the left side of Gaden's body, not the healthy, living skin beside it. Okonwe had been so panicked when they showed him the infection on their hand that Gaden had been resolved not to worry their adoptive father any further. Instead, they had gone to Zerdan and asked for assistance, and the old librarian had promised to search through the archives for any information regarding a blight that could affect both plants and scar tissue.

But as time passed, the old librarian forgot, and so did Gaden, for a time.

Until the undead struck.

And the infection had begun to . . . *itch*.

It was difficult to describe the nature of the Itch, as Gaden had come to think of it. The nerve endings of their scars were long since dead. Any part of their body that had been burned that night Okonwe stole them from the imperial palace felt nothing—nothing but a light sense of pressure where the scars covered their flesh. No pinching, no twinging, no aching. Once Gaden had accidentally cut themself with a knife while preparing dinner with the cook in Castle Dzong and had not noticed, not until they saw the spots of blood dotting the chopped onions.

But the Itch . . . the Itch lived in the scar tissue.

And it was slowly driving them mad.

Like the spots, the Itch had started small. A tickle in the fingers, something they could temporarily alleviate with a simple scratch. But as time passed, the Itch intensified. From a tickle to a torment, it was a near-constant presence in the back of Gaden's mind as they went about their day. There was no relief from the Itch, only distraction.

And sometimes it felt as though the Itch were turning them into a different person.

It was impossible to describe to anyone lest they think Gaden had lost their wits, but sometimes . . . they noticed thoughts that were not theirs flitting through their mind.

At first, the thoughts had been easy to dismiss. Fleeting, random notions that made them pause with the absurdity or strangeness of the idea. Sometimes the thoughts were merely bizarre, but other times they were violent. Gaden was no stranger to intrusive ideas that sometimes troubled them in the moments before sleep; they never affected their waking actions.

But these thoughts . . . did.

And they were growing louder.

The thoughts began as simple compulsions. *What if* . . .

Ever since Gaden was a child, they had been gifted with what Okonwe had called a *persuasive manner.* In arguments they had always been able to sway people to their point of view; it infuriated Lee-Lee even as it amused her how often they were able to get away with whatever they wanted, simply because they wanted it. But these days, it felt as though their persuasive gift was growing stronger, to the point where they could envision their charisma and charm concentrating in the chambers of their heart before speaking their desires into existence.

It scared them sometimes.

But it scared them even more how much they wanted to use this gift on other people.

The morning they were to set out for Mount Llangposa, Gaden noticed a spot near their chest.

One of the hardest things about travel had been cleaning and replacing the bandages on their chest, but Gaden knew the importance of keeping their bindings clean and dry, so had spent a good deal of time every morning making sure no infection or irritation was setting in on the skin. They had been diligent about this task every morning and every evening and had not found a single thing to concern them.

Until today.

The spot was small, more like a bruise or a burst blood vessel than a mole, so they had not noticed it the past few days. But instead of healing, the bruise was only growing darker. Thicker. Stonier.

Gaden swore.

"Is everything all right—oh." Han entered the shared room the two of them had been sleeping in to find a shirtless Gaden packing several rolls of clean bandages into their pack. "Oh, I'm sorry, I should have let you know I was here, I mean I should have known first—"

"It's all right." It wasn't the first time anyone had seen Gaden bind down their chest on the road, although most of the others had taken care to give them privacy to do so. "I was just . . ." They trailed off at the look of horror on Han's face.

"What's that?" he asked, pointing to Gaden's shoulder blade.

They craned their head and caught the glimpse of another mottled, scaly growth, this time sprouting from the scar tissue on their left shoulder.

"Are you all right? Should I go fetch a healer—"

"No," Gaden said quickly, pulling a shirt over their head and hiding the infection. "It's fine."

Han looked skeptical. "It doesn't look fine. It looks . . . blighted."

Gaden bit their lip. "It's fine," they said again through gritted teeth. "It's just a skin infection."

Han said nothing, and Gaden could feel the boy's judgment like the stinging rays of the sun on their back.

"Beast," they said quietly. "I think you should tell someone. Maybe you should tell my cousin."

"To what end?" they asked. "We don't have a cure."

Han hesitated. "But she does have *Songs of Order and Chaos*," he said. "Maybe she can find something in that text to help, or at least explain what is happening."

Gaden barked a laugh. "Pang Lok could tell you what's happening," they said. "My beastly personality is turning me into an actual beast."

"But you don't have a beastly personality," Han said.

Gaden laughed again, but softer. "I did when I was younger," they admitted. "And I was especially beastly to Lok."

"I still think you should tell Ami or Zhara," Han said. "If the infection is the same as the blight, maybe one or the other can cure it."

They hesitated. "I thought Jin Zhara could only cure abomination."

"Ami, then."

Gaden opened their mouth, then shut it again.

"Oh," Han said, reddening. "Are you . . . do you not want to . . . you know." He gestured to the bandages on Gaden's chest. "Show her?"

"What? Oh, no, it's not that," Gaden said, feeling the flush of heat brush across their cheeks as well. "It's just that . . ." They trailed off.

"You don't want to worry her," Han finished.

Gaden nodded. "Please don't tell anyone. Not yet."

Han looked skeptical. "Well, you know I wouldn't, but—"

"*Don't.*" Gaden put every ounce of will into the word, begging— practically pleading—for Han to keep quiet. They imagined that desire bursting like a ripple of energy from their chest. "*Tell no one.*"

Han's eyes were glazed as he replied. "I won't."

23

IT LOOKED LIKE SNOW.

The skies were dark and heavy as Zhara and company set out for Mount Llangposa from the Gyasol lands. Pang Lok had been elected to lead their expedition, as he was the only one of them familiar with the terrain and summiting at all. "I hope you are all prepared to face some cloud sickness and push through it," he said as they finished packing.

"Cloud sickness?" Han groaned.

Pang Lok nodded. "Aye. People can sometimes come down with nausea and lightheadedness when the air gets thin. When the altitude changes gradually, it's easier to push through, but the ascent up Mount Llangposa will be quite steep, so the change is quick. It's the tallest mountain in the Gunung range."

Han gave Zhara a sidelong glance, then pressed a spot three finger widths below his wrist. "I know how to handle nausea," he said.

She smiled, remembering when she had first taught him the pressure point on their jaunt to the ruins of Old Changxi. "Do you think we'll run into bad weather?" she asked.

"It's early yet for first snow down in the foothills, but it's always winter atop the Skyhold," Pang Lok replied, also eyeing the clouds ahead. "We could delay until the storm passes, although I'll warn you that with every day we delay, the colder it will be up there."

Zhara shivered beneath the furs Tenno Grandmother had gifted her. "It gets colder than this?"

"Oh, pretty one." Pang Lok grinned. "You haven't experienced real cold yet."

Zhara let that flirtatious remark slide for the time being, still trying to work through how she felt about his overtures. She didn't like the big youth, not in that way, although she couldn't deny that she occasionally felt flattered by the attention . . . especially as Han—dear, sweet Han—was nothing but chaste and courteous around her. She told herself that it was due to the situation they were in, that trying to save the world from the Mother of Ten Thousand Demons was hardly conducive to a romantic atmosphere.

Still, it was hard to keep that frame of mind when there were others who clearly did not share the same sentiment.

"Don't worry, dear, I packed you extra furs." Tenno Grandmother had outfitted them with provisions for the journey, including two yak to carry their equipment and food. "Take good care of them," the matriarch said, and although the smile was back on her face, the twinkle seemed to have left her eyes. "Pema and Ashok are their names."

"Which is which?" Han asked. He was enamored by them, petting their woolly heads and rubbing his nose against theirs.

"This is Pema." Tenno Grandmother pointed to the one on the right. "This is Ashok." She pointed to the other.

Pang Lok frowned. "But I thought the female was Pema and the male was Ashok. Pema is a girl's name and Ashok is a boy's name."

"How can you tell the difference?" Han asked. He made to bend over and peer at the pack animals before Zhara lightly punched him in the arm to make him stop.

"Does it matter?" Gaden asked. "Pema can be male and Ashok can be female. They're yak. They don't care. Unlike people," they muttered under their breath.

"What should we do about the weather?" Pang Lok asked.

Zhara was taken aback to find four pairs of eyes fixed on her for the answer. "Me?" she asked. "Why ask me? I'm probably the least equipped person here to make any decisions about mountaineering."

"Yes," said Ami, "but you are sort of our de facto leader in this fight against Tiyok."

Again, that terrifying and exhilarating rush of both pride and fear at being hailed as such overtook Zhara. "I'm flattered," she said, "but I repeat, none of that makes me equipped to make any decisions about our travel!"

"I know," Han said softly. He wrapped his mittened hand about hers. "But you're also the only one with any true sense of urgency about this quest, having experienced it firsthand."

She could not gainsay that. She looked from the skies to Lok. "What do you think?" she asked. "If we were to push through and be caught in a snowstorm, what would be the worst that would happen?"

"We would freeze to death." Pang Lok gave a nonchalant shrug.

"Oh," Zhara said in a choked voice. "Is that all?"

"Aren't you the Guardian of Fire?" the big youth asked with a grin. "I thought you could keep yourself warm. On second thought, perhaps you could keep all of us warm."

This time she set the edge of his jacket on fire.

"Aiyo!" he yelped. "I probably deserved that," he said ruefully.

"He did?" Han asked. "Why?"

Zhara sighed.

"I'll put it this way," said Pang Lok, seeing the aggrieved look on her face. "If we leave now and are caught out in the snow, there are at least seven different caves we can find shelter in near the foothills of the Skyhold. Farther up the mountain, there is no guarantee of shelter, and even if the storm passes, there's no guarantee another isn't on its way. The longer we wait, the worse the weather will get."

That made the decision a lot easier. "All right," said Zhara. "We'll leave today and pray for good weather the entire way."

Pang Lok clapped his hands together excitedly. "Let's go summit the tallest mountain in the world."

"I thought the Ever-Whites were the tallest mountains in the known world," Han said.

"They are the highest mountains in the world," Pang Lok corrected. "But here on the Gyasol lands, we pride ourselves on having the tallest mountain. Its peaks may not reach the same heights, but its roots reach deeper. Besides," he said, giving Zhara a wink. "It's not the height that matters; it's how it was used."

Zhara groaned.

"What?" Han asked in bewilderment. "What's wrong?"

"I can't believe you're with such an innocent," Pang Lok said. "Are you sure you don't want a real man?"

"Enough," Zhara said shortly. "Or I'll set more than your jacket on fire."

"Is that a promise or a threat—aiyo!" At that moment, the top of Pang Lok's fur hat burst into flame, sending the smell of burning hair everywhere.

"Can we stop flirting and get going?" Ami asked. Her face was scarcely visible beneath the hood of her fur jacket.

"All right," said Pang Lok with a hectic gleam in his eyes. "Let's go."

The storm hit halfway through their third day summiting Mount Llangposa.

It began snowing in earnest almost immediately upon them setting out on the trail, which was hard but manageable for the group. Tenno Grandmother had outfitted them all with snowshoes, which kept them atop the accumulating snow, although progress was still slower than they would have liked, as they continually had to break the new snow for the yak to follow. At first Sajah tried to melt the path for them, but Pang Lok asked him to stop, saying that the melted snow would only refreeze almost instantly into ice, which was infinitely more dangerous, especially on such a steep ascent.

Still, they would have managed the snow, if it weren't for the wind.

On the morning of the third day, the wind picked up, and visibility dropped to nearly nothing as the clouds descended and the snow blew sideways.

"Take heart!" Pang Lok called from the head of the procession. "We're not far from the nearest cave."

Zhara could scarcely make out his voice over the howling of the wind whistling through the rocks and crevices. She had only ever seen snow once in her life, back when her father was still alive. Winters in the southern provinces were usually mild and dry, and what precipitation they got every year was typically in the form of a cold, drizzling rain. But one year, instead of the typical freezing showers, Zhara had woken up one morning to snow.

The hush of the world after snowfall had been like nothing she had experienced. She remembered very little of the cold, only the memory of a runny nose and the icy thrill of brushing the snow off the statues in the garden. What she remembered more than anything was the silence, the lack of birdsong, the muffled crunch of footsteps, as though the entire world was holding its breath.

But that was not the snowstorm she was living through now.

She had never known weather could be *angry*. And the storm was furious, howling and shrieking and screaming as though the mountain had been given voice, personally outraged at the trespassers on its slopes. Zhara thought of the various trials and gates they were supposed to journey through on the way to the Root of the World, and could not imagine anything worse than this—freezing cold, unable to see past the tip of her nose, seeming as though they were all alone in the world. She wondered if the Unicorn of the West had preemptively judged them as unworthy.

A flash of lightning lit up the mountain, followed by a thunderous *boom!*

"Keep close!" Pang Lok shouted. "Don't lose sight of the person in front of you!"

Another flash, another boom.

"Hold!" Pang Lok shouted. "I think the path has collapsed up ahead!"

"What are we going to do?" Zhara called back.

"We may need to prepare to shelter in place until the storm passes!"

"Should we turn back?" Han yelled.

"I don't know." Pang Lok sounded uncertain. "I've never seen a storm this bad so early in the season before. Either way, we may need to stay put for the time being. That's likely going to be the safest course of action."

Flash! Boom!

And then . . . a crashing noise.

"What was that?" Ami cried.

There was a strange rumbling sound, something sonic that seemed to grind not in their ears but in their bones. The ground shook as the roaring, rumbling sound grew louder.

"Rockfall!" Pang Lok shouted, but his voice was whipped away by the wind.

And then the world came tumbling down.

24

DOWN WAS UP AND UP WAS DOWN.

When Ami opened her eyes, she wondered if she were dead. There was nothing but pitch-blackness around her, a darkness so complete that it had its own heft and weight. She had no eyes, no body, she was nothing but a ghost. If this was death, then all the religions were wrong, she thought. There was no great cauldron of the universe. There was no wheel of rebirth. There was nothing after death.

Then she became aware of the pain.

She still had a body.

She was still alive.

At first she was conscious of the stinging pain all down the right side of her arm, as though she had scraped it raw over some dirt or gravel. Then she was conscious of the bruising aches and sharp stabs along her ribs as she lifted her left arm, accidentally jabbing her fingers against what felt like solid stone above her head. The stars that burst behind her eyelids were the only source of light around her, and belatedly, she felt about her waist for her brush.

Gone.

Panicking, she reached around to her back, but the folios of *Songs of Order and Chaos* were still there, having protected part of her back from being shredded entirely. She allowed herself to relax and assess her situation. She was trapped somewhere close and dark, with scarcely any room to move. She could not sit up without hitting her head against something, nor could she stretch out her arms and legs beyond a few inches. She could do nothing but lie there, curled into a ball.

The events of the preceding minutes? hours? days? returned to her.

The scaling of Mount Llangposa with Pang Lok and the others, the storm that hit with such ferocity. The last thing she could recall was Pang Lok shouting something that got carried away by the wind before a deep grinding sound shook the ground beneath her feet, the path falling away entirely.

An avalanche.

"Yah!" she called. "Can anyone hear me?" The air was already stuffy around her, and she knew she must be buried under several tons of rock. "Gaden! Zhara! Han!" She knew she shouldn't be wasting her breath, but she couldn't help but cry out to the others in the hopes that they had survived.

There was no answer.

Tears stung her eyes, more painful than the scrapes and bruises she had endured in her fall, but it was the thought of having lost her friends that was the most painful of all. To be alive—for however much longer—and alone was so much worse than being dead. No one would be witness to her passing. No one would carry her memory back to her father. No one would know what had happened to her.

She was lost.

She curled up tighter into a ball and cried.

Presently, when the storm of emotions within her had passed, she rested her head against the rocks, feeling a sense of peace overcome her at the thought of impending death. She did not know what she believed, but she did not believe death was the end. She would either join the soul of her mother in the great cauldron of the universe to be reborn, or she would become nothing. Either way, it meant she would not be trapped beneath a mountain forever.

Ami?

There was a scraping sound above her, and she went very still. "Hullo?"

There was no response, but she could swear she could sense someone passing overhead.

"Hullo?" she called louder.

Ami!

She could hear the voice, but not with her ears. Somewhere deep in her soul, her ki, she thought she could sense someone calling her name. It seemed like her own voice, yet not, aside from it came from within her. Yet she didn't think the person speaking *was* her.

"I'm here!" she shouted, but her words did not travel far, and the air was so thick, so close, it was already getting difficult to breathe. A headache was forming about her temples, and the only thing she wanted to do was lie down and sleep.

No! You must live. Please!

Longing stirred Ami, again that sense that the longing both origi-nated within and without her. Did she want to live? Of course she did. But the longing felt almost compulsory, as though someone were forcing her will to live. She felt compelled by the desire to move, to push, to fight through the tomb of stone that had fallen around her, but part of her resisted at the foreignness of feeling her own will being used against her.

"No," she murmured. The air was close, and she was wasting breath.

Ami, please. Use your gifts. Move the rocks. Anything! Just . . . come back to me.

Come back to me.

Come back to herself.

She could do that.

Closing her eyes, Ami drew in a deep breath. Stars sparkled at the edges of her vision, and she knew she was running out of time. She felt for the place where her Guardian power lived and found it, the way she had found it the night Zhara named her for who she truly was. She sank into that place, and let her magic cocoon her like a parent swaddling their child.

When she opened her eyes again, all was still dark, but this time, she could see the threads of ki that bound the universe together. The stones around her were dull and flat, so she pushed her own gift through them to light them up. Life blazed through the inanimate matter, and slowly, surely, she began to push them away with her power. Of their own ac-cord, the rocks began quivering, tumbling, cracking, breaking, mov-ing aside, and clearing a path for her to emerge. The smallest of holes opened up in the fall and the rush of fresh air was so sharp and clean it felt as though it were piercing her lungs. She drank the air like water, feeling her blood suffuse with life again, and found the strength to push with her actual limbs.

"Ami!"

This time she heard the voice with her own ears, and felt strangely rough and stony hands grab her own to help haul her out of the rubble. She looked up, and a figure of brilliant white, so blinding she could scarcely stand to look at them, stood before her.

"Who——" she croaked, then coughed.

The world was still threaded with ki, but the person before her was more than ki, more than life—they were light itself.

Gaden.

"Ami," they breathed. "You're . . . you're alive."

Then they collapsed in her arms.

25

THE NIGHTMARE ALWAYS BEGAN WITH THE SMELL OF SMOKE and it always ended the same: a tiny Gaden in their mother's arms, feeling the soft press of lips against their forehead. Everything was black or red or white, glowing embers flying everywhere, the grit of ash in their lungs. Of all the details from that night that returned over and over again in their dreams, it was the smoke in their lungs that Gaden remembered the most. The rawness of their throat, shredded from both the smoke and their screaming, the pressure in their chest that made it hard to draw breath. The stars that sparkled at the corners of their vision—nearly pretty, if it hadn't been for the pain.

But this time, the dream was different.

This time Gaden watched as the smoke of time parted to reveal a cavernous chamber. A throne room. Gaden looked around to see an enormous throne upon a dais at one end, made of solid gold and carved with radial patterns that Gaden realized were sunbursts. Behind the throne hung a giant flag with a familiar device—a four-winged dragon on a golden field.

Everything in the room was gold. Gaudy and gold. The columns were gilded, and the ceiling—at least twenty-eight stories tall—was studded with golden stars. It was then Gaden realized that they were standing in the fabled Sunburst Hall of the Mugung Dynasty. They were too young to remember the glory of the imperial city before the Warlord razed it to the ground, yet the details rang with verisimilitude.

This was not a dream; it was a vision.

As the haze continued to clear, they saw that they were not alone in the Sunburst Hall. On the floor sat someone old, grizzled, and wearing the golden dragon robes of the Mugung Emperor, holding an enormous diamond the size of an egg in his hands. He appeared to be surrounded by several characters from the Language of Flowers written in what Gaden hoped was red ink and not blood. All around him were violet-robed imperial magicians holding their brushes before them at the ready, protective glyphs of many different colors hovering in the air between them. A summoning circle, Gaden thought, although they had never seen one before.

"Bring her forth!" gasped the emperor.

At the other end of the hall, the enormous doors swung open, and a pair of guards escorted a young woman wearing the golden headdress of the crown princess. Her belly swelled beneath her robes, and Gaden realized that she must be pregnant.

Mama. The thought rose unbidden in Gaden's mind, even though they did not recognize her.

"Be ready, daughter!" the emperor cried. "Be ready to receive the light!"

Slowly, carefully, the crown princess stepped across the glyphs painted on the floor, taking pains to hold her robes up above her ankles so as not to disturb what was written there. Once safely across, she knelt before the emperor and removed her headdress. The crown princess placed her hands on the diamond in the emperor's hands and Gaden watched in amazement as the crystal filled with light.

"One drop of will from every citizen of the Morning Realms," the emperor intoned. "I pass this on to you, Weiwu. The Star of Radiance, to bind the consent of all the souls who live in these lands under the aegis of Mugung rule."

Wielder of the Star of Radiance, Lee-Lee had said. Gaden had always thought it was another epithet for the one who sat upon the Sunburst Throne, but now they saw that the imperial gem was real, and full of a strange power. They remembered the stories of the Sunburst Warrior using the Star of Radiance to bind away the Mother of Ten Thousand Demons and wondered where this weapon had gone.

To bind the consent of all the souls who live in these lands under the aegis of Mugung rule.

It felt . . . wrong.

The crown princess took the gem and Gaden watched as the light slowly faded once more.

"May you wield this awesome responsibility with wisdom and judgment," the emperor intoned. "And safeguard the honor until the day comes when you will pass it on to your own child."

She nodded and bowed her head.

The emperor smiled. "Good," he said, rising to his feet. "Now, let us celebrate by—"

"Majesty!" one of the imperial magicians cried. "His robes! The spell—"

And then the Sunburst Hall was gone, swept away by another cloud of smoke, and Gaden found themself back in their old dream, back in the clothes cabinet where they had waited, sweat pouring down their face as they waited for their mother to find them.

And then the roof collapsed in all around them.

This was usually where the dream ended—the fall of the palace, the blaze of pain, almost icy in its severity rather than searing.

But for the first time, the mists parted with a beam of light and Gaden was conscious of an embrace. They were enveloped in someone's arms, someone who smelled of soot and smoke and the iron tang of blood.

The soft press of lips against their forehead.

You hold the star now, my child.

26

WHEN ZHARA OPENED HER EYES, IT WAS to unfamiliar skies.

The heavens above were dotted with constellations she did not know and the sky was moonless. That couldn't be right, she thought. They had only just passed the midpoint of the chrysanthemum month when they had left the Gyasol lands. While Zhara was no astrologer's daughter like Li Ami, she knew her calendar, and by her reckoning, the moon would have been only a few days past full when the storm had hit.

The storm.

She swiftly sat up and immediately regretted her decision. The events of the past several hours—days?—returned to her. She and the others were summiting Mount Llangposa when lightning struck the mountain, sending an avalanche of rocks tumbling down. She remembered nothing after that. Glancing around, Zhara could tell she had fallen into some sort of underground cavern. The air smelled mineral, almost damp, and if she listened carefully, she could hear the very distant roar of rushing water. Craning her neck, she looked up and realized that what she had taken for stars in the firmament had been glowing gemstones studded into the ceiling. Beneath her hands, Zhara noticed that the earth was pillowy and soft, and when she shifted it through her fingers, she saw it was sand. The grains seemed to glitter in the half-light of the cavern as though made of starlight themselves.

Getting to her feet, she assessed her condition. Aside from a few bruises, she didn't seem to be seriously injured. Her enchanted blade had also survived the fall with her, and it seemed a miracle that she didn't cut or stab herself during the storm. She made a note to make a scabbard for herself somehow, and to permanently bequeath ownership of the sword to Han when she found him. Wherever he and the others might be. Surely if she was alive, the others must be as well.

"Han!" she shouted. "Ami! Beast!"

A rustle somewhere to her left. Under the light of the false stars, it was actually quite bright, but the shadows they cast were vague, shapeless, and indistinct.

"Han!" she called again. "Ami! Beast!"

Another rustle, and then a groan. Zhara moved toward the sound, arms outstretched, feet shuffling carefully through the sand lest she accidentally run into something. There were large columns of stone all around her like pillars in a temple, formed of some sort of crystal that gleamed in the false starlight. Zhara had the sense she was walking through the abandoned places of worship of a civilization long since vanished, or the forgotten palace halls of a fairy queen. There were symbols carved on them, what looked to Zhara like ancient forms of the Language of Flowers. Although Zhara had been making steady progress through *The Thousand-Character Classic* on her own, her vocabulary of the magician's script was still limited to simple phrases and concepts like *light, dark,* and . . . *gate.* To her surprise, she recognized the glyph for *door* or *gate* carved onto the pillars beside a much more complex one she did not know.

"Han?" she tried again. The rustling had stopped, but she was sure she could sense someone else's presence. Like knowing someone was awake, even though their eyes were still closed. Zhara continued shuffling in the direction where the sound had come from, although she was now beginning to think whoever it was had moved to her right. "Ami?"

"Argh!" A shout and something bowled into Zhara's side, sending her crashing to the ground. "Oh, it's you."

At Han's voice, she relaxed. She was suddenly aware of the closeness of his face to hers; every feature was clear, as though etched in diamond. His breath was warm against her lips, and Zhara leaned forward to catch him in a kiss.

"Oh!" Han said, scrambling backward. "I, er, haha, I wasn't expecting that here of all places."

Zhara pulled back, trying to disguise the hurt and humiliation. "Yeah," she said, laughing awkwardly. "Not the right time, I know. Let's see if we can find the others and Sajah."

Opening her hand, she let a ball of flame blossom in her palm. In the increased light, more details of the cavern became clear. They *were* in a temple; she could see the prayers carved into the columns of glowing crystal like the prayer wheels she had spied in both Castle Dzong and during her travels across the outermost west. Strung across the tops of these ancient prayer wheels were half-rotted ropes with tattered bits of silk that still clung to the memory of color—red, yellow, blue, green, and white. Prayer flags.

"Ami!" Zhara called. "Beast?"

"Cousin!" She could hear Han's voice ringing several yards away. "Beast!"

But there was no reply.

After several long moments of searching, there didn't seem to be any way out or any sign of anyone but the two of them within the cavern. "I don't think they're here," Zhara said, sitting down on a nearby crystal.

"I think you're right." Han sighed, sitting down on the ground a discreet distance away. Her heart clenched, and although she could reach out and easily touch his hand, she felt the distance between them had somehow grown infinite.

"Come," she said, patting the crystal beside her. "Sit beside me and we can check each other for injuries."

"Oh." Han stirred and rubbed the back of his neck. "I'm fine. Some bruises, but nothing major."

The distance between them seemed to grow even wider.

"Ah." Zhara's voice was quiet, small, and scarcely audible in the enormous, echoing space. "Do you . . . do you not like me anymore?"

Han met her gaze with startled eyes before his glance slid sheepishly to the side. "Is this the proper time to be having this conversation?" he asked weakly.

Zhara laughed, gesturing to the cavern around them. "Do we have anything else to be doing right now?"

With a sigh, Han sat down at her feet, knees tucked up against his chest. "I thought this might come up," he said softly. "I just . . . I just thought it would happen at a more opportune time."

Fear and dread entwined their icy fingers through Zhara's heart. She knew it. She knew what was to come.

Tell me stories, nene. As long as all the love stories are yours.

It appeared as though her love story had come to an end.

"I see," she said, and she tried to keep her voice from breaking, the way her heart was breaking. "Well, I will respect whatever it is you choose."

Han was confused. "Eh? What do you mean?"

Zhara blinked. "What do *you* mean?"

"Hold a moment." Han's large eyes were even larger and rounder with surprise. "Did you think I wanted to . . . that I wanted to end this between us?"

"Did you not?"

"Of course not!" he said, and it was the indignation more than the words themselves that soothed Zhara's troubled heart. "I like you, Jin Zhara. I like you a lot."

It wasn't exactly the most romantic declaration of feelings she had ever heard; it wasn't even the most romantic declaration of feelings she had ever heard from Han himself. But it was honest and true, and that mattered more to her than anything else in the world.

"I like you," he continued, flushing a deep, dark plum color. Zhara smiled, her heart twinging a little to remember the flustered, blushing boy she had met in Zanhei's covered market all those months ago. It felt like another lifetime. "But frankly . . . I'm scared of what comes next."

"What comes next?" It was a moment before she understood what he was implying by how he was avoiding her gaze. "Oh."

She had always known Han was innocent, and despite his love of the romance serials of Jae Hyun, he hadn't gotten to the point in the story where the hero and heroine made love. She wasn't sure how to proceed. Ordinarily, she would tease him about being afraid of girls, but she suspected that it had taken a large amount of bravery for Han to confess this to her, and she wanted to honor his courage.

"You see," he went on, "for all that I seem like I'm terrified of women"—Zhara laughed quietly to herself—"I'm not. Or at least, not in the way you and Xu would tease me about."

"Then in what way?"

Han rested his chin on his tucked knees. "I'm not as innocent as I seem," he said at last. "It's not that I haven't been exposed to the physical intimacies that exist between people, or that I haven't read about it in books"—his ears reddened even further—"it's just that . . . it never really occurs to me. Attraction, I mean. Not like that."

Zhara frowned. "I'm not sure I follow."

Han rocked back and forth a little with nervousness. "You know how in *The Maiden Who Was Loved by Death,* the first meeting between Little Flame and the Dark was . . . well, *charged* with tension?"

Zhara nodded.

"I don't feel that tension. Not really. I mean, occasionally, yes, sometimes," he said shyly. "But generally? Not at all. In fact, I never really felt that way about anyone. Not until I met you."

Zhara tried to wrap her mind around what Han was trying to tell her. "So . . . you're saying you don't feel physically attracted to people?"

"I suppose so, yeah." He continued rocking back and forth. "I mean, I notice when people are good-looking. But the way Little Flame feels about the Dark Lord . . . I've never experienced that. Not upon first meeting, anyway."

"I see." Although Zhara did not quite understand the experience, she was trying her best to understand Han's heart, which was still pure and sweet and good.

"So . . . yeah. That's what I wanted to tell you." He placed his hand over hers, and once again, the sensation of touch soothed something deep within her soul. "It's not that I don't like you anymore, Jin Zhara," he said, and his eyes sought hers, warm and reassuring. "In fact, I like you more and more every day. But if I don't prove it to you in the ways you need me to, then . . . then I understand if *you* want to be the one to end things."

"Oh, Han." She slid from her perch on the rock and sat down on the ground next to him. "Thank you for telling me," she said. "Of course I don't want to end things with you."

"Oh good," he said, and it was the relief in his smile that thawed the dread around her heart. "Because I don't want to end things either."

"So where do we go from here?" she asked. "Do you not . . . do you not want to explore what comes after?"

"I don't know," Han said, squeezing her hand. "I think I do. Especially with you. But . . . is it all right if we take things slow? If we . . . if we stop if I'm too uncomfortable?"

"Of course," she said. "Of course."

His dimples deepened, and she felt all the tender places of her heart deepen in response. He lifted his hand from hers to rest against her cheek. As much as she wanted to push and press and melt against him, Zhara let Han take the lead, to set the pace of how he wanted the next encounter to go. Slowly, hesitantly, his lips brushed hers for the first time in an age.

Desire swept through her like a wildfire, but she kept still, kept it in check. Gently, she pressed back, parting his lips with hers, asking permission and taking it slow. The sliding of his hand from her cheek to cup the back of her head was a *yes*. The way he pushed against her was another *yes*. The way he softly gasped when she twined her fingers through his hair was another *yes*.

"So sorry to interrupt this tender moment," came a familiar northern-accented voice from the corner. Zhara and Han sprang apart to find the spirit of Yuli sitting on a rock beside them, a grin stretched from ear to ear. Beside her was Sajah, in ginger cat form, glaring at them disapprovingly with glowing golden eyes. "But I believe I have found you a way out."

"You always did have impeccable timing, Gommun Yulana." Zhara sighed.

"I do, don't I?" Yuli grinned. "Now as happy as I am that the two of you have made a breakthrough in your relationship, I did not consent to be part of the audience, so unfortunately I had to put a stop to it."

"Why?" Han groused. "You can spirit-walk. You could have just gone and come back and given us a moment of privacy."

"And where would the fun be in that?" Yuli shook her head and counted on her fingers. "There are only three great joys in life: a good meal, a good sleep, and giving the two of you a hard time." Then her face grew serious. "You have no idea how worried I was," she said. "Temur lost sight of you the instant the storm hit. I had no way of knowing if you had survived or not. I've been searching for the past three days, and my entourage is starting to get suspicious of the number of hours per day I'm spending napping. Temur and I had been searching the mountainside as best we could to get to you and guide you through it, but it wasn't until this one here"—she nodded at Sajah, who was primly washing his whiskers—"came and found us that we discovered you."

The cat turned his golden eyes on Zhara expectantly. She inclined her head. "May your good deeds return to you thousandfold."

Sajah sniffed and went back to his ablutions.

"Where *are* we?" Han picked up a rock the size of his head. It was studded with glittering flecks of crystal, and as it moved, it caught the light, flashing like embers in the cavern. Curious, Zhara drew near. It seemed to her that the stone gave off a faint illumination. "Wah! It glows!" Han yelped.

Zhara thought of all the legends of the Star of Radiance, of how the Immortals gifted the Sunburst Warrior with this gem with which to beat back the darkness. As she looked at these impossible crystals, it wasn't difficult to see the origin of such tales.

Yuli made a face. "As best I can tell, you are in the heart of the mountain. This peak is riddled with caves, and some of them connect, but others run straight into dead ends. You're lucky you fell into one of the connected systems; the others weren't so lucky."

"The others?" Zhara straightened. "Ami? Beast? Pang Lok?"

"I'm assuming the beast is the big brute with the yak," the princess said.

"No, the scarred one."

Yuli frowned. "I haven't found anyone else. This big fellow with the yak is perfectly safe at the moment; in fact, he's probably the best situated out of all of you to survive since he has both the animals and the gear. All he has to do is wait out the storm."

"Pema and Ashok are all right then," Han said in relief.

"The yak," Zhara supplied at Yuli's questioning expression. "But what of the Beast and Ami? If you've found us, surely we could find them. They can't be far."

Yuli looked thoughtful. "Well, there is a cave not too far from you, but I can't seem to get there."

"What do you mean you can't seem to get there?" Zhara asked.

"There's a sort of . . . force around it," Yuli said. "I can't explain it, but it feels almost like a shield. Utterly impenetrable, even by a ghost. Whoever is behind that force does not want to be disturbed."

"A shield? Made of what?"

The northern princess made a face. "Honestly? It feels like . . . it feels like ki, but its total and complete opposite."

All the hairs stood up on the back of Zhara's neck. "Anti-ki?"

Yuli was amused. "If you want to call it that."

Zhara bit her lip. "Then the shield must be made of pure demonic energy." She looked to Han.

"The Vale of Eternity?" he asked.

"Perhaps."

"What's the Vale of Eternity?" Yuli looked from one to the other.

"It's where the Root of the World is supposed to be," Zhara said. "And we believe it is where one of the portals to Tiyok was opened."

Yuli went still. "You believe one of the greater demons is there."

"Maybe." Zhara met Yuli's eyes. "Is the cave connected?"

"Yes."

"Well then," said Zhara. "Let's go see what—or who—does not want to be disturbed."

27

G ADEN."

    Someone was calling their name, but it was not the name with which they had been born.

"Gaden, please, wake up."

They recognized the voice, a little flat, a little affectless, but not without emotion. The voice of someone others had called *strange* and *eccentric* and sometimes even *uncanny*. They struggled to swim through the depths of unconsciousness, to surface again in the real world, but the darkness was wrapped so thoroughly around them they thought they would drown. It felt like the Itch, embedded not in their mind or their flesh but somewhere deep in their very soul.

"Gaden. *Beast!*"

With tremendous effort, they opened their eyes.

And found themself nearly about to step off the edge of a precipice. With a shout, they threw themself back, catching someone on the chin with the back of their head.

"Oof!" came a grunt. "Are you all right?"

Gaden turned around to find themself looking straight into the beautiful doe eyes of Li Ami, her face so close to theirs their noses nearly touched. "Ami?" They blinked, and for one heart-stopping moment, Gaden thought she might close the distance between them completely and press her lips to theirs.

And then they realized she was missing her spectacles and she was merely studying their face for any sign of injury. There was something endearing about her shortsightedness, something which made Gaden's heart go tender with affection. They wanted nothing more than to smooth the furrow of concentration from between her brows, to take her hand and describe the world to her. They wanted to be the lens through which she viewed the world. Without the barrier of glass between her gaze and everything else, Gaden found themself unexpectedly lost for words as the effect of her doe eyes struck them full force. They hadn't realized before just how much her spectacles had minimized the large, lambent elegance of her dark eyes, how they had obscured the intensity of her gaze. And a good thing too, Gaden thought, for not many could withstand the force of that gaze . . . not without falling in love.

They could have said something. They could have greeted her with a light joke or a smile. But there was nothing Gaden wanted to do more than to close the scant distance between them in a kiss. The feeling was so overwhelming it terrified Gaden, so they did nothing, paralyzed by both fear and want, staring up into Li Ami's eyes as she stared back.

They stayed there for several long moments, their breaths drawing in and out in time with each other.

"What . . . what happened?" Gaden asked.

"You don't remember?"

Gaden tried to dredge up the images of the past several hours, but the only memories they could recall were scenes from their usual nightmare—a woman crying, and flames. Flames all around. *You hold the star now, my child.* "I don't, I'm afraid."

Ami was silent for a long while. "I think . . . I think you saved my life. You pulled me out of the wreckage and I saw you with my Guardian eyes and you were . . . so bright. So . . . beautiful." She ducked her head, and Gaden wondered if she wasn't blushing. Warmth flushed their own cheeks in response. "And then you collapsed. You were dreaming and sleepwalking. I kept calling and calling your name, but you wouldn't wake or respond. It wasn't until I called you *Beast* that you woke up."

"I suppose it's because I've been called *Beast* far longer than I have been called *Gaden,*" they said softly.

Ami frowned. "Is Gaden not your name?"

"It is, but . . ." They trailed off, looking up at the ceiling studded with false stars. "It was a secret name for a long time. A name I had chosen for myself long before I ever shared it with anyone. I'm careful with sharing that part of myself, you see."

Ami said nothing, but her shortsighted eyes fluttered over Gaden's face, taking in each of their features as she gently ran her fingers over the scars running down the left side of their face. "Then I am honored to have been entrusted with that part of you."

Their faces were so close. So very close. One more breath and their lips could be met.

Gaden cleared their throat and withdrew. "So," they said awkwardly. "Where are we, anyway?"

They couldn't tell, but they thought Ami looked disappointed as she sat back on her heels. "As best I can figure," she said. "We are in some sort of cave with natural phosphorescence." She pointed to the false stars above them. "I think those must be glowworms. I would cast a spell for light, but I lost my brush in the rockfall."

"Do you need a brush to cast spells?" Gaden asked curiously.

Ami was surprised. "I've never tried. I suppose not." Tentatively, with the tip of her finger, she traced out the character for *illumination*. A faint green-gold trail of light shimmered in the air before fading into nothing. "Oh," she said. "Let me try again, it's just hard getting used to—"

There was a sudden blaze of brightness as every single false star in the cavern ceiling flashed.

Both Gaden and Ami gave shouts of pain and threw their arms over their eyes. As the luminance in the cavern evened to a soft glow, Gaden was better able to take in their surroundings. What they had initially taken to be the edge of a precipice had actually been the side of a massive stone bridge, at least twenty horses abreast, with no sides or railings, suspended by no supports that they could see. Below them, they could hear the muted roar of rushing water. To the right, near the entrance to the bridge, was a tumble of boulders and rocks, where they and Ami had fallen down during the snowstorm, and where Ami had become buried under rubble. Their heart constricted as they recalled the absolute terror of thinking they had lost her forever, that she had been crushed or would die slowly suffocating, cold and alone. On the other side, the bridge appeared to be connected to a set of ancient carved stairs, flanked by enormous carved animal-headed guardian chimeras holding stone tablets engraved with what looked like ancient forms of the Language of Flowers. They couldn't read one of the characters, but they recognized the other as a crude version of the glyph for *door* or *gate*.

"Well, we know they're not glowworms," Ami said, gazing up at the cavern ceiling with squinted eyes. "But I can't see what they are."

Gaden tilted their head back. "They're . . . crystals," they said in awe. "Glowing crystals. How . . . how is that possible?"

Ami rubbed between her brows. "There are stones that give off a light when subjected to heat or friction," she said. "Perhaps these are similar."

They shook their head. "But I thought these sorts of gems were just stories. Fairy tales."

"Like the Star of Radiance?"

A sudden dash of cold dread froze Gaden's veins. "Like the old imperial jewel of the Mugung Dynasty?" they asked in a careful tone. Bits of their dream returned to them, and the image of a gemstone filling with light hovered at the back of their mind. "Or the weapon said to be wielded by the Sunburst Warrior to seal the Mother of Ten Thousand Demons back in her realm?"

"Weren't they supposed to be one and the same?" she asked. "Because the Mugungs were said to be descended from the Sunburst Warrior, so the Star of Radiance was supposed to have been passed down from heir to heir."

Gaden frowned. "But if the imperial jewel was never found in the ruins of the palace after the Warlord razed it to the ground, does that mean we've also lost the legendary weapon wielded by the Sunburst Warrior?"

Ami rubbed between her brows, inadvertently pushing up the glasses that were no longer there. "I don't know," she said uncertainly. "The Star of Radiance wasn't always a jewel, not even in the stories about the Sunburst Warrior."

"It wasn't?" Gaden was startled.

"No. Sometimes the Star is a sword, sometimes it's contained in a box, or in a key, or even a lock." Ami reached behind her and pulled the battered but still intact folios from her sash. "It says in *Songs of Order and Chaos* that the people of the Morning Realms donated a single drop of will from each of them to the Sunburst Warrior to form the Star of Radiance. Whatever that is was never specifically defined."

One drop of will from every citizen of the Morning Realms to bind the consent of all the souls who live in these lands under the aegis of Mugung rule.

Suddenly the nature of the Star of Radiance was starting to become clear. Dread dug its icy fingers in Gaden's gut.

"What does that mean?" they asked. "One drop of will?"

Ami frowned. "I don't know. We're still missing two fragments of *Songs of Order and Chaos,* so we still don't have all the information. But as far as I can guess, I think it means the Star of Radiance is concentrated willpower. That whoever wields the Star can affect the will of others."

They thought of Han's glazed look as they impressed upon him their desire to keep their growing skin blight a secret, and guilt began slowly seeping down their spine. "Compulsion," Gaden whispered.

Ami was quiet. "That must be how the Mugungs controlled their imperial magicians," she said softly. "How they controlled my father. With the Star of Radiance."

"Your father?" Dread twisted its fingers even deeper into their heart. "Is that why he . . . ah . . ."

She nodded. "The night he broke that compulsion is the night he broke his mind."

Gaden said nothing. The guilt intensified, and they thought they might be sick.

You are the Wielder of the Star of Radiance.

They closed their eyes. All this time, they thought that if they could just change everything about themself, their name, their appearance, they could alter the destiny that fate seemed to have laid upon them. But there was no escaping fate. No escaping the life that they had apparently been born to, to be the person they loathed more than anything in the world.

"Gaden." Ami gently lifted her hand to wipe the tears from their cheeks, fingers lingering on the scarred side. "Are you all right?"

Slowly, without breaking her gaze, they lifted their own hand to rest atop hers.

For a long time, the two of them sat there without speaking, hands resting atop each other on Gaden's face.

"Ami," they breathed. "I—"

Desire blossomed within their chest, and that feeling of longing, of desire, of *will* that had forced Han to keep their secret overwhelmed them. *No,* they thought. They would not. They could not.

But Ami leaned forward and pressed her lips to theirs anyway.

For half a breath, Gaden let themself melt into her kiss, to savor it, to take it for what it was: a gift.

They pulled back. "I'm sorry," they whispered, their voice hoarse, scratchy.

"For what?"

Gaden lifted their hand to cup her cheek, either to push her away or bring her closer, they didn't know. "For—"

But Ami suddenly recoiled from their touch, her fingers coming up to brush the back of their bare hand. It was only then that Gaden realized their glove was gone—torn and shredded in the moments after the rockfall in a desperate bid to dig Ami out from beneath the rubble.

They pulled away, but Ami reached up with both hands to grab theirs.

"Gaden," she said. "Has it . . . has it gotten worse?"

They pressed their lips together and said nothing.

"It has, hasn't it?"

Gaden wanted nothing more than to pry their fingers from her grasp, to tuck their blighted hand behind their back so she wouldn't have to look upon the hideousness of the scaly growths. But her grip was firm, and instead of rejecting them in disgust, her touch was light along their scars.

"Let me," she said. "May I . . . may I try something?"

Gaden nodded. She held their hand between her palms and closed her eyes. A soft green-gold glow enveloped where their hands met and slowly, Gaden's breath caught as the entirety of her Guardian form was slowly revealed to them. They had seen Zhara in her full glory as the Guardian of Fire multiple times—a girl of living flame—but Ami's power was more subtle, less ostentatious . . . and more arresting. Shining through Ami's skin was a pure light, almost as though revealing the girl she was on the outside was merely an illusion and whatever form lay beyond was the truth. Her image shimmered, became translucent, and the figure beneath became visible, but the facade of the ordinary girl was still present. Beneath the gauzy image of the ordinary girl was a being whose skin was the palest chartreuse, a color exactly between the sweetest spring green and the sunniest pale gold. Her hair was a rich auburn, the color of freshly tilled earth, and Gaden could have sworn the tresses were entwined with blossoms—the pink and purple and white petals of the cosmos flower. If Gaden looked one way, Ami looked as she always had, but if they blinked another way, she was wholly the Guardian of Wood.

She opened her eyes and met theirs. Her irises were no longer brown but a stunning emerald green. But it wasn't the change in color that startled Gaden the most; it was how those eyes no longer saw them, she saw *through* them. Ami's human eyes were shortsighted.

"You have," she murmured, "such a light inside."

Kiss me again, and the thought crossed their mind before they could stop it, before they could snatch it back.

Immediately, the Guardian of Wood disappeared, leaving only Ami in her place. Her brown eyes were glassy and glazed.

"Ami—"

Suddenly, their lips met once more.

They were suddenly overcome with a sense of wrongness. This was not Ami kissing them. This was their own desire making Ami kiss them.

They pulled back so suddenly that the two of them tumbled over onto the ground. When Ami sat up, her gaze was clear. "What . . . did . . . did something happen?"

Whoever wields the Star can affect the will of others.

"Are you all right?" Gaden asked, avoiding her question. "You seemed . . . so far away."

She blinked rapidly, her sharp mind struggling to return to the moment, to pick up the thread of conversation she had dropped in the moment of their second kiss. "I . . . what . . ." She shook her head. "I'm sorry, I seem to have lost my thought."

They laid their left hand on her cheek. "I'm sorry."

She flinched at the brush of their scars against her skin. "Your scars," she gasped.

They snatched back their hand. "I'm sorry," they said again.

"No." She grasped their fingers in hers. "It's not that. It's that the flesh is dead around your scars."

Gaden nodded. "I know."

Ami shook her head. "Yes, but that's not what I mean. The dead flesh . . . it has the same emptiness that's within the undead."

28

To Zhara's surprise, the first thing she noticed as she followed Yuli's ghost out of the cavern was a faint but distinct perfume. The slightest whiff of a scent not quite floral, but something that reminded her of both warm breath and skin. Of steamed rice. In a cave deep in the heart of the mountain, there was nothing living that she could see that might be the source of such a fragrance, but there was something distinctly uncanny about Mount Llangposa that had nothing to do with the ordered magic of the mansions of Reason. The magic in the Skyhold was *wild*. Chaotic, even, but utterly unlike the chaos void of the demonic magic. Demonic magic felt like an absence or an emptiness, a hole within the fabric of reality. This . . . wild magic felt like *presence*. Like it proved the existence of a world beyond the one she knew.

Like the stones.

Every time she ran her fingers over the crystals embedded in the walls of the passageways, they glowed with light, visible even to the non-magical eye. To Han's disappointment, the stones went dim at his touch, but whenever Yuli or Zhara passed, they lit up immediately, as though responding to the presence of magic. She thought of the stories Mihoon had told her of ancient magicians summoning spirits to bind to vessels, but these stones did not contain any sort of supernatural ki. They simply *were* magic, as though the essence of their ki had been formed this way, the way the ki of magicians simply *were*. Zhara couldn't help but wonder at the origin of magic as she pocketed one of the fallen crystals, wondering if, since she as the Guardian of Fire could transform the nature of demonic ki into human ki, she could maybe transform the nature of mundane ki into something magical.

"Hurry up," the northern princess said, leading Han, Zhara, and Sajah, who was in mouse form, tagging along in Zhara's sleeve, through narrow intersecting passageways that seemed to wind endlessly atop one another like a labyrinth. "I don't know how much longer I can stay here with you without being called back to my body."

"Does that happen often?" Han asked with interest. "You being called back to your body. Is it involuntary?"

"Sometimes," Yuli admitted. "There is a . . . tether, if you will, that connects me to my body. It is infinitely long and can pass through anything, but it's still there, like a ribbon tied to my littlest finger. When I was younger, the slightest tug on that thread used to send me rushing back to myself, but as I practice spirit-walking, it gets easier to ignore the physical sensations requiring me to be present in my body."

"That doesn't sound very healthy," Han remarked. "Not being present in your body, that is. One of the things my fencing teacher used to always try to get me to do was be fully present when we sparred or exercised; it prevents accidental injury. What if someone harms your body while you're out spirit-walking?"

"There is always that possibility," Yuli said. "Which is why I usually have my auncle Mongke keep watch. They pretend that I have some sort of sleeping sickness to keep curious noses out of our business."

"Do you ever wonder," Han mused, "what would happen if you cut that tether to your body?"

Yuli was silent. "I don't know," she said. "Maybe I would become like some of the Sleepers who live on the Frozen Wastes."

"The Sleepers?"

Yuli squirmed, a gesture that was rather amusing for someone who did not feel physical discomfort in spirit form. "A story," she said. "Tales of bogeymen my mother used to tell me when I was a child. They were a group of thirteen magicians who had gone to see if they could harness the power of the Shimmer."

"The Shimmer?" Zhara asked. "What's that?" The passageways were getting increasingly narrow to the point where even she was starting to struggle to squeeze through the tight ingresses and egresses. Yuli could literally walk through walls in her spirit form, and she wondered if the Guardian of Wind sometimes forgot people had physical forms altogether. She picked up another one of the fallen crystals on the floor and it blazed like a torch in her hand, which she used as a source of illumination for her and Han.

"Up by the Frozen Wastes, there are ribbons of multicolored light that streak across the sky," Yuli said. "We call them the Shimmer. My people used to make pilgrimages onto the tundra to see them every year during the Endless Night as a way to celebrate the coming of spring again. But Obaji banned the practice since before the Just War, and the story goes that it was because of the Sleepers."

"Yah," Han called out. "Hold a moment, I think I'm stuck." He had managed to get one arm and one leg through the last pinch point, but the rest of him seemed caught.

"I keep telling you to enter sideways." Zhara sighed. "Your shoulders are too broad to make it straight on."

"I keep forgetting," Han said mournfully. "Can you . . . ?"

With another sigh, Zhara placed her hand on one of the rocks pinning Han in place and turned it into sand, setting him free. It was getting easier and easier now to manipulate the threads of ki, even without calling upon her Guardian form.

"Be careful with that," Yuli warned. "One of those rocks might be a support beam, and if you take that away, you might cause another rockfall, and this time I won't be able to rescue you hapless idiots."

"Surely there must be an easier way to get to this cave?" Zhara asked. "You may not feel how close and tight it is, but I worry we'll get to a point where we can't go any farther."

"It opens up ahead," Yuli said. "The center of the mountain is almost completely hollow, and filled with stairs and archways and bridges. We'll come upon a large cavern with an enormous bridge and stairs that lead through a doorway. Beyond that is the cave I can't enter."

"How much farther?" Han asked.

"A few more minutes."

"You keep saying that every time I ask," he muttered. "And you wonder why I have such trust issues with you."

But the northern princess's assessment was more accurate this time, for within moments, the tiny passageways gave way to broad boulevards and, finally, the cavern at the center of the mountain, its ceiling studded with hundreds of thousands of tiny crystals that glowed like twilight.

"Do you hear that?" Han asked. "It sounds like there's a river flowing somewhere."

Zhara could hear low whispering murmurs, water rushing somewhere, but to her, it sounded like the quiet conversation of two lovers somehow. A few times, she thought she could catch a word or two, but she dismissed those as the imaginings of her overactive mind, especially as the whiff of the curious perfume she had caught earlier was even stronger now. Now it seemed layered with a different fragrance—one that was both familiar and elusive all at once. She thought there was a stronger fruity-floral note now, almost sharp, but mellowing to a rounder, sweeter flavor almost instantly. Something about the scent made her heart race and her blood run cold, but she couldn't figure out why.

"It smells beautiful," Han said wonderingly.

"Does it?" Yuli asked, sounding envious. "I can't smell anything in my spirit form. Or taste anything. Or touch anything." She sighed. "As useful and awe-inspiring as my power can be, it sure does have its downsides."

"It smells like . . ." Han closed his eyes. "It smells like sweet grasses, fragrant waters, and cinnamon trees. Golden afternoons drifting by in a haze, dust motes like lanterns floating on the air."

"Why, Prince Rice Cake," Yuli said in astonishment. "Was that a poem?"

"Was it?" Han asked, then scowled. "Why is it always the things I say when I *don't* try that seem like poems but not any of the ones where I *do*?"

Zhara smelled none of those things, but she was beginning to identify the different notes in the fragrance. Charcoal, ash, and . . . osmanthus.

With a start, she realized that it smelled like the kitchen she'd lived in with Suzhan and the Second Wife back in Zanhei.

Like home.

"Shush." Yuli raised a hand for a halt. "Do you hear that?"

Both Han and Zhara paused, straining their ears. The whispered murmurs of what she had thought was a conversation between two lovers was even stronger now, and she seemed to be able to understand a word here and there.

The undead—

Emptiness—

Demons.

"Ghosts?" Han asked, looking a bit pale.

Zhara shivered. She thought of the caves beneath Mount Zanhei, the dead bodies gathered in tombs, the ki of magicians used to power the portal open, and wondered if they would come across a graveyard of the missing and abandoned here as well. Tenno Grandmother and Pang Lok had told her there were three gates to pass before coming upon the Root of the World—the Gate of Faith, the Gate of Humility, and the Gate of Reckoning, and that no one had returned from the Gate of Reckoning to tell the tale. Was she treading on the bones of pilgrims past, their restless ghosts lingering because no one had given them their last rites?

"There," Yuli said, pointing to two shadowy figures on the bridge ahead of them. "Do you see them?"

The light of the crystal in her hand was too bright, so Zhara tucked it into her jacket, allowing her eyes to adjust to the dimness. There were two definite silhouettes standing on the enormous bridge spanning what seemed to be a bottomless abyss, faces pressed close almost in a kiss.

Sajah poked his nose from her sleeve and gave the air a sniff. His mouse ears perked with interest and then he jumped to the ground, resuming his favorite ginger cat form and giving a *miaow* of greeting.

Niang! he cried, and the sound echoed off the rocks in the cavern.

The voices stopped, and the figures turned to face their way.

Niang! Sajah called again, and transformed into his Lion form. His mane glimmered under the light of the false stars, his flaming peacock tail swishing back and forth, leaving trails of flame.

"Sajah?" came a faint but familiar husky voice.

The Beast.

"Ami?" Zhara called. "Beast?"

The two figures got to their feet and began running across the bridge.

"Zhara?" came Ami's voice. "Han? You're alive!"

Zhara broke into a run and rushed toward the others, arms outstretched for an embrace, Han close at her heels. The four of them crashed into one another, a tangle of limbs and astonished laughter. "How—" Zhara began. "What—"

"Who," asked the Beast, staring at Yuli's spirit-ghost standing awkwardly to the side, "is this?"

The northern princess cleared her throat. "The Guardian of Wind," she said, clapping her right fist to her left shoulder. "But you can call me Yuli. A pleasure to meet you all."

Ami straightened excitedly. "You are the Guardian of Wind?"

Yuli eyed the other girl. "I am indeed," she said with a flirtatious grin. "And who is this rare beauty before me?"

"Li Ami," she said. "The Guardian of Wood."

"And my cousin," Han added. "This is Li Er-Shuan's daughter."

The northern princess eyed the girl with a slightly more critical eye. "She's prettier than you, Prince Rice Cake," she remarked.

"I'm sorry," said the Beast. "But can the Guardian of Wind explain what she's doing here and"—they gestured to her incorporeal presence—"why we can see through her?"

"That's her Guardian power," Ami said softly. "Spirit-walking."

"It's a spectacularly useless power compared to everyone else's." Yuli sighed. "All I can do is walk through matter. But as to what I'm doing here"—she gestured to the caverns around them—"I am here to guide my friends to safety."

The Beast narrowed their eyes. "Has the Guardian of Wind been spying on us?"

Yuli scratched the back of her neck. "Well, if you want to be technical about it . . . yes. But only because the Guardian of Fire and I have been working together for a while now to try to figure out how to defeat the Mother of Ten Thousand Demons."

The Beast crossed their arms. "Then why haven't you made yourself known to the rest of us before this?"

She tilted her head. "Between the abominations, the undead, and the rockfall as you summited this enormous death trap of a mountain, what opportunity did I have, exactly?"

"Fair point." The Beast uncrossed their arms and inclined their head. "Well, I am honored to make your acquaintance, Yuli." They pressed their palms together, touched their thumbs to their chin and forehead, and stuck out their tongue in greeting.

"What of Pang Lok?" Ami asked. "And the yak?"

"The brute and the beasts are situated well enough for now," Yuli said. "All he has to do is wait out the storm that's still raging outside."

"What of us then?" Ami poked at the empty space between her brows, pushing up a phantom pair of spectacles. "You were guiding us to safety?"

"Actually," Zhara chimed in, "I think we are closer to the Root of the World than we thought."

The Beast gave her a sharp look. "How so?"

Yuli gestured to the enormous stairway behind them. "At the top of those stairs is a doorway I cannot pass through, and the Guardian of Fire believes that it is because the shield is made of demonic energy."

The word *demonic* sent a shudder through the Beast, who shifted and tugged at the sleeve of their left hand.

"The Gate of Reckoning." All heads turned to Ami, whose face was alight with an epiphany. "That must be why no one has returned from the third gate."

"But what of the Gate of Faith and the Gate of Humility?" Han asked. "Shouldn't we have passed through those on the way to the Gate of Reckoning?"

She shrugged. "It may be that the avalanche and the subsequent cave-ins caused us to bypass those gates entirely, or we could have endured the trials of fear and guilt already."

Zhara and Han exchanged looks. Her greatest fear had been losing Han's love, and she had faced it. He smiled as though the same thought had crossed his mind. "I think we might have," she said softly.

"If the Gate of Reckoning is guarded by a shield of pure demonic energy," Ami continued, "then any magician would turn into an abomination if they passed through."

"What of non-magicians? Or anti-magicians?" Han asked.

Ami frowned. "We know that demonic energy can infect dead things," she said, and again, the Beast shifted, scratching at their hand. "But I don't know what demonic energy does to ordinary people. Oh!" She reached into her jacket and pulled out the battered leather folios containing *Songs of Order and Chaos*. "I suppose we can look it up."

"You have the book on you?" Zhara asked incredulously.

Ami looked nonplussed. "Of course. On my person is the safest place to keep it."

"But what if you had lost or damaged it during the avalanche?"

"But I didn't?" She looked from one person to the next, squinting hard to read their expression. "Anyway, I'm not sure I can read it without my glasses."

"Let's try to reason our way through this then," said Yuli. "If a demon is the opposite of ki—"

"Anti-ki," supplied Zhara.

"—if a demon is anti-ki, then what is it in opposition to?"

"The Guardians of Dawn?" Han suggested. "After all, the last time Tiyok tried to take over the world, the Guardians of Dawn were the only ones who could stand against the Mother of Ten Thousand Demons."

Zhara thought of the encounter with the Frog Demon of Poison and Pestilence she had had at Mount Zanhei, how the Lord of Tiyok had said the Guardians of Dawn were beings of pure spirit who had been reborn in human bodies instead of possessing them the way demons had to in order to access the physical realm. She looked down at her hands. She was Jin Zhara and she was not, for beneath the skin of a girl was a being of pure flame.

"The *taikhut*!" Ami said excitedly. "That's what it stands for!"

Five pairs of eyes—including Sajah's—turned to stare at the scrivener.

"What's a *taikhut?*" Yuli asked.

Ami pointed to the symbol etched onto the cover of one of the folios of *Songs of Order and Chaos*. "It means order in chaos, chaos in order. I couldn't understand why a book on demonology would have a symbol associated with the philosophy of the Way on the pages, but it's because the Way is about balance between dark and light, order and chaos. We've been so focused on the chaos part of it—the demons—we didn't think about what order represented." She looked up excitedly. "*Us.* We represent the positive force in the universe."

Zhara thought of the chaotic magic she had sensed all around her in the bowels of Mount Llangposa, how it had reminded her of demonic magic, only that it was filled with *presence* instead of *absence*. It was why her powers—and Ami's, and Yuli's—were different from that of mundane magic. Pure order. They did not use the void to do magic the way other magicians did; they used the opposite of anti-ki.

They used ki.

"Oh," Zhara breathed. "The powers of the Guardians of Dawn come from the ability to manipulate *ki itself.*"

She let Jin Zhara fall away and become who she truly was. The glowing threads of the universe appeared to her once more, and now that she understood the nature of her ki—her essence—a world of possibility opened up to her. She knew how to use her powers now.

She looked down at the crystal in her left hand. Concentrating, she slowly transformed the magical nature of the stone's ki into that of an ordinary rock. She watched as the light died in her hand before changing its ki back. Someone, perhaps her own soul, had enchanted these stones over a millennia before so that they would respond to magic. She could turn someone into a magician. She could change their ki. She could also take that ki away.

She let her magic fill the crystal again, and the stone blazed with light once more.

"What did you do?" Yuli whispered.

In response, Zhara placed the crystal in Yuli's hand. To the girl's astonishment, her fingers wrapped around the stone instead of passing through her hand to the floor.

"Ki," she said softly. "Our ki is pure magic. There is no void within us to manipulate, and because there is no void, we alone cannot be possessed by a demon."

"And that means we can pass through the Gate of Reckoning." Yuli breathed, understanding dawning over her features.

"What of me and the Beast?" Han asked.

"If my power is the ability to transform ki," Zhara began, "and Ami's is the ability to control ki, then the power of the Guardian of Wind is—"

"—the ability to untether ki from a physical vessel," Yuli said slowly. "The ability to create a state of pure ki, like my spirit-ghost." She looked down at her hand. "You know," she said, "I've never really tested the limits of my abilities. I can communicate from my mind to yours, and Temur and I speak spirit to spirit, soul to soul. But the shape of this ghost is one of comfort, really. I know what I look like, so I imagine my physical self as a ghost. But I suppose I could be any other shape. Including that of . . . a shield." The outline of Yuli's hand blurred, becoming an indistinct white-gold haze.

Han sucked in a sharp breath. "Do you . . . do you think that would work?"

Yuli shrugged. "Why not? What's the worst that could happen?"

"Oh, I don't know," he said. "The Beast could be killed, and I don't know what happens to anti-magicians who come upon demonic energy, but I can't imagine it's any good."

"True," Yuli said. "But do you really want to be left behind?"

Han and the Beast exchanged glances. "Not on your life," they murmured.

"Good." Yuli cracked her knuckles—or the idea of her knuckles—and gave a reckless grin. "Because I can't wait to give this a try."

29

IT TOOK SOME TIME, BUT THE GUARDIAN of Wind finally managed to imagine herself into the shape of a hollow sphere containing the bodies of both Han and Gaden.

Ami had suggested they start small before attempting the Gate of Reckoning. "Why not see if you can wrap your spirit around my cousin's hand?" she asked. "And then we can work toward something bigger."

Yuli tried wrapping her fingers around Han's fist, but her hand passed straight through his.

Han shivered. "So this is what it feels like to have a ghost whisper past your grave."

A furrow of concentration appeared between Yuli's brows. The outline of her fingers blurred and grew indistinct, the glow of her power growing bigger to encompass Han's larger hand. As the light of her magic trailed past his wrist, it appeared as though his fist were encased in a shimmering glove of white gold.

"My auncle Mongke would have a heart attack to see me hand in hand with a boy," said the Guardian of Wind. "The last time I was this close to a boy I was eight and throwing my fist in his face for daring to kiss me."

"Well, it's a good thing I'm not going to kiss you," Han said in a mild voice, staring at his hand.

"I mean, you're cute, Prince Rice Cake," said Yuli. "But I'm afraid you're not my type.

"How will we know if this even works?" Han asked worriedly.

In answer, Zhara stepped forward and wrapped her own fingers around Han's.

"Wah," the northerner exclaimed. "That feels weird. It's like you're holding my hand, which is holding Han's."

"Yes," Zhara said. "And I can't feel Han; I can only feel *you*." She turned her head and nodded toward Ami. "Come join me; I have a theory."

Curious, Ami stepped forward and laid her hand on her cousin's wrist as Zhara directed. Instead of passing through the glimmering glove of white gold as she expected, she felt as though she had come across an impenetrable force just a scant inch or so from Han's skin.

"Wah," Yuli said again. "That feels even weirder."

"I can touch your spirit-ghost because I am a Guardian of Dawn," Zhara said. "I can't pass *through* another Guardian's ki because we are both beings of pure magic." Ami could feel Zhara's dark eyes on her face, and although the other girl's features were blurred without her spectacles, she thought she could sense a questioning gaze. "What does this feel like to you, Ami?"

For the first time in her life, Ami felt rather slow-witted. She had come later to the understanding that she was a Guardian of Dawn than either Zhara or Yuli, and she felt the lack of knowledge keenly. The others could slip into their Guardian forms so easily, but she was still trying to find understanding between how she could be a being of pure magic and a human being at the same time. She learned more easily and quickly through books than through experience, and whatever theoretical knowledge about the Guardians of Dawn that was contained in *Songs of Order and Chaos* was yet to be deciphered, or even discovered.

"It feels," she began slowly, "warm."

The Lion of the South gave an impatient rumble, but Zhara placed a warning hand against his flank.

"Like . . . a current of air surrounding Han," she finished. "A warm breeze."

"There." Ami could see Zhara's cheeks bunch into a smile. "I think this is working."

It took several more tries before Yuli could imagine herself wrapping around Han and the Beast like a blanket. "I don't like this," the northern girl complained. "It feels wrong that I should be more intimate with a boy than I have ever been with a girl before."

Gaden gave a soft chuckle.

"I think we're as ready as we'll ever be," said Zhara. "Let's go see what this Gate of Reckoning is all about, lah?"

At the top of the large stairway was a blank wall.

"Well, that's anticlimactic," Han remarked. "All this work and we've come across a dead end."

"It's not a dead end," came Yuli's disembodied voice. Although Ami knew that she wasn't hearing the Guardian of Wind's voice with her ears, she still had difficulty coming to terms with the fact that the northern girl's words were appearing directly in her head. It was made slightly easier by the fact that Yuli the person was no longer standing with them but was wrapped around Han and Gaden in an amorphous haze of white-gold light. "There is some sort of . . . force there that's making it seem like a blank wall."

"An illusion," said Zhara. She lifted her hand as though to touch the smooth stone face, then paused. "Can you smell that?" Behind her, the Lion of the South padded up on velvet paws to give the wall a delicate sniff. He bared his teeth, peacock tail sending sparks as it lashed against the rocks.

Gaden closed their eyes. "It smells like the barley fields just before harvest," they said in wonder. "And butter tea candles in the library at Kalantze."

There was indeed a faintly green fragrance that permeated from behind the rock wall, but it smelled like neither barley nor steppe grasses to Ami. Instead she was put in mind of dust and the faint rice-water musk of Little Mother's little white blooms. Twined with that familiar fragrance was another smell—like sere, dry mountain air and the mineral tang of glacier water. It made her spine tingle faintly with pleasure. But beneath that perfume was a different scent, something nearly sweet, except it coated the back of her throat with a bilious aftertaste. Like flowers left to rot in a vase.

"Home," Zhara said softly. "It smells like home."

The tingle in Ami's spine grew stronger.

"I think it's the Vale of Eternity on the other side of this wall," Zhara went on. "For it doesn't smell like stone to anyone else, does it?"

Everyone shook their heads.

Zhara reached into her sash and withdrew a crystal that blazed in her hand like a star. As she brought it close to the smooth expanse, the light grew dim, before snuffing out entirely. "Huh," she said. "Not what I expected to happen. I would have thought this crystal would grow brighter in the presence of magic."

"Is it just me," Han asked, "or is the crystal making everything . . . darker?"

It was difficult to tell with any degree of accuracy or certainty, but Ami thought her cousin might have the right of it. In Zhara's hand, the luminous stone was no longer giving off any light; instead, it appeared to be turning an oily, inky black. Veils of shadow descended upon the group, not in response to brightness, but as though a mist of darkness had enveloped them all in a vague fog. Ami wrapped her fingers around Zhara's, and the darkness thinned, light returning in the depths of the crystal.

"I think the stone responds to ki," she said. "And if demonic energy is anti-ki, then . . ."

". . . then the light would dim," Zhara finished. She sighed. "That makes sense, although I will admit I had hoped a little light would give me some courage to step through that wall."

Ami drew close to the blank expanse. The rice-water and dust fragrance was even stronger and more familiar here, and if it weren't for the fact that she knew she was standing somewhere in the bowels of Mount Llangposa, she could have sworn she was back home in the little canal-house in Zanhei, sitting in the garden with her mother. And if it weren't for that ever-present stench of spoilage hovering just beyond her senses. Holding up her hand, she brought her fingers against the stone wall.

And brushed emptiness.

Ami gasped and stumbled back, as much in shock as in disgust.

Gaden called out her name and caught her before she fell, wrapping their wiry arms about her waist. The whiff of glaciers and mountain air brushed past her, and she was suddenly, acutely conscious of Yuli's presence between the two of them.

"What is it?" Yuli asked.

Ami had never had much difficulty with words, but she found herself at a loss to describe the sensations she had just experienced. With her physical body, she had felt nothing—just air, an illusion as Zhara had said. The rock face was nothing but trickery on the eyes, like a cleverly painted veil of magic. But with her Guardian self . . . every part of her elemental being had longed to fill the emptiness with herself, with her power, to give life where there was none, but she resisted, sensing that to do so would empty her body—her vessel—of the essence of who she was, leaving Li Ami vulnerable to demonic possession. For the briefest of moments, she had wanted nothing more than to give in to that impulse, and then profound despair and shame followed in its wake. The Gate of Reckoning was aptly named, for to pass through was to strip herself of everything she was and thought herself to be and be judged as who she was.

And she was terrified.

"Ami?" Gaden asked, their voice gentle with concern.

She glanced back at them, their scarred face so close to hers. She remembered the sensation of her lips against theirs, the varied topography of their skin, and the heat that had burned in her breast so hot that it had felt almost like compulsion. She could not feel Gaden, not with Yuli's magic between them, but the memory of that touch was nearly strong enough to cut through the shield.

Then she remembered the darkness in their blighted wounds. They carried that emptiness with them wherever they went, and it had not made them afraid; it had only made Gaden stronger.

"I'm fine," she said, and she laid her hand against their cheek. They turned their face away and the slight of that rejection stung. Something had passed between them between that kiss on the bridge and the moments afterward, but Ami could not remember.

But she couldn't dwell on that now.

Han coughed. "Not to sound like a baby or anything but . . . do you think we can hold hands as we cross a demonic threshold?"

Behind him, the Lion of the South gave a derisive snort.

"No, it's a good idea," Zhara said. "We don't know what will happen to us. What the Gate of Reckoning will ask of us as we pass through." She held her hand out to Han, who enveloped her fingers with his own glowing ones. "We'll go. Together."

"Yah," Yuli said. "I don't appreciate being turned into everyone's unwitting chaperone here."

Zhara stretched out her other hand to Ami. The void still clung to Ami's senses, but when she slid her palm against the Guardian of Fire's, she could feel the darkness burn away. Warmth suffused her bones.

"Together," she repeated.

And they all stepped through the gate.

Beyond the Gate of Reckoning was paradise.

Whatever Ami had imagined a demon portal to be, she had not expected to come across a lush, verdant valley beneath a sunlit sky. The terror of the void gate had lasted but a moment as they stepped through, the fear kept at bay with the burning feel of Zhara's fingers within her own. The feeling of emptiness could not claw at her hair, her eyes, her nose, her throat, her very bones, not with the protection of her friends beside her.

At last, they were on the other side.

The five of them—and the Lion of the South—stood on an outcropping of rock as mist flowed up from the waterfall at their feet, and Ami realized that the bridge in the cavern they had just left behind was also an aqueduct. The water sparkled as it caught the rays of the sun overhead, glittering like gemstones in the light.

Then Ami realized that the light was not that of the sun. There was no sun. They were still in the heart of Mount Llangposa. The light was coming from the myriad crystals studded in the ceiling, shining so bright in the presence of an impossible magic that it was as though the sun was high in the sky, held back by the mountain peak.

"The place where the sky was held back," she murmured.

Below them the valley opened up into gently rolling hills of green and lavender and pink and white. Ami squinted, trying in vain to bring the view into focus. At the center of this valley was an opaline lake, turquoise and teal and green and white all together at the center. Its color was impossible to discern, changing and shifting from moment to moment, like the flashing gemstones of a noble's headdress.

And there, on the other side of the lake, surrounded by mist, was the Root of the World.

Zhara sucked in a sharp breath. "There it is."

From her vantage point, Ami could just barely make out the shape of a large umbrella-type banyan that was several times taller and broader than several grown humans, its deep green foliage dotted with bits of white. Like the flowers crowning the branches of the Pillar back in Kalantze, she thought. The fragrance they had all smelled before they crossed the demon gate was even stronger, and now, surrounded by its unadulterated scent, Ami recognized that perfume. It was the perfume of Little Mother. It was the perfume her own mother had always worn.

Somehow, her mother had carried the heart seeds of the tree of life.

"Well," said Yuli, back to her ordinary spirit self. "For a place that's supposedly a portal to the chaos realm, it seems awfully peaceful."

No demons. No abominations. No undead. Nothing but a gentle, impossible breeze, almost as though the giant tree at the center of the vale breathed in and out. The tree of life indeed.

"Keep on your toes," Zhara warned. "We don't know if there are any traps."

The party carefully picked their way down the rocky slope and toward the Root of the World, but nothing disturbed their passage.

"I feel uncomfortable without a weapon in hand," Yuli groused. She bent and tried to pick up a fallen branch. Zhara picked up the branch herself, a thoughtful expression on her face.

"What's your weapon of choice?" she asked.

Yuli looked smug. "Anything you can name," she said proudly. "I've won the bear claws of the Gommun four years in a row at the

Endless Night Championships. But if I must choose . . . I suppose my best event was the bow and arrow."

Immediately the fallen branch transformed into a longbow within Zhara's hand. "Something like this?" she asked, handing the weapon to Yuli.

"How——" The Guardian of Wind shook her head. "Never mind." She took the bow in hand. "An enchanted weapon."

"May your arrows always fly true." Zhara grinned.

"You haven't made her arrows yet," Ami pointed out.

"Yah," she protested. "Must I do all the work?" But she dutifully began harvesting the tall grasses and rushes around them to turn into arrows, with Han and Gaden combing the fields for other items the Guardian of Fire could turn into weapons. "What about you, Li Ami?" Zhara asked. "Do you have a weapon of choice?"

"I'm a scrivener," Ami pointed out. "And a shortsighted one at that."

"Doesn't mean you're not also a legendary warrior of old," Zhara said playfully. She pressed something into Ami's hand.

A pair of glasses, she realized, then laughed. "Very clever, Jin Zhara." She put them on.

There was something to be said for enchanted spectacles, Ami thought. For the first time in months, Ami could see everything clearly—every blade of grass, every petal of every flower. What she had taken to be clouds or mist surrounding the Root of the World resolved themselves into statues of people and animals frozen in a scene of worship. With her new sight, she could marvel at the incredibly lifelike detail of the sculptures. But more than the clarity of her vision, Ami realized that she could see the threads of ki that bound the world together, without having to call upon her Guardian form.

"May your good deeds return to you thousandfold," Ami breathed as she took in the sights around her with new eyes.

There was something strange about the statues now that she could see them with her enchanted spectacles. She thought of the stories of Tenno Grandmother, the trials they were to endure before finding the Vale of Eternity and coming to the Root of the World. In a world aglow with ki, the sculptures of people and animals did not have the flat, matte light of stone and earth and other inanimate matter. They were . . . empty of any essence at all. The hairs prickled along Ami's arms.

If you were found worthy, then the Unicorn of the West would let you pass to lay your offerings at the Root of the World. But if you were deemed unworthy, then she would turn you to stone.

"It feels almost sacrilegious to arm myself in the presence of such holiness," Yuli remarked, stringing an arrow against her bow and testing the draw strength. "What dangers could we possibly come across in a place like this?"

"Yah, what about me and the Beast?" Han asked as Zhara distributed a quiver of arrows to Yuli. "Not that I doubt you ladies could more than capably protect us, but I do feel a bit naked without something to defend myself with." Zhara offered him her blade, but he shook his head. "No," he said softly. "That's yours."

"I don't know how to use it," she protested. "My hands are good enough for now."

He reluctantly took the weapon from her. "Fine, but once we've sealed the demon portal we are spending several weeks on your fencing lessons."

Beside Ami, Gaden quietly fingered the knife in their belt. "I'm good," they said at Zhara's questioning glance.

At last she returned to Ami. "Well, Guardian of Wood?" she asked. "What say you? Shall I make you a weapon as well?"

Ami looked down at her hands. In the past several weeks of travel, she had developed calluses in places she had never expected; as a scrivener, she had always had soft palms, even as her fingertips had been worn hard. But she no longer had the hands of a scribe or a clerk; she had the hands of a warrior. She wasn't sure how she felt about that.

"My skills have always lain with words, not weapons," she said softly. "I would only ask that you make me a brush, Jin Zhara."

The Guardian of Fire smiled. "Good," she said, and pressed one into Ami's palm.

The brush hummed with power beneath her touch. Holding the tool felt oddly like holding Zhara's hand: she could sense the other girl's ki running through the object, her magic made material. "Does it do anything?" Ami mused, brandishing the implement experimentally. "Does it shoot fire? I've never encountered an enchanted brush before."

Zhara laughed. "I don't know," she said. "We'll just have to see, lah?"

Ami slid the brush into her sash and gazed out over the Vale of Eternity. Between their party and the tree of life was a vast expanse of cosmos flowers and wild grasses. "All right," she said. "Let's go."

30

THEY CROSSED THE VALLEY WITHOUT INCIDENT.

Journeying across the Vale of Eternity was nearly a pleasure jaunt—the air was warm and thick, and their lungs did not struggle or strain with cloud sickness. The landscape was filled with gentle rolling hills instead of harsh peaks and crevices, and the waters they passed offered clean, crisp refreshment. After weeks and days of bitter cold, Ami found herself working up a sweat for the first time beneath her furs, and they each shed layers as they drew closer to the Root of the World.

"I don't like it," Yuli muttered as they walked. The others had all stowed their weapons away, but the northern girl had kept an arrow nocked on her bowstring the entire time. "It's too easy."

Of them all, the Guardian of Wind had had the most experience with fighting, but Ami couldn't help but agree. The Gate of Reckoning might have been meant to deter ordinary people from passing through to seek the Root of the World, but if the Vale of Eternity was indeed where a demon was supposed to have emerged, then she would have expected more traps and obstacles to prevent them from reaching their goal.

"I'm more surprised we have not yet encountered the Unicorn of the West," Gaden murmured. "Tenno Grandmother said she is rumored to guard the Root of the World from the unworthy."

The Lion of the South rumbled something as they walked. The big cat's brilliant fur and mane were calm, the lightning that flickered within its scarlet, vermillion, and crimson depths quiet and still. But Sajah's ears were pricked forward, occasionally twitching to the side, as though listening for faint and familiar footsteps.

"Could the Unicorn of the West be the demon Tenno Grandmother spoke about?" Han asked.

Ami looked to the Lion of the South—Sajah. She heard both Zhara and Han refer to the Guardian of Fire's celestial companion by a given name, but she didn't think she could bring herself to treat such a majestic creature with such disrespect. "I don't think celestial companions can be possessed," she said. "They are the essence of stars made flesh."

The Lion of the South rumbled again, but this time it sounded like a purr of approval.

"I thought the Unicorn of the West was the celestial companion of the Guardian of Wood," said Yuli. The redhead eyed Ami contemplatively. "But our lovely scrivener here does not appear to have an animal friend."

A sudden pang of loneliness overcame Ami. She thought of all the times she could have used a companion as a child—when she was the unwanted half-sister of two older girls, when she was the too-wise and too-canny child among all the other children in the neighborhood, when she was Li Er-Shuan's equally odd daughter in the palace. She had only ever had the plants in their garden for company, and those friends had been sold off along with the little canal-house in Zanhei after her mother had died and she and her father were whisked off to the palace.

"Sajah appeared to me when he was just a little kitten," Zhara said. "But I admit I didn't think much of it. Cats are sacred in the south. It's considered a blessing to have one grace your doorstep and adopt your family as its own." She turned to Yuli. "Have you always known Temur was the Eagle of the North?"

"Yes," said Yuli. "But because she and I met on the astral plane. When I spirit-walked for the first time, Temur was there to guide me, to make sure I returned to my body."

"What does your family say about the fact that a giant white four-winged bird of prey hangs around you all the time?" Han asked.

"Nothing." Yuli grinned. "Like me, Temur can spirit-walk. Unlike me—or rather, unlike me until somewhat recently—she can change the appearance of her ghost. Most of the time she sits on my shoulder as a kestrel while her actual body is elsewhere."

Ami thought about the legends of the Unicorn of the West she had read about in *Songs of Order and Chaos*. Unlike Sajah and Temur, or even Yongma, the Unicorn was the one Celestial Symbol without a name that she could find. And unlike the others, the Unicorn of the West was the only one of the animals without the ability to disguise its true form or nature. Perhaps that's why legends had sprung up around it as the guardian of the Root of the World in addition to being the companion of the Guardian of Wood.

The Root of the World. Through her enchanted spectacles, Ami could see the tree of life ahead, still quite a distance away, but every detail of its leaves and branches was clear to her. Its bark was smooth, the limbs straight and young despite its ancient age. She could see now why the Pillar was considered the only living sapling, for the two trees could be identical, save for a rather impressive difference in size. Where the base of the Pillar had been as wide around as six people holding hands, the Root of the World was at least ten times that size. The umbrella-shaped canopy bent down to brush the hill from which it grew, but Ami could also see how the uppermost branches spread even farther above them, supporting the peak of Mount Llangposa like the beams of a palace hall. It was both ordinary and awe-inspiring, and Ami couldn't help but compare this first view of the Root of the World to the first time she had set her eyes on the Pillar in Kalantze. A trickle of uncertainty wound its way through her veins as she remembered the blight upon its roots, the emptiness and void that felt so like and unlike the blight afflicting the barley yield and the scars on Gaden's arm.

"Is it just me, or are the stones around here getting more . . . lifelike?" Han asked.

Although there was no path or trail that led from the Gate of Reckoning to the Root of the World, their way had been marked by the occasional limestone rock carved with ancient forms of the Language of Flowers that read *life*. The stones had begun appearing with increasing frequency the closer they drew to the holy tree, and Ami realized with some discomfort that her cousin was right—the forms were becoming increasingly more like statues of people and less like amorphous, shapeless stone as they drew close.

If the Unicorn of the West deemed you unworthy, then she would turn you to stone.

Horrified, Ami looked again to the circle of statues surrounding the base of the Root of the World, overcome with a wave of unease as she noticed once again that the forms were not threaded with any ki. Unlike with demonic energy, there was no absence that had its own presence pressing against her magical senses; they were not filled with anti-ki. They were empty of any essence at all. Then with a prickling of dread, she thought of her own powers. She looked down at her hands, shimmering with green-gold light. If the Guardian of Wood could give life where there was none, could she also take it away again?

"Yah," Han said as they passed by yet another rock, this one even more realistically human than those that came before. "This is starting to get creepy."

They were at the foot of the hill leading up to the Root of the World now, in a garden of stone warriors. Ami recalled reading in the annals of the reign of the second Mugung Emperor of how he had—late in his declining years—grown paranoid from drinking infusions of quicksilver and insisted on finding the Root of the World in search of its fruit, one bite of which was said to grant immortality. The statues they passed were clad in what seemed to be ancient armor, of a style and fashion that would be found only in barrows and other archaeological finds.

"They were judged and found unworthy," Gaden breathed, lifting a scarred hand to touch the nearest statue with an expression of wonder and reverence. They snatched back their fingers with a hiss of surprise.

"What is it?" Zhara asked.

"It's not . . . stone."

"What?" Zhara reached out toward the closest statue herself. "Aiyo," she murmured disbelievingly. "Beast is right. It's not stone, it's . . . it's . . ."

Ami raised her own hand to run her fingers along the cheek of the nearest warrior. She sucked in a sharp breath through her teeth. Based on the texture and gray color of the figures, she had expected solid statues of granite or limestone, but instead she felt—

"Flesh," she finished. "It's flesh."

Suddenly, beneath her fingers, the statue came to life.

The sound of the warrior's hoarse, torn scream was almost worse than the silence of the undead. The roar was high-pitched, almost reedy, like the whistle of a flute, and so, so painful to hear. Ami could feel centuries—a millennia—of thirst parching their vocal cords and her hands flew to her own throat, gulping air as though it could quench the sudden dryness there.

"Ami!"

Someone barreled into her side just as the warrior brought down their broadsword, missing them by a hairsbreadth, followed shortly by the *sssssssss-thunk!* of an arrow thudding into an ancient bronze breastplate. Ami scrambled out from beneath her cousin, who had already sprung to his feet, brandishing the blade Zhara had given him.

"What demonic sorcery is this?" Yuli cried, nocking another arrow to her bow and letting it fly.

All around them, the garden of statues was beginning to come to life. The ground rumbled beneath their feet as what Ami had taken to be lumps of stone buried in the earth began to shake and twist themselves free, uncurling themselves and standing upright, lurching and lumbering toward them.

"Back!" Han shouted. With a great cry, he swung his weapon, decapitating the nearest warrior crawling out of the dirt. The head went flying, but there was no blood, no squelch of flesh, nor snap of bone. Instead, all Ami had heard was the grind of steel against stone as Han's blade cut through the warrior's neck. Over the years these warriors had become not just mummified but fossilized. Reaching into the earth with her power, Ami sent green tendrils of her Guardian magic to wrap themselves about the stone warriors' feet, rendering them immobile. With effort, she forced them farther into the fossilized flesh, causing it to crack and crumble from the inside out, in much the way weeds could choke the cracks of great stone edifices over time. Within moments, the warriors crumpled and fell into a thousand pieces.

An eerie whispering sound rose up all around them.

It was a moment before Ami realized they were words.

Kill us. Free us from our misery.

The shouts from the fossil warriors' mouths were garbled, crackled, their vocal cords too stiff to vibrate or produce much sound, but their pleas were unmistakable.

End our suffering. An eternity of half-life is worse than death.

Was this demonic magic? Her enchanted spectacles showed nothing of the void, nothing of the blackness of the anti-ki threading through these bodies. They were not possessed, not like abominations, not like the undead. Despite the strangeness of the magic that had left these warriors neither living nor dead for a millennia, this was not the work of a demon.

Ami glanced back at the Root of the World spreading out on the hilltop above her. A cold drip of dread slithered down her spine. If this was not the work of a demon, then . . .

All around her, her companions were engaged in battle, but the fossil warriors were not putting up much of a fight. Instead, a chorus of begging rose like a storm around them, *kill us, free us from our misery,* a litany of cajoling that made Ami's heart twist with compassion. She ignored it all, running up the hill toward the Root of the World, hoping against hope that her suspicion about the portal wasn't true.

Panting, she crested the slope to find a familiar scene. At the center of a large, flat top was the tree of life, star-shaped blossoms making constellations across a forest-green canopy, and in that instant Ami was transported back to Castle Dzong in Kalantze, to the moment she first stood beneath the Pillar and gazed at its flower-dusted branches. But it was more than the tree of life's similarity to the Pillar that made the hairs on the back of her neck stand on end. The familiarity of the scene went deeper than memory: it dove into dream.

She had dreamed this moment.

Curled up at the foot of the tree was another statue, and although her waking mind could not comprehend what she was looking at—a delicate gazelle-like animal with the tail of a fox, the mane of a horse, and a singular horn sprouting from its head—she knew she had seen the creature before. And from the depths of her dream, she knew what—or who—it was.

The Unicorn of the West.

And she was waiting for Ami to bring her back to life.

As she approached, all sound seemed to fall away entirely, leaving nothing but the gentle susurrus of a breeze through leaves. The scent of rice water and warm skin was everywhere, and she knew now that this was the perfume of the tree of life, the flowers giving off the fragrance of home to anyone fortunate enough to come within its presence. A gentle rain of white petals drifted down around her, and even the light beneath the Root of the World was softer and more dreamlike, the harsh glow of the crystals above diffused through greenery. The Unicorn of the West did not stir as she drew close, as still and as calm as though she had been carved of earth by a mysterious hand.

Ami knelt beside her.

She was the celestial companion of the Guardian of Wood. Being in the Unicorn's presence gave Ami a sense of profound relief, as though she had been waiting all her life for the friend she had known in another life. And in a very real way, she supposed she had. Unlike the Lion of the South and the Eagle of the North, the Unicorn of the West had no way to walk among the ordinary beasts of the world. Like Ami, she was separate and apart from her peers. Like Ami, she had been alone for a very, very long time.

She laid a hand on the Unicorn's head.

A clear light filled the single horn between the creature's brows, which almost seemed to be made of quartz instead of bone—pale and nearly translucent. A soft intake of breath and the Unicorn opened her amber eyes. Through Ami's enchanted spectacles, she was nearly blinding to look at in her majesty, for beneath the mirage of hide and fur was a beast made of star fire.

"Hullo," Ami said in a soft voice. "What is your name?"

The Unicorn did not reply, merely blinked her impossibly long pale lashes at her.

"Ami!" Zhara came running up the hill behind her. "There you are!"

It took Ami several moments before she remembered where they were, and what they had been doing. "Zhara!" she cried, guilt at having abandoned her friends during the heat of battle crawling up her throat. "Are you all right?"

The other girl nodded, looking flushed and not a little harried. "The warriors have all been put down," she said. "They weren't interested in killing us, so we made quick work of them, but I have to admit I felt a bit bad about it."

The memory of their pleas still rang in Ami's ears. *End our suffering. Free us from our misery.*

"And the others?" she asked. "Are they all right?"

"They're fine." Zhara started when the Unicorn of the West rose to her feet beside Ami. "Mother of Demons," she gasped. "Is that . . . is that . . ."

"Rinqi." It was her mother's name. "The Unicorn of the West." Ami glanced at the Unicorn, who blinked her lashes once more, but with an approving air, she thought.

There was a roar that shook the branches of the Root of the World and the Lion of the South came bounding up the slope. The Unicorn immediately reared onto her hind legs, her forelegs pawing the air before her in joy. The two celestial companions frolicked and gamboled around each other, a reunion over a millennia in the making. Sajah was nuzzling Rinqi so hard that the Unicorn nearly fell over in his enthusiasm.

To Ami's surprise, Zhara was trembling. "Is everything all right?"

"Yes," Zhara said in a quivering voice, watching the Lion and the Unicorn play beneath the Root of the World. "No. I don't know. This is all so much." The glowing sword in her hand thudded to the soft grass at their feet, the flames dying away the instant the blade left her grasp. "We made it," she said softly, looking around them in awe. "We are at the Root of the World. We survived."

Although Ami had never been especially demonstrative or comfortable with physical affection, she wrapped her arms around the other girl's slight, wiry frame and gave her a hug. At first Ami was afraid Zhara would pull away, but the other girl brought her own arms up to return Ami's embrace, and the two of them stood there for a long moment, drawing strength and reassurance from each other. Beneath Ami's touch, she could feel the awesome power of the Guardian of Fire, the power that called to her own, but what astonished Ami more was the revelation that while Jin Zhara might have been an elemental warrior of legend, she was also still an ordinary girl—a girl who had, seemingly against all odds, led them to triumph.

"You did it," Ami said hoarsely. "You kept us safe. You brought us all here, hale and whole."

Zhara sagged in Ami's arms, and she could feel the extraordinary burden of unwitting leadership that had weighed her friend down.

"You did it," she repeated. "And I'm so, so proud of you."

A bright strength enveloped Ami's shoulders and she turned to find the freckled face of the Guardian of Wind beside hers. "We did it," Yuli said. "We're here. Although," the northern girl said in mock reproach, "we could have used some help back there with those fossil warriors."

Zhara gave a watery laugh as Han and Gaden also crested the hill behind them.

"Yah," Han complained. "You girls are having a cuddle party and no one invited us?"

"I thought you were afraid of women," Gaden remarked. "And who is this?" they asked as Rinqi approached. The light of her horn had grown dim, as though she were unsure of these new interlopers.

"I should think the horn would have given it away." Han gave the Unicorn of the West a courteous bow, which Rinqi returned with equal gravity. Behind her, Sajah rolled his golden eyes.

"The Unicorn of the West," Yuli said with a bow of her own. "It is an honor."

Rinqi shifted on her hooves, as though both flattered and shy.

"So this is the Root of the World," the northern girl said, looking from the Unicorn up to the tree of life. "It's . . . not what I expected."

"How so?" Han asked. His large round eyes were even larger as he took in the immense size and scale of the Root of the World. "This is the most impressive tree I've ever seen in my life."

"I don't know," Yuli said with some discomfort. "I just thought . . . well, the crater at Mount Zanhei felt so . . . so . . ."

"Empty," Zhara finished quietly. A wrinkle of concern appeared between her brows as she glanced around them. "Aside from those fossil warriors, I would have expected the demon to be here, trying to stop us from sealing the portal to Tiyok."

Indeed, now that Yuli had mentioned it, Ami thought that the Vale of Eternity was . . . calm. Peaceful. Her previous encounters with demonic energies—abominations, the undead, the blight—had felt distinct. The scent of rot that she associated with demons was not present here. In fact, the air was sweet and clean, and the fragrance of home that had suffused the vale had surrounded them all with a feeling of safety instead of unease.

"Could this all be a trick?" Han asked uncertainly.

The three Guardians exchanged glances. "There's only one way to find out," said Zhara. She held out her hands to the others.

Ami linked her fingers with hers. Between their palms, the glow of their magic mingled, turning a brilliant, pure white. Yuli enveloped their joined hands with hers, her faintly transparent ghost as solid to their magical senses as actual flesh.

Together, they walked toward the Root of the World.

Zhara placed her hand on the trunk of the tree of life and closed her eyes. Through Ami's enchanted spectacles, she could see the ki pathways light up beneath the other girl's touch, but it was the realization that she could sense what Zhara was sensing through their linked powers that was more astonishing.

And the Root of the World was not a portal to a demon realm.

The Root of the World was simply an ordinary tree.

"How—" Yuli began, and Ami knew she was feeling what she was experiencing too.

"There is no corruption here," Zhara said in confusion. "No void, no anti-ki."

"But how is that possible?" Gaden asked. "I thought the portals would be at the resting places of the spirits of the Guardians of Dawn."

Ami thought about the translation she had worked on in *Songs of Or-*

der and Chaos. The characters for the final resting place of the Guardian of Wood had been ancient forms for *tree* and *life,* which she had taken to mean the Root of the World.

But there was another tree of life in the outermost west.

"What is it?" Zhara asked, studying Ami intently. "I can feel your . . . doubt."

Doubt and dread and disbelief bubbled together in Ami's mind, muddying the waters of her realization. But she thought of the courtyard in the middle of Castle Dzong, and the first time she had stood beneath the only living sapling of the Root of the World. The sensation that it had not been a living thing, but a vessel that nothing could fill. The blight dotting the branches and roots of that tree had been like pinpricks into an abyss, a depthless emptiness that had been worse than death.

"The Root of the World isn't the portal to Tiyok," she said softly. "It's the Pillar."

PART 3

THE STAR OF RADIANCE

NO ONE EVER WROTE ABOUT THE JOURNEY home in any of the novels Zhara read. It was always about the journey *to* a place, the journey of a quest to retrieve something or to save someone. There was never anything to be written about the journey *back,* once a quest was done. The mundanities of travel and hardship were interesting only when in service of a goal, but boring and tedious once the goal had been achieved.

There were no stories about what happened after the heroes failed to achieve their goals. The descent to the Gyasol lands was easier than the ascent; the storm had subsided, leaving the skies clear and blue. The air was still bitterly cold, but the sun shining down on the rocks and snow made the chill somewhat bearable, even for Zhara's thin southern blood. It might have even been something of a pleasant excursion, if it weren't for the pall of failure that hung over them all.

"One step at a time," Zhara murmured. They had been taking one step at a time down the slopes of Mount Llangposa for days now. Once they determined that the Root of the World was not, in fact, the portal to the demon realm, they decided they would have to return to the Gyasol lands to recoup, regroup, and plan their next course of action.

But failure soured everyone's mood.

And it was especially noticeable in the Beast.

At first Zhara had thought their irritability was due to some sort of discomfort; they kept scratching at the skin of their left arm during their journey, sometimes so hard that she was afraid they might draw blood. Along the way, Zhara had noticed bruise-colored sores affecting the scar tissue of their hand and worried that the Beast might be suffering from chilblains. Zhara did not know much about treating cold-related ailments, but she had rudimentary medical knowledge from her work with Teacher Hu back in Zanhei. The party had little in the way of salves to soothe pain, but the least she could do was wrap their wounds with some bandages. But the instant she offered, the Beast had jerked away, suddenly snappish and short-tempered.

"It's none of your business," they snarled, and with such venom that she felt the unexpected sting of tears in her eyes. The Beast must have noticed, for they were instantly contrite and apologetic.

"A thousand pardons, Jin Zhara," they said. "I just . . . I've a lot on my mind."

It wasn't much of an apology, but she sensed she wasn't going to receive any better. "So do we all," she said softly.

They nodded. "I know." Their hand went to the small pouch of seeds they'd carried about their neck ever since the party had left Kalantze. "I'm sorry. Don't mind me. I'm just . . . I don't feel much myself these days."

She peered at them. "Is everything all right?"

They bit their lip. "Yes," they said. They scratched at their arm again. "It'll be fine."

Behind the Beast, Han met her eyes. There was something in his large, dark gaze that seemed askew to Zhara, as though Han were desperately trying to communicate something to her that he could not recall.

"I'm sure a few days' rest once we get back to the foothills will lift my mood," the Beast said, by way of reassurance.

They found Pang Lok holed up in one of the caves near the summit, having survived the storm quite nicely with five people's worth of supplies for food and two yak for warmth. He was disappointed to have missed the action but was more than willing to return home.

"Eating meal after meal after meal of tsampa gets pretty old pretty fast," he said.

"Yeah." Han sighed. "You'd think that after all those weeks of eating this stuff on the road, I would have gotten used to how nothing it tastes." He rubbed his belly. "My stomach is full, but my mouth still waters."

"That could be a poem," Ami said.

"Truly?" Han seemed pleased. "Uncle Li always said that I had the makings of a poet," he said. "But that I wouldn't know it until I was older. He said it was because I hadn't done any living. Not really. All I had ever known was the palace. *The years season our appreciation, like the seasons age our wine.*" He laughed softly. "Oh. I understand that now."

"Was that another poem?" Zhara asked with a smile.

"From *A Peach Season Chronicle* by Phan Weng-tsai," he said. "They were my mother's favorite. I have each poem memorized, but I didn't understand them until this moment. Not truly. She was right," he said, his voice trembling a little. "Their work grows with you."

Ashok and Pema eyed Rinqi with disinterest as the Unicorn of the West joined the party. If Zhara had expected some sort of astounded reaction from their briefly estranged party member, she was sorely disappointed, as Pang Lok took all their new developments in stride.

"The outermost west is crawling with the undead, abominations roam the south, and there are two"—he squinted—"three? Guardians of Dawn with me in the flesh. Well," he amended, glancing at Yuli, "almost the flesh, anyway. Just one more impossible thing to believe isn't going to flummox me, I promise."

"I can't stay," Yuli said. "I've got to return to my own body. I've been away too long as it is. Obaji is on his deathbed, and by all rights, I should be there to say goodbye, if it's not too late already."

"The Warlord?" Han asked. "He's dying?"

A stunned silence fell over the company.

"The Gommun Emperor," Pang Lok growled. He straightened to his full height, which was a full half-head taller than Han. "You mean to tell me that this northern chit of a girl is the granddaughter of the man who has persecuted and slain our loved ones for decades?"

Yuli glared at Han, who looked sheepish when he realized that it might have been the better part of discretion not to reveal that bit of information to a member of the Heralds of Glorious Justice.

"That is not her fault," Zhara said. "She's as much the Guardian of Wind as the granddaughter of the Warlord, and she's on our side."

"*Our* side?" Pang Lok raised his brows. "And what side is that, Guardian of Fire?"

Zhara was taken aback. "Defeating the Mother of Ten Thousand Demons," she said, looking to Yuli and Ami. "And restoring balance to the Morning Realms." She blinked when Pang Lok did not respond. "Is it not?"

"Oh, lovely one." The big youth shook his head with a sigh. "We have the same aims, but perhaps differing ideas as to the means."

She frowned. "How do you mean?"

Pang Lok gazed out over the mountain peaks of the Gunungs topped with glacier snow. The view from the summit of Mount Llangposa was stunning. On a day as clear as this one, it was said one could see all the way from the kingdom of the Sindh in the west to the Azure Isles in the east from its heights. "What do you know," he said in a quiet voice, "about the Star of Radiance?"

The Beast stiffened.

"The imperial jewel?" Han asked.

"No." Pang Lok shook his head. "The weapon."

"Weapon?" Han furrowed his brows. "Do you mean what the Sunburst Warrior used to seal the Mother of Ten Thousand Demons back into her realm all those years ago?"

The big youth nodded. "Do you know why we are called the Free Peoples?" he asked, using the collective name to refer to all the various tribes and clans of the Zanqi Plateau.

"Because the Free Peoples swear allegiance to no sovereign but the Sunburst Throne," said Han. "But I don't follow."

Pang Lok heaved his broad shoulders and patted Pema between her horns. "It is because the one who sits on the Sunburst Throne is the Wielder of the Star of Radiance, the one force that keeps the Mother of Ten Thousand Demons trapped in her realm for millennia."

The Beast stirred and shifted on their feet.

"Hold a moment," Yuli said. "Are you saying that without the Star of Radiance we cannot defeat the Mother of Ten Thousand Demons? But the imperial gem was lost." The northern girl glanced at Zhara. "Well, we're doomed."

Pang Lok eyed her with distaste. "Didn't you hear what I said?" he said. "The Star of Radiance is a weapon—a force—not some pretty little trinket."

"Then how do we find it?"

Pang Lok glanced significantly at the Beast, who shook their head. The big youth opened their mouth to speak, then closed it again. He seemed to be struggling with himself, deciding whether to tell them.

"The Star," he said through gritted teeth, "is—" His face purpled and his eyes went glassy in that moment, and for one heart-stopping breath, Zhara feared he was suffering some sort of apoplectic fit. Then his gaze cleared once more and he shuddered. "Apologies," he said. "I don't know what came over me."

The light in Rinqi's horn flared, almost as though in warning. Ami was studying the big lad through her enchanted spectacles with a troubled look on her face. "Lok," she said. "When you tried to speak just then, there was some sort of magic that stopped you."

Zhara startled. "What sort of magic?"

A furrow appeared between the scrivener's brows. "I'm not sure," she said. "But it's not demonic. It was like"—she struggled to find the right words—"the light of his ki suddenly concentrated about his mouth, stopping the words there. His . . . his life force. His own . . . living essence creating a lock or a knot." She made a face. "Ugh, sorry. That doesn't make sense."

The Beast stepped forward. "Why don't we take a rest?" they suggested. "We've all been through a trial these past several days."

None of them could disagree. They found a semisheltered spot on the trail to sit and take a breath while Zhara unearthed a box of tea and a jug. She filled the jug with snow and melted it into hot water before adding several pinches of strong Sindhalese tea, which was more intense and aromatic than the more delicate teas found in the south. Ami passed around several cups and they each poured themself some tea, with Pang Lok and the Beast adding a dollop of yak butter to theirs.

"I've always wondered how butter tea tasted," Yuli said with interest. "Back home on the steppes, we make a brew of fermented mare's milk."

The Beast offered their cup to the Guardian of Wind, but she shook her head. "I'm not here, remember?"

"How are you still alive?" Pang Lok asked. "How has your grandfather not killed you for being a magician?"

Yuli sighed. "Obaji doesn't know."

"Then he must be as stupid as he is cruel."

Something in the northern girl's expression hardened. "I cannot deny his cruelty," she said. "Nor his willful blindness when it comes to the ones he loves. But I'm not without protections. My auncle is a shaman, and I am apprenticed to them. We hide our magic beneath a veneer of mysticism."

Pang Lok grunted. "You should join the Heralds of Glorious Justice," he said. "We could use someone close to the Gommun Emperor."

"The terrorists?" Yuli shook her head. "No, thank you. I would rather achieve my aims by less violent means."

"Violence is merely a tool," the big youth said. "And one only to be used as a last resort."

"And what would you have me do if I were to join your organization?" Yuli asked. "Assassinate the entire Gommun bloodline?"

Pang Lok looked away.

"I thought as much," she said with disgust. "But say that I were to join you. Even if the entire line of succession on my grandfather's side were destroyed, that would not stop civil war. There is no Mugung heir to sit on the Sunburst Throne."

He opened his mouth, then shut it once more. The light in Rinqi's horn flashed again.

"There's that strange magic again," Ami said. "Can no one else see it?" She turned to Zhara and Yuli. "Can you see the threads of ki that bind the world?"

"In my Guardian form," Zhara said. She let the flames within her emerge, and the scene before her was awash with light. It was getting easier and easier to call upon her unique powers, but it never failed to both surprise and thrill her every time she used her magical sight to view the world anew. Before her eyes, she could see the muted royal blue that coursed through Han, the shimmering mirage of beauty and spring green that was Ami, and to her shock, she could scarcely make out Yuli for the blinding white-gold, vaguely human-shaped figure standing beside her. Yuli's ghost was her ki, entirely detached from her body except for the thinnest, barest thread that wound northeast, toward where her sleeping form was traveling with her party to the imperial city.

The non-magicians among them—the Beast and Pang Lok—did not have colored ki; instead their bodies were lit with a clear glow, like beams of sunshine cutting through the shadows of their physical forms. The Beast's ki in particular was incredibly bright, and seemed to be concentrated around their heart, radiating light like the crystals in the caves beneath Mount Llangposa, like the ones Zhara carried in her sash that she had taken from the Vale of Eternity.

But it was the spots of darkness dotting that light that made the cold hand of dread squeeze Zhara about her ribs. "Beast," she breathed, "your scars—" But there was a blinding flash that pulsed from their chest, and once she blinked her eyes, the spots had cleared away.

"What are you talking about?" Yuli asked. "I don't see anything."

"Here," Ami said, taking off her spectacles and handing them to Yuli. "Maybe you can see through these—"

The northern girl laughed. "It's charming that you think I'm actually seeing you with my eyes," she said. "I have no eyes in this form. I'm seeing you all with spirit senses."

"What do we look like through spirit senses?" Ami asked with curiosity.

Yuli shrugged. "You don't *look* like anything. You *seem* like yourself, though. That's about as best as I can put it."

The furrow between Ami's brows deepened. "That makes no sense."

"Magic makes no sense, oh beauteous one." The northern princess grinned.

"Wait, if you can't see me, then how can you tell—"

"Enough," said Pang Lok. He drained the last of his butter tea and rinsed the cup with snow. "I've rested enough. We should get going again. I'd like to find us some proper shelter before the sun goes down."

While the Beast, Han, and Pang cleaned and gathered their things, Yuli drew Ami and Zhara aside to say her farewells.

"Here," she said, handing Zhara the enchanted bow and quiver of arrows she had transformed from branches and sticks in the Vale of Eternity.

"Take it with you," Zhara said.

"I can't," Yuli said with a wry smile. "Your power might enable me to touch this incredible weapon with my ghost, but since I don't know what will happen to it once I return to my body, you'd best hold on to it for now. Keep it safe for me."

Zhara flung her arms around the northern girl. "You watch out for yourself." Even though she knew Yuli wasn't truly there, she thought she could feel the Guardian of Wind's arms tighten about her middle. "It's especially dangerous for magicians now that the Warlord is ill."

"I know." Yuli looked grim. "To say nothing of how dangerous it is to be in the running for succession." She turned to Ami and gave a bow. "And you, little scrivener. I will be in touch soon. We've got our best people in the Guardians of Dawn searching for the other fragments of *Songs of Order and Chaos*. We'll compare notes when we can."

"Best people?" Ami asked.

Zhara smiled. "She means the Bangtan Brothers."

"The performance troupe?" Ami wrinkled her nose in confusion.

Yuli laughed. "One and the same." Then she turned to the others. "Hoi, Prince Rice Cake!" she hollered. "You make sure to take care of Bubbles for me!"

Tears stung Zhara's eyes as a pang of worry stabbed her through the heart. Of them all, Yuli walked the most dangerous path—directly behind enemy lines, as it were, in the Warlord's camp. Although the northern princess had claimed that her bloodline offered her some protection from her grandfather's edicts, now that he was dying, she was afraid he could no longer protect his favorite grandchild.

"Don't be a stranger," Zhara said, voice tight.

"I'll be back," the Guardian of Wind said with a grin. "For that bow and for more opportunities to interrupt you and Han in a romantic moment, if nothing else."

Zhara gave her a pinch.

"Aiyo!" Yuli said ruefully. "Why do I keep forgetting you can do that?"

And with that, she was gone, as though she had never been there, leaving nothing but a faint breeze and the crisp, near-mint scent of ice flowers behind.

32

AMI WAS AFRAID SHE HAD SOMEHOW OFFENDED Gaden.

They had been fairly silent on their journey back to the Gyasol lands, and Ami wondered if she wasn't somehow to blame. Friendships frequently turned awkward for her, and she wasn't sure how or why, only she had some sense that she was standing on the outside of understanding at all times. But she thought that perhaps this time, she had something of an inkling.

It was the kiss beneath the caverns of Mount Llangposa.

Even now, the memory of their lips against herself sent tingles down Ami's spine. In the evenings, when they stopped to shelter for the night, she often found herself reliving the moment—the utter terror that she might lose them off the edge of that precipice, and the bone-deep knowledge then and there that the loss of Gaden from her life would wound her forever. The fear of their loss cut her to the quick and she understood in that moment just how precious they were to her.

She had no words for the feeling, or at least, not words she had grown accustomed to reading in those dreadful romance serials she had copied out for Master Cao back in Zanhei. She had never understood their popularity; the sentiments contained within seemed too easy or shallow to convey any true depth of feeling or connection, and despite everything, she felt *connected* to Gaden in a way she had never felt connected to anyone. She thought of the stories of the red thread of fate that connected lovers together by their littlest fingers, no matter the distance, and although she had always had difficulty with figurative language, she thought now that she understood a little of what it felt like.

Wherever Gaden went, she felt that little tug on her heart.

She was entirely too conscious of where they were at any given moment, as though she had a dedicated sixth sense attuned solely to their presence. Ami tried to recall if she had ever felt like this before, or even the moment she had become aware of it, but she both mistrusted and reveled in that connection. With so many of her peers and those around her, Ami often felt as she did without her spectacles, only it was that sixth sense of understanding that was muted and unclear. With Gaden, it was as though she saw them—*truly* saw them, their expression and actions as decipherable to her as a book written in her native tongue, whereas all else took work and study and painstaking effort.

With them, being herself was effortless.

Perhaps Ami understood figurative language better than she thought.

But a curious mood had befallen Gaden ever since their escapades in the caves beneath Mount Llangposa. They were silent, sullen, and short-tempered, and for the first time since she had met them, Ami could not understand the language of their actions. She watched them snap at Zhara for offering to tend to the blight on their scars and snarl at Han for standing too close to her once. Although Gaden's relationship to Pang Lok had always had something of an antagonistic bent, she once watched Gaden insult the big youth's intelligence and size with such viciousness that she felt sick. She didn't think they were capable of that sort of cruelty.

"Gaden," she had said reproachfully.

The moment they met her eyes, she was struck with a sudden fear that perhaps she never really knew them at all. Their gaze was hard, and that effortlessness she had always felt around them was gone, lost to the judgment she read in their gaze. She thought of the carved boar-chimera mask they had worn as the Beast of Kalantze, and the similarities between their fierce, unforgiving expressions struck her in that moment.

"Gaden," she said again, and the judgment disappeared from their features, almost as though they had slipped off a mask. Instead of mollifying her, Ami felt even more uneasy.

"I'm sorry," they said. "I don't know what came over me." They scratched at their arm with bruised and bloodied fingers, and with a start, Ami realized she could see the spots of darkness that dotted the dead flesh growing, spreading, and expanding through her enchanted spectacles.

The demonic infection was getting worse.

Beside Ami, Rinqi pawed at the trail with her hoof in agitation. She met the Unicorn's amber eyes, which were shadowed with concern. The light in Rinqi's crystal horn flickered with uncertainty, and her black-tipped ears twitched nervously.

"I know, friend, I know," Ami said. "But what should I do?"

She wanted to say something to Zhara and the others about Gaden's scars. She *needed* to say something to Zhara and the others. But as she had been so many times before, Ami was unsure of the right thing to do. If Gaden continued to refuse to engage with her, did that mean she should go over their head and tell the others in their party without their consent? She wished there were a handbook for this sort of thing, but the etiquette manuals she had pored over and studied in Master Cao's bookshop had been more about good comportment than ethical dilemmas, and she was afraid of being wrong more than anything else.

Rinqi nudged at her with her snout, pushing her in Gaden's direction. When Ami held back, the Unicorn blew out an impatient breath.

"But what if they don't want to speak to me?" she murmured.

Rinqi nudged her again.

If Ami were being truthful with herself, it was she who felt awkward around Gaden. She thought of the moment they had come together beneath the false stars in the caves beneath Mount Llangposa, and thought of the moment they had pulled away, and the rejection in that moment was so sharp, so painful to recall that she instinctively shied away from its memory.

I'm sorry, they had said.

"Gaden," Ami said, and this time, the youth did not avoid her company.

"Yes?" they asked softly, and in that moment, all was effortless between them once more.

"Can we . . . can we talk about"—Ami tilted her head toward the bloodied bandages wrapped around Gaden's left hand—"that?"

The effortlessness vanished as Gaden covered their damaged hand with their right, hovering protectively over their scars. "There's nothing to talk about," they snarled.

Ami flinched, her entire being smarting from the rebuke. Behind her, she could feel Rinqi's warm, solid presence, encouraging her to take heart and be brave. "I think you know there is," she said softly. "The infection, it's—"

There was a flash of magical light so blinding that Ami cried out.

"I'm sorry!" Gaden said in a stricken voice. "I didn't mean—I didn't want—"

"Ami?" Zhara asked, rushing to her side. "Is everything all right?"

Eyes watering, Ami took off her spectacles. The world was blurred around the edges, but there were no streaks of dead vision still recovering from the brightness. When she put her spectacles back on, the darkness returned, and she couldn't see the threads of ki that bound the world.

She removed her spectacles again. Aside from her shortsightedness, her vision was clear. Something had injured her magical vision, but not her physical sight.

"I . . . don't know," she said. "Did anyone else see that?"

Zhara frowned. "See what?"

Ami looked to Gaden. Without her glasses, their features were vague, indistinct, but she thought she could read something of guilt in them.

"I don't know," she said softly. "I don't know."

If Ami thought Gaden's unsociability would improve once they happened upon Gyasol lands, she was proven wrong almost immediately.

It was the sight of the Four-Winged Dragon planted into the ground that proved to be the last straw.

There were rather more people in the settlement than when they left—survivors from the undead attacks at both the Heralds' encampment and Kalantze. Ami spotted Captain Okonwe's dark skin and tall, broad form in the distance speaking with Tenno Grandmother, along with a handful of other ragtag people congregated around the cook fires. To Ami's surprise, she saw the barley aunties from the refugee shantytown gathered with the other elders of the Gyasol clan, sitting on platforms in the common square and carding wool.

"Ami-yah!" they hailed when they saw her. "You're alive! Come, come, let us look at you!"

Ami exchanged glances with Zhara, who nodded and gave her an encouraging smile. "Go," the other girl whispered. "Come find me and the others after you've made your greetings."

Ami approached the carding platforms hesitantly. As a child, she had always been uncomfortable being petted by those older than her, for all they had ever wanted to do was coo over her looks as though she were a doll or a plaything, but the affection and relief in the eyes of the barley aunties overcame her initial reserve.

Auntie Tsong, the oldest and kindest of them all, grasped Ami's fingers in her cool, callused ones, bringing them up to her face to kiss the backs of her hands. "Child, child," she said. "We thought we had lost you."

"How—" Ami began, at a loss for words. "When—"

"The librarian led a handful of survivors from the castle, including your father, out through the catacombs to safety," said Auntie Tsong. "But when you weren't numbered among them, we feared the worst. What happened up at Castle Dzong?"

"Baba?" Ami's heart soared. Her father was still alive! "Where is he?"

"Shush, shush, all in good time," the barley auntie soothed. "He spends his time out in the meadows, talking to that little fairy tree of yours. We'll send someone to fetch him. But in the meantime, tell us what happened before I die of old age waiting for your reply!"

Ami opened her mouth to relate all that had befallen her and her companions since fleeing Kalantze before shutting it again, suddenly overwhelmed by everything that had happened. She did not know where, or even how, to begin her tale. The Qirin Tulku had been killed by a child that returned from the dead. The blight, the undead, and the abominations were all due to a demonic infection, the cause of which she and the Guardians of Fire and Wind believed was due to a portal to Tiyok being opened at the Root of the World. They had even managed to travel to the site of the tree of life at the summit of Mount Llangposa, fighting fossilized warriors and finding the fabled Unicorn of the West, oh, and did she mention she was also the Guardian of Wood?

"The monastery was attacked by the undead and abominations, so we fled with Captain Okonwe to the Heralds of Glorious Justice" was all she said. "What happened to Kalantze?"

Auntie Tsong's face darkened. "Gone," she said hoarsely. "The town is overrun by those . . . those *things* that escaped the castle."

Ami could feel the blood drain from her face. "Gone? Then how . . ."

"Zerdan." The barley auntie pointed with her chin toward the tiny, bright-eyed librarian conversing with Captain Okonwe. "He gathered up what refugees had made it out of Kalantze and led them here, to land where his heart seeds will be buried."

"Zerdan is of the Gyasol clan?" Ami was surprised, although she supposed she shouldn't be.

Auntie Tsong nodded. "It's a miracle the librarian made it this far; he's even older than I am."

"What of the catacombs beneath the castle?" Ami asked. "The Free Peoples don't bury their dead."

"Ah," Auntie Tsong said dismissively. "It is not our custom to bury the dead anymore, but back in the days before memory, the people used the ashes and bones of the deceased to build monuments to their legacies instead of enriching the land. We haven't kept that tradition since the Sunburst Warrior brought the faith of the Great Wheel to the outermost west from the kingdom of the Sindh."

Ami thought of the stories of the Sunburst Warrior sealing the Mother of Ten Thousand Demons back into her realm with the Star of Radiance with the Guardians of Dawn. For her, growing up in the southern provinces, the Sunburst Warrior was just a hero of legend, the supposed founder of the Morning Realms themselves. But here in the outermost west, the Sunburst Warrior was revered almost as a religious figure, someone who had brought the radiance of enlightenment to the people, and the reason the Free Peoples swore no allegiance to any sovereign but the Qirin Tulku, and the Qirin Tulku swore fealty only to the Sunburst Throne.

No, Ami thought, remembering what Pang Lok had said on the descent from Mount Llangposa. They swore fealty to the one who wielded the Star of Radiance. The Mugungs, the descendants of the Sunburst Warrior.

This reverence for the deposed dynasty among the westerners was strange to Ami, whose father's mind had been broken by the Star of Radiance. The thought of being compelled to do anything was repulsive to her, and seemed like the greatest violation one could endure—to have one's consent and free will taken away.

"And what of my father?" Ami asked, scanning the fields and meadows beyond the common where one of the barley aunties had gone to fetch Li Er-Shuan. "Is he all right?

A shadow passed over Auntie Tsong's eyes. "He is . . . well. You'll see."

Ami flinched. On his best days her father had been difficult, and on his worst, he had been a danger to himself and others. "May your good deeds return to you thousandfold," she said, pressing her palms together and bowing to the barley aunties. "Many thanks, for keeping him safe."

"It'll do him a lot of good to know you are alive," the old woman said, although the deepening creases between her brows made the words feel like a lie. "I'm sure of it."

But the barley auntie who had gone to fetch him had returned alone. "A thousand apologies," she said. "But he's not in the meadow."

Alarm raced up Ami's spine, but Auntie Tsong held up a consoling hand. "He's perfectly safe on Gyasol lands," she said. "And there are not many places he can hide. We'll find him in no time, Li Ami, never you fear."

It was then the shouting began.

33

THE TIME IS RIGHT TO STRIKE!" Pang Lok's voice echoed across the common. "The Warlord is dying, and the moment to make ourselves known is now!"

"No." Gaden crossed their arms. "Absolutely not!"

The last thing Gaden wanted was a spectacle, but a crowd was starting to gather around the two of them, watching the shouting match take place in much the same way the spectators would enjoy a sport. Gaden had been afraid this would happen; Pang Lok had been agitating for a confrontation ever since Gaden stopped them from betraying their identity as the Wielder of the Star of Radiance to the others on the trail from Mount Llangposa. The news that the Guardian of Wind had revealed about the Warlord being ill and on his deathbed was merely an excuse for Pang Lok to rile Gaden up and get beneath their skin. They had fought like this ever since their days together in the Heralds of Glorious Justice—first for Lee-Lee's attention, then due to their fundamental differences in philosophy: Pang Lok believed in magical liberation at all costs, while Gaden . . . Gaden wasn't entirely sure what they believed. Not anymore. If they even had a system of belief in the first place.

"Don't you understand the meaning of *at all costs*?" Pang Lok asked, pressing close. He had always known how to get a reaction from Gaden, using his superior height and breadth to loom over them, trying to intimidate and dominate through sheer size alone. "The Warlord had no compunction about destroying all magicians to further his own ends. We should merely return the same courtesy now that we have the chance. We cannot sit idly by and let the northerners dictate the parameters of battle."

"But we are not at war," Gaden said.

"Yet," Pang Lok said in a dark voice.

"What's going on here?" A deep, thunderous bass rumbled through the crowd, and Gaden stiffened. Okonwe. The sight of his dark skin and broad shoulders towering over the others sent a jolt of conflicting emotions through Gaden—relief that he was still alive and resentment that he had to come to their rescue . . . again. The Itch flared through their scars, and inflamed the irritation already lying within.

"None of your business," Gaden said. They were startled by the snarl that had come from their mouth. They hadn't intended to sound so snappish.

Okonwe met their gaze, and guilt washed away the Itch, a cold wave that made the tips of Gaden's fingers tingle and go numb.

"We need to decide our next course of action now that Auntie Lee-Lee's gone," said Pang Lok. "The direction the Heralds of Glorious Justice need to go."

"Then take the Heralds in that direction yourself," said Gaden. "And leave me out of your plans."

"How could you possibly step away from your destiny now?" Pang Lok asked, and they were right back in their previous argument. "Auntie Lee-Lee bestowed the leadership of the Heralds upon you before her death."

"And now I bestow the stewardship of this movement to you, Pang Lok," Gaden said. "I don't want it. I've never wanted it!"

"And yet you want to stop me from taking matters into my own hands?"

"You're not thinking things through!" The Itch was back, and Gaden curled and uncurled the fingers of their left hand, trying their best not to scratch. "What do you think would happen if the Heralds of Glorious Justice were to reveal themselves and declare their cause?"

"More people would rally to our banner!"

"And what banner is that?" A flare of searing pain coursed up Gaden's arm, over their left shoulder, and up the left side of their neck. Anger surged in its wake. "The Four-Winged Dragon?" They had made their wishes clear to everyone before they left the Heralds—their true identity as the Wielder of the Star of Radiance was not to be known or shared with anyone. The fact that Pang Lok dared to even entertain the notion of revealing who they were to the world was intolerable. "To what end?"

"Does it matter?" Pang Lok retorted. "Once the Warlord is gone, then we can put the empire back to rights!"

"What are you going to do?" Another flare of fiery pain shot up their arm. "Assassinate the old man?"

"If necessary," Pang Lok said seriously.

"And then what?" Gaden couldn't stand it anymore. They dug their fingers into the flesh of their shoulder, and scratched. "Who do you propose we install on the Sunburst Throne?"

Pang Lok did not respond, unable to give an answer even if he wanted to. A wave of vindictive delight surged through them, but the feeling was strange, as though it both belonged and did not belong to them. As though the emotion did not originate from them. A prickle of uncertainty ran down their spine, but the tickle was immediately subsumed by the Itch, which was starting to take over every moment of Gaden's waking existence. The unbearable torment was beginning to drive them mad, making the Star of Radiance burn within them.

"Tell me, Lok," they continued, digging their fingernails into the dead scar tissue running up their left arm. "Once we destroy the Gommuns, just who is it you expect to take over the Sunburst Throne?"

They had compelled the Heralds to stay silent, but Gaden was curious now whether they could compel Pang Lok to speak. What would happen if two opposing desires met within the same person? Would it tear them apart? Or would the two commands simply render the other obsolete? The Star at their breast pulsed like a second heart, drawing upon the willpower of everyone around them.

Pang Lok's face purpled as they struggled to obey. "The . . . Mu . . . gungs . . ." he choked out.

"Yes, that's right," Gaden said mockingly. They held their bandaged hand out toward Lok, as though holding the big lad in place with a gesture. They could feel the concentrated force of their will pouring out from their fingertips. "The Mugungs. Now, tell me, Lok . . . are there any Mugungs yet alive?"

They could almost imagine bright ribbons of light being pulled from the Star in their chest through the meridian pathways of their body to wrap around Pang Lok's mouth, forcing themselves down his throat. If they pushed harder, they could move the flesh of his body like a puppet. Pang Lok clutched at his throat as blood suffused his face, bloating and swelling his cheeks. The whites of his eyes bulged and reddened as he heaved, air straining through constricted pathways.

"Gaden!" Ami cried. "Enough!"

It was the horror, more than the sound of the scrivener's voice that broke through their reverie. Gaden relinquished their hold on Pang Lok, who fell to the ground, gasping and gulping for air. The Itch was gone, and in that brief moment of clarity, Gaden saw what they had done.

"Lok," they said, and their voice did not sound as though it belonged to them. They held out their hand to help the other boy to his feet. "I—"

"Get away from me." The big youth scrambled backward, rage and hatred and . . . terror in his bloodshot eyes. No. Gaden had never wanted this. They had never meant to make the other boy afraid, just annoyed and intimidated enough to step down, to leave them alone.

"Lok, please, I didn't mean—"

"My liege." It was Okonwe. The former captain of Castle Dzong's guard knelt and offered Pang Lok his shoulder to lean on, heaving them both upright. "That's enough."

"But I haven't done—" Gaden choked on their words. They could taste the lies on their tongue, coated with the power of the Star of Radiance. *Concentrated willpower,* Ami had said. It tasted like bile. "I'm sorry, Lok."

The other boy merely nodded his head and turned away, hobbling off into the crowd. "Auntie Lee-Lee was wrong about you," Pang Lok said softly as he walked away.

"Wrong about me?"

"She said you would never abuse your power. Not like this."

Gaden said nothing, uncertainty, doubt, and confusion churning their gut, making them feel sick. The Itch had subsided for now, but they could feel it lingering at the back of their mind, waiting to return. They couldn't continue on like this. They had to find a cure. "What are you going to do?" they asked.

"I'm going to do what you are too much of a coward to try," Pang Lok said in a grim voice. "I'm going to try to save the Morning Realms."

And he walked off into the crowd.

Spectacle finished, the people began to dissipate, leaving only Okonwe, Ami, and their other companions from the Vale of Eternity behind.

"Gaden," Ami said softly. "What was that about?"

"Nothing," they said mulishly.

At once a look of dismay crossed Ami's face. "You're lying," she said, her large eyes filling with tears behind the owlish shine of her spectacles.

They knew how sensitive Ami was to what she perceived as people being untruthful. "I'm not," they began, then shut their mouth again. If they were not being untruthful to her, then they were being less than truthful, which was nearly as terrible a sin to the scrivener. "It doesn't have anything to do with the rest of you, I promise," they said instead.

Zhara spoke up. "It may have everything to do with us, and our fight against the Mother of Ten Thousand Demons," she said quietly.

"What do you mean?"

Zhara and Ami exchanged glances, and the Guardian of Fire gave the other girl a little encouraging nod.

"You are," Ami said hesitantly, "the Wielder of the Star of Radiance."

Gaden went still. "How—"

Ami fiddled with her glasses, the enchanted pair Zhara had given her in the Vale of Eternity. "I saw it," she said softly. "Your power. How it wrapped itself around Pang Lok when he tried to tell us about the Star of Radiance before. And I saw that power once again just now, when he tried to both tell us and not tell us about the Mugung heir."

Gaden's heart sank, and they could not meet her eyes. "I see." And now they knew. They all knew the truth of who they were. Not Princess Weifeng, not the Mugung heir, but someone who could compel and control the wills of others. Of all the secrets their true identity carried with them, they had not expected the fact that they carried the Star of Radiance to be the worst revelation in their eyes. That Gaden had been born another person, that they had been expected to sit on the Sunburst Throne, those were all the secrets they had expected their friends to revile them for. But then Gaden remembered what Ami had said of her father, of his mind being shattered by breaking the compulsion their grandfather had had over Li Er-Shuan's will, and knew this, more than any other truth of their identity, was the biggest betrayal of all.

"You can . . . you can compel us," Han said. "To do your will?"

Gaden looked away. "Yes."

"Have you ever used your power on any of us?"

They could not meet Han's eyes.

"You have." It was not a question.

"Yes."

"When?" came Ami's voice. "When have you used this power on us? And on whom?"

Gaden looked away. "On all of you," they whispered.

The silence that fell over their group was heavy. "Beast," Zhara said, her voice gentle. "We want to be able to trust you, but . . ." She trailed off.

"I know." Their voice was scarcely audible for the shame. "I know."

"When?" Ami demanded. "When did you ever use that power on us? And can you take it off?"

"I . . . I don't know."

Ami sucked in a sharp breath. "What about . . . what about the cave? Did you . . . make me feel the way I feel about you?"

Zhara gasped and threw her hand over her mouth.

"No!" Gaden burst out. "Never! I would never—" They choked on this last, remembering the second kiss—the one they had stolen.

Ami did not miss their hesitation. "Was it . . . was it ever real?"

she asked, and it was the anguish in her voice that drove the dagger of despair deeper into their heart. "Or was it a lie?"

"I never lied to you, Ami," they said softly.

"But why do I not believe you?" she asked. "Why does this feel like a lie as well?"

"Ami—"

"Don't." She backed away from them, and it was the discomfort in her eyes that hurt the most. "I need . . . I need to go."

And she turned and ran.

34

AMI FOUND HER FATHER IN THE PLACE he had been trying to find ever since they arrived in the outermost west: a place to bury her mother's heart seeds in the earth.

A place to plant Little Mother.

A place to return her to her people.

Ami's father was lost, in more ways than one.

She discovered Li Er-Shuan in the shadow of Mount Llangposa, in a small banyan grove that was more shrubs than trees, puttering among the vines and roots, muttering to himself and the little fairy tree in his hand. In the weeks Ami had been apart from her father, Little Mother had become more flower than branch, its crown pure white with lightly musky petals.

"Baba," she said softly, but her father did not hear her.

Of course he didn't hear her. He never had. All her life, her father had been elsewhere—among the heavens and the past, preferring the slips of time he still had command of his senses. In that respect, she supposed she could not blame him. But in all others . . .

"Baba," she said again, more firmly.

This time, he raised his head. "Rinqi?" he asked, squinting through cracked spectacles at his daughter.

Despite everything, Ami's heart squeezed bitter tears. Her mother, her mother, it was always about her mother. Sometimes she wondered if her father even remembered he had children. It was the one thing she had in common with her older half-sisters—the absentminded and benign neglectfulness of their upbringing. The two great loves of Li Er-Shuan's life—astrology and Rinqi—could not compare. "It's Ami, baba," she said. "Your youngest daughter."

She watched him struggle to find his footing in the present. "Ami?" His eyes slowly sharpened into focus. "Ami."

"What are you doing?"

Li Er-Shuan clutched Little Mother's vase close to his chest. "I'm looking for a place to lay your mother to rest."

Ami looked to the Gunung Mountains casting long shadows over the plain. "But Mother was not from the Gyasol lands," she said.

"No," he said. "Yes. I don't know."

There was so much of her own mother Ami did not know. Rinqi had been part of a trader's caravan selling incense from the outermost west in the imperial city when she met Li Er-Shuan, a young woman with no past and an uncertain future. She had been an orphan, the only keys to her origins carried in a pouch around her neck. Although she had grown up with no knowledge of letters, she had a sharp mind for ciphers and the ability to calculate the movements of the stars without charts. *A navigator,* Li Er-Shuan had said. *Blessed by the Second Immortal.*

Like her father, Ami's mother had been fascinated by the heavens, although more for pragmatic reasons than for prophecy. It was Rinqi who had taught Li Er-Shuan the asterisms of her people, the significations of the wandering stars, and the stories of celestial watchers, now aspects of her father's practice. With Rinqi, Li Er-Shuan had known love again after the death of his first wife, and of that love, Ami had been born. The little family had had a few blissful years together before the wasting sickness took Rinqi away from them, a loss that devastated Li Er-Shuan because he had not foreseen and prepared for it.

He had become obsessed with death and doom after that.

"If you don't know where Mother was from, why choose to bury her heart seeds here?" Ami asked.

"Because," he said, growing increasingly agitated, "this place is filled with her scent. Because"—his voice broke—"it smells like home."

"Home?" For the first time in a long time, the word no longer conjured the scent of their little house along the canals back in Zanhei. No longer the fragrance of warm skin, rice water, and herbs. No longer the perfume of her mother.

"Yes," her father whispered. "Safe." He held Little Mother to his nose, inhaling the fragrance of the white flowers crowning its branches. Then with a cry, he tossed the little fairy tree to the ground, sinking to his knees.

"Baba!" Ami gathered up Little Mother to her breast, hands glowing as she used her power to settle the fairy tree back into its miniature vase. "How could you?"

"No!" he shrieked, grabbing her hands with his own. "Hide your light! How many times must I tell you to hide your light?"

"A thousand times over!" she burst out, unable to check her fury. "And you've never explained why!" She thrust her right hand to her father, the glow of her power illuminating the shadows between them. "This! This light! I know what I am now and I don't want to hide it anymore!"

At her words, a sudden calm fell over Li Er-Shuan. "You know?" he whispered. "The truth?"

Of all things it made her want to laugh. Not with mirth, but with despair. "Yes, baba," she said acidly. "I know the truth. I am the Guardian of Wood."

He slumped to the ground. "Then you must know," he said. "You must know the reason I had to keep you hidden."

"Keep me hidden?" she scoffed. "From whom?"

"The emperor."

She blinked. "The Warlord?"

"No." He shook his head, clutching at his ears. "No. The Mugung Emperor."

The word *Mugung* sent a throb of anger and betrayal through Ami. Gaden. Gaden was the Mugung heir. The Wielder of the Star of Radiance.

The Star of Radiance.

Ami fell back on her heels beside her father. All his ramblings about the Star of Radiance now made sense, and for the first time in a very long time, she felt such sympathy and sorrow for the suffering he must have endured. If his torment was just a fraction of the emotional agony she was feeling, then the mire of his mind must be a terrifying place.

"Listen to me." With enormous effort, Li Er-Shuan brought himself together. "Please, listen while I can still"—he ground his teeth and screwed his eyes shut—"still hold my thoughts together. Please. Please."

Ami stiffened, but forced herself to pay attention.

"When I was an imperial astrologer," he began, and his voice was clearer than she had ever heard it, "I once cast a chart for the emperor that foretold doom and destruction. The return of the Mother of Ten Thousand Demons." Li Er-Shuan opened his eyes, staring into the middle distance between them at horrors only he could see. "At the time I was young, full of arrogance and pride, so smug and pleased with myself and my work that I had not foreseen the implications of what this information might do to an already unstable man." He shuddered. "That was when he called upon four of his best magicians to go forth and summon the Guardians of Dawn."

"But the Guardians of Dawn cannot be summoned," Ami said, thinking of what she had read in her fragments of *Songs of Order and Chaos*.

"No," Li Er-Shuan agreed. "But they can be reborn."

Ami thought of Zhara, of Yuli, and of herself. The souls of elemental warriors, reborn as ordinary girls. Extraordinary girls. She wondered what else the stars had foretold about their births. "Do you . . . do you know the identities of the reborn Guardians?"

Her father brought his hand up to brush Ami's short locks behind her ear. His gaze was the clearest she had ever seen it, and for some reason, it made her more afraid than if he had been lost in the mists. "Yes." Then, shaking his head: "No." He brought his hand down to cover hers. "Only you," he said in a trembling voice. "I cast the chart the night you were born. That was the night I discovered your true identity."

Ami sucked in a sharp breath.

"After that," Li Er-Shuan continued, "your mother and I tried to hide you from the emperor. If he had known, he would have taken you from us. Compelled you to fight for him against the forces of chaos with the Star of Radiance. But I couldn't do that to—I wouldn't let them . . ." He swallowed, his eyes flitting from side to side as he fought to remain in the present. "The night the emperor found out my sin was the night I fled the imperial city."

Ami covered her mouth, horror and sympathy holding hands within her.

"He tried to force me to stay." Li Er-Shuan closed his eyes and turned his head to the side, as though he could not bear to watch the scenes of memory playing out in his head. "He tried to force me to give you into his possession. But I couldn't let him. I, who had been enslaved to his will ever since I passed my imperial examinations, I could never subject my daughter to such cruelty. That night was the first time I ever dared defy him . . . and it burned out my mind."

Tears scalded the back of Ami's throat. Her father was *here,* he was with *her.* He saw *her.* For the first time since she could remember, her father was not lost to her.

"Oh, baba," she said, her voice thick. "Oh, baba." She wrapped her arms around him and buried her face in his shoulder. "Why did you never tell me?"

"Because," he said hoarsely, "I thought that the only way to keep you safe was to keep you ignorant. The fact that you are a magician was troublesome enough. Do you not remember the day the Chancellor discovered your magic? How much worse would it have been if he had known the truth of your power?"

Ami remembered the day they fled the palace as though it had been seared into her mind like a brand. She had been sitting in the Royal Consort's meditation garden with her father and their cousins—the Royal Consort and her children. The Royal Heir—Han—had been playing with his little brother, chasing him through the flowers and bushes, a game of tag with rules so opaque they were known only to each other. Although she and Han were near to each other in age, she had never been especially close to him, especially as he was the sort of easygoing child whose thoughtless charm was the most intimidating to her.

That day, her father and the Royal Consort had been discussing matters in low voices that did not carry. She sat a little ways off in the moon-viewing pavilion, comparing a translated book on Azurean history to the original text, trying to teach herself a bit of the original language of the peninsula. Languages were easier for her to understand than people sometimes; there was a reason and rhythm and rules to language that people did not have.

Now what do we have here? came an amused voice behind her. *A little scholar, perhaps? What's your name, learned one?*

She recognized the seal of office before she recognized the person: a jade pendant with a laughing monkey. The Chancellor of Zanhei. The second most powerful person in the city, save Prince Wonhu himself.

Ami didn't know to be afraid, not then. *Li Ami,* she replied.

The Chancellor raised his brows. *Not a very polite little scholar, I see.*

She never could remember when to use honorifics or not. *Li Ami, Your Eminence.*

The official took her hand. *It's all right, child,* he said. *Courtesy is not a virtue all the time.*

When the Royal Consort saw the Chancellor about to take Ami's hand, she cried out and intervened. But in that moment, he touched her, and in that touch, the Chancellor recognized the Royal Consort for what she was.

The Royal Consort had died by fire not long after that.

"Oh, baba," Ami said, eyes watering. "Oh, baba."

"I'm sorry I could not be here for you as much as you needed me to," Li Er-Shuan said. "I promised your mother I would look after you, and I failed in that, just as I failed her."

She tensed at the mention of her mother; she couldn't help it. She feared she was on the verge of losing her father again, just when he had found his way to her.

"She . . . she was cursed the night we fled," he said. "By one of the imperial magicians. She stole one of his fragments of *Songs of Order and Chaos* because I had asked her to. But I didn't notice . . . I didn't see . . . not until it was too late. She was gone before I could help her, because I spent all my time poring through *Songs of Order and Chaos* for a way to fix what I had started."

Ami thought of her father's obsession with the book of demonology. Her interest in old texts was through language, through translation and uncovering layers of meaning. But Li Er-Shuan's fixation had been because of guilt, because he believed he was the cause of all the trouble in the realm. "Oh, baba," she said again. "It's not your fault."

"But it *is* my fault!" He was growing more and more upset now, and Ami could see his grasp on the present moment slipping away. "I could have said no. I could have kept this information from the emperor. I could have foreseen the outcome!"

"But you couldn't have," she said. "The Mugung Emperor bound your will to his. You were compelled to comply with his every wish." Again the memory of Gaden admitting that they had used the Star of Radiance on her rose up like bile in her throat, hot and choking. The anger returned, burning through her temper like a fuse. "No one's will should be controlled by another, not even by the gods. The Star of Radiance is evil; it is a power no one should have."

At that moment, her father looked at her, his gaze steady and fixed. "No one person should have that power," he agreed. "That power should be returned to the people of the Morning Realms."

Ami was taken aback. "What do you mean?" *A single drop of will from every person in the Morning Realms to the Sunburst Warrior to form the Star of Radiance.* "The power can be returned?"

"Consent, once given, can also be revoked," Li Er-Shuan said seriously. "The people would have to reclaim that power for themselves." He groaned and brought his hands to his head, crying out in agony. "No one is ever entirely powerless against the will of another," he said weakly. "I know that better than anyone."

"How did you do it?" she asked softly. "How did you break the compulsion magic of the Star of Radiance?"

His eyelids were drooping shut and she knew she needed to get him somewhere to rest soon. Nights in the outermost west were now colder than the bitterest of winter days back home in Zanhei, and her father's frail body would not be able to handle it.

"Love," he said simply. "Love is the one force in the world that cannot be compelled."

Ami went still. "Love?" she asked. "How so?"

Li Er-Shuan lifted his hand to rest it against her cheek. "I love you, Ami-yah," he said hoarsely. "And it was that love that gave me strength to pull away. The Mugung Emperor could command me to do whatever he desired, but the one force he could never control or take away was my love for you. He could take all else, but never my love."

Tears slipped down her face, and her father gently wiped them away with his thumb.

"Love cannot be compelled," her father said, stroking her hair as gently as he had when she was a child. "Remember that, Ami-yah. Remember that."

35

THE STARS WERE EVEN BRIGHTER IN THE foothills of the Gunungs than they were out on the Poha Plain, steady and strong.

It was a strange phenomenon, Gaden mused, that the stars did not twinkle in the highest places of the world. Zhara had told him that back in the southern provinces, what little they could see of the stars not obscured by the lamps and lanterns of the city winked and blinked from the heavens.

You hold the star now, my child.

Gaden pressed their bandaged hand to their breast, over the pouch of the Qirin Tulku's heart seeds they had carried with them all the way from Kalantze. The worst had happened. Their friends now knew the truth of who they were, and the world hadn't ended. And yet, in some ways, why did it still feel as though it had?

They thought of Ami's tear-filled eyes as she ran off, and they could still feel Zhara's little hands wrapped around their arm, preventing them from following after her, to explain, to beg, to plead, to ask what they could do to fix this, to make everything as it had been between them. As it was about to be between them. They brought their hand up to their lips, the memory of the kiss—the real kiss—they had shared beneath the caverns of Mount Llangposa still lingering on their skin. The taste of her lips was nothing like what the romance novels said. It was better. Better because it had been real. Because *she* had been real.

As Gaden walked among the cosmos flowers, they searched for an appropriate place to honor their old teacher's last wishes—to bury their heart seeds at the foot of Mount Llangposa. They glanced at the waning moon above and wondered if the Qirin Tulku's soul had incarnated yet again in the body of another child. How many weeks had it been since his death now? Two? Three? As the Left Hand of the Unicorn King, it would have been Gaden's duty to search the lands of the outermost west far and wide for their teacher's next incarnation while the Right Hand governed until the new Qirin Tulku came of age. Indeed, Gaden would have waited to find this child before burying their teacher's heart seeds, to ask them if they knew of their previous incarnation's final wishes. The correct answer would determine who they would be bringing back with them to Kalantze to learn at the Right Hand's feet.

That was the destiny they would have had, had they not been the last Mugung heir.

Had they not been the Star of Radiance.

"Oh, Teacher," Gaden murmured to the pouch in their palm. "Why didn't you tell me?"

If Okonwe had been their first father, then the Unicorn King had been their second and the first person to teach them about a world bigger than mere survival. A world bigger than the need to hide their identity, bigger than the struggle for magician liberation, bigger than the petty politics of the Heralds of Glorious Justice. The Qirin Tulku taught them not just about magician liberation, but the meaning of liberty itself. The Unicorn King had also taught them the politics of the Morning Realms themselves, helping them understand that all politics are the result of both history and unrest. Of all people who should have told them the truth of who they were—about what being the Wielder of the Star of Radiance truly meant—it should have been the Qirin Tulku.

"You, of all people, could have told me the significance—the weight—of it all," they said softly. "*One drop of will from every citizen of the Morning Realms,*" they quoted. "*To bind the consent of all the souls who live in these lands under the aegis of Mugung rule.*"

Something rustled the hedges behind them. Gaden turned to see if they were followed, hoping against hope that it might be Ami. But there was no one there. Perhaps it had simply been the wind through the leaves.

Sitting down on a rock surrounded by blooming cosmos flowers, they carefully opened the Qirin Tulku's pouch and poured the seeds into their palm. To their surprise, the seeds were more like dried flowers than actual seeds, like the dead heads of a dandelion flower before it returned to the earth and blossomed anew next spring. A faint fragrance still clung to the dried petals—a musky white perfume that unexpectedly put them in mind of the rich tallow scent of the yak butter candles they frequently burned in the library back at Kalantze.

"You once told me, Teacher," Gaden said to the seeds in their palm, "that though we may plant for the next harvest, there is no telling what yield may come. I wonder what harvest you intended in me, to plant all these histories and philosophies of what it means to be free."

Gaden scratched absentmindedly at the scars at their neck. Out here, closer to the mountains and the wilds of the world, the Itch was diminished, more the memory of a tickle than an active, present torment. Beneath the tips of their callused fingers, they could feel the hardened, scaly bits of flesh that had grown to cover their neck and were starting to spread up their jaw to their cheek. Soon there would be no hiding the spread of the affliction from anyone.

Another snap of a branch and Gaden leaped to their feet, swiping the bone-handled knife from their boot and brandishing it at the intruder. To their surprise, a soft glow filled the glade, originating from a slender, curled horn set between a pair of amber eyes.

"Rinqi?" Gaden lowered their blade as the Unicorn of the West approached. They weren't sure if it was proper to address the celestial companion of a Guardian of Dawn so informally, but they had been caught off guard. "Is Ami with you?"

Rinqi tilted her head quizzically. All at once Gaden remembered the stories of the Unicorn of the West being able to cure all illnesses with a touch of her horn and wondered if Ami's companion had come seeking them to do that very thing. If this meant that Ami forgave them for the transgressions they had wrought against their loved ones by being the Star of Radiance.

But Rinqi did not reply.

"Er," came a different voice. "Not to disappoint you, my friend, but I'm not Ami."

Stepping into the circle of light cast by the glow of Rinqi's horn was a tall, trim, athletic figure. Han.

"But if I'm not Li Ami," the southern boy continued, "then would her cousin suffice?"

Despite everything, Gaden could feel the edges of a smile curl the corners of their lips, then they winced. The bunching of their cheeks pulled at the scar tissue on their left side and it hurt.

"It's getting worse, isn't it?" Han said softly.

Gaden raised a hand to their face. "Has it spread this far already?"

Han shook his head. "I don't know," he said in a serious voice. "Ever since you . . . did that . . . star magic or whatever on me, I haven't been able to see it. But I'm also not stupid, no matter my charmingly obtuse manner, and I can see that you are in an increasing amount of pain."

Gaden cringed. "I'm sorry, I didn't mean to—"

"Force my mouth shut?" Han's expression was uncharacteristically hard. "I wasn't going to say anything, you know."

"I know," Gaden whispered, guilt crawling up their throat to leak out their eyes. "I didn't mean to hurt you."

"You knew I wasn't going to betray you and you still forced me anyway?" Han asked, horrified. "What a beastly thing to do."

Gaden flinched. "I panicked," they said, and even to their own ears, the excuse sounded flimsy, weak, petulant.

Han said quietly, "How many times have you used that star power on us?"

Gaden opened their mouth, then shut it again. The Star of Radiance burned in their chest, and they rubbed at it with a bandaged hand. "More than I'd like to admit," they said at last.

"How many?"

They looked down at their feet. Rinqi drew up beside Han and gently nuzzled her snout against his hand. Gaden was alone in their shame, and they knew they had to stand up to it and own it.

"I think . . . before I knew just what it was, I must have used the power of the Star of Radiance on the Heralds of Glorious Justice," they said softly. "To prevent them from revealing the nature of my identity as the Mugung heir to anyone."

Han nodded. "I suppose that's understandable," he said. "That person isn't who you are anymore."

Despite the shame roiling through Gaden, Han's casual validation of their true self was incredibly gratifying. It was all they had ever wanted to hear from Lee-Lee, from Okonwe, from all the people who claimed to love them—one final, decisive acknowledgment of their lived existence so they could move on. Move forward. Perhaps they might have even been able to untangle the concept of their destiny as the Wielder of the Star of Radiance from their old self, and they wouldn't have been in this mess in the first place.

"You are right," they said, their throat clotted thick with emotion, "I'm not that person anymore." Saying the words aloud was far more empowering than they had realized. "I am Gaden now."

"Gaden," Han said softly. "It's a nice name."

They laughed. "It means *handsome*."

"Like I said, a nice name."

Gaden smiled. "Thank you, friend," they said. "May your good deeds return to you thousandfold."

Han sighed. "While I am honored to have been given your true name," he said, "that doesn't mean I forgive you, Gaden." He crossed his arms. "You still magically compelled me to keep my mouth shut."

Guilt rushed back in, overwhelming the gratitude warming their insides with cold dread. "I know," they said. "I'm sorry." When Han's glower did not disappear, they ventured meekly, "Shall I remove the compulsion magic?"

"Yes," said Han. "But what I want to know is why you couldn't trust me to keep your secrets. I thought we were friends. That's what friends do."

Gaden couldn't meet his eyes. "Because I'm a coward," they said. "Because I was afraid. I know it's no excuse, but I had spent a lifetime believing that I had to be perfect in hiding my identity, lest someone trample over my wishes to be seen as I truly was." Now that Gaden had said the words aloud, they knew the depths of the wrong they had done to Han, and to everyone else. "By the Great Wheel," they murmured. "What have I done?"

It was the pity, the empathy, and the kindness in Han's eyes that was Gaden's undoing. The tears they had unsuccessfully been trying to keep at bay finally broke through their fragile hold, and they started crying in earnest.

"I'm sorry," they said. "I'm sorry, I'm sorry, I'm sorry."

Han draped an arm over Gaden's shoulders and said nothing, merely offering the solid comfort of his presence to them. When the storm of emotions subsided, Gaden got to their hands and knees before Han and bowed, pressing their forehead to the ground.

"Wonhu Han," they said in formal tones. "I apologize for the wrong I have done to his person by violating his consent, his free will, and by forsaking his trust. I know I cannot make sufficient amends, nor can I expect forgiveness, but in a gesture of remorse and reproach, I remove the compulsion magic I have set upon Wonhu Han, and humbly beg him to hear my honest heart and know my actions to be done in good faith."

It was a long moment before Han replied. "I accept your apology," he said, sounding impressed. "I should take notes from you on how to make one."

Gaden gave a watery chuckle. "May your good deeds return to you thousandfold," they said again. "And . . . thank you. For being my friend."

The smile on Han's face was brighter than the light of the moon and the stars above. "So," he said. "What about this star power of yours? Do we know how powerful it is? How you can control it?"

"I don't know," Gaden said. "As far as control goes, I think I can." At that precise moment, the Itch returned, and part of Gaden's mind was blotted out by its ever-present agony. "As far as power . . . I don't know. I've never really consciously tested its limits. I don't know if there is a limit."

"There isn't," came a thin, querulous voice from the shadows. "Not even the Mother of Ten Thousand Demons can withstand the force of one drop of will from every living person in the Morning Realms."

Whirling around, Gaden brandished their knife and Han slid into a fighting stance at the sight of a slim, slight silhouette standing before them. There was scarcely enough light to make out the stranger's features beneath the silver sliver of the moon, but Gaden thought they looked familiar.

"Relax, children." The figure emerged from the shadow of the mountains, and for the first time, Gaden could see clearly the wizened wrinkles and twinkly eyes of Castle Dzong's ancient librarian. "I mean you no harm."

"Zerdan?" Gaden sheathed their blade back in their boot. "You're here!"

"I may be old, but I'm not dead yet." The librarian grinned.

"How did you survive Kalantze?"

"Well, I couldn't give you all the library's secrets, now, could I?" They smiled. "But you are aware of the catacombs beneath the monastery, yes?"

Gaden nodded. Much of Grombo Hill, onto which the village of Kalantze and the fortress-monastery had been built, was in fact an ancient catacomb system of caves and passageways. Before the peoples of the Zanqi Plateau buried heart seeds, they buried the earthly remains of their ancestors.

"The catacombs lead out onto Poha Plain by way of a concealed exit," the librarian continued. "I led everyone I could out through the entrance in the library."

"How did you end up here?" Gaden asked. "How did you know we would end up in Gyasol lands?"

"Think so highly of yourself, do we, child?" Zerdan chuckled. "The truth is, I did not know you would be here, but I did know of an ancient protection upon these lands and thought it would be the safest place to bring the survivors and refugees."

"You did?" Han asked. "How?"

The old librarian grinned. "Because I hail from these lands myself, my friend," Zerdan said. "I am Gyasol Dzenar."

"What?" Gaden was astonished. "You never told me that."

Zerdan tilted his head to study Gaden's face. "Of course not," he said. "I didn't think it was important. Did I ask you where you came from, who your family is, or what it means for you to be the Star of Radiance?"

He had not. It was one of the reasons they had liked to spend time in the library; Zerdan had never asked them about their past, and was instead content to remain in the present with Gaden instead. But something the librarian said stuck in their ear and they could not shake the little niggle of doubt loose from their mind.

"Zerdan," they said, "how did you know I was the Star of Radiance?"

A strange look crossed the old librarian's face—half guilt, half eagerness.

"Dzenar," Han murmured. "Why does that name sound so familiar?"

Realization struck both of them at once. "The demon . . ." Gaden said.

Zerdan—Dzenar—grinned. "Very clever, you two. Truly, I didn't think anyone would remember. It was over twenty years ago, and I would have thought anyone who remembered my deeds would have gone. I am the Locust Demon of Scarcity and Starvation. A pleasure to meet you."

Gaden swiped their bone-handled knife from their boot. "Run, Han," they said in a low voice. "Go fetch the others."

"Now, what makes you think you could stop me with such a little blade?" Zerdan was amused. With a movement too fast for them to follow, the librarian disarmed them. "Even if I couldn't do that, no mortal weapon could harm me."

"We're still two against one, ancient one." Han had picked up a rock and held it in his hand, standing ready in a loose but comfortable fighting stance.

"Are you sure about that, child?" Suddenly, Zerdan grabbed Gaden by the wrist, igniting the Itch in their veins. With a cry of pain, Gaden fell to their knees, but their scarred left hand began moving of its own accord. They were overwhelmed by the uncanny sensation that someone else was wearing their hand like a glove, wriggling their fingers, trying their skin on for size.

"Interesting," said Zerdan, wriggling his own fingers, causing Gaden's hand to twitch and tremble. "I really did think you would put up a harder fight, my child. This is almost as easy as manipulating the undead." Then, with a swift gesture, the librarian curled his hand into a fist, the movement echoed by Gaden's own limbs, and punched Han across the jaw, knocking the other boy out cold.

"What . . . is . . . happening?" Gaden said, struggling against the invading force that had colonized their body. If this was what it felt like to have their will overridden by the desires of another, then Gaden swore never to use the magic of the Star of Radiance against anyone but the Mother of Ten Thousand Demons. Never. Never.

"Did your pretty little scrivener never tell you the powers of each of the Lords of Tiyok?" the librarian asked. "My siblings and I each have a particular . . . gift, you can say. Mine is the ability to infect and manipulate dead matter."

Their scars. The dead tissue on their flesh. "What do you want from me?" Gaden asked.

"Me?" Zerdan looked thoughtful. "Nothing. I've satisfied my curiosity with you." He wriggled his fingers again, and Gaden's hand involuntarily mirrored the gesture. "But I'm afraid my mother is most interested in you."

"Why?"

For a moment, the librarian looked almost . . . regretful. "Because you are the Star of Radiance. Because yours is the power of every living person in the Morning Realms, and it is only the combined force of the collective will of the people that can seal my mother away in her domain. I didn't know until I overheard you talking with your unconscious friend there. I'm sorry."

And then Gaden knew no more.

36

AFTER SHE HELPED HER FATHER TO BED, Ami returned to the foothills of Mount Llangposa. She sat on an outcropping of rock, naming the asterisms in the mansions of the heavens. The Fan, the Brush, the Inkstone, and the Well in the mansion of the First Immortal. The Compass, the Ship, the Labyrinth, and the Mirror in the mansion of the Second, and so on and so forth, naming all those she had studied over and over as a child at her father's feet. The Immortal Dragon circled the pole to the north, the seven stars of its serpentine body the Seven Immortals of Reason, keeping watch on the march of life on earth. Her father was an astrologer, but their peoples had ever been star worshippers, ever since they first set eyes upon the night sky. She had walked him back to the Tenno homestead after his fit had broken, falling into a peaceful sleep for the first time in his life.

A soft glow illuminated the glade around her. "There you are," said the Guardian of Fire, riding up on Sajah's back and holding up one of the crystals from the Vale of Eternity. "I was worried about you."

Ami roused herself as Zhara and the Lion of the South approached. "I'm fine," she said.

"Are you?" The other girl dismounted and sat at Ami's feet, tucking her knees up to her chest. "Because you don't seem fine."

"How can you tell?" Ami looked down at herself, wondering what about her had given away the turmoil she was feeling inside. "Am I showing it somehow?"

Sajah huffed and settled down beside Zhara. "No, not so much." The Guardian of Fire laid a gentle hand on Ami's leg. "But that's what worries me sometimes."

"Why?"

"Because," Zhara said, "it does no good to bottle up your emotions inside. You can tell me how you feel, Ami. There's no shame in that."

"Isn't there?" Ami thought of her father, of how much of a burden he had sometimes felt with his emotional needs. She both resented him and regretted her resentment of him, knowing how much care he needed. "I have to be strong."

"A single reed is easily snapped, but a bundle of reeds can withstand the force of thousands."

Ami frowned. "I don't follow." She shifted on her seat. "I'm not very good with figurative language, sorry."

Zhara sighed. "What I mean is that it's easier to talk about feelings sometimes, to share the weight and burden with friends."

"Why do friends tell each other what they feel?" Ami said. "I don't really like to talk about my feelings. It makes me feel . . . odd. Eccentric. It's like my feelings are wrong, or grow against the grain from everyone else's in the world, and it's a burden to others."

Zhara considered this, turning the glowing crystal in her hand over and over. "Your feelings aren't odd, Ami. It's just that you feel things so much and you are so aware of them in ways that the rest of us are too self-conscious to even think about."

No one had ever told her she was too aware before. If anything, most people seemed to think she was too obtuse, too esoteric. Ami curled and uncurled her fingers, wishing she had a crystal to fiddle with as well. She didn't always like being in her body, the too-muchness of her flesh, her feelings, her form. The sensations around her were sometimes too much, and she often needed a distraction to hold her focus. To be present. As though sensing this, Zhara wordlessly handed her the stone, which glowed beneath Ami's touch as well.

"I think," Ami said after a while, "I think too much."

Zhara laughed. "You do, but that's all right. It's charming."

Charming. That was the first time anyone had ever called her that. Some of the tightness in her chest eased with the warmth that blossomed there. The girls sat in silence together, with Sajah keeping watch, and Ami could sense Zhara waiting for her to open up.

"I don't know how to talk," Ami said. "What do you talk about?"

"Whatever you want." Zhara studied her face. "Can I ask," she said slowly, "if you like Beast?"

It was a moment before Ami remembered she was speaking of Gaden. "Why do you call them Beast?" she asked.

Zhara seemed surprised. "Because that was how they introduced themself to me."

"But you know their name. You've heard me use it several times."

"Yes." Zhara pulled her mass of dark wavy hair over her shoulder to braid it. Ami watched the strands twine together, feeling soothed by the repetitive motions. "But they never gave it directly to me. It would feel presumptuous to use it without express permission."

Permission. All at once her irritation and her discomfort at the revelation that Gaden was the Star of Radiance rose up again like bile in her throat, and the tightness in her chest returned. It felt curiously like the tightness she felt whenever she remembered the pleasure of that kiss they shared beneath the caverns of Mount Llangposa, only now it was complicated and muddied by betrayal. Had they compelled her to kiss them? She *had* felt compelled in that cave, she had felt that gravity between them, the sensation of falling slowly toward inevitability just before their lips met. She had wanted to press her lips to theirs, wanted so badly the desire felt almost outside herself. Almost. She gripped the crystal tightly in her hand.

"I . . . don't know if I like Gaden," she said in response to Zhara's earlier question. "I thought I did."

"What changed?" the Guardian of Fire asked softly.

"They are the Wielder of the Star of Radiance."

Zhara frowned. "Why does that matter?"

Ami laughed without mirth. "Why does it matter? You know what the Star of Radiance does."

The other girl took the enchanted stone back from Ami. "Yes, but now that we know Beast is the Wielder of the Star, we stand a better chance to win our war against chaos. We need them, Ami. I don't understand why that's a bad thing."

"That's not it," Ami said in frustration. She wished she had her fragments of *Songs of Order and Chaos* with her to show the passage to her friend. "The people donated a single drop of will to the Sunburst Warrior, who gathered it with the consent of the governed to fight back the hordes of chaos. Remember? The Star of Radiance is concentrated willpower. It can compel us to do things."

Zhara gave her a wry smile. "Not all of us have your prodigious memory for text." Then she sobered. "And you think Beast somehow compelled your feelings for them?"

"Yes." Ami nervously picked at her fingernails. "No. I don't know."

Zhara got to her feet. "It's a dangerous power, to be sure," she said thoughtfully. "But perhaps Beast didn't fully understand what their power could do. Not until recently."

"They still should have told us."

"Yes," she agreed. "But sometimes we keep things to ourselves because we feel they are a burden to others. And sometimes we have to wait until we are ready before we can speak."

Ami could hear the echo of her feelings expressed by Zhara's words. She did not want to feel sympathy with Gaden in that moment; she wanted to linger in her anger because it was easier to understand. Safer.

Zhara tilted her head. "Haven't you ever kept a secret from someone because you weren't ready to tell them yet?"

"Never," Ami said decisively. "It would have been akin to a lie. And I don't like lying."

"Truly? You've never had to hide your magic from people?"

Ami blinked, shading her eyes from the light of the crystal in Zhara's hand. "That's different."

"How so?"

"I was doing it to keep myself safe. And it wasn't hurting anyone." But then she thought of the night she and her father fled Zanhei Palace all those years ago, the night the Chancellor discovered the Royal Consort was a magician. She was the reason Han's mother was dead. And she had never told him. Ami opened her mouth to confess to Zhara, then shut it again. Zhara was not the person with whom she had to make things right. It was her cousin. Doubt cooled the anger in her body.

But Zhara's searching gaze did not miss Ami's change in posture. "You've remembered something, haven't you?"

"Yes." She did not elaborate. The anger she had clung to as protection from feeling the full brunt of her emotions dissipated, leaving her exposed and vulnerable. Ami hunched in on herself, wanting the sensation to go away. Sajah curled up his enormous bulk against her side, and she drew strength from his furry presence.

"You don't have to tell me," Zhara said kindly. "Only remember that none of us are perfect. Here." She handed the crystal to Ami.

"What's this for?"

"I want you to have it. I gave the others I had to Beast and Han. They can't make it light up without magic, but in the presence of demonic energies, it goes black."

Ami examined the stone more closely then. It resembled unpolished clear quartz and the light it gave off seemed to originate from its depths. She removed her spectacles. It looked the same with her ordinary eyes and through her enchanted vision. "Magical ki made stone," she murmured. She tucked the crystal into her sash. "What is everyone going to do now?" she asked.

Zhara looked troubled. "Pang Lok and a handful of the Heralds of Glorious Justice are going to try to march on the imperial city, gathering other supporters along the way."

"That's a terrible idea," Ami said.

"I know, but there's really nothing we can do to stop them. I think we should go back to Kalantze and find some way to seal the portal at the Pillar. You're certain you felt it there?"

Ami nodded. "There's an . . . emptiness at the heart of that tree. A nothing so deep as to almost have a presence of its own."

"That definitely sounds like a demon portal," Zhara said ruefully.

"How did you seal the one at Mount Zanhei?"

The other girl bit her lip. "To be honest . . . I'm not sure. It all felt like a fever dream. But maybe there will be something in *Songs of Order and Chaos* that can help us."

Ami was about to rise to her feet when the thundering patter of hooves interrupted her. Sajah gave a warning rumble. "What was that?"

There was a bright flash of light, and the girls turned to find Rinqi, the Unicorn of the West, with an unconscious Han on her back.

"Han!" Zhara cried, running to his side. Rinqi knelt beside her, allowing the boy to gently slide onto the ground.

Ami jumped to her feet. "Is he alive?"

"Yes," Zhara said, and the relief was nearly palpable in her voice. "There is a pulse. Han," she said, gently patting his cheek. "Han, wake up."

Ami's cousin stirred and groaned. "Gaden," he croaked, sitting up with another groan. "Gaden——"

"Shush," Zhara soothed. "Don't overwork yourself. What happened?"

Han's hand went to his jaw. "Dzenar," he said. "The old castle librarian——"

"Zerdan?" Ami asked incredulously.

He shook his head. "He said his name was Dzenar. Don't you remember? The story Tenno Grandmother told us about the shaman who——" He cut himself off. "Gaden!" he gasped. "He took Gaden!"

"Slow down," Zhara said. "Who took Gaden?"

"A demon," Han said grimly. "He called himself the bug demon of something and something."

Ami went cold. "The Locust Demon of Scarcity and Starvation?"

"One of the Lords of Tiyok," Zhara said in shock. "Are you sure?"

Han nodded. "He did something to Gaden. He took hold of the dead flesh of the scars on their body and manipulated them somehow. They punched me." He rubbed the darkening bruise along his jaw. "I don't remember anything after that."

Ami felt the blood drain from her face. "The Star of Radiance is the only thing that can bind the Mother of Ten Thousand Demons back into her realm," she said. "And if the demon took Gaden, then there's only one place they could have gone." She thought of the Pillar, and knew Zhara was thinking the same.

The Guardian of Fire was grim. "Kalantze."

37

BY ALL ACCOUNTS, RETURNING TO KALANTZE SHOULD have been a homecoming of sorts, except for three things:

One, the last time Zhara had been there, Castle Dzong had been overrun by abominations and the undead.

Two, she didn't know what had happened to those who couldn't escape the village after that.

Three, therefore there was a high likelihood that the entire village of Kalantze was now overrun with abominations and the undead.

The third assumption was proved to be correct the closer Zhara and her party drew to the village. They had not encountered any revenants along the way; indeed, they had barely encountered any life at all. All the incense plants and crops had turned into that strange rocklike coral, and all the wildlife had moved on in search of better pastures. The entire world was eerily silent, empty of the calls of birds of prey or even the locusts singing their sad song of autumn's end. The homes of Kalantze stood empty, the gates to the paddocks left open and unlocked. Laundry hung from drying lines, the clothes turned ragged by the elements. The streets had not been flushed for several days, perhaps even weeks, and the reek of death and shit was sharp and acrid. The insides of Zhara's nostrils burned and she buried her face in Sajah's lightning-and-petrichor-scented mane.

"How are we going to get to the Pillar from here?" she asked in dismay, surveying the carnage around them. "And Beast?"

"Carefully?" Han asked.

"There are only two entries into Castle Dzong from here," said Okonwe. "One from the catacombs, and the other through the 888

Steps of Meditation." The former captain of the guard studied the lonely hill from their vantage point on the plains.

"Surely the catacombs are the safest?" Zhara suggested.

"Even if someone could show us where the entrance was hidden, those catacombs are a labyrinth," Okonwe said grimly. "You could easily get lost and wander among the bones until you turned into a skeleton yourself."

Zhara made a face at the gruesome image. "So you're saying the only option is to assail the village itself?" She took stock of their numbers: thirty-four survivors of the original undead attack on the Heralds' camp had agreed to come with them to try to retake Kalantze instead of following Pang Lok to the imperial city. Each of the volunteers was a seasoned warrior—both in battle magic and with weapons—but none of them knew just what obstacles they would encounter in the village. "Do we have enough forces to get through?"

"With the Guardians of Fire and Wood, not to mention the might of the Lion of the South and the Unicorn of the West, I think we might have a fighting chance," the former captain said drily.

Zhara's fingers twitched. Although she was coming to better understand her Guardian powers, having to face an entire horde of both the undead and the abominations still seemed a greater task than what she could handle. She looked to Ami and Han, the two of them gazing at her with such trust her heart felt both heavy and light with the weight of their belief that she could lead them. In her moment of doubt, she felt as though it were a duty thrust upon her and wished someone else could take responsibility instead.

But no. Of them all, it was she who had faced down a greater demon before, she who had even faced an incarnation of Tiyok. Of them all, it made sense for her to take the lead. Only . . . she wasn't sure how. She was no battlefield general; she was still just an apothecary's assistant from the Pits of Zanhei with a love of romance novels, still just an ordinary girl as much as an extraordinary one.

"Do you think we can draw the undead and abominations out here?" Han asked. "To give the girls a better chance of entering the castle?"

"I don't know if they have the presence of mind to think for themselves anymore," Ami said darkly.

Zhara turned her focus back to Grombo Hill. Although she knew little of fighting tactics, she knew that the position of the monastery rendered it nearly impregnable due to its isolated location. Although they wouldn't be facing an intelligent horde who could pick them off one by one, there would be no way they could overwhelm the village through sheer numbers alone. "We need to be strategic about it," she said. "There's no point in wasting our strength fending off the undead and abominations one by one if we have nothing left to defeat the demon and seal the portal. Stealth is our best option, and I think it's best we try the catacombs anyway."

"If you say so, Guardian of Fire," said Okonwe dubiously. "I'll send scouts to find the entrance."

"I still think we need some sort of diversion," Han said. "Find some way to lure the enemy out onto the open field. We won't need all of us to enter the castle—just Zhara and Ami and a small force to guard and watch their backs."

"Will you be able to handle it?" Zhara asked the former captain.

The old soldier gave her a grim smile. "All of us were around for the Just War," he said. "And many of us were fighting monsters long before you children were born. Give us some credit, Guardian of Fire. We are not entirely helpless."

"Then let me give you what I can," she said. "Hand me your weapon."

Bemused, Okonwe handed her the ax he wore slung on his back. The weapon was much heavier than she expected, and she nearly dropped it, almost taking off her foot in the process. Closing her eyes, Zhara concentrated, calling on the fire that was her soul. Feeling along the ki of the ax in her hand, she imbued it with a touch of her transformative magic before returning it to the big man.

"I put a bit of my power in your blade," she said. "I don't know if it's enough to transform any abominations you encounter back into magicians, but hopefully it will be enough to slow them down."

Okonwe nodded in approval. "What of the undead?" he asked.

Zhara looked to Ami, who shook her head. "I can't enchant things like you," she said. "I can only give life where there is none, remember?"

Ideas began forming in Zhara's head. "Wait," she said. "Do you remember the fossil warriors we came across in the Vale of Eternity?"

Ami screwed up her face with distaste. "As if I could forget."

"I think I've found a way to bolster our numbers."

···᠅᠅᠅···

The next morning, they were ready. Or as ready as Zhara felt they could be based on her limited knowledge and abilities. Thirty-four warriors had become at least two hundred, although the vast majority of them were made of mud and dirt. Zhara and Ami had spent the night arming their forces for battle—Zhara by enchanting their weapons with her fire, Ami by bestowing a drop of life into each mud soldier the others had made. Their new forces were crude—a torso with arms and legs—with nothing but a bundle of branches and barley stalks as the barest suggestion of a head. But they each held an even cruder weapon in their hands, enchanted from the rocks and twigs Zhara had found, and could be directed by one of the Heralds of Glorious Justice to fight at their behest. She had also distributed the last of the crystals she had taken from the Vale of Eternity to some of the magicians, who made them light with their power.

"It will have to do," Zhara said. She worried it wasn't enough.

"Zhara," Han said softly. "Remember our purpose."

"To rescue Beast and to seal the portal at the Pillar," she said. It was a refrain she had repeated often enough through the night when she felt like fretting over the responsibility of having so many lives depending on her. "I know. It's just . . ."

"I know," Han replied gently. "But you have to trust them, and trust yourself that you have done enough. They each know what they came for. They each believe in the cause. And that gives them the strength to fight."

"Mugung restoration?" she asked in confusion.

He laughed. "No. Restoring order to the Morning Realms. They've just come around to our side of thinking about it, not Pang Lok's."

"I don't want anyone to die."

"None of us want anyone to die," he said. "But sometimes, that is the way of war."

War. The word sent a shudder down Zhara's spine. They were at war, whether they wanted it or not. Against demons, against Tiyok, and against the forces of chaos that threatened the balance of the world. She could feel Han's gaze on her face as she looked out over the Heralds and their mud soldiers. It was so strange; just a few weeks ago she had been so against them and their tactics, but on the eve of battle, they were just people she had come to know. They were parents and siblings and friends and lovers, and none of them deserved to die, no matter the differences between them as to methods of revolution. Han was right; they still believed in the same cause.

"They'll be fine," he said. "Sajah and Rinqi will be fighting with them."

There was a sudden liquid cry, clear as a bell, like a dewdrop pinging against glass. Han and Zhara looked up to see a sinuous white shape, circling around and around, growing larger and larger as it resolved into a four-winged bird. "Temur?" she asked incredulously as the Eagle of the North landed with a gentle flutter beside them.

The giant white raptor chimera bowed her head.

"Is Yuli all right?"

Temur bobbed her head again, both in affirmation and in annoyance.

"Have you come to fight with us?"

Another nod.

Zhara's heart lifted. Although Yuli could not be with them in either person or literal spirit, her presence was with them nonetheless. "Thank you," she whispered to Temur, tentatively scratching her beak. The Eagle's eyes slid half-shut with pleasure, her four wings beating with affection. "Keep them safe," she said, meaning Sajah and Rinqi. "I know you are all celestial beings, but . . . keep safe."

Temur huffed her wings and butted her head against Zhara's, nearly knocking her over. She laughed, and she swore she could almost hear Yuli's voice in her mind.

Southern softies, the lot of you.

Presently, the scouts came from searching for the entrance to the catacombs. "We are ready you when you are, Guardian of Fire."

Zhara, Ami, and Han would be escorted to the catacombs by a handful of Heralds acting as their guard. Okonwe drew up behind them. He was staying with the Heralds to fight on the battlefield, and Zhara felt a sharp stab of fear that she would never see him again. No, it would do no good to dwell on her anxiety. She could only move forward.

"One step at a time," she murmured.

The old soldier inclined his head. "One step at a time," he repeated. "Are you ready?"

She was not ready. But she would never be ready.

"Yes."

Okonwe had been right.

The catacombs beneath the castle were a labyrinth, and Zhara was afraid they were lost. As far as she could tell, the tunnel system beneath Grombo Hill consisted of one main channel, with several small pathways branching off into darkness and the unknown, but she wasn't entirely sure they hadn't just been going around in circles for the past hour. The entrance to the catacombs had been well-hidden indeed, the ingress so small everyone had to hold their breath to squeeze past. Han had almost gotten stuck again, but he remembered to turn his shoulders sideways at the last minute. They had spent the first several moments crawling around on all fours, and although Zhara was not afraid of enclosed spaces, she had been terrified that they would all be stuck there forever, like rabbits in a warren, with no way to turn around and escape if need be.

But presently, the warren-like tunnels had broadened into a large boulevard-sized space, with a narrow channel of mineral water trickling down the center. Zhara reached into her sash and withdrew her crystal, the catacombs filling with a soft, clear light. Holding the stone up high, she attempted to illuminate the farthest corners with magic, trying to take in as much of her surroundings as she could. The light doubled when Ami pulled out her own stone.

"Where to, Guardian of Fire?" one of the scouts asked. Poche or Botze, Zhara couldn't quite remember.

She glanced left, then right. Both sides curved around and disappeared out of sight, but she thought the path to the left might slope upward a little. She turned to the Guardian at her side. "Left?" she asked. "What do you think, Ami?"

Ami pushed her spectacles farther up the bridge of her nose and squinted at the ceiling above her. "I can't tell," she said softly, "but I feel as though I can see a light to the left." She slid her glasses back down again and tucked her crystal back into her sash, gesturing for Zhara to do the same. She peered over the rims with her ordinary eyes, then pushed the lenses back up. "Can you see it?"

Zhara slipped into her magical vision. All around her the threads were dead, dull, matte—either stone or bone. No life. No magic. No demons. But Ami was right, somewhere to the left, high above them, was a point of clear, bright light. It twinkled almost like a star. The Star of Radiance.

"Beast?" she asked.

"I think so," Ami whispered.

And so they had been traveling left for the past hour or so with what felt like no progress whatsoever. By now, she both hoped and didn't hope that the battle had started outside on the Poha Plain, with Okonwe and the others drawing whatever abominations and undead from the village they could.

"You'd think we would have run into some skeletons or something by now," Han said, sounding almost disappointed.

"The dead are all around us," Ami said. "Their bones are buried in the floors, the walls, and the ceiling." She pointed with her crystal at what Zhara had initially taken to be the roots of some intrepid tree, only to realize that it was the finger bones of a skeletal hand pointing to the left.

"Ugh, never mind," Han said with a shudder. "I shouldn't have asked."

The slope of the tunnel had steepened considerably now, and the company fell silent, conserving their breath as they made their way uphill. Shallow stone steps had been carved into the ground beneath their feet to aid their climb, but soon even the steps grew larger and taller, and they were beginning to crawl hand over hand.

"Is it just me," Han panted, "or is it getting darker the higher we go?"

Zhara glanced at the crystal in her hand. He was right: the light was growing dimmer the more they climbed, and she was suddenly struck with the memory of the Gate of Reckoning in the caves beneath Mount Llangposa, of how the glow in the stone snuffed out entirely in the presence of anti-ki. All the hairs rose along Zhara's arms.

"Watch your step," she said to the others. "We may run into some trouble."

"The castle shouldn't be too far above us," said Poche or Botze. "At the rate we've been ascending, we should be coming up to the summit by now."

The darkness was growing thicker by the moment.

"Does anyone smell that?" Ami asked. "It smells like . . . rot."

Neither Han nor the other members of the guard could sense it, but Zhara thought she could also smell something sickly-sweet with her Guardian senses. But as far as she could see, there was nothing living around them—no flesh left on the bones of the dead to decompose or decay, not even mold or mildew from the constant drip, drip, drip of the water she could hear below them.

The shape of the walls around them also began to change as they continued on their trek. Instead of smooth tunnels, the floor and ceilings warped and rippled, and instead of rock, there was sand and dirt beneath her palms as they climbed. Although the catacombs were not damp, there was a persistent scent of moisture to the air now, which made the breath going in and out of Zhara's lungs less dry and painful.

Ami gave a sharp hiss of surprise. "The walls," she said, looking around her through her enchanted spectacles. "The walls of the cata-combs are held up by the roots of a tree."

"A tree?" Zhara asked. "What sort of tree can grow this far underground?"

"It's the root system of a tree," Ami said.

Through her Guardian eyes, Zhara could see Ami was right. Streaks of the warm light, the light of life, threaded all around them. "But there's only one tree in Castle Dzong," she said in awe.

"The Pillar," Ami whispered. "We are surrounded by the roots of the Pillar."

The portal to Tiyok. "Be on your guard," Zhara warned. Now that she looked closer, she could see the spots of darkness blotting out the light of life within the roots. The crystal in her hand flickered, like a candle flame struggling against a strong breeze. Reaching behind her, she drew her sword from its sheath, which shimmered beneath her touch.

The crystal went black, leaving only what faint light emanated from her blade.

"Um, not to alarm anyone," Han said to her right. "But . . . does anyone hear that?"

There was a soft grinding sound all around them, the sound of a thousand bones vibrating against ancient stone. Above their heads, sand and dirt shuddered and fell as dusty rain, choking and dry.

"Something's moving beneath our feet," Han warned. "Keep watch, it might be—"

An explosion of undead hands burst through the dirt, and Zhara screamed as the catacombs collapsed around them.

38

IT WAS THE ITCH THAT FINALLY WOKE Gaden.

They had been dreaming before, but the dream was muddy, disjointed, strange, more sensation than image. They dreamed of a formless dark cloud with glowing red eyes surrounding them like so much smoke. Everywhere the black mist touched burned, like the Itch but ten thousand times stronger. The aggravating, near-painful tickle was not just in their scars, but everywhere—their hands, their feet, their cheeks, their eyes, and most especially their mind. Gaden was formless and without a body, they could not use their fingers to scratch, to claw, to tear at the Itch, and yet they could feel their physical self somewhere close, somewhere nearby, just out of reach.

They're strong, this one, came a voice that was both their own and not. *And I am not yet recovered enough to take their shape.*

Then they awoke.

It smelled like the library. Dust, mold, mildew, and the faint, sour tang of yak butter tallow candles burning somewhere in the distance. But when they opened their eyes, they did not come to in the library. The space was dimly illuminated by a handful of those yak butter candles lining shallow grooves in the wall of some sort of ancient antechamber without windows or doors that they could see. The Itch had not subsided with the dream; if anything, the sensation was *in* their flesh now, and they were acutely conscious of every part of their body, but especially their wrists and ankles, which were bands of fire.

It wasn't until Gaden tried to get to their feet that they realized they were chained to what appeared to be some sort of stone table. A tomb? Sarcophagus?

They were in the catacombs beneath Castle Dzong.

The stone table seemed to be in the tomb of an ancient leader, one who had lived long before the conversion of the Free Peoples of the West to the faith of the Great Wheel, before they had gotten into the practice of burning their dead. All around them, the walls were painted with murals, most of which were astonishingly well-preserved, as though they had been painted just the day before. At their feet was a portrait of a leonine beast, its mane a wreath of fire, with lightning shooting from its eyes. The Lion of the South. Craning their neck, they saw at their head was a mural of the Eagle of the North, and then the Unicorn of the West and the Dragon of the East on either side. Oriented this way, Gaden tried to work out where they were in relation to the rest of the castle.

Overhead, the antechamber fell away into darkness, the ceiling wrought with what looked like bones . . . and roots. To their amazement, they realized that the entire antechamber they were in was encased by these giant roots, each as thick as the torso of a warrior. What they had taken to be rocks or stone embedded in the living matter were actually blight-growths—their bruise-like color similar to the ones on Gaden's scars.

The Pillar.

They were *beneath* the Pillar.

"Ah, so you're finally awake, child," came a familiar voice. "I was wondering when you'd come to."

Garden stiffened. "Zerdan." To their surprise, the librarian had been standing in the antechamber with them the entire time, hidden by the flickering shadows. "Dzenar."

Zerdan pressed his palms together, fingertips touching his nose as he bowed in what seemed like a tasteless mockery of the clerics in the castle monastery above. "At your service. Well," he said. "I am at someone's service, but it's not yours, I'm afraid."

"Tiyok."

The name thudded in the antechamber. Zerdan shuddered. "I really would rather you not refer to my mother by name," he said primly. "It's awfully rude, you know." He sighed. "I do apologize for all this," the greater demon said. "I really am rather fond of you, insofar as I can be fond of anyone. But I serve a greater mistress than affection, alas."

"What is all this?" Gaden brought their wrists closer to their eyes to examine the material. The manacles felt solid and ordinary to the touch. At first glance they had supposed the bonds to be made of steel, but upon closer examination, Gaden realized they were chains of bone and ivory. They yanked on the chains experimentally, but the bone was as hard as any stone.

"Demonic manacles," Zerdan said, and despite everything, their tone sounded regretful. "I wasn't sure they were going to work on you, to be honest. They dampen the magic of ordinary magicians, but I've not quite tested them on other powers."

"Other powers?" Gaden was confused. "But I'm no magician."

"No," Zerdan said with a smile. "You, my friend, are so much more. You are the Star of Radiance."

The Star of Radiance. Gaden remembered suddenly that the power of the Star could compel even demons to do their bidding. They struggled with their bonds and tried to remember how it felt to use that power on other people. But the only thing they could think of at the moment was the Itch, which was everywhere and nowhere and they wanted to howl with frustration and agony at being unable to relieve it.

"Why am I here?"

"Well," Zerdan said in delight. "After the Guardian of Fire defeated my brother the Frog Demon in Zanhei, we lost a portal for my mother to enter the world. She needs a physical vessel to be present in this plane, much like the rest of us. But no one wants to summon the Mother of Ten Thousand Demons, so we have to do it ourselves. That's where you come in."

"Me." Gaden tried to reconcile the cheerful librarian they had known for most of their life with the knowledge that they were now possessed by a greater demon. One of the Lords of Tiyok. "A vessel for possession."

"Yes," Zerdan said happily. "You're a good candidate, especially since once she's possessed you, she can go on to claim the Sunburst Throne and begin her rule of one thousand years of darkness."

"But I am not a magician. I thought only magicians could be possessed by demons, greater or otherwise."

"Yes, but I have found a workaround for that." Zerdan ran his fingers lovingly over Gaden's scarred left hand. The hand was now almost entirely mottled black and brown, scaly and strange. "See?" With a gesture of his hand, Zerdan caused Gaden to lift their arm, much to their horror. "That's how I got you here," he said. "I walked you here."

"Why not kill me? You can possess the dead."

"Yes, I did consider that." Zerdan tapped his chin thoughtfully. "But the problem with the dead is that they're just empty husks, really. No living ki, therefore no power to manipulate. You have to be alive when my mother possesses you, so that she will be able to wield the Star of Radiance herself. Of course, she will have to prove she is the lost Mugung heir afterward in order to claim the Sunburst Throne, but that is a problem for another day."

A lump rose in Gaden's throat. "So the Mother of Ten Thousand Demons will possess me through my scars." They thought of Lee-Lee's belief in Gaden's destiny to protect the Morning Realms, and would have laughed, if it weren't for the profound emptiness of despair that hollowed their heart.

"Yes." Zerdan beamed. "Brilliant, isn't it? It's not ideal, of course, as there will always be some part of you screaming out from the void."

Gaden shuddered. The irony of their fate was not lost of them; they who could strip the will of others would forever have their own will torn from them, lost to the service of a dark mistress from the chaos realm.

"I truly am sorry about all this," Zerdan said. "I've known you a long time, child. I watched you grow up. That is an odd experience for a demon. We don't grow or change. We just *are*. But that is the unique thing about life, isn't it?" He clenched his fist, twisting the demonic energy in Gaden's scars, and the expression on his face was truly sad. "It ends."

Gaden screamed as Zerdan worked his dark magic. It wasn't pain coursing through them, not physical pain at least. It was agony of a different sort, spiritual, perhaps, a dread so potent it was a force within their body that overtook them. In a dim corner of their still sane mind, they were horrified to see the veins of black spread from their scars into the healthy living skin. They could feel it crawling up their limbs, over their heart, up their neck, over their eye, and into their mind.

Their soul.

Then Gaden was no more.

39

THE DEAD BURST FORTH FROM THE WALLS, their skeletal hands grasping and tearing at any bit of life and flesh they could reach.

"Han!" Zhara cried. "Ami!"

Shouts of surprise and horror rang out all around her as the others found themselves entangled in the bones of the ancient dead. Zhara gave a yelp of terror as fossilized teeth snapped down at the spot her foot had just been. Lashing out with her power, she sent the skull up in a crackle of fire, but bones, like stone, were slower to catch fire and burn. The flaming skull rolled toward her, sending up sparks wherever it went.

"Han!" she called again. "Ami!"

There was a grunt and crash beside her as Han swung out with the enchanted staff he had brought with him, the skeleton he had been grappling with turning black with scorch marks wherever the wood made contact. With a roar and a mighty blow, he sent the revenant flying, shattering into a thousand pieces on the far wall. Then he turned and grabbed her hand, dragging her upward through the rubble.

"This way!" he shouted. "There's open air above!"

Zhara clawed her way out of hell, following a shaft of light that had broken through the ceiling of the catacombs. She didn't know where the other members of their guard had gone—Poche or Botze, Hama, Tse-mao, Junghwan, or Ami. There was a growling sound behind her. The undead were silent: an abomination? But she had no time to turn around and make sure they were all right, for another skeleton dropped down from above her, teeth clacking as it tried to rip out her throat.

Smash! The skeleton burst apart as Han's staff careened through its bones.

"Hurry!" He had made it out of the catacombs and was leaning down through an enormous hole, reaching out for her hand. Behind and above him, the skies were blue and clear. "Jump!"

Shoving the remains of the rattling dead aside, Zhara sheathed her sword and scrambled to her feet and took off at a run, crying out with the pain of a twisted ankle. Ignoring it, she found her footing on the edge of a stone and leaped into the air. Han's fingers just brushed hers before they slipped through his grasp and she was plummeting, right before she was stopped by a tremendous force about her torso. The sword. Han had managed to grab her sword and was hauling her over the lip. They collapsed onto the smooth cobblestones of Castle Dzong's courtyard.

The growling had grown louder.

Below them was a snarl and a snap and then enormous claws burst through the shattered courtyard a few feet away from where they lay, followed by the slither of a slimy coil. Another explosion to Zhara's left, then another behind her as more tentacles erupted all around them, the seeking, searching arms of an abomination from the depths. Hama? Tse-mao? They were magicians and they could have been infected by the undead, but Zhara couldn't think about that, couldn't do anything but throw herself to one side as the nearest tentacle came smashing down a hairsbreadth from where she had been.

"The sword! The sword!" Han swung blindly at what he could see of the creature, his staff sparking and sending up plumes of stinking smoke where it struck the slimy skin. "Draw your sword!"

Zhara pulled the sword free of its scabbard with a ring, and it blazed to life beneath her hand. With a wild cry, she brandished her blade and cut through the nearest tentacle, spattering herself with hot, reeking blood. Some of it landed on her mouth and she tried not to gag at the taste—foul and rotten. The momentum of her swing had sent her flying, and she tumbled to the ground as shrieks of pain rose from the catacomb, a high-pitched whistle that faded to nothing as the coils slithering around them shriveled to nothing.

"If we survive this," Han gasped, "we are definitely having those fighting lessons."

They had a moment to catch their breath, but the commotion had roused the remaining inhabitants of the castle. The stench of spoiled meat filled the air and there was a shuffling, scraping sound as myriad torn and broken hands and feet crawled down the stairs of the castle to the courtyard. The undead clerics and clerics-turned-monsters.

"The Pillar!" Han cried. "You've got to seal the Pillar!"

The tree of life stood in the center of the courtyard as it always had, its crown now entirely white with blossoms. The sweet scent of osmanthus perfumed the air as Zhara drew close, gasping down gulps of freshness to get away from the vile reek of decomposing flesh. She tossed Han her blade and placed her hands on the trunk of the Pillar, falling into her Guardian form.

She went up in flames.

Beneath her touch, she could instantly sense the anti-ki at the heart of the Pillar, that portal to the realm of demons that was open and leaking infection into the world. Down and down and down she went with her power, searching out every bit of blight she could find and cauterizing it with her fire. She remembered all the times she had transformed the ki of a magician from that of chaos back into order—Thanh, Yao, Taeri—and concentrated, pushing her power through the roots of the tree of life.

But the tree of life was dead.

For every spot of darkness she could seal, another opened up in its flesh, the dead matter of its body vulnerable to the demonic influence of the Locust Demon unleashed on the world.

"It's not working!" she cried.

Ami, Ami, where was Ami? *The ability to give life where there was none.* She needed the Guardian of Wood to help her seal the portal, to push away death so Zhara could transform the tree's living ki. Down and down and down beneath the catacombs, Zhara followed with her magic the roots of the Pillar that reached deep beneath the foundations of Castle Dzong. Through its dying tips she could sense the world with her power, and in her mind, she thought she could see a faint green-gold figure near a clear, bright light.

"Ami," she gasped. "Beast!"

But they were far beyond reach, and she was alone.

40

THE GROUND GAVE WAY AND AMI WAS FALLING.

"Zharaaaaaaaaaaaaaa!" she screamed, flailing for something, anything to slow her down and break her fall. Her hands brushed roots and rock, fingernails scraping ineffectually at nothing.

Thud!

The landing knocked the wind from her lungs. There was the sound of tumbling rock and stone, the patter of pebbles as they rained down around her. She tried to move, tried to curl up into a ball to protect herself, but it was as though an iron band had squeezed her ribs, and she was unable to draw breath. She rolled over onto her side and coughed, retching up dust and dirt.

"Zhara!" she croaked. "Han!"

But there was no reply. Presently, as the unbearable pressure about her lungs began to lift, Ami sat up and took stock of herself. She appeared to have escaped mostly unscathed from her fall, save for a few scrapes and bruises, although she'd lost the crystal Zhara had given her for light. Out of habit, she reached for a brush tucked into her sash, but there was nothing; she appeared to have lost that as well. She was alone, weaponless, and lost.

"Zhara?" Ami tried again, choking on dust. "Han?"

Nothing, not even an echo. She thought of Mount Llangposa falling down around them in the middle of that blizzard as they ascended the slopes and remembered the absolute certainty that she would die there trapped under several tons of stone. But she was not buried in rock now; in fact, she seemed to have fallen into a chamber of decent size.

She could stretch her arms and legs, but more important, she could breathe, even if the air stank of spoilage.

No, the reek was not in her nostrils, but in her magic. Ami shuddered.

Demons.

"Zhara?" she called, even though she did not expect a response. She thought of the voice that had saved her at Mount Llangposa, the sensation that it had come from within somehow, and wished she could hear it again, if only to stave off the fear that threatened to choke her.

Come back to me, she thought to the voice. In her mind's eye, she imagined calling out to Gaden. *Come back to me,* she thought. *Wherever you are, come back.*

But no one replied. Not even the demons.

Ami could feel the void all around her, pressing in on all her senses, both physical and magical. She felt numb all over, as though someone had placed an enormous blanket of silence over her magic, and everything was muffled. But despite the dampening sensation, to her surprise, the chamber into which she had fallen was not pitch-black. There was a faint golden glow coming from somewhere to her right, scarcely illuminating the space she was in. As her eyes adjusted to the darkness, she could see a set of stairs to her left beside her leading up in a spiral above her head, disappearing entirely into black. She pushed at the bridge of her nose, only to discover her enchanted spectacles were no longer there either.

Squinting, Ami followed the source of the light. It seemed to be coming through a crack at the bottom of the far wall from where she stood. A door? There seemed to be a seam on one edge, where more light escaped. Tracing the crack with her fingertips, she thought she could feel a faint breeze coming from the other side. She gave a look over her shoulder at the spiral stairs disappearing into darkness, then decided to follow the light instead. Giving the wall an experimental push, she was astonished when it gave way. Slowly but surely, the door slid open, revealing a room surrounded by candles. Blinking as her eyes adjusted to the light, Ami slowly became aware of enormous tree roots snaking down through the stone to encircle an antechamber painted with murals on four sides. The Pillar. Any other tree would have eroded the foundations of Castle Dzong, but Ami had the sensation that the Pillar was embracing the building, supporting it, keeping it from collapsing in on the dead below.

In the center of the antechamber was a sarcophagus. And on top of the sarcophagus lay the prone, still body of the Beast of Kalantze.

"Gaden!" She ran to their side, grabbing their wrist before falling away with a cry, her fingers tingling with numbness. "Gaden!"

"It's no use, child," came a voice from behind her. "They won't wake."

Ami whirled around find the librarian of Castle Dzong—no, the Locust Demon of Scarcity and Starvation—standing behind her. His bright eyes twinkled at her in the dim, flickering lights of the yak butter candles, and if it weren't for the void she could sense within him, whirling like a maelstrom, she could almost believe he was harmless— tiny, shriveled, and wrinkled as he was. "You," she breathed.

"Me," the demon agreed. As he stepped closer into the light, his form seemed to ripple and change, and Ami thought she could just make out another shape beneath his skin, trembling and pulsing like a moth about to emerge from its cocoon. She shuddered with revulsion. "And you. Although I am a bit disappointed not be to facing the Guardian of Fire. I had hoped for a bit of a challenge. I did not expect an ordinary magician to come to the Beast's rescue."

Ami blinked. Could it be possible the demon did not know who she truly was? Could Zerdan not sense the ki of the Guardian of Wood within her, the way she could now sense his demonic self? If so, that could be to her advantage.

"Zhara has more important matters to attend to," she said. "Like sealing the portal to Tiyok at the Pillar."

"Oh?" Zerdan—Dzenar—laughed. "Is that so? Then I'm afraid she's got quite a challenge ahead of her."

A cold trickle of dread dripped down Ami's spine. "How so?"

The demon waved his hand dismissively. "Her powers, however impressive, are no match for mine. The Guardian of Fire may be able to transform ki from one essence to another, she cannot give life where there is none. And as long as the Pillar remains dead, I will continue to mold its matter to my liking."

The power to give life where there is none. The power of the Guardian of Wood. Ami's power. "The Pillar is dead?" she asked.

"Undead, if you will," Dzenar said. "It is my particular gift."

The Locust Demon of Scarcity and Starvation was her ancient nemesis, and now Ami understood why. His abilities were a corrupted mirror to her own. Their powers were like the *taikhut,* the dark and the light side of the same gift. Life and death. Order and chaos.

"Is that what you've done to Gaden?" she demanded, looking down at their body, lying so still and lifeless on the slab. "Have you killed them?"

"Me? No, my mother needs them alive." The demon peered at her, his enormous eyes seeming to grow bigger and more buglike by the second. He approached her, arms tucked and back hunched. "But I will admit the temptation to kill them is growing greater by the second. It would be easier to control them if they were dead."

"Why control them at all?" she asked. "Why did you kidnap them and bring them here?"

The little librarian studied her, his enormous eyes seeming even bigger in his wizened face than before. "The Star of Radiance is one of the few forces in this world that could seal my mother back into her realm, and I can't let the Beast use their power on her," he said. "So they're in my safekeeping at the moment. Don't worry," he said, and in a strange way, Ami thought he meant to sound reassuring. "They won't come to any harm. Or at least, their body won't. I'm not entirely sure what will happen to their soul, though."

"What do you mean?"

"You know, I've never known what happens to a soul once a demon possesses a living body," Dzenar said, sounding almost jealous. "One of my siblings, the Frog Demon, could possess magicians and turn them into monsters, and one of my others, the Moth Demon, can displace the ki of the living. Me? I can only control the dead, so I have had to work around that a bit by infecting the dead flesh of the Beast's scars. It is," he said petulantly, "all rather taxing, but useful, since not even the Guardian of Fire can counter my power."

No, but Ami could. The dead flesh of Gaden's scars. If she could touch them, if she could heal those scars on their body and push the corruption away—

"Now, now," the demon tsked. "I can see a clever mind working behind those beautiful eyes of yours. You're going to try something, aren't you? Well, let me assure you it won't work, whatever you're thinking. Only the Guardian of Wood can counter my power and seal the portal to Tiyok."

Ami went still. "How?" she asked. "How would the Guardian of Wood be able to seal the portal?"

The little librarian scratched at his arm. A large chunk of skin flaked off and floated to the ground like a giant dust mote. Ami shuddered as she thought she could see the shine of beetle-black through the patch on his wrist. It was as though he was molting. "By bringing the Pillar back to life, of course," he said. He wriggled his fingers. "I can't manipulate the living, as you know. Alas."

She looked around the chamber. They were surrounded by the roots of the Pillar. If she could just get to them without alerting the demon to her intentions, if she could just get her hands on—

"Hold a moment." Dzenar began approaching her. With every step, his physical form seemed to shrink, but his presence loomed even larger than ever. She could feel the noxious aura emanating from the demon, smothering and choking, searching for the ki at the heart of her. "I recognize you."

Her power writhed in response, threatening to reveal her true identity. *Hide your light.* She had to hide her light. Keep it lying in wait, and if the demon got close enough, she would lash out.

Ami slowly backed up toward the western wall. "Of course you do," she said. "We've met before, when Gaden hired me to translate some texts in the library. You told me about the *taikhut*."

"Ah yes." Even more wrinkles sprouted over the librarian's skin, and his flesh seemed to collapse on itself, and another pair of arms emerged from his midsection. "I do remember that, but no." Each eye blinked independently of the other as Dzenar squinted at her. "But no . . . I *know* you. Your soul . . ." He trailed off and those buglike eyes widened impossibly large. ". . . has been reborn." He sucked in a sharp breath. "Guardian of Wood."

At that moment, Ami leaped forward to grab those grasshopper-like limbs, but the demon knocked her aside.

"No," Dzenar said again. "Nice try, Guardian of Wood. But I know how to counter you."

Gaden rose from the table.

Their arms and legs moved jerkily, stiff and unnatural. A puppet manipulated by undead strings. One shuffle step forward, and another, hands outstretched, fingertips curled into claws, reaching for Ami's neck.

"Gaden!" she cried out, but the words were cut short by the pressure on her throat.

Gaden's eyes were blank, their features slack, empty of any expression. They were alive, but the stillness of their face made it feel as though she were staring into the face of death. As though the soul she knew were gone.

"Gaden," she choked out. "Please . . ."

But there was no reaction, and like the undead, it was their silence that was the most uncanny. She grabbed their wrists and managed to prize their grip off her neck, throwing herself to the side to avoid their next attack.

"Fight me," taunted the demon. "Take control of the Beast's body. You can do it, Guardian of Wood; we can make their flesh our battleground. Let us see who is stronger."

She thought of the times she had mingled her power with others, the times she had overtaken another's ki with her own, and was overcome with sudden, sharp revulsion. She couldn't do it; she couldn't usurp Gaden's will with her own. Gaden was not like the mindless mud soldiers she had created for the Heralds of Glorious Justice; they were a person with their own thoughts and desires. It was a violation. Casting about desperately for some sort of makeshift weapon, her glance fell on the columns of yak butter candles. She ducked out of the way just as Gaden lunged toward her, toppling the candles over and sending the molten wax spilling all over the ground. Calling upon her power, she reached out with her hands, sending her gift through the melted butter. Life blazed through the candle matter, and shapeless forms pulled themselves out of the mass. The candle soldiers swarmed Gaden's feet as they lurched toward her again, cooling again immediately into hardened, solid lumps. Gaden struggled against the morass of melted butter but was held fast.

"Clever," Dzenar remarked. "But limited. You could do so much more with your power. When I last knew you, you were in the prime of your glory. You could command the very earth to dance. But I have a few tricks up my sleeve too."

Thud! Boom!

The chamber shuddered, sending dust and dirt cascading down from the ceiling. The roots of the Pillar were quivering, shaking, ripping, tearing themselves from the stone to writhe all around them. Dzenar lifted his hands, then brought them down with a sharp gesture, the points of the roots turned sharp and stabbing. Ami threw up her arms against the attack, pulling an armor of rocks around her. The roots burst through the stone, coiling and wrapping around her neck, choking her, dampening her magic. The void was pressing against every part of her—her eyes, her mouth, her nose, her ears, crawling into her body, draining her power away. She was tired, so tired, she couldn't think, she couldn't move, she was trapped. Unbidden, her eyes went to Gaden, who had managed to work their feet free.

"Gaden," she tried again. "Help me."

They rushed her, hands digging into her collarbones. Her fingers scrabbled at theirs, trying to pry them loose. The give and press of their flesh contrasted with the dead wood strangling her, and she was overwhelmed by the sensations. Rough, soft, hard, yielding. She couldn't breathe, and she didn't know if she was struggling with her body or with her magic. The touch of their skin against hers, of *life* in their bones, kept the worst of the demonic energy at bay, and she stared into Gaden's unseeing eyes, begging, wishing, reaching with her power for the person she knew was trapped inside. She thought of the shining heart of them, the Star of Radiance, and thought of the voice within her that had called her out of the rockfall back at Mount Llangposa.

"Gaden." Ami coughed. "Come back to me . . ."

They paused.

"Gaden," she said again, and this time she reached for the brightness within them with her power. "You can fight this." It felt as though she were reaching for them on the other side of a chasm, if she could stretch just a little bit farther, a little bit harder, she could just brush their fingertips with hers. She could see that light within, the glow of the Star of Radiance, and she could just about touch it . . .

The pressure in Gaden's hands lifted ever so slightly. For a moment, she felt their ki, felt *them*—their candor, their kindness, their temper. *This is not who you are,* she thought. *You know who you are.*

She had a grasp on them. A grasp on their soul. Ami kept her eyes on Gaden's, as slowly, light returned to their gaze, as the power of the Star of Radiance reached back to twine with hers.

A single drop of will from every person in the Morning Realms, she thought. *But beneath that power is* you. *Your will. Your soul. Your own destiny. I see you.*

A sudden rush of air into her lungs as Gaden backed away. "Yes," she breathed, voice hoarse. "I see you. Come back to—"

She choked as the dead roots of the Pillar slithered and tightened about her neck. At once her connection to her magic was severed, and that unsettling numbness fell over her again.

"Interesting," said Dzenar, observing the proceedings with a tilt of his head. "You are stronger than I thought."

She almost had them. She had almost called Gaden back from the dark, from the grips of Dzenar's demonic possession. Tears leaked from her eyes as stars burst on the edges of her vision, blackness filling her gaze. Ami kept her eyes on Gaden's as Dzenar continued to squeeze the life from her. She lifted her hand and placed her palm on their scarred left cheek. She wanted their face to be the last thing she ever saw. She thought of their kiss beneath the false stars in the cavern at Mount Llangposa.

Please. Please, please, please, she thought to the light in their eyes. *I am asking. I am begging. Yes, please, yes.*

The light in Gaden's eyes brightened, the shadows clearing from their gaze.

Their lips met.

Her power blazed once more as their ki mingled with each other's. And this time, it was Gaden's soul that met hers halfway. The roots wrapped around Ami's arms withered, the stiffness of dead wood becoming pliant, falling away like cut ropes from her limbs and neck.

Dzenar gave a shout of surprise, then clenched his left hand into a fist. Gaden cried out as the scars on their body went black, stumbling back as they struggled against the invading force of the demon's power.

Ami rose to her feet and gathered the fallen roots and vines of the Pillar, slipping her magic into their forms and lashing out. But the roots were heavy and she was tired, so tired. She could feel the encroaching void of the Mother of Ten Thousand Demons making its way through every part of the tree of life, and knew she lacked the will— the power—to drive her back. Slowly, surely, death crept through the Pillar once more, and Ami lost her hold. The roots crawled over her arms and legs, pinning her to the floor.

Ami.

Gaden. Their souls were still connected.

Use your gifts. Use the Star of Radiance. Use me.

Her eyes met theirs again and she felt their permission as a gift.

And she surrendered her own consent.

The force of pure will filled her body, the power of the Star of Radiance, giving her strength.

"No!" Dzenar cried as his hold over Gaden dissipated. With a scream of frustration, he leaped atop them both, grabbing Ami by the hair and pulling her off Gaden. She felt the touch of the demon like heat, like drought, drying up her wellspring of magic. But she was one with Gaden now, her power now working Gaden's limbs, their arms, their hands, their fingers. Together as one. Abandoning her body, she poured herself into Gaden, feeling their soul wrap around hers like a warm embrace.

"Dzenar," she said, and she spoke with Gaden's voice, felt with Gaden's power. "I banish you back to Tiyok."

The Star of Radiance flared from their chest.

The demon howled and buckled in on himself as the combined force of pure willpower and Ami's Guardian gifts struck him. There was the cracking sound of snapping bone and desiccated flesh as the little librarian's transformed body crumpled, crushed like a bug beneath the pressure. The sounds turned grotesque, the squish of guts, the wet squelch of splattered body parts as cosmos flowers burst forth from eyes, ears, and every other orifice. The little librarian was gone.

All around them was a storm of demonic energy being drawn back into the roots of the Pillar, which writhed and wriggled as though in pain.

Seal the portal, Gaden said from within her. Within them.

Ami grabbled one of the flailing roots. Immediately there was an unholy scream in her ears and she felt an ice-cold rush of anti-ki freeze her. The blackness of the void assailed her magical senses and she struggled to maintain hold of herself, of her identity, discrete and whole.

Then she felt the warmth of the Star of Radiance like a spring rain, melting the frost, and beneath that, the warm embrace of Gaden's soul. Her power turned liquid and she flowed through the ki pathways of the Pillar, up and up and up, like a sprout reaching for the sun, leaving life in her wake. She could feel the heat of another power on the other end, a pure burning fire.

Zhara.

Ami!

She met Zhara's magic with hers and Gaden's, green-gold and rose-gold and blinding white together.

You have to bring the Pillar back to life, Zhara said through their connection. *I cannot manipulate the dead. I can only burn corruption from the living.*

Ami knew what she had to do, but she wasn't sure if she had the strength. The Pillar was enormous, but it was not the size of the vessel that frightened her; it was death itself. The vastness of the unknown was bigger than her mind could encompass. She remembered trying to follow her mother down the abyss after Rinqi had died, and was afraid of the enormity on the other side. She had to pour and pour and pour herself into the darkness, and she wasn't sure if she was enough.

You are enough, came a different voice through the bond. Gaden. *And where you are not, I shall be there.*

Closing her eyes, Ami let her Guardian self emerge from the restraints she had placed around her magic her entire life. Her father had told her she had needed to *hide her light,* but she was done with that now. She was no longer a body; she was the Guardian of Wood.

She began pouring her power into the void at the heart of the Pillar, pushing death away with her green-gold glow. Life flourished in the wake of her magical touch, but there was more and more and more and more death to overcome. No bottom, no end. As she explored the edges of the darkness with her light, she was dismayed to discover that she was not enough. Not enough.

And then, all around her, the loving embrace of more life.

Gaden.

She could feel their life force, their ki, entwined with hers, and their gifts were doubled, tripled, quadrupled. Together, they were enough to chase away the shadows, even as the light of Gaden's life was growing fainter with each passing moment.

No, she thought, feeling the strands of Gaden's ki slip through her fingers. *You can't—*

I can, said Gaden. *We must finish this.*

Slowly, surely, they beat back the darkness together. Above them, the Pillar burst into green, shedding its blooms in a shower of white petals. Scaly gray bark took on a rich brown hue, the blight and growths smoothing and disappearing altogether.

The Pillar had returned to life.

Now, Zhara!

Through their magical bond, Ami could see the Guardian of Fire place her hands on the trunk of the Pillar, could see the flames of her power attack the demonic corruption that ran deep. Zhara burned away the dark spots on the fabric of the universe, binding the tears, leaving nothing but light and life and ki behind.

The portal was closed.

And the demon threat was sealed.

It was several long moments before Ami returned to her body.

It felt strange after having been bigger than her physical self while closing the portal at the Pillar, as though she were returning to a well-loved pair of shoes she had not worn in years, only to discover they were still the same size as they had always been. Her arms, her legs, her lips, her shortsighted eyes were all the same as they had been before, but she was now conscious of everything—the feel of her skin, the weight of her tongue in her mouth, the feathery strands of her short hair tickling the back of her neck. The sensations were almost too much, and for a while, Ami simply lay there, trying to readjust to existing.

"Ami," came a weak voice beside her.

Turning her head, she saw Gaden on the ground, collapsed in a similar position of fatigue. Her first thought was simply to lie there, to relieve herself of the burden of will, but she gathered herself together and sat up. She reached for Gaden's hand in hers, but their fingers did not curl to entwine with her own. The corruption had cleared from their scars, and no traces of Dzenar's demonic poison remained, but the rest of their body felt . . . hollow. The soul that she had felt before was faint, flickering, as though spent by the awesome effort it had taken to seal the portal. She remembered the feel of their ki slipping through her fingers and her breath hitched.

Their life was fading.

"No," Ami said, tightening her hand around theirs. "No, no, no, you can't die."

Although the Star of Radiance still glowed steadily in their breast, the light of life was dim within Gaden. Ami wanted to rail at the cruelty that this force, this *thing,* that had enslaved so many people should continue when the person who carried it should die. She wanted to rip the Star of Radiance out of Gaden's chest, but did not know if it was possible without killing them, even if she did know how.

"Please," she whispered again. "Please live."

She could force the issue. She could push her power through their veins, to leave more life in her wake, but to do so would be a betrayal of the very same kind as the one that had put so much distance between them in the first place. She could not compel them when consent did not exist.

"Gaden," she said, her voice breaking. "Gaden, Gaden, Gaden."

Ami got to her hands and knees and crawled closer to them. Gaden's other hand came to cover hers. Their left hand, the one that had been scarred when they had been but a baby, trapped beneath the still-burning rafters of the imperial palace all those years ago. Although it was dim in the catacombs beneath the Pillar, she could see the dark spots of corruption had cleared, leaving a shiny, almost silvery expanse of flesh behind.

"Ami," they said, and their voice was faint, so faint. "I'm sorry."

"Sorry?" she asked. "For what?"

"For kissing you."

She blinked, the haze of tears obscuring her vision. "What?" She thought of the kiss they had shared during their battle with Dzenar, the kiss that had brought her power back to herself. "Why?"

"You asked if I had ever used the Star of Radiance on you," they said, their voice so thin as to be scarcely audible in the dark. "And I have. Once. In the cavern beneath Mount Llangposa. When we—" They coughed. "A second time."

A kiss, she realized. They meant they had stolen a kiss.

"Shush," she said, placing a finger on their lips. "It doesn't matter now."

"But it does." Gaden's lashes fluttered. "I don't want to die without your forgiveness."

Her forgiveness. It felt like a lifetime ago that she had felt so betrayed by their actions. She understood better now the urge, the fear that could drive someone to force others to do their bidding. She wanted to do that now, to grab the threads of Gaden's fading life and thrust them back into their body.

"Shush," she said again. "Don't talk. Save your strength."

"No." The words came a bit more forcefully. "Please. I took from you something to which I had no right."

Beneath her hand on their breast, beneath the bandages that bound their chest flat, she could still sense the awesome power of the Star of Radiance. She had been afraid, so afraid, that they had somehow created her feelings for them with that power. But there was a force greater than that, one that could not be compelled. She knew that now.

"It's all right," she said softly. She knew how the heart of them was pure, how they had never meant to control her. There was the Star of

Radiance, but there was also the soul of Gaden—generous and kind and strong. "I forgive you."

They smiled as their eyes began drifting shut. "Thank you," they murmured, so soft Ami thought she might have imagined it. "May your good deeds return to you thousandfold."

Gaden's hand went limp in hers.

"No." She tightened her fingers. "No, please."

She leaned down and pressed her lips to theirs.

Light blazed at their touch, and once again, Ami had the sensation of standing on the other side of a chasm from Gaden. She thought of her terror that they would fall off the edge of the precipice beneath Mount Llangposa, the realization of the true depth of her affection for them. She had reached out with her power then, only she had not realized it it. She reached out for them now.

And just as it had before, Gaden's ki reached out across the abyss.

Please, and she could no longer tell if the thought was hers, or theirs. *Please.*

As she deepened their kiss, she could feel herself filling the empty places. With Rinqi and with the Pillar, she had been terrified she was not enough to fill the void of death. But with Gaden, she knew she was enough.

Because they met her desire with their own.

As her magic lovingly traced the ki pathways of Gaden's body, she understood the difference between giving life where there was none and asking someone to return from death. Ami felt their lips press against her own, and she closed her eyes, reveling in the sensation.

Yes.

Presently, she opened her eyes to find Gaden's gaze staring at her.

"Ami," they breathed.

"Gaden," she returned. "You . . . you came back."

They lifted their hand and pulled her face even closer to theirs for another kiss.

"Yes." They laughed. She could feel the tears wet upon both their faces. "Of my own free will, I came back."

EPILOGUE

THE DAY DAWNED BITTER AND COLD WHEN Ami finally laid her mother to rest.

It had taken a few weeks to set Kalantze to rights after the battle of the Pillar. Once the portal to Tiyok had been sealed, all the magicians who had turned into abominations returned to their former selves, but the undead were once again lifeless bodies. The Right Hand had spent a good deal of time to gather everyone's heart seeds and send emissaries to their homelands to bury them in the earth of their ancestors. The days had smelled of ash and mud, the smoke from the funeral pyres billowing for miles around them as the first snows of late autumn began to fall.

"What of the harvest?" Ami had asked the barley aunties once they returned. "Will there be enough to get through the winter?"

Auntie Tsong had looked around at the destruction of Kalantze with sorrow. "I think," she said softly, "there will be now."

There was an incalculable loss of life, and it was not life that Ami could return to the people.

Once matters had been settled, the party journeyed back to the Gyasol lands to bury the heart seeds of Li Rinqi and the Qirin Tulku.

"Why the Gyasol lands?" her cousin asked as he and the others helped Ami dig a hole in the hard, frozen earth. "Was your mother a member of the clan?"

Ami looked up to the Gunungs, their peaks casting deep shadows on the plains and valleys below. "No," she said. "But it feels right to bury a new tree of life near the old one."

Gaden rubbed their hands together, blowing warm breath over

their frozen fingertips. "Let's hurry up," they said. "Before it gets dark and any colder."

"You mean it gets colder than this?" Zhara asked miserably. She was so bundled up in leathers and furs that only the barest tip of her nose was visible, red and chapped from the flapping wind.

"It doesn't feel as bad if you relax your muscles and stop fighting the cold," Gaden advised.

Ami met their eyes and they smiled at her, and she felt a compulsion that had nothing to do with the Star of Radiance. She wanted to kiss them.

"Yah, is anyone going to help me here, or am I going to do all the work?" Han complained, kneeling over a tiny hole he had managed to scrape in the frozen ground.

They laughed and helped Han with the digging. Ami then planted Little Mother in the hole, while Gaden gently laid the seeds of the Qirin Tulku around its roots.

"The plants will survive, won't they?" Zhara said anxiously. "It's so cold."

"They're native to these parts," Ami said. "But if it eases your mind, I can help it and the Qirin Tulku's heart seeds along."

She placed both hands, palms down, on the newly covered mound of earth that marked where Gaden had buried the Unicorn King's seeds. Closing her eyes, she fell into her Guardian form. While she might not yet have mastery over her powers like either Zhara or Yuli, it was getting easier with practice to access the part of herself—her soul—that was not Li Ami but another being altogether. Burrowing deep into the ground with her magical senses, she found the little seeds that had once been worn in a pouch around the Qirin Tulku's neck. As she had done with the herbs and flowers in her mother's garden back in Zanhei, she pushed her power through the little husks and into Little Mother's roots.

Please. Live.

She offered her gift and the plants accepted it, beginning to grow tall and large. Zhara and the others fell back as Little Mother's trunk thickened, the roots rippling and pushing the earth away. Beneath the ground, little tendrils emerged from the Qirin Tulku's heart seeds, twining around the fairy tree, secure and warm. So they would both rest until spring, filled with the life that only the Guardian of Wood could give them.

"There," Ami said softly. "They will survive."

"And thrive?" Zhara asked hopefully.

Ami shook her head. "That will be up to them."

Their tasks finished, the party returned to someplace warm with alacrity. The ruins of Kalantze would not be rebuilt easily, but several makeshift shelters had been erected in what reminded Ami of the refugee shantytown.

"I suppose we are all refugees now, of sorts," she said.

The four of them sat cross-legged on a low platform back in the heart of the Gyasol homestead, sipping cups of butter tea and drinking bowls of ginseng chicken soup. Han heartily tucked into a plate of warm barley bread with various spreads, including a ginger-and-mint chutney that was Zhara's particular favorite.

"What is our next course of action?" he asked through a mouthful of bread.

Ami and Gaden looked to Zhara.

"I . . . don't know," she said. "But I suspect there is more travel to be had in our future."

Ami thought of the tasks they had left to fulfill. Find the other fragments of *Songs of Order and Chaos*. Find the other two portals and seal them. Find the last Guardian of Dawn. Defeat the Mother of Ten Thousand Demons. Her father had promised to assist in what way he could, calculating and charting the stars of the past seventeen years to see where and when the Guardian of Water had been born. Although his mind would never be what it once was, a measure of calm had overcome him when Ami had offered to plant Rinqi's heart seeds in the shadow of Mount Llangposa, where her remains would help nurture the next tree of life. But the wounds of his trauma still ran deep, for when he was in Gaden's presence, the Star of Radiance pained him.

"What of Pang Lok and the other Heralds of Glorious Justice?" Han asked. "Has anyone heard word of them?"

Gaden shook their head. "The last I heard, there were reports of the Four-Winged Dragon flying on the road to the imperial city. Why they persist in this foolhardy endeavor is beyond me."

"The northern hordes are some of the most fearsome warriors in the land," Han agreed. "Even if they did have the number to assail the imperial palace, I'm not sure they will get very far."

"Even if they had the numbers, they don't have the claim," Gaden said softly. "I'm not with them."

Silence fell over the group at their words.

"What will you do, Beast?" Zhara asked. "With the Star of Radiance?"

They looked down at their chest, almost as though they could see the light that burned within them. "I . . . don't know," they said at last. "If I knew how, I would return the power to every living citizen in the Morning Realms. It was a gift that has become corrupted to selfish ends."

"But," Han said, "don't we need the Star of Radiance to seal the Mother of Ten Thousand Demons back in her realm?"

"Yes," Gaden said. "And I am committed to you all now. But . . ." They sighed. "I wish I could get rid of this destiny and just be me. Not Princess Weifeng. Not Beast. Just . . . Gaden."

Ami twined her fingers through theirs. "You don't have to be anyone or anything you don't want to be."

"But is that true?" they asked. "Even if we defeat Tiyok, the realm is still under the thrall of an anti-magic tyrant. Magician liberation is still a cause I believe in, even if I don't always agree with the means."

"Do you mean to reclaim the Sunburst Throne?" Zhara asked in surprise.

They shook their head. "No. But Pang Lok did have one thing right— the Morning Realms cannot continue under the Warlord's rule."

"One step at a time," Zhara said. "I'll start by writing letters to the other Guardians of Dawn—the mutual aid society, not us." She laughed at Ami's expression. "The Bangtan Brothers may have found the northern fragment of *Songs of Order and Chaos* by now."

"The nearest message waypost is Mingnan," Gaden said.

Han made a face. "I'd rather avoid having to deal with the Le sisters again, if you don't mind."

"The other border towns will have safe houses," they said. "The closest one after Mingnan would be farther to the north, near the Dzungri basin." They shuddered. "And I'm telling you now I don't relish the idea of having to deal with the freezing temperatures they have up there. It may be chilly on the Zanqi Plateau during winter, but it's absolutely frigid up by the steppes. I don't know how Princess Yulana could have grown up there."

"It was difficult," came a familiar voice behind them. "But it's not as bad as all that."

"You always did have impeccable timing," Han remarked. "Well met, Yuli. We were just talking about you."

But the redhead's countenance was serious, unlike her usual smirking self.

"Obaji is dead. He's been assassinated, and the northern kangs blame the Heralds of Glorious Justice."

"But that's not possible," Gaden said. "Pang Lok and the others only just left a few days before. They would not have reached the imperial city just yet."

Yuli nodded. "I thought the story was suspicious as well, but either there are more cells of the Heralds than we thought, or someone is framing them to cover their own dark ambitions." Her lips thinned. "And I think I know who."

"Who?" Zhara asked.

Yuli shook her head. "Not now. But suffice it to say, the northern kangs have made their move."

"So what happens now?" Han asked.

The northern princess looked grim. "And now the realm falls to chaos and civil war."

My most darling Suzhan:

A thousand pardons. The messenger with whom I have sent this is a member of the Guardians of Dawn.

I'm sorry it's taken so long to write, mimi. You said you wanted love stories and I finally have one to tell. Don't worry; it's not a romance. Love exists in all forms, and continues on after the fairy-tale-ending kiss for a little cinder girl and her prince—growing, maturing, changing, spreading to encompass so much more.

The story starts like this:

Once there was an odd but beautiful scrivener and a Beast who lived in a castle on a hill . . .

In the Lands
of the Bitterest North . . .

KHO KNEW THE INSTANT THE WARLORD HAD DIED.
There was a great storm of messenger birds, blowing in on ill
winds from the south. She watched the swirling clouds of black wings
and black feathers circle the rookery tower to the northeast, coming in
to roost one by one like vultures diving for carrion.

More than birds of prey had been circling for the past several weeks.

Although she would never admit it to her mother, Kho had been
enjoying the relative peace and quiet of the Warlord's illness. The
northern steppes had never been so empty of intrigue, and for the first
time in years, she felt as though the air she breathed was as clean as the
bitter winds from the Frozen Wastes. But as the firstborn daughter of
the Lady of Wild Things, she was expected to be mired in the muck
of politics, and the birds winging their way north were as much a message for her as they were for the other northern kangs.

Her mother was about to make her move.

And she had to be ready.

"The winds of change are upon us," said Ogodei. Kho's older brother
had just returned from a hunt; he was still dressed in his leathers, the
blood still staining his skinning knife. "Can't you smell it, mimi?"

"The scent of change has been on the wind for weeks now, *gogo*," she said, "what with the news of the undead from the west and the abominations from the south. The Guardians of Dawn have awoken."

"You don't still believe in that, do you?" Her older brother looked down. "All that fairy-tale nonsense about greater demons and elemental warriors?"

Kho studied her brother with sharp, keen eyes. "I don't know; do you still believe all that nonsense about Princess Weifeng still surviving to this day, gogo?"

The muscles along Ogodei's jaw tightened. "The Mugung heir is still alive," he said in a near growl.

"You have no proof!"

"Don't I?" Ogodei's smile was sly, which made Kho's stomach twist with unease. Her brother was one of the least subtle people she knew, and she mistrusted this new coyness.

"Out with it, gogo," she said. "What have you heard?"

He glanced at the rookery tower. "A little birdie told me," he said, "a very interesting story about a famous naval queen and a lost little girl."

Kho narrowed her eyes. "Are you speaking of the lost daughter of the last Marquess of the Azure Isles?"

"The very same." Ogodei grinned, holding out a slim bamboo tube to his sister.

Kho took the reed from her brother and tapped one side. A rolled-up piece of paper slid out into her hand. She knew who it was from without having to look at the seal. A cold drop of dread slid down her spine as she scanned the message. The first part was addressed to Ogodei, detailing intelligence about the political situation in the Azure Isles beyond the Bay of Dragons and across the Azure Strait. Always fractious, the island suzerainty was in one cycle of rebellion after another. During the Just War, the Marquess, the last elected naval queen, had been allied with the Mugungs, but she had been betrayed by her sister, the Fleet Queen, who had thrown her might in with the Warlord. The peace achieved in the years afterward had been tenuous, only as strong as the Fleet Queen's command of the Baron Flotilla. It appeared as though rumors of the last Marquess's daughter had been surfacing in recent months, and many of the barons were rallying behind this girl as the next potential leader of the flotilla.

"Gogo," Kho said slowly. "Are you suggesting that the Marquess's lost daughter may be Princess Weifeng?"

The rest of the message gave away the girl's location as being in a nunnery of the priestesses of Do somewhere in the remote mountains of the Azure Isles, as well as an order for Kho. She crumpled up the paper and shoved it angrily into her sash.

"Why else would Mother want us to hunt the girl down and kill her?" Ogodei asked.

"The Fleet Queen remains allied to the anti-magician cause, and the girl is an unknown," Kho said. "Mother is simply being pragmatic."

"You have no imagination, mimi," Ogodei pouted.

Kho crossed her arms. "Would it appease what little conscience you have left, gogo, to believe you are murdering the last Mugung instead of an innocent little girl?"

His lashes flickered, and Kho knew she had landed a blow. It was increasingly rare these days; the last time she had managed to score a hit on her brother was when she was ten and he was eleven, and he had yet to come into his growth spurt.

"The Marquess's daughter is no little girl," Ogodei said darkly. "She would be at least sixteen years old by now."

"I'm sixteen."

"And you're no child, Kho-yah, not anymore."

She knew that. She knew that by the way the elders of the kangs had started treating her, the way they eyed her with both surprise and suspicion, and the way offers for her hand had started to come in by the droves. She knew she was grown now, when just last year she had still been one of the youths racing each other on the steppes.

"And you don't have to be Mother's Huntsman anymore either, Ogodei," she said. "You've won your place in the kang. Let it go. You no longer have to be at her beck and call."

Her brother's lashes flickered again. "It's different for you, mimi," he said, his voice soft. "Your honor doesn't have to be proven."

Kho said nothing. Her brother carried the affliction, although he could not wield it as other magicians could. If he had been born to a different kang, a different family, he could have joined the Falconer as one of the Kestrels. But he was a Maltak Wolf, and magic was not a weakness to be borne in their bloodline.

"When do you leave for the Azure Isles?" she asked instead. "You'd have to leave soon, before the winter storms set in."

"Not until spring. You saw the message; Mother wants us down in the imperial city when the matter of succession is settled."

Kho fiddled with the fang strung on a chain about her neck. "That could be days or even months from now. You know the kangs; it will take at least four weeks for everyone to have said their piece if it will take a day. Has Mother even said who she would cast her stones for?"

There were two possible heirs to the Sunburst Throne now that the Warlord was gone—three, if one were daring enough to throw their support behind the shaman Mongke. The surviving child and grand-child of the Gommun Emperor. The people of the northern steppes had ever been democratic in their own ways; leadership was not simply a matter of kin, but of worth and honor. The Grand Kang of the northern families was chosen from a handful of warriors willing to prove them-selves in the Grand Game—racing each other to the Shimmer beyond the Frozen Wastes to bring back one of the golden eggs of the northern rocs. She imagined the choice for emperor would not be too different.

Ogodei fell silent. Understanding dawned over Kho.

"She doesn't mean to cast her stones for anyone," she said in quiet realization. "She means to advocate for herself."

Her brother did not reply, and his silence was answer enough.

"What of the Grand Kang?" Kho asked. "If she's empress, then you . . ."

Ogodei met her gaze. No, despite his position as eldest, the Lady of Wild Things would never suffer magic to taint her legacy.

"No," Kho breathed. "I don't . . . I never—"

"You've still got enough time to train for the Grand Game before Princess Yulana returns home." He gave her a lopsided grin.

Kho sighed. Princess Yulana. Yuli.

Her days of peace were coming to an end.

ACKNOWLEDGMENTS

I **AM IMMENSELY GRATEFUL TO AND GRATEFUL *FOR*** the following people who have stood and supported me and my writing from the very beginning, for without them, this entire series could never have happened:

My editor, Eileen Rothschild, and the entire team at Wednesday Books, including Meghan Harrington, Rivka Holler, and Brant Janeway. My agent, Katelyn Detweiler, and the wonderful people of Jill Grinberg Literary Management, including Jill Grinberg, Sam Farkas, and Denise Page. May your good deeds return to you thousandfold. I don't know where I would be without you.

To the Ca$h Money Coven, as our group chat is so lovingly named— Lemon, Renée, and Rosh, another round of drinks is on me. And to the members of Bangtan Sonyeondan, or BTS, not only for inspiring a certain troupe of perfomers in the book, but for quite literally saving me during a dark time in my life.

Last but not least, all my love to my family—Sue Mi, Michael, and Taylor Jones. And to Bear, always Bear. Thanks for taking care of our chaos clowns, Castor and Pollux, so I could write. For you, I will always return of my own free will.